Ma
Pearson

DEATH
ROW

arrow books

Published by Arrow 2010

4 6 8 10 9 7 5

I Walk The Line
Words and Music by John R. Cash © 1956 (Renewed 1984)
HOUSE OF CASH, INC. (BMI)/Administered by BUG MUSIC
All Rights Reserved Used by Permission
Reprinted by permission of Hal Leonard Corporation

First published in Great Britain in 2010 by
Arrow Books
Random House, 20 Vauxhall Bridge Road,
London SW1V 2SA

www.rbooks.co.uk

Addresses for companies within The Random House Group Limited can be
found at: www.randomhouse.co.uk/offices.htm

The Random House Group Limited Reg. No. 954009

A CIP catalogue record for this book
is available from the British Library

ISBN 9780099550877

The Random House Group Limited supports The Forest
Stewardship Council (FSC), the leading international forest certification
organisation. All our titles that are printed on Greenpeace approved FSC
certified paper carry the FSC logo. Our paper procurement policy
can be found at: www.rbooks.co.uk/environment

Mixed Sources
Product group from well-managed
forests and other controlled sources
www.fsc.org Cert no. TT-COC-2139
© 1996 Forest Stewardship Council
FSC

Typeset by SX Composing DTP, Rayleigh, Essex

Printed and bound in Great Britain by
CPI Cox & Wyman, Reading, RG1 8EX

For Kim, Curt and Tami

'The percentage of adults who experienced sexual abuse as children and have had long-term side effects is not known. However, in one British study, thirteen per cent of the sample of such adults reported that they had been permanently damaged.'

Counselling Directory 2009

They all say it's a physical thing. An urge. An uncontrollable desire that builds and swells, like an ocean at high tide, until action must be taken. A slow boiling of the blood. As uncontrollable and devastatingly powerful as a tsunami. But that isn't it: it was part of it but just that – a part. It's a mental thing, he knew that as well as any. Thoughts scuttling and skittering in the brain like hundreds of small crabs in a tin bath, climbing the sides with scratching, feverish claws, falling back into the writhing, clicking mass. Memories crawling through his mind like shickle in a turning drum.

Billy Thompson. Just eight years old and his first trip to the seaside. His first trip anywhere more than five miles from where he was born and had lived his entire life. It was deep in the cold-hearted grip of a brutal winter and he was huddled against the passenger-seat window, shivering against the cold. It was a boxy, draughty, metallic rectangle-on-wheels of a car, with a hard bench seat and the wind whistling through gaps in the doors and window frames. It bounced and clattered on the uneven road, jolting him and sending needles of pain shooting though his thin, bony body. The wipers were scratching thick, flurrying snow from the windscreen and tears were pricking his eyes so that his vision of the changing landscape outside was softened, blurred. His life behind him fragmenting like the flakes of snow scattering into pin-points in the rear-view mirror.

Billy's uncle was a crab-and-lobster fisherman living in a small village on the south-east coast between Southend-on-Sea and Herne Bay. This trip was the first time Billy had ever been away from his family home and he would never be returning. His father had been sentenced to three years in prison for battering his wife once too often; his mother had been hospitalised for three weeks, during which time Billy was looked after by his next-door neighbour, Grace Williams, a woman in her late sixties with a houseful of cats and a forgetful nature. When Billy's mother returned from hospital she decided she couldn't bear to look at her son's face any more – she said he looked just like his father – and arranged for him to live with his Uncle Walter, her elder brother, who was looking to take on someone he could train as an apprentice. Billy had never met Walter before, a tall lean man with a face like a rusty hatchet, battered by sea and sun and wind, carved lines of cruelty written into it like the scratchings of a blunt bradawl.

Billy was bundled without ceremony from the car, shivering with the cold, the tears near-freezing on his cheeks, into a house that was only marginally warmer. He was put to bed with barely a grunt of welcome and a cold glass of water and then shaken awake at four in the morning to help his uncle at work. Cold, wet and hungry, he huddled in the back of the small craft as it slapped and danced on the yawing waters. Waves splashed over the sides, chilling his wind-blasted and sore face. He had made the mistake of complaining once – he didn't want this, he wanted to go home – and his uncle had hit him. Not rebuked him or slapped him. But punched him. Hard, in the side of his face with a hand fashioned of sinew and muscle, knocking him to the floor where he whimpered but didn't cry. He had long ago learned not to cry out. Then the boat was anchored. 'Inside' as his uncle called it, a mile out to sea. He was huddled against crates filled with shickle, the remains of the crabs and the lobsters after they had been processed. Empty, broken shells, claws, legs, eyes. The smell filled his nostrils, and the sound as his uncle tipped the crates emptying the eviscerated carcasses back into the cold water was like the sound of an army of cockroaches skittering on a dance floor.

Like the thoughts dancing in his head now. Building like a symphony as the blood roared in his ears and he remembered how it all began. Back in that boat shed with the smell of the shickle still ripe in his throat and his uncle tall in the shadows as he pulled the door behind him closed and looked down on Billy, with the inhumanity of a feral thing, his eyes empty. Billy remembered the sharp cuts in his knees as he was forced to kneel, the slivers of lobster and crab shell cutting through the thin fabric of his jeans.

His uncle crossed to the workbench and turned on his new transistor radio; music played. The one everyone tipped for number one that Christmas. Johnny Ray, 'Walking in the Rain'. It was nineteen fifty-six and it seemed to Billy that it had never stopped raining . . .

He remembered hearing the music and looking up and seeing his uncle's eyes that were no longer empty. He felt the soft touch of the man's hand on his head now that was almost like a benediction. He didn't remember crying but he could feel the moisture trickling into his mouth, the sweet salty taste and the *lingering fetid smell of rotting flesh. He looked across at the small window, stained green with algae so that the light filtering weakly through made him feel like he was at the bottom of the ocean.*

He shook his head, clearing the ancient memory, and looked down at his twitching hand, arching it so that the sinews stood out like cord and made the blood vessels move below the translucent skin like thin blue slugs. His fingers curled inward, making his hand a crab.

The Year of Our Lord 1995.
Time to feed.

FRIDAY NIGHT

Jack Delaney handed the last of the plates to Siobhan, his seven-year-old daughter and the bright-eyed light of his life. She rubbed a tea towel quickly over it and then handed the plate to her Aunt Wendy, who dried it properly and put it in a wooden plate-rack that was mounted over the counter to the right of the sink.

'Last one,' said Delaney, pulling the plug out of the sink to release the soapy water.

Siobhan pointed to the old-fashioned penny that was set into the base of the plate rack. 'Why do they put a coin in it?'

Delaney ruffled her hair. 'The lady who makes them, it's like her signature.'

'It's like Kate's, isn't it?'

'It is. She helped me choose it.'

'Just as well,' Wendy said as she looked around the kitchen. 'She has a good eye.'

Delaney grinned. 'Obviously.'

Wendy laughed and flicked the towel at him. 'I wasn't talking about you, big-head. What do you reckon, Siobhan? If he was any more of a doughnut . . . sure he'd be eating himself.'

Siobhan laughed. 'He'd be an apple doughnut.'

Delaney fixed her with a serious look. 'Why apple?'

'Because they're my favourites,' she said, with a musical laugh, and hugged him around the waist.

Wendy cast her gaze around the room. 'Seriously, though, Jack. You've done a good job here. It actually feels like a home here now.'

'Thanks. But, like I say, I had help.'

'And like I say, just as well.'

'Are you saying I haven't got good taste?'

'Only in women, Jack, only in women.'

Delaney looked around the kitchen himself, a slight smile playing on his lips as he realised how far he had come since meeting Kate. It was furnished now with a range of styles: a sturdy wooden farmhouse table, a Scandinavian rocking chair in the corner with a tapestried cushion on it, an antique dresser. Some original framed watercolours on the wall. If it had just been down to him he would have gone to IKEA and got the lot from there, but Kate had put her foot down and made him take his time to work at finding the right pieces of furniture. In just a few weeks he had the whole house decorated and furnished and his sister-in-law Wendy was right, he realised. It did feel like home. In a way he was sad to have finished. He had really enjoyed hunting down pieces with Kate: from antique shops and auctions, from bric-a-brac stalls – photos and prints and original watercolours, sofas, chairs, sideboards, cutlery, crockery, glassware, wine rack and wine, whisky decanters and – most important of all – a big sled-style rubberwood bed they had bought from John Lewis that sat in the middle of Delaney's wooden-planked master bedroom with antique mahogany pot-cupboards either side like a statement that Jack Delaney was back and open for business.

Delaney realised that his daughter had asked him a question. 'Sorry, darling, what's that?'

'I was saying . . . can I stay the night? Aunty Wendy said it was all right.'

'Sorry, darling, not tonight.'

'Oh please.' Siobhan pulled her most pleading expression, her beautiful big eyes plucking at his heartstrings like Segovia on a banjo. She reminded him so much of her mother. At least he could see the resemblance now and take comfort in it. Months back and he'd have been in pieces, but things had changed. Kate had done more than just help decorate his house; she was helping him rebuild his life.

He ruffled his fingers though his daughter's curly dark hair again and felt the guilt.

'Sorry, poppet, I've got a really early start tomorrow. But soon, I promise.'

'What about a fairy story? You haven't told me a story for ages.'

'Just a quick one, then.' Delaney sat at the table and picked Siobahn up, plonking her in his lap.

'One with magic in it.'

'All stories have magic in them, darling.'

'Proper magic. Not just silly words. Anyone can make up silly words.'

'All right then, I'll tell you the story of the desert rose.'

'Okay.'

'Once upon a time, long, long ago, in a time before man had taken metal from the earth and

9

cracked the bargain they had made with the ancient gods—'

'What bargain?'

'They gave us fire so long as we burned only wood. When we took the metal from the earth and burned it we broke that bargain.'

'You can't burn metal, silly.'

Delaney's voice softened, his childhood brogue creeping back in with a sad and lyrical cadence to it. 'But you can, darling. That magic wasn't man's to take, however, and the gods have been angry with us ever since. You see that anger in the melting of the icecaps so the polar bears have nowhere to go, and the angry seas rising in New Orleans and across the world to punish the poor and the defenceless.'

'That's global warning.'

Delaney chuckled. 'It *is* a warning, yes, darling, not that anyone's listening, but this happened long before we stole the metal from the underground gods, in a time when tree braches shaking in the wind made music, and the stars overhead sang in the coal black of night.'

Siobhan cuddled back comfortably against Delaney's chest, listening, her eyes wide.

'Long, long ago and far away' – he began again – 'there blossomed a single red rose. It grew in the middle of the never-ending desert within a ring of sharp-edged rocks in a bed of bleached white sands, and the rocks sheltered her from the biting winds that would spring up as suddenly as a sneeze. Cutting, swirling, hissing winds that raged and howled and danced across the desert like a swarm of angry killer wasps.'

Siobhan frowned. 'I don't like wasps.'

'But although they rasped and scraped and laid low all before them . . . the winds also carried the little rose seed hundreds of miles from the fertile lands of Araby and left it in the little hollow in the middle of the desert, before vanishing again, in the way of all winds, as suddenly as they appeared. Like a candle being snuffed out. So the little seed was safe where it had been placed, and the tears of the moon in the cool night sky watered it, and the sheltering rocks that ringed her were like stone guardians, so the rose grew tall and proud and beautiful. And the desert loved her. Never in his vast regions had he ever seen something so lovely. So that when the storms raged and the sands blew, the desert stood with the rocks and made sure there was an oasis of calm around the lovely rose.'

'What was she called?'

'Just Rose, darling. The rose of the desert.'

'And what happened to her?'

'Well, time passed and the little rose flourished. Her delicate red petals were so bright that they seemed to glow in the afternoon sun and her scent was so rare and fragrant and she was so beautiful that the heart of the old desert was nearly broken and he fell even more in love with her. The rose, however, became bored and restless. Nothing ever happened in her tranquil patch and so she wanted to see more of the world. Finally the little rose, sighing with boredom, plucked up her courage and decided to venture out of her little shelter in the eye of the desert. The winds had returned and the rose was overcome with curiosity about what could be making such strange and wonderful sounds. So the rose delicately pulled up her roots and stepped forth, around the corners of the standing stones and out of her patch. And the winds swirled around her, fluttering her delicate leaves so that she almost seemed to dance, and then – as suddenly as a thought – she was gone.'

'Cheery story, Jack,' said Wendy, one eyebrow critically bent.

'What happened to her? Did she die then?' asked Siobhan, her eyes still wide but a crease crunching her smooth forehead now.

'Well, darling, the old desert caught a last lingering smell of the rose's beautiful fragrance and then it was gone, vanished in the swirly air as quickly as you can snap your fingers.'

Delaney snapped his own fingers, making Siobhan jump. 'And the old desert was heartbroken because he had destroyed the very thing he loved.'

'Yeah, don't give up the day job, cowboy,' said Wendy, frowning.

'So the rose died because she left home?' asked Siobhan.

'Not at all, pipkin,' said Delaney, grinning broadly. 'The wind swirled around the rose and lifted her from the floor but cradled her in its airy arms and carried her high, high above the desert and far, far away. Across glittering seas that sparkled like wet turquoise and translucent jade. Over mountains topped with snow so bright and white that it would dazzle you to look at them, over countries with woodland so thick with forests it was like a carpet of branches that stretched from coast to coast, and finally they hovered over a land far below her that was as green as the brightest emerald you had ever seen.'

'The emerald isle?' said Siobhan, smiling delightedly once more.

'Ireland!' said Delaney, with an emphatic nod. 'And the wind danced downwards, swirling slower and slower, and laid the rose to rest in the rich and fertile soil below, the sea ahead of her and the rolling hills behind, in a spot that was later to be called Cork in a nook by the sea.'

'Ballydehob?'

'No, darling. In a place that was to be called Cunnamore.'

'Where Mummy came from?'

'She did indeed, sweetheart.'

'And roses were her favourite flower.'

'So they were.'

'Well, then, that's a good story.'

Delaney kissed his daughter on the forehead and set her on her feet. 'Time to get you home for bed. And I have to get to bed myself, pipkin – got an early start in the morning.'

He picked up her coat, which was hanging on the back of one of the mismatched penny chairs he had bought at auction, and helped her shrug into it.

Wendy looked at him, suddenly very serious. 'Tomorrow morning, Jack, are you involved in the—'

Delaney shot her a warning look to interrupt her. 'Nothing she needs to know about.'

'What don't I need to know about?' Siobhan asked.

Delaney grinned as he buttoned up her coat. 'The price of snowshoes in the Sahara.'

'What?'

'Just work stuff, darling. Boring old work. Nothing to worry about.'

'When can I stay over again, then?'

'Like I say, soon. I promise.'

'You shouldn't promise things unless you mean it.'

'I know.'

She pointed a finger at him sternly. 'It's a sin!'

'Cross my heart and hope to die, should I ever tell a lie.' He made a crossing gesture over his heart.

Siobhan grinned. 'You'll keep your promise, then.'

'I always do, sweetheart.'

'Come on then, mischief, let's get you home and let your daddy get some sleep,' said Wendy as she led Siobhan to the kitchen door leading to the garage and the street off from it. Delaney noticed her wincing a little as she walked, holding her left hand to her side. It wasn't so long since Wendy had been attacked by Kate Walker's degenerate uncle. Attacked in her own house, stabbed and locked in an under-stairs cupboard and left to die. Attacked because she was looking after Delaney's daughter and Jack had got in the evil bastard's way.

Delaney put his hand on Wendy's arm as she opened the door. 'Are you really doing okay, Wendy?'

She smiled, and his heart fluttered again as he could see his dead wife's lovely smile echoed in it. 'I'm mending, Jack. It's what we have to do, isn't it?'

Delaney nodded, leaned in to kiss her on the cheek and hugged her – carefully though, as if she were made of tissue paper. 'Come and see us soon.'

Delaney closed the door and walked up the steps

back into the kitchen. He looked at his watch and then went into the lounge. A fire was roaring in the clearview log-burner that Kate had insisted he buy, the dancing flames clearly visible through the glass screen, but the house still felt colder somehow, much colder now that his daughter and Wendy had left.

He pulled out his mobile phone, flipped it in his hand a few times and then sighed and punched in some numbers. After a few rings the familiar smoky voice answered.

'Speak to me.'

'Hi. It's Jack.'

'Hey, cowboy, what can I do for you?'

Delaney looked at his watch again. 'Thought it might be time for another go.'

'You going to pay me this time?'

Delaney smiled. 'I'm certain sure we can come to some sort of arrangement.'

'When do you want it?'

'Right now.'

'You better get your riding boots on and saddle up, then, cowboy.'

'Oh, and one last thing.'

'What's that?'

Delaney's voice was suddenly all business. 'You don't tell anybody about our little arrangement.'

'Of course not.'

'I mean it, Stella, nobody! None of your friends, none of your colleagues.'

'You got it, Jack.'

'Good. I'll see you in twenty.'

He closed the phone and looked at the fire, the

15

reflection of the flames dancing in his eyes like tiny elementals.

*

Roger Yates was a man accustomed to getting his own way. Since childhood he had lived a privileged life and whereas others might have felt some guilt in being born with a silver spoon in their mouths, the idea never even once crossed his mind, certainly not at boarding school and not even at university when he'd been forced to rub shoulders with people from all manner of backgrounds. He wasn't a snob, though – he didn't look down on poorer people, just didn't allow their worries to trouble him. In fact, he had shagged quite a lot of working-class women at university. He had found their vulgarity of expression in times of intimacy extremely arousing, had encouraged it, in fact, directing their outbursts like Mike Leigh would direct an improvisation in one of his working-class films that his wife seemed to enjoy so much, although he saw little point in them himself. If you wanted to look at drab lives, pop down the laundromat or listen to the inane conversation between people on a London bus. So Roger Yates didn't bother with the poor people. There are those who have and those who have not. That is a simple fact of life.

Or it was.

Roger was pacing in the long hall, gripping his mobile phone hard in his right hand as he held it to his ear. Whisky sloshing in a glass held in his left. A flush was rising in his face and he loosened his collar. 'Everything is in hand, trust me on that,' he said, as stridently as he could manage. 'And I'll take care of him as well, believe me. He won't be a problem for much longer.' He loosened his collar a little more, then took a swallow from his glass. 'Like I said, there really is no cause for concern.'

He started as the door opened and Siobhan burst into the hallway, singing.

'One two three, my granny caught a flea, she roasted it and toasted it and had it for her tea.'

'Can you keep the bloody noise down!' Yates shouted to Wendy as she followed her niece into the house.

'Yeah, all right, Alex Ferguson, wind your neck in,' Wendy snapped back, far from impressed.

'I'm on the telephone here – it's business!'

'Go on upstairs; I'll be up in a minute,' Wendy said to Siobhan, who pulled a guilty little grin and scampered up the stairs, singing again quietly when she reached the last step. Wendy took off her coat and hung it on the coat-stand that stood by the large Victorian door of their hallway. She looked across, concerned, at her husband as he finished his call.

'Like I say, it's all in hand, you have my word on it.' He nodded. 'Okay, goodbye.' And he hung up.

'What's up, Roger? This isn't like you.'

Roger spun round and glared at her, holding his glass of Scotch forward.

'You want to know what's wrong? You're what's wrong, Wendy! You and that niece of yours upstairs, and particularly that black bog Irish brother-in-law of yours! That's what's wrong!'

'Roger, what are you talking about?' Wendy asked, perplexed and not a little worried for him.

Yates gestured with his free hand, sweeping it around. 'All this, Wendy. That's what I'm talking about. *Paying* for all this. I'm talking about my work.'

'What's that got to do with—'

'Nothing. All right? Nothing. Forget I ever said anything.' He took another gulp of his whisky and choked a little.

'Roger.'

'No.' Yates waved a finger at her. 'I'm going to read my book.'

He walked into the downstairs study to the right and slammed the door behind him.

Wendy stood looking at the door, bemused, for a moment or two and then sighed. 'Hi, honey,' she said. 'I'm home.'

*

'Puta!'

Kate Walker held out her hand and smiled disarmingly; the man was speaking in Spanish but she knew the language very well herself. Her fingers were splayed and stiff, warning the wiry and red-faced Mexican standing in front of her to keep his distance. He was smaller than her, five foot six, somewhere in his early thirties, she figured, and he was already at simmering point, ready to boil over again. Kate did her best to keep her voice level, trying to pacify him.

'*Just stay calm, and keep your distance – let's not make matters any worse for you.*' She replied to him in his own language.

Not that he had much room to manoeuvre. The small bedsit with kitchen off was probably no more than ten metres square in total. It housed a bed, a

18

sofa, an old television and a battered wardrobe with peeling blue vinyl panels on the door.

'Yeah, calm it down, Chico.' Bob Wilkinson stepped up beside Kate, not really helping the situation.

'*And fuck you too, you son of a bitch.*'

'What did he say to me?' the sergeant asked Kate.

Kate crossed to the woman sitting on the threadbare sofa. She had her head in her hands and was bent forward at the waist. Long luxurious dark curls spilling around her hands to the floor, she was taking in gulping breaths of air and sobbing. Kate guessed her to be somewhere in her mid-twenties, with beautifully unblemished ivory skin and a delicate, elegant bone structure. For some reason she couldn't quite place, the woman reminded Kate of some delicate exotic bird. She looked back up at Bob. 'He's commenting on modern policing techniques,' she said.

'He can comment on my boot up his arse he doesn't watch himself.'

The Mexican snarled challengingly at Bob. He didn't speak English but he could recognise the tone in his words. '*You old man,*' he spat in guttural Spanish. '*Save your brave words for your bitch of a whore, you pussy!*'

Kate put a reassuring hand on the woman's knee. 'Are you okay?'

'I'm fine. We don't need you here. Please to go.' The woman half spoke, half sobbed the words, her tiny hands still covering her face.

Kate spoke soothingly. 'We received complaints. Fighting. Shouting. A woman screaming. Your neighbours called us. They were scared for you. We want to help.'

'Please, you go now.'

Kate gently lifted the woman's hands away. The woman was younger than she'd first guessed, beauty still there somewhere in the frightened, despairing eyes and despite the ugly bruise that marred the right side of her face with puffy swollen tissue. Kate looked at her for a moment, the anger inside her simmering. 'Did he do this to you?'

'No. I tripped up. I hit my head on the door.'

Kate looked across at the door to the small room. There was no handle, just a simple Yale lock. Put your key in and push. She already knew the woman was lying but that confirmed it for her – you couldn't get the kind of injury she had sustained from a flat door. The skull was designed that way to protect the eyes. She took the woman's hand. 'We can help you, Maria. We can protect you.'

The woman's eyes flicked nervously to her boyfriend and she shook her head. 'I hit the door, is all. These neighbours, they should mind their own businesses.'

'*You heard her, puta! Time for you to leave.*'

Kate sighed and stood up. It wasn't the first time she had reached this kind of impasse in a domestic-abuse situation. She was getting pretty sick and tired of not being able to help people because they weren't able to help themselves. A vicious circle of fear, abuse and misery that all to often ended in tragedy, people only coming to their senses when all reason had been knocked out of them, and by then it was too late. She took a business card from her pocket and gave it to

20

the woman. 'Come and see me in the surgery tomorrow. I'll treat you for that eye.'

'I'll be fine.' The woman held the card out but Kate shook her head.

'You keep it. Call me any time you need anything. Any time.'

'You heard her – she don't need your fucking card. What are you, some pussy-eating lesbian ain't got no man to do her right? Maybe you should come back one night, just you and me. I'll sort you out.'

Kate turned round and looked at the Mexican stepping closer, watching his nostrils flare, watching the jaunty jut of his chin, the cockerel breath swelling his thin chest. She knew exactly what he was capable of, exactly what would happen when she left, and she pretty much decided there and then that this was one time she wouldn't walk away. She looked at the man and spat on the floor. *'What are you, some homo with balls the size of peanuts? You think you're a man hitting a woman, I think you're a faggot pansy who can't get it up and takes it out on her because you know what you really are and despise yourself for it.'*

'What did you call me?'

'I called you a cock-sucking faggot.'

And the Mexican lunged forward, his fist flying towards Kate's face. Time slowed for her. She watched the punch coming and flicked his arm away at the wrist with an open left palm. As it passed she drove her right fist hard into his sternum. Years spent keeping fit with karate paying off in spades. The man grunted and fell to his knees, his face beetroot-red now as he struggled to draw breath, his eyes flicking with shock and panic. Kate had to fight really hard to suppress the urge to kick his head and really hurt him. She took a deep breath and calmed herself. She turned and nodded at Bob Wilkinson. 'He just attacked an officer of the law. That's an offence, isn't it?'

Bob grinned back. 'It is in my book. What did you say to him?'

'I was just asking him what he recommended on the menu in the restaurant he works at. Thinking about picking up some takeaway. I might have pronounced a word wrong. It's been a long time since I vacationed in Spain.' Kate smiled innocently.

Bob nodded dryly. 'These Latin types, they sure do fly off the handle sometimes.'

'It seems so. It's the climate, no doubt. Maybe the chillies?'

Bob Wilkinson pulled out his radio 'I'll call for backup.'

As the sergeant moved to the door and put the call through, Kate turned back to the woman, who was still holding her card, clutched hard in her small fist – crumpling it, but not wanting to let it go. 'Come in and see me tomorrow. He's not going to be doing anything for a while.'

The man on the floor was making a whistling sound now as he finally managed to coax some air painfully in and out of his lungs. His hand was clutched to his stomach as he rocked back and forth on his knees, like one of the faithful called to prayer, and a low mewing groan could be heard under his rasping breath. Bob walked back to him as the man struggled to his feet, putting one hand on the table and wiping tears from his eyes with the other. Bob winked at him as he unclipped handcuffs from his belt. 'They're going to take you for a little ride in the nice police van. And then, when we've got you nice and cosy in a little room of your own, we'll see if your papers are all proper and correct. You wouldn't believe it but some people try and sneak into this country without proper permission.'

*

Twenty minutes later, downstairs and outside on the pavement of Camden High Street, the sound of a police siren dwindled into the distance. It was twelve o'clock but the night was bright and raucous with noise. Laughter, raised voices and music spilling from the pubs that were starting to close and the late-night clubs and pubs that were beginning to fill up. Takeaway fast-food joints were doing a roaring trade as burgers, kebabs, greasy fried chicken, chips and pizza slices were ordered to assuage lager- and alcopop-fuelled hunger. Doctor Kate Walker was no stranger to the sight of feeding time when the pubs closed, except that in Hampstead, where she lived, you could also get crêpes with your choice of filling, sweet or savoury, or toasted panini or ciabatta rolls with all kinds of exotic fillings. And the people queuing to eat them had probably had a glass of bubbly too many rather than too much vodka and Red Bull. Jack Delaney might be among them, she thought, with a small smile to herself; they weren't all Hooray Henrys in Hampstead, after all. Jack Delaney with a glass or two of whiskey in him, hugging her warmly to him as they waited in line for a takeaway pizza from Pizza Express. Arguing whether they should go up to the hill to her house or down the hill to his new place in Belsize Park. The area was certainly a lot better with him in it. Her life was a lot better with him in it.

Breathing in the rich smells wafting out of a kebab shop as they passed it Kate realised she was pretty hungry herself. It had been a long shift – she'd grabbed a quick sandwich before coming on duty at six but that seemed like a lifetime ago now and she was thinking she might just pick up a crêpe Suzette herself to enjoy with a well-earned and well-chilled glass of Viognier when she got home. Loaded with calories, she knew, but hey, she had just had a work-out and, after the day she had had, she reckoned she deserved a treat or two. She smiled to herself as they passed Big Enchilada, the Mexican restaurant Rodrigues Sanchez worked in, where a chicken-and-ribs joint had once been. She glanced at the menu – tacos and burritos and her favourite, chicken quesadillas, marinated and grilled chicken meat fold-ed in toasted tortillas with three kinds of melted cheese and fiery jalapeño sauce. Kate felt her mouth salivating and her arteries hardening at the same time and considered for a moment buying some takeout to bring home to share with Jack. And then she remem-bered the haunted battered face of the woman who worked long hours waitressing here to pay the rent on the squalid bedsit that they had just left. Remembered the pain written into her fragile flesh and the hurt branded in her eyes and Kate's appetite disappeared. Besides, Jack had an early start tomor-row and would probably be sound asleep in bed. And as for her glass of Viognier? She was pregnant so that was going to have to wait a long while; it would be quite a good few months before she could look forward to that luxury again.

Kate pulled her coat tighter around herself, shivering with the cold as they continued walking past the restaurant towards Regents Park Tube station. She enjoyed her shifts as a police surgeon but on nights like this she wondered sometimes if she had done the right thing – giving up her job as a forensic pathologist. But she chased the thought away: she'd had many cold, late nights in that career too and general practice and teaching at the university gave her variety, gave her new challenges and, more importantly, it put her into contact with people. Living people. She'd been among the dead for too long in too many ways and for the first time in a very long while she felt a proper part of the real world again. She felt she *belonged* again. Beside her Bob Wilkinson was talking, but she wasn't really listening. She was still thinking about Jack Delaney. Earlier he had taken a call from one of his Irish cousins and it had clearly affected him. She had pressed him for details but he had fobbed her off. She knew him well enough by now to know when he was concealing something, and she knew him well enough to realise that he was as stubborn as a rock when he wanted to be. He'd tell Kate what was going on when he was ready to, she guessed. Bob Wilkinson stopped and she realised he was waiting for her to say something.

'I'm sorry, Bob. I was miles away. What were you saying?'

Wilkinson laughed. 'I was just saying you were miles away and wondered what was on your mind?'

Kate opened her mouth to reply but at that

moment a loud scream, piercing and terrified, came from a side road just ahead of them. They both ran and quickly turned the corner. A woman in her mid-twenties was leaning back against a wall, one hand to her mouth, her legs buckling at the knees, looking as though she was about to topple over. Further up the road, and disappearing fast, a youth in a hooded top was running away. Bob turned to Kate. 'You see to her and I'll get him.'

The sergeant set off at a run and Kate jogged quickly over to where the woman was gagging into her hand. 'Did he hurt you? Has he robbed you? What's happened?'

The woman took her hand away from her mouth, her eyes wide with fear, with shock. She shook her head, unable to speak, and stumbled a couple of yards to throw up in the gutter. Kate stepped across to help her but she pointed with a shaking finger to the alleyway behind them, a narrow passage running between two houses. Kate walked back and looked – she had missed it as she ran up but now she could see what had distressed the woman. A young dark-haired and dark-skinned man, she couldn't tell his nationality in the shadows, lay slumped face up on the ground. He was maybe Middle Eastern, she thought, it was hard to tell in the dim light, but what she could tell from the blood staining his bright white shirt and dripping onto his outstretched and motionless hand was that he had been stabbed or shot and left to die.

She rushed over to kneel beside him, putting a slender finger on his cooling throat, checking his carotid artery for signs of life. She gently felt the wound, determining that he had indeed been stabbed, and took off her white woollen scarf – cashmere and a present from Jack. Folding it, she made it into a compress which she held against the wounded man's chest.

A short while later a breathless Bob Wilkinson returned.

'The little bastard got away. Oh shit . . .' He didn't finish the sentence when he saw what Kate was attending to. 'Is he dead?'

Kate looked up at him. 'There's a faint cardiac rhythm. Very weak. An ambulance is on its way.' She took off her coat to drape it around the cold and unconscious man and Bob immediately took his off and offered it to her.

'I'll be fine, thanks, Bob.'

'Yeah, you may well be but I won't. Jack Delaney would have my balls for conkers and dangling on two bits of string if he found out.'

Kate smiled briefly. Then she turned back to look at the man on the ground. His eyes cold, his dark skin looking pale in the moonlight, his lips thin and bloodless. This city, she thought.

This bloody city.

*

The girl turned in her bed. Voices had awoken her, raised voices. Voices fat with alcohol and drugs. Slurred with anger and cruelty. She put an arm over her head and sighed – she couldn't blot out the sound. She heard a slap and a gasp of pain. And then the woman's voice shouting back and another slap and a thump. And then silence.

27

She looked across at the window, the curtains not fully closed. She looked out at the dark night sky, brooding clouds swelling low over the city like the belly of some alien creature. She'd seen *Doctor Who*, seen London threatened by monsters time and time again. She was fourteen years old, nearly fifteen and she already knew that monsters didn't come out of the sky or from the back of wardrobes or portals in time and space. They came from now. They came from next door. They came from downstairs.

She heard the creak on the steps and knew what was coming next. Better her, she thought. Better her.

The door opened, a spill of light from the downstairs lounge threading its way across the dust-laden carpet of her bedroom. The man peering through the light, unsteady on his feet, his shirt hanging untidily half in and half out of his trousers. His face looking like it had been moulded from wax and been left too long under a hot sun, his eyes small and cold like a guinea pig's. She could smell his rank odour coming off him like waves of heat. His mouth opened in a crooked cruel smile, and she could imagine the fetid breath, could remember the crude words whispered in her ear. It wasn't pain any more, at least not in a physical way.

'It's all right, darling, she's asleep,' he said, smiling and stumbling forward, bracing himself with one hand against the door frame. He tried to make his voice seductive, inviting her to be complicit in her own abuse.

The girl rolled onto her front again and lifted her nightdress. There was no point talking. She had learned the hard way that to pretend to want him just meant it was worse when he had finished. That she was to blame. That it was all her fault. She knew better, and she knew the angers that raged within him were beyond his control. She knew why her aunt had got drunk and shitfaced and had taken herself away with needles in her arm until one day she just took herself away for good. She knew why he only wanted her like a boy. The thought of it now chilled her to the bone as she realised that everything was changing. Time was running out.

She heard the porcine grunt, felt his filthy hands hold her, felt him enter into her. Her eyes pricked with the pain at first, tears that she blinked back, willed back, and then her eyes went as cold and dark as the sky outside, as flat and still as water under a full moon.

Better her, she thought. Better her.

His time was coming.

*

Kate closed the door quietly behind her. It was one o'clock and the house was quiet. She glanced into the lounge, but the lights were off. She eased off her shoes with her feet and went quietly into her bedroom. A soft gentle snoring told her that Jack had let himself in, and she was glad. She slipped out of her clothes, shrugged into her bathrobe and, closing the door quietly behind her again, walked to the bathroom, a foolish smile playing on her lips. Jack was all kinds of trouble, she knew that. It was like bringing a whirlwind into her life, but the thing was . . . she couldn't picture life without him any more. She held a hand to her normally flat stomach and felt a slight swelling there now, as though she ought to be cutting back on the four-seasons pizzas. Except that Kate knew it wasn't due to an unhealthy diet, it was due to Jack Delaney. The father of her child.

She let her bathrobe fall to the floor stepped into the cubicle and turned the shower on, adjusting the temperature. She stood underneath the powerful jets of water and felt the tension easing from her body as the water pummelled her flesh. A few months before and she would have had the water a lot hotter, punishing her flesh. Scourging the demons within. Burning the pain and the hurt and the guilt away. Now she just had it hot. Hot enough to wash the smoke and the grime and the smell of the city off her, but not hot enough to hurt. Not any more.

Kate gasped as a large powerful hand snaked around her waist and pulled her backwards against him. She had been so lost in her thoughts that she hadn't heard him enter.

'Room for a little one,' said Jack Delaney.

Kate laughed. A musical, deep-throated laugh that came from deep within her.

'I thought you were getting up early?'

Delaney leaned in and whispered in her ear. 'I am.'

Kate pressed back against him and smiled again as she reached around with her own hand. 'That you certainly are.'

SATURDAY

Outside Bayfield Prison. Morning. Six-thirty. The dawn only just about breaking. Dark but getting lighter by the minute. Not getting any warmer, though. Dampness hung in the air like a very fine mist. Not raining, at least, which was about the only good thing you could say about it, thought Melanie Jones as she adjusted the belt on her raincoat, folded her arms and flapped her hands against them, trying to coax some warmth into her shivering body. The raincoat had been bought from Aquascutum on Piccadilly for a small fortune and might well have kept the rain out but it certainly didn't keep any heat in. It wasn't the money she'd spent that she objected to, either: it was the fact that she needed to buy a raincoat at all. Bloody England – that was the problem. London in particular. Sodding London. Sodding rain-sodden London. She was still here! If she had her way she'd be out on the west coast of America where the news stations knew how to respect talent and you only saw a raincoat on late-night reruns of *Colombo* on a golden-oldies channel. America, the land of opportunity – *that* was where a woman like her rightly belonged. You wouldn't catch Fox America putting old battleaxes front of camera in a month of sunny bloody Sundays, would you, she thought bitterly as she stamped her feet in a little dance to keep warm. At least she was with Sky and not having to put up with BBC intellectuals past their sell-by date, banging on about age discrimination. That kind of approach to the industry belonged in the 1930s when you had to wear a bow tie even to read the news on the radio!

Anybody could be intellectual if they read enough books. Oxford and Cambridge had about sixty colleges between them, for goodness' sake. Brains were ten a penny. But what Melanie Jones had was looks, and she knew it. God-given beauty. And you couldn't buy that, no matter how good your plastic surgeon was. Just ask Michael Jackson. She looked up at the sky, growing increasingly more pregnant with the possibility of rain, scowled, and thrust her hands deep in her pockets.

'Here you go, Melanie. Milk, no sugar.'

Melanie took the cup of tea and nodded at Simon Harvey, the eager cameraman who had just handed her the drink. He was in his early thirties but still dressed like he was a film-school student, wearing black jeans, a black jacket and black Doc Martens on his feet. He was smiling at her with puppy-dog eyes. If he'd had a tail she reckoned it would have been wagging nineteen to the dozen. Men! All driven by urges they couldn't control. Every single last one of them.

They were among a crowd of press and TV journalists and a large mob of the angry public who were waiting outside the prison that morning, despite the cold and the early hour. The anger simmering through the crowd like tidal energy. An anger that had been building for days, ever since the press had splashed across the front pages the news that one of the prison's more famous inmates, Peter Garnier, had finally broken his vow of silence. The fury had been building for fifteen long years and for the last three days it had simmered to boiling point. Today was the day that he had agreed to take the police to his last burial ground. He was going to take them to the bodies.

Even his name sounded distasteful to Melanie Jones. Peter Garnier, she thought, with an involuntary shudder that had nothing to do with the cold, damp air. Peter Garnier. There was a man who certainly couldn't control his urges.

A loud trilling sound startled Melanie Jones out of her thoughts. She pulled her mobile phone from her pocket and read the message on it.

She clicked it shut, put down her cup of tea on someone's car bonnet and nodded excitedly at her cameraman,

'Come on, Jimmy Olsen. We're out of here.'

Simon Harvey had a good five inches on her but he had to lengthen his stride to catch up with her.

*

Graham Harper, seventy-six and feeling every year, set his cup back on its saucer. It rattled a little as his trembling hand fought to keep itself steady. The volume went up on his television as it always did when the ads came on. He picked up the remote control, pushed mute and then, his hands still shaking, as they did permanently now, he picked up

35

a packet of cigarettes. His tired eyes blinked as he fumbled a cigarette out and into his mouth and searched in his dressing-gown pocket for his lighter.

He was sitting in the lounge of his two-bedroom end-of-terrace house. A cluttered room, dark with the curtains drawn, and a single lamp and the television providing the only illumination. His daughter had been on at him for ages to sell the place. Put himself in sheltered housing. But he'd worked hard all his adult life and now he was retired he'd be damned if he'd be put in another home again. They'd carry him out and up the street in a wooden box before he'd let that happen. He found his lighter and held it cupped between his knobbly hands, scarred and twisted with arthritis, and after a few rolls of the wheel managed to spark a flame and light the cigarette. He inhaled lightly and after a couple of hacking coughs cursed under his laboured breath as he heard a key turning in his front door and footsteps clattering on the tiled floor of his hallway.

'Only me and Archie.'

Rosemary Woods was a tall strident red-haired woman in her forties. She came into the room, tugging an eight-year-old boy behind her. While her hair was a tamed auburn, hanging straight to her shoulders, her son Archie's hair was wild and curly, such a dark brown that it was almost black. He had hazel, impish eyes, and was tugging on his mother's hand, clearly not happy to be there. Rosemary shook his hand angrily and glared at him and Archie let go. Rosemary took off his padded coat.

'Now you just behave for your grandfather.'

Beneath the coat Archie was wearing the brand-new Chelsea strip, bright blue with SAMSUNG written in bold white letters across it, over a pair of jeans and black and white trainers. 'I want to go to Johnny's house,' he said. But he quietened as his mother turned to him with another exasperated look.

'Well, for the hundredth time, you're not! You're staying here with Grandpa this morning like we arranged.' Rosemary reached into her bag and brought out a coloured jumper with a large cartoon giraffe on the front. 'If you get cold, put this on.'

She handed him the jumper and stepped smartly over to her father's chair, whipping the cigarette out of his trembling hand and stubbing it out forcefully in an old pub ashtray he kept on the table by his side.

'Rosemary . . .' He started to object.

'Don't "Rosemary" me. You know what the doctors have said.'

'Doctors. What do they know?'

'They know what an X-ray is. And they know how to read them. What are you trying to do, kill yourself?'

'Well, it would make you happy, wouldn't it?'

'Don't be ridiculous, Dad!'

'And your husband. Maybe he wouldn't have to be away from home so much. Sell the house and he could cut back on all those trips to the Continent. Maybe sell the truck and open a little café. That's what you want, isn't it?'

'What I want has got nothing to do with it.'

'See me in my grave and you'd be frying eggs and flipping bacon before the sod's even settled.' Graham let out another hacking cough.

Rosemary shook her head as she crossed to the

wall and turned the dial on the thermostat up. 'Daft old sod, more like.' She turned to her son. 'Sit quietly on the couch and Grandpa will let you watch your cartoons in a minute.'

The boy hopped up on the sofa, crossing his arms resentfully. 'I could have just gone to Johnny's.'

'Stop looking like that,' she said, looking at her watch. 'I told you it's too early. I'll be back by eleven and you can see him then.' She picked up the ashtray from the side table and emptied it into the fireplace that had been set but not lit. 'And what would happen if you fell asleep and dropped a cigarette?' she snapped at her father. 'Do you want the whole house to go up in flames with you in it?'

Graham shared a sympathetic look with his grandson. 'We're all going to hell. It's just a question of when.'

Rosemary buttoned up her coat. 'Why don't you take him down to the allotment if the weather improves? But make him wear his jumper – it's cold out!'

'Maybe.'

'Though why you have still got it is beyond me. You don't grow anything on it any more.'

'I keep it neat, don't I?'

'Well, if it gets you out in the fresh air it can't hurt, I suppose.'

'It's what the doctors said.'

'If it's not cold or raining is what they said! And just so long as you don't just sit in that filthy shed smoking your lungs to ruination.' Rosemary picked up his packet of cigarettes and put them in her pocket. 'Why don't I take these with me, just to be sure?'

She turned to the TV as the news came back on. A picture of Peter Garnier filled the screen and Rosemary shuddered. 'Can't you turn that over? Just the thought of it makes my blood run cold.' She looked over at her son and back at her dad. 'Put the cartoons on for him.'

Graham Harper fumbled the remote control into his hand and changed the channel.

'That's better. I'll be back for eleven – be good for your granddad, Archie.'

Archie nodded but didn't turn back, his attention now fixed on the television screen, where futuristic vehicles were transforming themselves into different shapes.

Rosemary sketched a wave in the air and left.

Graham watched her go, sighing resignedly, and looked across at his grandson, his eyes a little wet now. He coughed again, hacking so hard that it hurt his ribs as though they were fractured. He held his hand to his lips and coughed again. Then he looked at his palm, expecting to see blood. He wiped the back of his twisted crablike hand across his damp eyes and fumbled into his other pocket to bring out another pack of smokes.

'Shit!' he said as he took out the last remaining cigarette and crumpled the packet. Then he put the cigarette between his lips and scowled at the TV. 'Shit it all.'

*

About seventeen miles west of where Melanie Jones and her cameraman were firing up the engine of their car was a stretch of woodland called Mad Bess

Woods that lay between the towns of Ruislip and Northwood. Covering some 188 acres it had been compulsorily purchased by the local council from a highly disgruntled Sir Howard Stranson Button in 1936. It had been part of the new Green Belt initiative to contain the creeping urbanisation from London and so protect the countryside. And it worked, to some extent. But while the Green Belt might well have held back housing development it was no protection against the wicked desires of men or the foul acts they committed in pursuit of satisfying them. Some said that the Mad Bess of the wood's name was the ghost of a headless horse-woman, some said she was a lunatic wife of a gamekeeper. The truth was that no one knew for certain. But Jack Delaney knew one thing very much for certain. There was a presence of pure evil in the air that morning, permeating the clearing in the heart of the woods like a sulphurous mist. He remembered that John Brill, a fifteen-year-old boy, had been murdered in 1837 just twenty yards from where Delaney now stood. Murdered for collaborating with the police, ironically enough, and the investigation into his killing had been the first time that Scotland Yard had ever sent an officer to assist a murder enquiry. Delaney thrust cold hands deep into his jacket pockets and shivered slightly. He knew that the palpable sense of evil in the air had nothing to do with the unquiet dead . . . but everything to do with a living man.

Peter Garnier.

*

Delaney pulled out his packet of Marlboros and snapped one into his mouth. He took it out, deliberated for a second, then put it back in his mouth and fumbled in his pockets for a box of matches. Sally watched amused as he lit the cigarette, seeing his frowning expression soften somewhat as he drew the smoke deep into his lungs.

'I thought you were giving up, sir?'

Delaney grunted. 'Thinking of giving up. I'm not a man to rush into things, Sally.'

Sally lifted an eyebrow. 'That's right, sir. You look up the word "cautious" in the dictionary and sure enough there's Detective Inspector Jack Delaney's photo right there underneath it.'

Delaney nodded. 'And you look up the words "degenerate scum" and that dead man walking is right there too.' He gestured with his cigarette. 'Just the sight of him makes my skin crawl.'

Sally looked across to a clearing where a small army of police – uniformed, detectives, armed officers – stood by watching as Diane Campbell led a slight manacled man, with grey hair and thin stooped shoulders, across the wet ground. He was dressed in prison uniform and had wire-framed spectacles that made his pale blue eyes look larger than they were, like fish eyes. He glanced across at Delaney as if he had heard what he'd said, looking at him for a long unblinking moment. A shaft of sunlight breaking through the clouds made his spectacles shine and then with a quick reptilian flick of his head he looked down at the ground again. Scanning it. Remembering. Stirring the leaves with the toe of his shoe as though stirring his memories. His thin lips curving into something resembling a smile as his foot moved back and forth and the leaves rustled.

Peter Garnier.

*

In the summer of 1995 Delaney was just a few years out of Hendon, a foot soldier in uniform working at the Wealdstone police station near Harrow on the Hill. Practically every other lamp-post that he passed as he walked had on it a picture of the two children who had gone missing.

Samuel Ramirez was just ten days away from his tenth birthday. He lived next door to a corner shop in Carlton Row, a little side street a mile or so away from the main shopping centre of Harrow. It was within walking distance of a large bingo hall that had once been a cinema that his mother went to every Friday night. And every Friday night, she brought him back fish and chips from the shop next door to it.

But at six-forty-five on this particular Friday night in mid-August his mother Laura Ramirez, a young widow and a nurse of English/Spanish descent, had sent him out to buy a fresh box of eggs, since she was making him pancakes for his tea. His favourite sort, with maple syrup, lemon juice and ice cream. He had passed his cycling proficiency test that day and his proud mother declared that he deserved a special treat because of it. Samuel Ramirez was wearing white shorts, a blue-and-white-striped T-shirt, a lime-green cardigan and a Mickey Mouse watch on his wrist. It was a thing he treasured because it was the last present that his father had given him before dying six months earlier from a brain embolism. He'd sit and watch the gloved hands telling him the time and he liked to think it was Mickey waving directly at him. Sometimes he'd even wave back.

Samuel Ramirez was never seen alive again.

The shopkeeper next door, Patrick Nyland, a single man of forty-two with a slight stammer and sometimes painful eczema that was visible on his hands, claimed that he had never seen the boy come into his shop when he was questioned by his worried mother ten minutes later. The police were called and an hour after Laura Ramirez had sent her son for eggs, Ellie Peters, another single mother, who claimed never to have known who the father of her child was and who lived three houses up from the Ramirez home, woke up from a liquid lunch she had been sleeping off and realised that her daughter was also missing. Alice Peters was nine years and five months old. With blonde curly hair and eyes like chips of sapphire flashing in bright sunlight.

Patrick Nyland was questioned exhaustively at Harrow police station on the Northolt Road, and the search for the missing children intensified. Nyland was kept in custody for twenty-four hours and his story seemed to stand up to rigorous interrogation. His house was searched and no sign of the children was discovered nor any evidence linking him to them. No witnesses came forward to say that they had seen the children, let alone to say they had been seen entering his shop. He was released without charge but events had been set in motion and his private life became the object of scrutiny – and not just by the official forces investigating the children's disappearance. His shopfront window was smashed and the store petrol-bombed when information that he had been charged with a sex offence some years before became public knowledge. The policeman who leaked the information was never charged or disciplined for it. The fact that Nyland's offence was not related to children – he had been found guilty of indecent exposure to a mature woman on the fields south of the medieval church on the hill – made little difference to an increasingly angry and vigilante-minded local populace. Two schools were near those fields where he had been exposing himself: a Catholic primary school and, of course, the more famous Harrow School further up the hill. In fear for his life, Patrick Nyland went into hiding while his insurance company fought his case. The police initiated an enquiry into the perpetrators of the arson but their efforts were minimal. All eyes, ears, feet, hearts and minds of the force were focused on finding the missing boy and girl. Television appeals were made, newspapers ran daily updates – genuinely keen to help, perhaps, but profiting nonetheless from the increased sales that their lurid headlines engendered. The children's faces appearing in those papers were poster models of innocence. Samuel's hair was every bit as curly as Alice's but his was jet black and his eyes were the warm brown of rich caramel, and the hearts of the entire nation went out to the parents. *Almost* the entire nation. Many dark-hearted people looked at the pictures of those children with feelings very far removed from pity or compassion. Men and women both. Society waking up to the chilling knowledge that one in every four of those sexual predators was a woman. And one forty-seven-year-old man in particular collected the pictures as they appeared in the papers. He would cut and paste them into a scrapbook with hands sculpted by the harsh weather and salt air into cruel things. His eyes would glitter as he pressed the cuttings hard into the pages of the book, his hands stroking the children's faces as he smoothed them flat, fixing them. They glittered with a green cast, like an old bottle, like the ocean.

A month passed and still there was no sign of the abducted children, no witnesses came forward. No contact or ransom demand was made. Although it was clear from the outset this was no abduction for financial gain. It was as if the boy and girl had simply vanished off the face of the Earth in a moment, in a heartbeat. Only of course it hadn't been a heartbeat and every waking minute since they'd disappeared represented an eternity of suffering for the boy's mother Laura Ramirez. Nightly she would seek peace in her dreams but found heartbreaking tragedy instead. She would see her son walking into her room, climbing into bed with her, snuggling up to keep warm and she would smooth his hair, realising it had all just been a nightmare. And then she would wake up and the horror of it all would hit her again, turning her stomach muscles liquid, her mind reeling so that she gagged and dry-retched, her body shuddering with the inconsolable pain of it. Ghost-walking through the days, her nerves shredded, she would look at every boy out on the streets and for a desperate moment she would dare to hope. And at home she would sit and look at the front door as though mesmerised, and at every knock she'd say a prayer and close her eyes before she opened it. The hope ate away at her like cancer.

As for Alice's mother, to the outside observer the loss of her child had seemingly little impact on her behaviour. She had been an alcoholic drug abuser before Alice had gone missing and the sad tragedy of her daughter's disappearance had no seemingly redemptive effect on her. She sucked up the pity she was offered like she sucked up cheap wine, until she was tired of having to put on a brave face, and the charity of strangers that had at first fuelled her alcoholic emotional anaesthesia dwindled to frosty stares and muttered comments whenever her back was turned, comments loud enough for her to hear, whispered fingers of blame poking right at her. *What kind of an addict falls unconscious and allows her angel of a nine-year-old daughter to roam the streets alone like that . . .* Finally she had had enough. She changed her name and moved so that she could put it all behind her and forget she had ever lived in Carlton Row.

But human conscience is an organic and mutable thing. Wired differently in the individual mind so that two people could be almost from different species.

Two years after the summer evening in mid-August when Samuel Ramirez and Ellie Peters had disappeared into the ether, Laura Ramirez killed herself by stepping front of a high-speed train at a level crossing. Her existence wiped out in a thunderous moment.

Three weeks after that Peter Garnier was arrested. It happened like this.

*

On a late Sunday afternoon Garnier had approached a small eight-year-old boy – who was seemingly on his own – in some wooded parkland bordering the Ruislip Lido. It was common land, like the Mad Bess Woods a mile or so away. The boy's father, unobserved by Garnier, was in the trees attending to a call of nature. As he came out Peter Garnier moved swiftly away but when the father learned that the man had asked his son to help him look for a lost dog he swore loud enough to startle the boy and set off in furious pursuit. Garnier, seeing that he was being chased, took off at a fast run, but he was a slight man, never a sportsman, and was certainly no match for the enraged father, who was a plasterer from Northolt, a weekend footballer and a fan of the *Sun* newspaper. When he was finally pulled off him, Peter Garnier required hospital treatment for multiple injuries including internal bleeding, fractured ribs and a broken jaw. While being treated in hospital and unable to speak, his car remained on a road with no parking restrictions at the weekend but which came into force from eight a.m. the following Monday.

At ten past nine on that Monday morning Arthur Ellis, a fifty-nine-year-old traffic warden and chronic arthritis sufferer nearing retirement, was ticketing the car when he heard a soft whimpering sound like that of a small frightened puppy coming from inside the locked boot. Calling for assistance, he tried to open the boot himself. Becoming ever more frantic as the whimpering sound had faded away and now there was only a chilling silence. He tried to open the boot using a Swiss army knife that he carried but to no avail. He ran to the nearest door and banged on it but there was no reply. He ran to the next door along and had better luck. A puzzled middle-aged unemployed man in his dressing gown answered and let the traffic warden use his phone to call the police.

Ten minutes later and PC Jack Delaney, who had been on patrol with his sergeant Rosemary Dawlish, arrived. They prised open the boot with a metal bar, which they had confiscated fifteen minutes earlier from a bald-headed tattooed man who had been using it to smash up his lover's car. The woman had been unfaithful to him with a number of people from his football team while he'd been in prison. The man was even then scowling at them through the barred windows of their patrol car, clearly eager to return to secure accommodation.

Inside the boot there was no puppy, but an olive-skinned seven-year-old girl with brown hair and almond-shaped hazel eyes was huddled against the back, looking up at the young constable. Her tired eyes were wide with fear and her tiny hands were clutching a large teddy bear as though it were a powerful talisman that could protect her from all the evils of the world.

Delaney smiled at her reassuringly and stepped aside to let his female sergeant bring her out. But when the woman reached in with arms outstretched the little girl screamed, almost soundlessly, and backed deeper into the boot. She looked at Delaney, almost pleading for his help. The sergeant shrugged and stepped back.

'Why don't you give it a try, constable?' she said.

Delaney stepped up, smiling reassuringly again. The

girl scampered forward and climbed into his arms, hugging him around his neck. As Delaney stood up and brought her out a bright light flashed in front of them. The homeowner, still in his dressing gown, fired off another shot before a glare from Delaney made him lower his camera. The first picture, however, was on the front page of almost every paper the following day and the man in the dressing gown, whose breakfast had been so rudely interrupted, made more from the sales of it than he had all year.

The picture of Delaney holding 'the girl in the boot', as she became known, was wired around the world and earned him no small amount of ribbing from his colleagues. But Delaney didn't care: that moment, holding the small, vulnerable, terrified girl, now safe in his arms, was exactly why he had joined the police force in the first place.

Later that day, the real horror of what might have been struck home to him as he stood guard watching as a SOCO team led by CID went through Garnier's house. In the basement they found three boxes of photographs. All children. They found videos and Super-8 films. Home-made. In a locked cupboard they found several items of clothing. Children's clothing. And they found a cardigan that had once belonged to Samuel Ramirez, the cardigan he had been wearing two years previously on the day he was abducted from Carlton Row.

Later they would find the bodies of six children aged between six and ten buried in the ground underneath his garden shed. None of them would prove to be either Samuel Ramirez or Alice Peters.

When Garnier awoke in prison the next day after

being assaulted on the common he was arrested and moved to a secure unit. He would never enjoy life as a free man again.

The same day that Peter Garnier was arrested Police Constable Jack Delaney put in his application to join CID.

In the thirteen years since his arrest Peter Garnier had refused ever to disclose where the missing children were or where the girl in the boot had come from.

Five months ago he had converted to Catholicism.

Three months ago he had been diagnosed with progressive supernuclear palsy. A disease which over time could rob a person of the ability to walk, talk, feed themselves or communicate with the world around them. And yet their brain would remain alert.

Fourteen days ago he had agreed to tell the police where the children's bodies were buried.

*

Delaney scratched another match to light a cigarette and watched as a team of forensic anthropologists excavated the ground that Garnier, after twenty minutes of deliberation, had indicated to be the place where the bodies of the murdered children were buried. Garnier himself was sitting on a fallen tree trunk some twenty yards away. His fishlike eyes watching dispassionately, glancing across occasionally at Delaney and Sally Cartwright. But no emotion showed on his face.

'Does he know who you are?'

Delaney shrugged. 'I doubt it.'

'What happened to the girl you found alive?'

Delaney took a long drag on his cigarette. 'We never found her mother or father. No relatives at all ever came forward and that degenerate slime refused to say where he had taken her from.'

'Poor thing.'

'She didn't speak for six months and when she did it was in halting English.'

'Where was she from?'

'Eastern Europe somewhere. Originally, anyway.'

'And where is she now?'

Delaney smiled at her. 'Safe.'

Sally raised an eyebrow. 'Wherever that may be nowadays.'

Delaney ground the half-smoked cigarette under his heel. 'True.'

Diane Campbell came storming up, her eyes glittering with anger. 'Give us one of those, Jack!'

Delaney fished out his cigarette packet again and handed her one. Then he stuck another in his mouth, smiling wryly. 'I guess I picked the wrong day to give up smoking.'

Diane flicked her Zippo lighter under his cigarette. 'Jack, you picked the wrong fucking life!'

Delaney nodded towards Garnier. 'Anything?'

Diane Campbell shook her head derisively. 'He's just pulling on our chain. The sick bastard. He's jerking us around – depend on it.'

'Why now, though?' Sally asked. 'After all this time.'

Diane shot her a look. 'The guy rapes and strangles young children. You want to try climbing in his shit-soup of a brain and make sense of what motivates him?'

Sally shrugged, conceding the point. 'I guess not.'

Diane blew out another angry breath of smoke. 'Who the fuck knows? Maybe he's developed a conscience.'

'Yeah, and maybe you've grown a pair of balls, Diane,' said Delaney.

Diane looked back at him coolly. 'Remember I'm still your boss, cowboy.'

Delaney considered it for a moment. 'That's right . . . you've *always* had balls.'

His mobile phone rang, muffled in his jacket pocket. Delaney took it out, looked at the caller ID and walked away to answer it, his voice barely more than a whisper.

'Hi, Mary. How is she?'

He nodded, listening. 'Has she remembered anything else . . . ?' Delaney put his other arm out and leaned against a tree. 'No, there's nothing here. I think he's just playing mind games with us.'

A loud commotion sounded behind him and he looked across as a couple of uniforms started shouting and running over with their arms outspread. Armed officers formed a protective group around Garnier as Melanie Jones and her cameraman came striding into the clearing, the bright light mounted on top of the video camera causing Peter Garnier to blink and shield his eyes.

Delaney cursed under his breath. 'Look, Mary. I've got to go. Something's come up. Tell her that I'll be round later to see you both.'

He closed the phone and headed back towards the group, his foot sliding a little in the wet mud and leaves beneath so that he stumbled forward and onto one knee. As he did so a shot rang out, cracking through the air like a shin bone being snapped. Ahead of him Delaney could see the cameraman who had been pointing the camera directly at him stagger backwards as though he'd been punched in the chest and then fall over, his camera crashing to the ground, and the only sound left ringing in the air was that of Melanie Jones screaming.

Delaney clambered back to his feet as Diane knelt down to put her hand on the fallen man's neck.

'Is he alive?' Melanie asked in a horrified whisper, her face now as pale as a dead fish as she cowered on the ground, her hands over her head as though they could protect her.

Diane Campbell ignored her. 'He's still breathing. You, get an ambulance!' she called over to a uniformed constable who quickly pulled out his radio.

In the distance the sound of a motorbike firing up and roaring away could be heard as the armed units set off clattering through the trees in pursuit.

Delaney gripped Melanie Jones by the upper arm and swung her around to face him.

'What the hell are you doing here, Jones?'

She smiled sarcastically. 'Oh, I can't get enough of you, Jack. You know that.'

Delaney shook her arm, not gently. 'I asked you a question!'

Melanie jerked her chin towards Peter Garnier. 'What do you *think* I'm doing? My job!'

Diane Campbell glared up at her. 'Arrest the stupid bitch, Jack.'

'On what charge?'

'Just get her out of here!'

Delaney steered Melanie back to the car park just off the Ducks Hill Road as Sally came across to join them.

Melanie angrily shook Delaney's hand off. 'You can't do this. I have the right to be here.'

Sally looked at her incredulously. 'You want him to take another shot at you?'

Melanie shook her head. 'Whoever it was out there wasn't shooting at me, you bloody idiot!'

Delaney glared at her. 'You want to watch that mouth of yours, lady!'

'Or what?'

'Or it's going to get slapped.'

'It's all right, sir.'

'Strikes me, Delaney, that if you hadn't stumbled when you did it would have been you face down in the mud.'

'What are you talking about?'

'He was standing right in front of you. I told him to get some shots of the hero who found the only child who lived.'

'I didn't find her.'

'You got her out of the car. Garnier must hate you for that.'

'I doubt he thinks about me at all.'

'Well, someone clearly does.'

Delaney subconsciously put a hand to his shoulder where he had been shot some weeks earlier and then shook the thought away. The man who had tried to kill him then had been killed himself. Shot twice and then blown to high heaven and hell with half a pound of Libyan Semtex. 'You've probably made some powerful enemies yourself. I've seen some of the crap you broadcast, Miss Jones.'

'Rubbish.'

Melanie tried to laugh it off but her gaze darted around nervously and she flinched involuntarily as Peter Garnier, surrounded by a phalanx of gun-wielding officers, was brought across to the heavily armoured police van that was waiting to take him back to Bayfield Prison.

Sally jerked her thumb in his direction. 'That's who he was after, you ask me. Vigilante justice.'

Delaney wasn't so sure. 'Shame he was such a lousy shot, then. And how did he know Garnier was going to be here?'

'I don't know, sir – how did *she*?' Sally jerked a thumb at Melanie Jones.

Diane Campbell walked across to them as the armoured door slammed shut, incarcerating the serial child-killer once more. The sound of an ambulance with its sirens wailing could just be heard now, growing louder. Diane fixed a dark, angry stare on the blonde reporter. 'It's a good question. How the hell did you know where we would be?'

'It's no secret that Peter Garnier had agreed to help you find the missing bodies. It's been all over the news, twenty-four seven.'

'It should have been a secret!'

'But it wasn't, was it? It was leaked.'

Diane fought the urge to slap her. 'So who leaked that, and who told you where we'd be this morning?'

Melanie Jones shrugged. Insouciant. She could have been deliberating over a cappuccino or a latte in a Hampstead boutique café. 'He was arrested further down the road near the Ruislip Lido. There's acres of woodland all around. I took an educated guess.'

'Bollocks!'

Melanie was taken aback by Diane Campbell's response, but only for a second. 'I don't have to talk to you. My sources are confidential.'

Diane nodded to DI Jimmy Skinner and PC Danny Vine who had joined the group. 'Bring her down the nick.'

Skinner smiled. 'Be a pleasure.'

Melanie glared across at Diane. 'You can't do this.'

The DSI smiled. 'Watch me.'

As Skinner and Wilkinson led her towards a squad car she called back over her shoulder. 'You'll be hearing from our lawyers.'

Delaney threw his boss a quizzical look. 'Good idea taking her in? She's right – if she doesn't want to disclose her source there's not a lot we can do about it.'

'We have a right to question her.'

'Yeah, we have that right.'

'Meanwhile, while she is helping us with those inquiries we can examine the footage her cameraman shot before he was.'

Delaney nodded. 'Good thinking.'

'It's what I'm good at.'

Sally gestured, not quite holding her hand up. 'Maybe check if Garnier had any visitors over the last few days, too?'

'Good idea. See you back at the factory.'

An ambulance came into the car park at speed and stopped abruptly, spraying gravel behind it. Delaney turned to Sally.

'Come on, constable.'

'Where to?'

'See if the sniper left any clues.' He flashed her a sardonic smile. 'Get out your magnifying glass.'

They stepped aside as the paramedics rushed past with a stretcher. Delaney and Sally walked back into the woods, past the clearing where Peter Garnier had falsely claimed to have buried the bodies of the dead children and further into the trees beyond.

A few steps into the darkened woodland and the numerous primeval ferns seemed to crowd together in a natural screen, the hubbub behind them fading away slightly. Delaney looked back to check his bearing and walked forward, trying to keep in a straight line. Sally followed behind. Mindful of the tumble Delaney had taken earlier, she picked her way carefully through the bracken and over fallen branches that littered the uneven ground.

'How far away did that motorbike sound to you, Sally?'

The detective constable shrugged. 'Close. Maybe a few hundred yards.'

'And the shot? What kind of rifle do you think?'

'I wouldn't have a clue, sir. Why? Do you?'

'Me? Fuck, no! I grew up in Southern Ireland, Sally. Not Belfast. Sounded like a car backfiring to me.'

'Lucky you slipped when you did.'

Delaney looked back at her. 'Don't go paying any attention to what that bubbleheaded news monkey was saying.'

'She might have had a point.'

Delaney snorted dismissively. 'If that woman was any more full of shite she'd be a Portaloo at the fucking Glastonbury Festival, Sally.'

'I didn't know you were a Glastonbury fan, sir.'

'There's a lot about me you don't know, Sally.'

Sally nodded quietly in agreement to herself. Probably best keep it that way, too.

Delaney walked further into the woods, stopping every now and then to look upwards. After a couple of hundred yards or so he stopped under a group of trees – thick oaks, the boughs gnarled and knotted. He looked upward, shielding his eyes with the flat of his hand, and then down at the ground. Sound was all around them. The sound of sirens in the distance and the clatter and shouts of police, uniformed and plain-clothes alike, as they searched for the shooter. But the sound of the motorcycle had faded away long enough ago for Delaney to believe they wouldn't trace him. The area was a warren of woods and commons and led into the urban sprawls of Ruislip at one end and Northwood at the other. The shooter would be long gone by now. Delaney bent down to pick up a stick and moved some of the undergrowth away at the base of one tree.

'Anything, sir?'

'Nothing useful.'

He held the stick up, dangling a pair of women's underwear from it. Then he flipped it down again, discarding them.

Sally grimaced. 'And they say romance is dead.'

'It is in Ruislip.' Delaney looked up at the tree again and then used the stick to move more of the grass and bracken aside. He took out a pen and knelt down to pick something else up.

Sally leaned down to see what he was doing. 'What have you got?'

Delaney held the pen forward. A brass shell casing

hung on the end of it. 'That's what you call evidence, constable.'

'How did you know where to look?'

Delaney pointed upwards. 'There's a broken branch there – newly broken, too. Not quite sturdy enough to take his weight, obviously.'

Sally looked up to where he was pointing. A medium-sized branch about four inches in diameter had snapped but not broken clean through: the white inner wood was in marked contrast to the moss-covered outer part of the branch. 'He broke it while hurrying down, you think?'

'Maybe. Maybe he broke it when he took his shot. Maybe that was why he missed.'

Sally nodded thoughtfully. 'Yeah . . . maybe.'

Delaney took a small plastic evidence bag from his pocket, slipped the casing into it, sealed it and put it back in his pocket.

'Let's get back to the office.'

'See what Melanie Jones has to say?'

'No. I've heard enough from that woman today. I want to listen to any more shite I'll stick prime minister's question time on the radio.'

'What's the plan, then?'

'The plan, Sally, is to go and talk to Roy Smiley, king of the burgers.'

'You hungry, sir?'

'And that.'

*

Roy Smiley was a larger-than-life character in all senses of the word. He ran a burger van called Bab's Kebabs parked in a side street just around the corner from the White City police station although he never sold kebabs and had never been married to a woman called Barbara. He was, in fact, married to a woman called Janet, had three children, all daughters, and cooked the best bacon-and-egg sandwich north of the river. He had also spent eighteen years in the Royal Fusiliers. So, while fat slices of bacon sizzled on the hotplate behind him, he bowed his head to look at the shell casing that Delaney was holding up in the transparent bag.

'Am I going to get paid for this?'

'I'll get Sally here to give you a smile and pay you for the bacon butties – how's that?'

Roy smiled at Sally. 'Sounds reasonable. What you have there is a shell casing from a standard-issue military rifle. Bolt action.'

'Current?'

'Yeah, it's current.'

'Long time since you were in the army, Roy.'

'Long time since you dragged your sorry arse out of the peat bogs of Ballydehob. Doesn't stop you being a miserable Irish bastard.'

'You pretty certain, then?'

'I keep up to date. Jack. You don't just hand your Fusiliers badge in like a punched train ticket.'

'So the man up the tree was ex-army?'

Roy shrugged. 'Could be. Could be current army. Could be neither. Might have bought the rifle off someone who was. Could be stolen. Want to leave it with me, see what I can find out?'

Delaney looked up at him incredulously. 'Yeah, why don't I do that, Roy? I'm sure when we catch the fucker his lawyer wouldn't object in the slightest.

You ever heard of something called chain of evidence?'

'What is it? A Stephen King novel?'

Delaney put the evidence bag back in his pocket. 'Just make sure my egg is runny.'

Roy grinned and picked up a couple of eggs, the fat hissing and spitting as he cracked them over the hot griddle and flipped the bacon.

*

Back at the station Delaney and Sally approached the entrance as the door swung wide and an angry Melanie Jones swept out. She stormed up to a waiting taxi, finding time to throw Delaney a withering look as she passed before jumping in the back seat and slamming the door hard enough to make him wince.

As they walked into the station Diane Campbell was handing some files over to Dave 'Slimline' Mathews, who was behind the desk.

'Someone's not a happy bunny,' Delaney said.

The chief inspector flashed him a quick smile. 'Then my job is half done.'

'How's the cameraman?'

'Stable. They've got him at the Royal South Hampstead. He'll live – just have a sore shoulder for a while. Missed all the vital organs. High-velocity bullet. The shock was the most danger to him.'

Delaney, on reflex, rubbed his own shoulder again. 'I know how that works. So, Melanie Jones. She give up the source?'

Diane shook her head. 'She stonewalled for a bit, giving it the big confidentiality-of-her-sources crap. But finally she caved in and admitted she hadn't

61

spoken to anyone at all. It was her editor who called with the information of where we'd be.'

'He give us anything more?

Diane shook her head again. 'He claims he got an anonymous e-mail. I've sent Jimmy Skinner over there to check it out.'

'Right.'

'Not holding out a lot of hope, though. The internet's easier to hide in than a tick in a flock of unshorn sheep.'

Delaney put his hand in his pocket. 'The sniper left something behind.'

'A calling card?' Diane asked wryly.

'Maybe,' Delaney replied as he pulled out the evidence bag and handed it across. 'Maybe forensics can get something from it.'

Diane looked at the shell casing through the clear plastic. 'What is it – pistol, rifle?'

'It's a . . . rifle-shell casing. Bolt action: as you load another cartridge it ejects the one before.'

'Army?'

'It's standard military issue yes.'

'Current?'

'Yep. There's thousands like that littered all over Afghanistan.'

'Melanie Jones. She do anything on the Afghan war?'

'What war? That's a fucked-up police operation, that's all.'

'Yeah, spare me the political analysis, Jack. Did she do anything on the war? Wind up some comrade of a fallen soldier? Make some comment a disgruntled and disaffected soldier would take the wrong way?'

'I don't know.'

'A tenth of all prisoners in this country are ex-military, you know.'

Delaney shrugged. 'I know, but I get my news from Chris Evans or Roy Smiley at the burger van. I certainly wouldn't pay good money to watch that bubbleheaded slapper.'

Sally smiled apologetically at Diane Campbell. 'Do you want me to look into it, boss?'

'Yeah, you do that.'

'You seriously think she was the target?'

'I don't know, Jack. Who would want to shoot the cameraman?'

'Someone with an axe to grind with the channel?'

'No, I don't buy it. He's an anonymous nobody. Melanie Jones is the name, she's the face.'

Delaney shook his head, unconvinced. 'It doesn't ring true. If someone wanted to take her out they could have done that any time, anywhere. Why now? Why there? Why Peter Garnier?'

Diane looked at him steadily. 'Maybe you can find that out.'

'What do you mean?'

'There's been a development.'

'A development?'

'He wants to speak to you.'

'Peter Garnier?'

Diane nodded. 'In the flesh.'

Delaney looked at her blankly for a beat. 'You *are* fucking kidding me?'

'Do I look like I'm smiling to you?'

'What the hell does he want to talk to me about?'

Diane shrugged. 'He wouldn't say. Said he'd talk to you.'

'And that charade in the woods today? What was that about?'

'Don't know. But the morning he leads us a merry dance in Mad Bess Woods is the same day someone takes a shot at him and he decides he needs to speak to you. Maybe he wants to unburden his soul.'

'How the hell does he even know who I am? What does he want from me?'

'What am I suddenly, the oracle of fucking Delphi? Go and speak to him, Jack. Find out.'

*

It was Jennifer Hickling's fifteenth birthday that morning, but if she was at all pleased or excited about it then it didn't show in the brown eyes that looked back at her from the mirror. She was dressed in a quasi-goth style, with dyed black hair and black make-up around her eyes but not her lips. Her lips were ruby, thick with lipstick. She looked about twenty-two and felt half a century older. She put down a plastic hairbrush matted with different-coloured hair and practised a smile. Her face felt waxen somehow, its muscles not quite under her control, the corners of her mouth twitching down-ward. A reflex that she couldn't control, like a knee being tapped with a hammer.

She smoothed down the front of her short dark denim skirt and held her Doc Marten-booted foot up, looking at it along the line of her dark stocking leg, and felt like kicking it straight into the man sleeping on the sofa. His mouth was open, drool gumming the corner of his mouth, and Jennifer felt like slamming the boot straight into his head. Breaking his teeth. Stamping on his face so it looked like raw hamburger. He was twenty-eight years old, with long greasy hair, two days' worth of stubble on his pockmarked chin and stains on his jeans where he'd pissed himself during the night. The sight of him made her almost physically sick.

A wet sigh escaped from the lips of the sleeping man and Jennifer curled the corner of her own lip again. The guy was a pig. She picked up a short-bladed knife which she had put on top of the sideboard moments earlier and not for the first time thought about slicing him from ear to ear across his scrawny throat. Slaughtering him like the hog he was.

She looked back across at him, the knuckles on her hand whitening as she gripped the knife, and a younger girl's voice cut across her dark imaginings.

'Jennifer?'

Smoother than a seaside conjuror, she palmed the knife into the side pocket of her skirt and turned to smile at her nine-year-old sister Angela.

'Wassup, kidder?'

'I'm hungry.'

'Come on, then. Let's get you breakfast.'

She put her arm around her sister's shoulder and steered her towards the kitchen.

'Are you coming to school today?'

'No. I'll take you there, then I've got some things to take care of.'

'You going up Camden again?'

'Yes.'

'What do you do up there?'

Jennifer looked down at her sister without replying, her gaze hardening and then softening again in a blink. She ruffled her fingers through Angela's curly hair and smiled.

'You want toast or cereal?'

'Toast.'

Jennifer led her through to the kitchen and opened the fridge. Inside was a can of lager and half a pint of milk. She closed the door and smiled at her sister again. 'How about an egg McMuffin? My birthday treat.'

*

Jennifer stood in the queue, looking at the menu to the side of the counter. Everything was so complicated – what about a simple list of burgers?

'Help you?'

Jennifer looked at the bored eighteen-year-old who was addressing her. His face was slack, his eyes lifeless until she turned round and he saw her. Then they became mobile with interest. His dirty blond hair looked like it had been cut by his mother with a pair of garden shears and there was a faint whiff of body odour coming off him, almost but not quite disguised with cheap aftershave. He looked familiar somehow – Jennifer was sure she had seen him around the estate. Maybe she'd given him a hand job. He looked the type and the way he was shiftily looking at her, not meeting her gaze, made her suspect as much. Just another loser from the estate ending up in a dead-end job with no future, no life ahead of him. Shit, she thought, was this going to be her in three years' time? Not if she could help it, she knew that much. But what options were there for her? If you were born on the Waterhill estate there weren't a lot of prospects ahead. Drug dealing, petty crime, prostitution seemed to be the careers of choice for many. She'd had enough of two of them and had no intention of trying the other. She saw where it ended. Dead. One way or another.

'Give me an egg McMuffin and a quarter-pounder with cheese and two large fries to go.'

'You want to go for a meal deal and get a—'

Jennifer cut him off. 'Just get me what I said!'

The youth nodded and scuttled away to fetch the food. Men, Jennifer thought. They were all arseholes. Every fucking one of them. She looked back at her sister, who was sitting quietly at a table. She remembered a time when Angela hadn't been so quiet. She remembered her running around laughing, squealing, enjoying life. Before her mother met *him* and everything changed. She realised the burger boy was saying something to her and as she turned back he was holding out a bag of food for her. She reached into her pocket for the money but the boy leaned forward and whispered conspiratorially: 'On the house. You know. Old time's sake, Jennifer. Maybe see you around.'

He winked at her and the smell of his body odour once again assaulted her nostrils and for the second time that morning she felt like being physically sick.

Men. Every one of them pond scum. Jennifer slipped her hand into her pocket and closed her hand around the comforting handle of the knife. It had already killed one of them – maybe there was time for one more before she made her move. One more for luck.

*

Kate Walker stifled a yawn as she walked along the corridor, past the geriatric ward and up to the intensive-care unit. She nodded to Bob Wilkinson, who was standing outside one of the rooms looking in through the window. Kate joined him and watched as a doctor and a nurse inside checked the patient's vitals, took the readings of the machines that were keeping him alive, made sure the drips were still connected properly and functioning.

'No change, then?' Kate asked.

'No,' said Bob Wilkinson. 'Still touch and go.'

'And the prognosis?'

Bob shrugged, a world-weary who-can-tell gesture that he had spent most of his life on the force perfecting. 'Doctors. They ever tell you anything you want to know?'

Kate gave him the bent eyebrow.

'Sorry, present company excepted . . .' He paused for a moment. 'Some of the time, anyway.'

'Who caught the case?'

'DI Bennett.'

Kate looked at him blankly.

'DI Tony Bennett. I kid you not.'

'Never heard of him.'

'A flashy-tied immigrant from up north somewhere.'

'Immigrant?'

'To London. Just transferred down.'

'He around?'

Bob Wilkinson shook his head. 'Been and gone. Early hours.'

Kate cast a critical gaze over him, seeing more than the usual world-weariness in his eyes. 'You been here all night?'

'Yeah. Three more stabbings came in after this one.'

'You know what I think they should do?'

'Go on.'

'Ban knives.'

Bob laughed dryly. 'Why not? Sure as shit worked for drugs.'

Kate turned and held her hand out to the intern who was coming out of the high-dependency room. He was in his twenties with a face still shy of the pessimism she imagined he would soon learn to develop. Hospitals boiled the optimism out of you as powerfully as they tried to wipe out germs. The nurse in her forties behind him looked as though she could eat him and three more like him for breakfast.

'Doctor Kate Walker. I'm a police surgeon.'

The doctor shook her hand with a surprisingly powerful grip, glancing back at his comatose patient. 'I'm Doctor Hake.' He smiled slightly self-consciously. 'Timothy. You were the first person attending at the scene?'

'I was. The sergeant and I were on our way back from a domestic call and found him unconscious off the road. If a slightly drunk young lady hadn't tried to take a pee in the alleyway there we might never have found him.'

The young doctor nodded. 'You probably saved his life.'

'He's going to come through?'

Doctor Hake gave his shoulders the slightest of lifts. 'I don't know. That's why I said "probably". You don't know how long he was out there before you found him?'

'No idea.'

'He lost a lot of blood and there were hypothermia complications because of it. We're trying to stabilise him, but there are internal bleeding issues – together with the wound, the shock, the possibility of serious infection.'

'I know the score, doctor. I was a forensic pathologist for quite a number of years.'

Hake looked at her, puzzled. 'You were? And now you're a police surgeon?'

'Not just that. I work here on the teaching staff and in the students' clinic.' Kate smiled. 'I'm a multi-tasker. The police-surgeon work is just the odd shift here and there.'

'Voluntary.'

'More or less.'

'So isn't that . . .' He hesitated. Trying to find the right words.

'A backward step?'

'Well, yeah. I'm looking to make consultant by the time I'm your age.'

Kate laughed. 'Good luck. And yeah, in career terms maybe it is a backward step. But I prefer working with people when they still have a chance to make it, if you know what I mean,'

Timothy Hake smiled back. 'Yeah, I can see how that works.'

'So. If you had to make a call . . .' She nodded

towards the patient in the room. 'He going to make it?'

'I could give you all the statistics, my medical background, my professional analysis . . .'

'But?'

'You might as well flip a coin.'

He nodded apologetically and moved off, the nurse ahead of him like a linebacker running defence.

Bob Wilkinson ran a hand through his thinning hair. 'Fifty-fifty. I'd take those odds on the dog track sometimes.'

'You would on a red-hot favourite. But you wouldn't bet your mortgage on it. Or your life.'

'True.'

'We know who he is yet?'

'Nope. No ID on him. No one's come forward to report him missing.'

'And what's the new DI doing about it?'

'He's got uniform canvassing the vicinity but this is Camden Town we're talking about. North London. Monkeyland.'

Kate shot him a quizzical look and Bob Wilkinson put his hands over his ears, eyes and mouth in succession. 'Only not so wise,' he said.

Kate looked back at the patient. The steady beat of the heart monitor like a grandfather clock counting down.

'Did you read the story last year about the chimpanzee in a zoo in Sweden?'

'No. What about it?'

'Called Santino. He started throwing pebbles and bits of concrete he'd shaped up like discs at visitors.'

'So?'

'So there were no stones in his compound. The keepers couldn't work out where he was getting them from.'

'And where was he getting them from?'

'From the moat that surrounded his compound. He had a stockpile of rocks at the ready.'

'I'm sure you're going somewhere with this.'

'He had them ready to throw at human visitors.' Kate nodded through the window at the stabbed man. 'It seems that premeditation is not now a solely human trait.'

'So what's your point?'

'Maybe *Planet of the Apes* got it right. Maybe our time on this planet is coming to an end. Maybe it deserves to.'

'You know what I think?'

'Enlighten me, Bob.'

'I think you spend too much time with miserable bleeding Irishmen.'

Kate laughed. The warmth of the sound should have been a tonic to the unconscious man in the intensive-care bed but he was now in a place beyond human emotion and a long way from home.

*

Jennifer held her hand out at the bus stop. Technically, she didn't need to. Technically, buses were supposed to stop automatically. Technically, we were still in an ice age, according to her English teacher, who thought he knew everything. It was bleeding cold, she knew that sure enough. Last year there might have been an Indian summer, this year England seemed to have skipped autumn altogether and headed straight into winter. So technically it was still autumn, technically the bus should halt at a designated stop but if Jennifer Hickling had learned anything in her fifteen long years on this Earth it was that 'technically' didn't mean shit, not in this city.

The single-decker hopper bus pulled up and the doors swung open with a mechanical clang and a hiss of compressed air. Jennifer flashed her bus pass at the twenty-something-year-old African-English driver, who smiled at her with perfect teeth and genuine good humour.

'Nice day for the ducks,' he said.

But Jennifer ignored him and headed down the bus as it pulled away from the kerb and into traffic. What the fuck has he got to be so pleased about? she thought to herself. The bus was nearly full but half-way down on the right a seventeen-year-old youth wearing baggy jeans, a hoodie and a fatuous smile plastered across his pale white face winked at her, spreading his legs wider, and patted the vacant seat next to him. She flipped him the finger and walked to the back where an elderly woman was sitting tight against the window staring out at the rain. She had a loose canvas shoulder bag in her lap, was wearing a smart raincoat and had her hair covered in a floral scarf.

Jennifer sat down next to her and the woman looked across at her for a moment, blinking as if to pull her eyes into focus. Then she smiled at her.

'You going to be late at school?'

Jennifer shrugged dismissively. 'It's a field-studies day.'

'Oh, I see.' The woman nodded and looked at her again.

'Vampires is it, dear?' she asked.

Now Jennifer blinked herself. 'You what?'

'What with the hair and the make-up. What do you call yourselves? Geemos. I know you're all into it now. I have a granddaughter your age Kirsty.'

Jennifer didn't have a clue what the daft old bat was going on about. 'Whatever.'

'Stephanie Meyer, isn't it? She's all the rage. I have to get one of hers for Kirsty for Christmas. Maybe you can tell me what the latest one is?'

'I have no idea.'

'In my day it was Errol Flynn.'

Jennifer sighed, exasperated, and turned to her. 'What?'

'That had all the girls swooning. Mind you, he just wore green tights and the like. Maybe he should have dressed in black and gone out at night.'

'Yeah.'

'I wouldn't have minded him biting *my* neck. That's for sure.'

Jennifer's lips curled. 'Yeah, too much information.'

'I wasn't always old, you know,' said the woman, smiling, lost a little in her nostalgic reveries. 'Like they say, *tempus fugit.*'

Jennifer would have responded, pretty sure that she had just been dissed by the old woman, but she stood up before Jennifer could say anything.

'Anyway, this is my stop.'

As Jennifer shifted her legs sideways to let the woman pass, the bus swerved to the side and came to a sudden stop, throwing the old woman against her

74

and causing her to drop her bag. Jennifer muttered under her breath and bent down to pick it up, sweeping the contents back into it. She stood up, handed it to the old woman and let her pass.

'Thanks, dear, and good luck with the undead.'

Jennifer watched her go and waited for the doors to close and the bus to pull out into the traffic again. Then she opened her left hand and looked at the small purse that she had neglected to return to the old woman's bag.

Maybe the woman's granddaughter would have to wait for her bloody vampire novel or whatever it was that the daft old bat had been wittering on about. Some people liked to read horror stories, Jennifer reckoned, some people were already living in them. She opened her own bag, put the purse in and checked the contents: her own purse, five packets of condoms, a pepper spray she had bought off one of the other girls, some amyl-nitrate poppers. She closed the bag and stood up as the bus came into Camden.

Yeah. Time for field studies.

*

The governor of Bayfield prison, Ron Cornwell, a tall, thin man in his fifties, always felt nervous in Delaney's presence and couldn't quite put his finger on the reason. Some of the most dangerous criminals in the country were incarcerated in his prison and yet he felt more uncomfortable under the Irishman's probing gaze than he did among them. It was to do with power, he guessed – he had complete control over the men in his care. He wasn't sure whether anybody had control over this particular man and from what he had heard of him he couldn't believe, even if only half the tales were true, why Delaney hadn't been kicked off the force long before. He did get results, though, that much Cornwell knew. There were a lot of his inmates right now who would have dearly loved to get their hands on Jack Delaney.

They were in the segregated wing of Bayfield prison. An inner sanctum reserved for those prisoners most at risk from their fellow detainees. Maybe some of them would have been better off in the secure facilities at Broadmoor but what distinguished the criminally insane from the criminally and murderously perverse was a fine distinction that didn't trouble Ron Cornwell's conscience. And if the perverts were targeted and hurt or even murdered because of it – if there was no honour among thieves, then what should pass for honour among these lowest of the low? – then he didn't have a problem with that, either. The segregated wing was a sanctum from the normal prison population but when rabid dogs turned on each other a handler was well advised to stay clear. After all, these were the prisoners that even the most morally reprehensible of the prison's general population found repugnant. Child killers. Child molesters, rapists, torturers. And the worst of the lot, as far as some of the inmates were concerned, were ex-policemen.

People like Charles Walker. Delaney's old boss and Kate's uncle, who was awaiting trial on various counts of murder and the sexual exploitation of children.

People like Peter William Garnier.

Delaney cleared his throat and the governor realised he had been staring. He nodded to the two guards who stood beside him, one of whom took out a key and unlocked the door of the interview room.

'We have him handcuffed as well as shackled by the legs.'

'He's a danger to young children, not to me,' Delaney replied.

'It's standard procedure. Body fluids can be a dangerous weapon in a prison nowadays. It keeps him at a distance.'

Delaney nodded. 'Let's just get this over with.'

The governor looked at him again. The curiosity was written plain on his face. 'And you have no idea why he asked to speak to you?'

'None at all.'

'And the woods this morning . . . ?'

'There was nothing there. It was a wild-goose chase.'

Ron Cornwell gestured to the guard, who opened the door for Delaney to enter the room. 'The guards will be just outside.'

Delaney ignored him, walking straight into the room and closing the door behind him. At the end of a ten-foot wooden table and facing the door sat Peter Garnier. His magnified, watery eyes, which stared at Delaney as he entered, were as emotionless as those of a fish looking out of a bowl.

Delaney pulled out a chair and sat down, looking back at him. Assessing the man. He'd been forty-two years old when he'd been arrested eighteen years ago, and he looked older than his present sixty years. Frailer, his skin papery so that the pale blue of his blood vessels beneath filtered through. The pale blue of death, Delaney thought, and the sooner that happened the better – although the disease could take up to seven years, so maybe not. He revised his opinion. The man deserved a slow and painful death.

'I saw you watching me this morning, detective.'

Garnier's voice wasn't what Delaney had expected. It was quiet but confident, more powerful than his thin legs and wasted frame would have suggested.

'That a fact?' Delaney said.

'Watching me quite closely, Detective Inspector Delaney. I could feel your eyes upon me and when I looked over into them I saw the darkness of your desire. We have something very much in common, don't we, Jack?'

Delaney felt his hands forming into a fist underneath the table but he kept his eyes level, his voice steady.

'The only thing we have in common, you little piece of shite, is that we are both going to die and you're going to do that a long time before I do.'

The corner of Garnier's mouth quirked in something resembling a smile.

'You seem very sure of that fact.'

'Depend on it, Garnier, I'll be pissing on your grave sooner or later. What do you want from me?'

Garnier twisted his head to look at the solid wall, as if there were a window there. 'Things can happen when we least expect them,' he said. Ignoring Delaney's question as he looked back at him.

'You know, Garnier, you open your mouth and I get the smell of raw sewage in my nostrils. What am I doing here?'

'Do you believe in vengeance, inspector? Do you believe that revenge is a dish best served cold? No, I can see it in your eyes. You don't wait, do you, Delaney? You're an Irishman driven by passions you can neither control nor live with. You're an addict, aren't you, just like me?'

'You're a bug. A cockroach. I'm nothing like you. I'm a human being, Garnier.'

Garnier looked at him for a long moment without replying. 'You believe in a final judgement, don't you, Inspector Delaney?'

'What I believe or don't believe has got nothing to do with you. Either tell me what you want to tell me or I am leaving. Right now.'

'What's the time?'

Delaney glanced at his watch. 'It's ten o'clock and I'm out of here.' He watched Garnier, waiting. Sometimes it was all about waiting. Delaney didn't know why he was there but Garnier was after something. He could see it in the glittering of his eyes, in the moistness of his breath, in the hot flush that was suffusing his pale flesh like a rash.

Garnier quirked the corner of his mouth again. 'The girl you rescued.' He gestured as if searching his memory. 'What's her name now?'

He asked the question in an innocent enough way, but his eyes had focused and Delaney was sure that this was the question he had been brought here to answer.

'Your fifteen minutes of fame, wasn't it? The girl rescued from a monster by a handsome young policeman. The girl in the boot. Whatever became of her, I wonder?'

Garnier tilted his head slightly, like a bird, looking at Delaney. Watching his reactions.

Delaney held his gaze, the muscles in his neck tightening visibly. When he spoke his voice was heavy, laden with threat.

'You attempt to put yourself in my life and you will regret it, Garnier.'

'You put your own self in my life, inspector, the day you took that young girl.' He coughed into his hand, his whole body suddenly racked with spasms. Then his body shuddered and grew calm again. 'She was the last,' he said and looked up again at Delaney, the corner of his mouth twitching once more like a grub exposed to sunlight. 'And I know what you did with her.'

'You know nothing about me.'

Garnier smiled almost fondly. 'See, you and me, Jack. We're alike in so many ways. I'm a Catholic too now – did you know that.'

'No. I must have missed the memo on that one,' said Delaney sarcastically. 'While I was busy having a life.'

'Busy indeed, Jack. Busy indeed.'

'You call me Jack one more time and I will break every fucking tooth in your mouth.'

Garnier looked up at the security camera mounted on the ceiling.

'It's switched off.'

Garnier shook his head. 'I doubt that, but no matter. It's the violence in you that I admire, inspector. All that rage, all that fury lashing out at the world. It's a coping mechanism. It saves you from those thoughts you have. Those desires.'

'You've become a psychoanalyst as well as a Catholic, have you? Did you learn anything in your studies about a man who rapes children and then strangles them as he climaxes?'

'Indeed I did. Our God is a violent god, inspector. A slaughterer of innocents. There's more blood in the Old Testament than love. You know that to be a fact. Sex and blood. It's always been there. You understand this.'

Delaney looked at him, not responding. Waiting.

'See, both you and I know, detective, that the world is made of chaos, not order.'

'That so?'

Garnier nodded excitedly, warming to his theme, oblivious to Delaney's sarcasm. 'And there is an imperative in the human psyche either to embrace that chaos or to try and tame it. The first is irrelevant and the second is a fool's errand. God knows that. The God of the Old Testament. Our existences are scattered fragments of meaning. You try to fit the shapes together, resolve the randomness of things, like a jigsaw puzzle building bit by bit to make a perfect picture. You have to get each piece in order to make sense of the world, don't you?'

Delaney shifted uncomfortably. 'I have no idea what you are talking about.'

'Yes, you do. It's like that perfect portrait of Christ and his disciples on the jigsaw your mother bought for you when you were seven years old and had just had your first holy communion.'

Delaney snorted. 'You know nothing about me.'

'I know you have to make the pieces fit. It's everything about you because you broke it in the first place.'

'And you?'

'Me? If I wanted to make a piece fit I'd cut the head of it till it did. It's my picture that is important. No one else's. God knows this.'

Delaney stood up and walked to the door. 'Like I said, talking to you, Garnier, is like swimming in a cesspool. We're done here.'

As Delaney put his hand on the door handle Garnier called after him.

'Look after your girls, Jack. They're a precious gift . . . But you know that, don't you?'

Delaney could hear the catch in the man's voice. He looked back at him, could see Garnier's wet-eyed stare fixed on him now, one hundred per cent focused.

He shook his head. 'You're not worth the spit.'

And Garnier sat back in his chair and smiled. 'You don't know, do you? You really don't know.'

Delaney went through the door and closed it behind him. The guard threw him a questioning look, checking if everything was okay, as he turned the key in the door. Delaney nodded but as the guard locked the door Delaney felt a shivering unease run through his nervous system, like the ghost of a malarial sickness long ago cured. He took a couple of deep breaths and ran his hand across his forehead, damp now with perspiration. He put a hand against the wall and took in some breaths.

The other guard looked him. 'Everything okay?'

'Yeah. Just need a cigarette. Some fresh air.'

'I know what you mean. I had my way, Peter Garnier would have been flushed a long time since.'

The first guard tested that the door was secure and turned to Delaney. 'He tell you where the bodies were buried?'

'No.'

'What did he want, then?'

'To give me his views on God, the universe and family life.'

'Funny how they all find God when it comes near their turn to meet him.'

'He could have years ahead of him but his kind have always found God long before that sort of need.'

The guard looked at him quizzically.

'Not any kind of God you and I would recognise. The kind that lives in their heads and puts rat poison in their veins.'

Delaney looked at his own arm, his own veins proud on his hand and forearm, a slight tremor still visible. He fished in his pocket for a packet of cigarettes and gestured to the guard.

'Take me outside. I think I'm going to throw up.'

*

Kate Walker was standing by the water-cooler in the corridor just down from the CID briefing rooms, taking a long swig from a clear plastic cup, draining it. She was about to throw it in the bin when a medium-height man in his thirties, with short brown hair and amused brown eyes, approached her. He favoured his right leg, the hint of a limp in his left. An accent she couldn't quite place.

'Any chance of you pouring me one of those, darling?'

Kate looked up at him, feeling her face tighten as her eyebrows raised. 'Come again?' she said, her voice like a taut wire.

'Thirsty work, being a detective.' He winked.

Kate shook her head, shrugged and pulled out a cup for him, filling it with cold water. 'Let me guess. You work in the political-correctness division?'

'CID, for my sins.'

Kate still couldn't quite place his accent. A hint of northern in there somewhere. 'Transferred down from Doncaster, I take it?'

'My fame precedes me, Doctor Walker.'

Kate blinked again, not managing to hide her surprise.

'I was told to look out for a strikingly attractive dark-haired woman with come-to-bed eyes and a ready temper.'

'Is that a fact?'

The detective laughed. 'Well, no, not really. Bob Wilkinson told me you'd just gone to get a drink of water. Master detective that I am, I worked the rest out.'

Kate laughed despite herself. 'So you'd be the famous Tony Bennett.' She pointed at his leg. 'Invalided out of the horse division, were you?'

'I took a tumble, all right. But not from a horse.'

Kate tilted her head and sighed. 'Go on, then?' She couldn't bet on it but she thought he coloured slightly.

'I fell off my pushbike, if you must know.'

Kate laughed and the DI held his hand out.

'I'll be all right in a day or two. And I might not be the famous Tony Bennett. But I am one. I blame my dad.'

'Your dad?'

'For not telling my mum it was a ridiculous idea. She's a huge fan.'

84

'Clearly.'

'Could have been worse – she could have been a Gordon Sumner fan.'

Kate poured herself another cup of water and took a sip. 'Have you identified the stabbing victim yet?'

'No.'

'Seems odd that no one has come forward. How old would you say he was?'

Bennett shrugged. 'Eighteen or nineteen.'

'A single stab wound to the chest. A mugging, do you think?'

'Unlikely.'

'Why?'

'The location, so close to the main street. That time of night in Camden Town the place would have been jumping.'

'True. But there was no wallet on him.'

'You saw someone running away.'

'That's right. Constable Wilkinson set off in pursuit but couldn't catch him. I stayed with the victim.'

'Just as well, by the sounds of it.'

'I hope so.' Kate shrugged too. 'Still touch and go.'

'But you didn't get a good look at the assailant?'

'Just his back as he was running away – he had a hood on, dark clothes . . .' Kate held her hands up apologetically.

'What about on his feet?'

'Don't know.'

'Ethnicity?'

'Like I say, he was wearing a hooded top.'

'Height?'

'Hard to tell from the distance. Not tall. Medium height, I'd say.'

Bennett nodded and threw his cup into the bin. 'When we know who the vic is, might give us somewhere to start.'

'Usually helps.'

The detective gave her an appraising look. 'How about I shout you lunch later, as we're going to be working together?'

'No can do, I'm afraid.'

'Back to the day job, then. What is it, medical centre at the university?'

Kate nodded. 'That and the odd lecture. But not until next Wednesday. The students have half-terms nowadays, reading weeks.'

'Not in my day.'

'Nor mine. Sad to say. Still,' she smiled, 'at least the policemen aren't looking younger.'

'Ouch. So . . . lunch?' Bennett obviously didn't give up easily.

'Prior arrangement – sorry.' Kate smiled again, over Bennett's shoulder this time, as Jack Delaney came walking down the corridor towards them.

'Morning, Jack. This is Tony Bennett, the new DI.'

Delaney nodded and held his hand out. 'Pleasure to meet you,' he said, his voice clipped, all business.

'Likewise.'

They shook, the briefest of handshakes. Kate looked at Delaney, sensing his troubled mood. 'Everything all right, Jack?'

'Fine as. Why?'

'You look like someone's just walked over your grave.'

Delaney smiled humourlessly. 'Dancing on it, more likely. I've just been to visit Peter Garnier.'

Bennett whistled through his teeth. 'I heard about what happened this morning. Someone took a shot at him.'

'That's right. Shame they missed.'

'How'd anyone know he'd be there?'

'Good question. Someone leaked it to the press, too.'

'Someone on the force?' asked Kate.

'Exactly.'

'Why?'

Delaney poured himself a cup of water. 'Garnier was just telling me people do things for all sorts of reasons. That the universe itself makes no sense and is designed that way. Working here . . . ?' He shook his head and took a gulp of water. 'I don't know, maybe he's right. There's no sense to half the fucking things people do to one another, after all. And we're just here to pick up the pieces, not make sense of any of it.'

Kate look across at him, concerned. 'What's going on, Jack? Why did that man want to see you?'

'I honestly don't know, Kate.' Delaney shrugged and looked puzzled as Sally Cartwright came running up the corridor.

'Sir. You'd better come quick,' she said in a breathless rush, clearly very agitated.

'What is it?'

'A child's gone missing.'

'And . . . ?'

'An eight-year-old boy, sir.'

'When?'

'About an hour ago.'

'An hour. Surely that's too early to start panicking about—' DI Bennett started to say before Sally held up her hand, cutting him off.

'He was taken from Carlton Row, sir. Harrow on the Hill. The same street where Peter Garnier abducted those children all those years ago.'

'I know where it is, Sally.'

'From a house just across from where their houses were.'

Kate looked across at Delaney. His gaze was impassive. His dark eyes a mystery to her once more.

Delaney looked at his watch and the action stuck a spike in his heart. 'The son of a bitch.'

'What is it, Jack? What the hell is going on?'

'I have no idea.' He took his sergeant by the arm. 'Come on, Sally.'

They strode off down the corridor.

'Jack!' Kate called after him but to no effect.

'You got any idea what that was all about?' DI Bennett asked her.

'Not the first thing.'

'Looks like your lunch might have been cancelled.' He raised a questioning eyebrow hopefully.

'Yeah. Nice try.'

She turned and hurried after Delaney.

Bennett stood there a moment or two, watching after them thoughtfully. Then he crushed the plastic beaker tightly in his fist and threw it into the bin.

*

Any copper knows that the first forty-eight hours of an investigation into a murder are critical. And the same applies to an abduction. Perhaps more so, as the longer the investigation continues the higher the probability that the child will not be returned home unhurt. Sexual predators who prey on children act on impulses that they cannot control. Some don't wish to control them, but when the moment has passed, when their actions have brought them relief from their uncontrollable urges, they are left with the child. And the child is evidence. Evidence that can bring the howling pack right to their very door. For some it is not about the killing. It's just evidence disposal. For other people the killing is very much a part of it. People like Peter Garnier.

Jack Delaney knew that better than most. There was a babble of concerned chatter around him in the briefing room that morning, but he wasn't listening to it. Tuning it out like so much white noise. He knew all about sexual predators and the morning's events had sent him back to places that he had never wished to revisit. His own daughter, Siobhan, had been taken by the worst kind of sexual predator. Kate Walker's uncle, a man who not only treated children as objects for his foul lusts, he treated them as a commodity, making films and distributing them to the worst sort of deviants like himself, who somehow seemed to recognise each other and form networks. Like the nursery-school club that formed on Facebook and distributed images between themselves up and down the country. Delaney couldn't even begin to imagine how these people did it, how they recognised their own types and made contact with each other. And, like them, Kate's uncle had taken the rape of children and made it a commodity. But he had also, like Garnier, taken it further and made murder part of the sick mix. Had it not been for Kate's intervention, putting her own life at risk,

Delaney shuddered to think what would have become of his own precious daughter. He certainly hadn't been able to protect her. His vision was clouded with guilt, with self-loathing, with a self-pity that made him a shambles of a father, a shambles of a man. He looked up from the printed report he was reading as Kate came into the room and felt a small flashback of fear as he read the concern in her eyes. The human form was such a delicate thing, such a fragile vessel. His gaze dropped to her stomach; her jacket was buttoned and he knew she wasn't showing yet, but he still felt he could see the signs. Such a soft, vulnerable, defenceless form for such precious cargo. He met her gaze again and knew that his heart would break if anything ever happened to her and to the child she was carrying. His hand clenched inadvertently, crumpling the paper he was holding.

'Is it bad?' she asked.

'I don't know, Kate.'

The hubbub died as someone turned the volume up on the television in the corner of the room and Melanie Jones's face filled the screen.

'Breaking news just in. In another bizarre twist in the Peter Garnier story, police sources have confirmed that a young child has gone missing from a house only a few doors away from where two children were abducted by Garnier in 1995. DNA traces linked Garnier to their abduction and murder and although he has confessed to it he has never revealed where their bodies are buried. A further six children's bodies were discovered buried under his garden shed in 1997 but the mystery of where the remaining bodies are has never been resolved. Dramatically, two weeks ago

Peter Garnier broke his vow of silence and promised to lead the police to the two children's burial ground. This morning, in a covert operation that myself and Sky News had access to . . .'

Delaney snorted, shaking his head with disgust.

'. . . Peter Garnier led a group of detectives to Mad Bess Woods, a wooded conservation area outside Ruislip. No bodies were discovered but, as Sky News revealed to you exclusively earlier, someone fired a shot at Garnier, injuring our cameraman in the process. It can be no coincidence that only a few hours later a child of around the same age as Garnier's previous victims was abducted from Carlton Row. Police sources have also revealed that an ongoing police investigation into the leaks . . .'

Diane Campbell strolled into the briefing room, her loud voice cutting across the reporter's. 'Someone shut that woman up.'

A remote was pointed at the television and muted the sound.

'Okay, everyone. Listen up.'

Any muttering and whispered speculation subsided as the DCI walked up to the front of the gathering and swept her gaze around the assembled staff, uniforms and detectives alike.

'Paddington Green are taking the lead on this, for obvious reasons. We are not treating today's events as pure coincidence. Somebody tried to take out Peter Garnier, and someone else, or the same man, has decided to copycat him.'

'We don't know that yet, boss,' Delaney spoke out.

'If you've got something to share, detective, don't wait for the speaking stick.'

Delaney shrugged. 'It's been an hour or so. The kid could yet turn up. The grandfather says he nodded off in his shed for just a minute.'

'Yeah. Just like Ellie Peters did in 1995.'

'The difference is that Ellie Peters was an alcoholic junkie who couldn't have told you the time of day if you shoved a cuckoo clock up her arse and set the chimes for twelve.'

Laughter rippled around the room and Diane glared at her detective. 'Save the jokes for when we get the little boy back, safe and sound. All right?'

'I was just saying maybe we should wait till we start joining dots and get a picture that is completely different from what we think we should be looking at.'

'Here's the dots, cowboy. 1995, two kids are abducted from Carlton Row. 1997, Peter Garnier, a serial predator, a child rapist and murderer is arrested by chance. Clothing and DNA connect him to the missing children. 2010, he takes us to where he claims to have buried the bodies and someone takes a shot at him. A couple of hours later a kid in the age range he prefers is taken from the same street. What does that tell you?'

'That maybe he had a partner in crime all those years ago.'

Diane looked at him thoughtfully. 'Did he tell you anything in your interview with him this morning that we don't know about?'

'He told me that God killed children and that the world is designed as a place of chaos, and that by trying to impose order upon it we are going against God's divine will and therefore the misery and pain and loss we suffer we have called down upon our own heads as a direct consequence of it.'

Diane looked at him for a moment. 'Have you been drinking this morning, Jack?'

Delaney's voice thickened, the soft Irish burr of his childhood accent becoming more noticeable. 'I swear when I left that man's presence I felt like taking a bath in surgical spirit and downing a bottle of Bushmills without benefit of glass, ice or soda, boss. But the answer to your question is no, I have not had a drink this morning.'

'Then do you mind translating what you just said into English?'

Delaney shrugged impassively. 'It's what he told me. I am a simple detective, Diane. Not a charmer of snakes or a reader of the offal he has cast in his own brain to see into the future.'

'You're anything but simple, Jack. What do you think he meant?'

'Exactly what he said. He is a sociopath. The worst kind of degenerate sociopath. He was telling us that he operates without a moral compass.'

'We already knew that.'

'He was telling us he can do anything he likes and we are powerless to stop him. And he can do it because he has a true understanding of the real nature of the universe, and the Divinity that created it is on his side.'

Diane shook her head, disgusted. 'God help us, another politician.'

Delaney nodded. 'You make a good point, ma'am.'

Diane Campbell turned back to the room. 'Like I said, Paddington Green are taking the lead on this –

serious crime unit because of the possible links to Garnier. We'll be assisting with CID backup and uniform, likewise uniform from Harrow, Pinner, Wealdstone and the Met generally. It may well go national. The main thing is that we find this missing boy and we find him quickly.'

Chairs were scraped back as people stood and the hubbub started again as they took this as a sign of dismissal.

Diane held her hand up and spoke loudly. 'One other thing before you go. Someone on the force has been leaking information to the press. That person will be identified . . . and if I find out it's someone from our watch then I will personally have them strung up and left to dangle. And Jack, Paddington want to speak to you asap. Detective Inspector Robert Duncton. I believe you know him.'

Delaney nodded. 'Tell him I'll be at Carlton Row. Come on, Sally, get your chauffeur's cap.'

As Sally hurried off to get her jacket, Delaney turned to Kate, who was standing nearby talking to Bob Wilkinson. 'Sorry about lunch.'

'You're good for a rain check.'

'Believe it.'

'And Jack . . .' She hesitated.

'Go on.'

Kate stepped in closer and spoke quietly. 'Your cousin Mary. She's tied up in this somehow, isn't she?'

Delaney looked around the room, then leaned in and put his hand on Kate's upper arm. 'I'll explain later.' He gave her arm a squeeze and headed out, followed by Sally Cartwright.

DI Tony Bennett watched him leave, deep in thought. Kate caught the look on his face and he smiled broadly. 'Seems like I picked an interesting day to move to White City,' he said to her.

'Well, you know what they say.'

Bennett bent an enquiring eyebrow. 'What?'

'If you're tired of White City, you're tired of life.'

'Who says that?'

'Nobody who lives here,' said Bob Wilkinson.

*

A light but steady rain had started to fall and Sally switched the windscreen wipers on, the rubbers scratching loudly at first before settling into a gentle swishing rhythm that was almost hypnotic.

Delaney looked out of the passenger window as they slowly progressed west, snarled in heavy traffic that was the norm now on Western Avenue.

'You ever think about how many hours you've wasted on this particular stretch of road, Sally?'

'Not particularly, sir.'

'You're young yet. If I was to sit and add up all the hours I've wasted sat in traffic on this miserable stretch of tarmac I'd probably cry.'

'I like to keep my mind active, sir. Use the time to think.'

'And what conclusions has that active brain of yours come to?'

Sally turned to him and smiled. 'Take Peter Garnier, for example.'

'What about him?'

'The fact that he lied about taking us to find the bodies. The fact that he wanted to speak to you.'

'Go on.'

'He's interfacing with us, sir. He hasn't done that for fifteen years.'

'So?'

'So he's on the radar. We only catch them if they're on the radar, don't we? If they're in the system somewhere, somehow. There are hundreds of them out there that we don't know about. Thousands. Some we never catch. Hundreds of crimes we don't know about. Rapes. Assaults. Murders we'll never know about.'

'And this is good? Why?'

'Well, it's not good, is it, sir? That's my point, that's what you should take from what you told us Garnier said to you.'

'Sally, you want to cut to the chase here?'

'We don't catch a lot of sociopaths because they have no conscience, no desire to be caught. But some do. People like Ted Bundy, they want to be caught, they even want to be killed and they want to control that as well. They play games with the police because in the end they want us to catch them. In America maybe they want to be caught so they can be killed. In those states where they have the death penalty, anyway.'

'Go on.'

'Well, nothing's ever black and white, is it, except in a police uniform. Sometimes people want to be caught because they want to be stopped.'

'Peter Garnier was caught a long time ago.'

'But if he had an accomplice like you said, maybe he's going to lead us to him. He's talking to us, sir. Well, he's talking to *you*, anyway. It's a thin thread, sir, but it's something to hold onto. Something to develop.'

Delaney threw her an appraising glance. 'You've learned a lot from me over these last few months, haven't you?'

'I already knew how to drink, sir.'

Delaney grunted. 'Including a proper respect for authority.'

'It's a line, sir. From *The Sting* – I like that film.

'Well, then just keep thinking, Sally. It's what you're good at.'

'Sir.'

'And pull off at the next left.'

'That's not the way to Harrow.'

'I know that, Cassidy. It's not the way to Amarillo, either. We're going to Pitshanger to see someone first.'

'Who?'

'One of my cousins.' Delaney paused for a moment. 'One of my cousins on the respectable side.'

*

Kate was sitting in the police surgeon's office, which was a small room downstairs just off the custody and booking area. She looked up when there was a knock on her door and DI Bennett stuck his head round.

'Got a minute?'

Kate gestured with her hand. 'Sure. Come in. Just catching up with the paperwork.'

'Don't get me started on paperwork. Cut down the number of forms we have to fill in and we'd raise our solve rate exponentially, you ask me. '

'Who was it who said bureaucracy is the bedrock of incompetence?'

Bennett shrugged. 'I don't know but if he was in the Met I imagine he'd have been fired.'

'What do you want?'

'I'm on my way over to part of your university. Thought you might like to tag along.'

'I told you I'm not working there this week.'

Bennett smiled. 'I know you did.'

Kate looked at him. 'You're not hitting on me, are you, Inspector Bennett? I thought we cleared all that up.'

Bennett laughed. 'No. No. I don't swing my truncheon on another man's beat.'

Kate looked at him coolly. '*Swing your truncheon on another man's beat*?'

'I was speaking metaphorically.'

'Let me guess . . . Germaine Greer is your godmother.'

Bennett shrugged. 'When I am with attractive women, I just use humour as a defence mechanism. What can I say?'

'You can say what you're doing here. I am busy. It's paperwork but I'm busy.'

'Someone has come forward. From the university. We might have a name for your stabbing victim.'

'Go on.'

'A fellow student across the corridor from some fellow in their hall of residence called the police because he was concerned. This guy hasn't been home since last night, he missed his lectures this morning and he matches the description.'

'Who is he?'

'Jamil Azeez. Second-year student. Studying law. An Iranian.'

Kate looked at the paperwork on her desk and stood up, pulling her coat, a tailored black cotton jacket that matched her skirt, off the back of the chair. 'The paperwork can wait.'

'Bennett nodded 'Good call. I'll drive.'

Kate threw him a cool look, snatched up her car keys off her desk and rattled them at him pointedly. 'We'll both drive.'

'Shame. I thought we could have got to know each other better on the way there, and you could tell me all about Inspector Delaney. He seems a fascinating character from all I hear.'

'I wouldn't believe half of what you've heard. He's a lot worse than that.'

Bennett pointed at her jacket. 'You'll need something warmer than that on. It's cold out there.'

Kate grabbed her black parka with its faux-fur trim and sailed out of the office, leaving DI Bennett to follow in her wake.

*

Pitshanger Village is a small area some miles west of Central London, just outside Ealing and off the Western Avenue. Hidden in the scar of housing that runs from well east of the city to the borders of the Green Belt in the west, it is a little-known but exclusive area. Like a miniature version of Greenwich Village in New York it is home to artists and writers, to musicians, cameramen, actors, lawyers, business-men and businesswomen. It has boutique bakeries, independent bookshops, organic pizza-parlours. A bit like Hampstead Village, Delaney thought as they turned along Pitshanger Lane, but not that much, not by a long chalk. Well heeled by Prada, though. Christ, he thought to himself, I'm turning into one of them. Maybe moving to Belsize Park hadn't been such a good idea, after all: he'd be wearing Hunter wellies next and buying the *FT* and discussing the Nasdaq with Nigel in the Holly Bush over croissants and coffee on a Sunday morning. He shuddered.

'Something up, sir?'

'It's cold, Sally. That's all. Sure, I'd never have left the sun-kissed shores of Cork if I'd have known the weather was going to be this bleeding miserable year in and year out.'

'We had a cracking summer, sir.'

'Seems like a lifetime ago now.'

Sally looked through the softly thwumping wind-screen wipers at the rain-drenched urban landscape of West London beyond and couldn't help but agree. London in the summer was a different place. No doubt about that.

A short while later, Sally pulled the car to a stop on the street across from the library, next door to the bookshop that was painted Tardis blue and was busy with customers, seemingly defiant in the face of the recession and the competition from Amazon and the supermarkets. Maybe people in Pitshanger could afford to pay the full price for books, or maybe they just didn't want to be seen shopping in Asda or Tesco. 'Do you want me to wait in the car?' she said.

Delaney shook his head. 'Not at all, Sally. Come with me. We might need some thinking done after all. And you're the girl for that.'

'Woman, sir.'

'Jeez, you're all so keen to grow up. I don't know what's wrong with the youth of today, I surely to God don't.'

'I sometimes think you were born a grumpy old man, sir.'

'Nah,' said Delaney. 'A proper miserable personality is like a good beer belly – it takes many years and serious application to achieve it.'

Sally glanced across as Delaney levered his tall athletic frame out of the car, at his flat stomach and powerful shoulders. 'Well, at least you've got time for the beer belly, sir.'

Delaney closed the car's passenger door and pulled the collar of his jacket up against the cold rain that was slanting across the street. Then he led Sally across the road, past the bookshop and through a double doorway to a staircase leading up into a group of flats called Kenmure Mansions that ran above the shops that lined the street. They both shook the moisture from their hair as they climbed upward. Delaney's shoes clattered loudly on the bare concrete steps and Sally's curiosity was piqued. She knew better than to ask him what they were doing here – she'd find out soon enough, she was sure of that. Must be pretty important for him to delay getting to Harrow, she knew that much. Or then again, maybe she didn't, she realised. Who knew with Jack Delaney, after all? The man was about as predictable as the weather in barbecue season.

Delaney walked past a number of doors, all black, all well kept, before stopping and tapping on one that was painted bottle green and had a shiny brass knocker. There was a small metallic plaque on the wall beside it. Sally kept her expression neutral but flicked her glance sideways to read it.

DR MARY O'CONNELL.

Before she had a chance to ask Delaney if that was his cousin the door opened. A tall woman in her late forties with long honey-coloured hair and sparkling blue eyes looked Delaney up and down critically and then smiled. 'It's good to see you, cousin.'

'And you, Mary.' He gave her a hug.

'Well, you'd best come through.' She looked at Sally and tilted her chin teasingly. 'And who is this beautiful young thing with you? I hope you're not up to your old tricks again, Jack Delaney?'

Sally blushed despite herself and held her hand out. 'I'm a detective constable. I work with Inspector Delaney. Sally Cartwright.'

'Pleased to meet you, darling.'

Mary shook Sally's hand in a warm grip, clasping the other hand over and patting it.

Delaney gestured that they should go in. 'She's my right-hand woman, Mary, and that thirsty, more importantly, that she can barely speak for the dust in her throat. Let's get the kettle on.'

'Come in, come in, then! It's you that's standing there on the step like a kidnapped garden gnome who's lost his fishing rod.' Mary waved them in, laughing. 'And kettle, you say? Are you sure you're my cousin? What have you done with him, Sally? Signed him up for the pledge?'

Sally laughed. 'Not in this life.'

Mary led them through into a beautifully decorated and surprisingly large lounge. Large windows looked out onto the street below but the double glazing muted the noise of the traffic so that it barely registered. A young woman stood up from the couch as they walked in. She had thick curly hair that was midnight black and shiny, flawless olive skin and beautiful almond-shaped eyes that seemed to shine. If she was one of Cleopatra's hand maidens, Sally thought, she'd have probably had her killed.

'This is Gloria, Sally,' said Delaney.

The woman smiled and held her hand out. 'I'm the girl in the boot,' she said.

*

Whitefriars Hall was a brick-built building, constructed sometime in the early 1970s to house the burgeoning population of students in the ever-expanding West London University. The university had several buildings spread throughout the west of the city: old technical colleges, art colleges and a polytechnic that had been assimilated under the banner of West London University at the beginning of the 1990s. The Conservative government's idea for getting more people into university by simply renaming the polytechnics.

'More universities, that's what the world needs isn't it, Kate?' said DI Bennett as he pulled his car to a stop in the car park outside the halls of residence. 'Never mind if there's no jobs for the poor sods when they graduate. Half of them would be better off studying to be mechanics.'

'Is that meant to be a dig?' asked Kate frostily as she snapped open her seat belt before letting it zip back into place with a definite clunk.

'Not at all,' said Bennett, enjoying her

discomfiture. 'You are clearly a successful driven woman. It's not your fault that your car wouldn't start – you probably flooded the engine.'

His smile did little to appease Kate. 'There *are* jobs to be had and I thought we were supposed to be out of the recession,' she said.

Bennett climbed out of the car and sniffed dismissively. 'Twenty to thirty grand of debt and no job. Where's the sense in that?'

Kate closed the car door, tempted, but resisting the urge, to slam it. 'I take it you didn't go to university, detective inspector?'

'You take it wrong, then. But I did a proper degree, not some Mickey Mouse degree in media studies or the like,' Bennett said as they walked toward the halls of residence.

'As in?'

'Criminology.' Bennett jiggled his car keys in his hand as they walked along. 'University of Kent. Vocational, linked to work. No debt at the end of it and a job.'

'Some people believe it's healthy for a culture to have people studying simply for the pleasure of studying.'

'Some people believe little green men from Mars are running our government.'

'They may be right.'

'Did you know you can get a degree in stand-up comedy now?'

'I teach medical students, Inspector Bennett. I know all about stand-up comics.'

They approached the building, stepping between three white concrete posts just outside the entrance that allowed bicycles through but no vehicles. A high arch bisected the building and led through to a square, surrounded on all sides by separate buildings that provided three floors of accommodation each. Around the arched tunnel, the fourth wall of the square housed the staff quarters and the Dean's office. A woman in her early to middle fifties bustled up towards them as they came through into the square. She was dressed in charcoal-grey trousers with a matching jacket and a mauve blouse underneath. Silk, Kate thought, and expensive.

'Doctor Walker? I'm Dean Anderson . . . Sheila,' the woman said.

Kate nodded and held out her hand. 'This is Detective Inspector Bennett.'

The woman shook her hand and turned to Bennett to do the same.

'Tony,' he said.

The Dean removed her glasses. Oliver Peoples, Kate couldn't help noticing, liking her style.

'I would make some sort of feeble joke, but I am sure you have heard them all and this doesn't seem the right time for levity, does it?'

'No,' the detective inspector agreed. He reached into his jacket and pulled out a six-by-four photo of the man lying a mile or so away in the intensive-care wing of the hospital that was attached to this same university.

'Is this him?'

The Dean took the photo and studied it, dipping her head and blowing out a sigh. 'Jamil Azeez. Yes, it is.' She handed the photo back. 'Do we know what happened?'

Kate shook her head. 'He hasn't regained consciousness yet.'

'And it was you who found him?'

'Yes.'

'Last night?'

'Yes. In Camden.'

The Dean frowned. 'And what time was this?'

'Just before midnight.'

'What was he doing in Camden?'

'We don't know,' said Bennett.

'Especially that late at night.' The Dean shook her head, puzzled.

'It was a Friday. A lot of people socialise on a Friday night,' said Kate. 'Camden is a very popular place for people of his age, particularly at the weekends.'

'But Jamil never drank.'

Bennett cleared his throat. 'Forgive me, but as a Dean of the halls of residence how would you know that?'

'Because of his religion. He was very devout. We know because students with special dietary requirements inform us of it, for obvious reasons.'

'He was a Muslim?' DI Bennett pulled out his notebook.

'Yes.'

'He wouldn't be the first Muslim to drink and it may well be that he wasn't drinking anyway. They do serve soft drinks in the pubs and nightclubs.'

'I get the sense he was pretty devout.' She caught herself. 'Sorry, that he *is* pretty devout. How is he, by the way?'

The Dean seemed a little embarrassed to be asking that question only now. Kate put a reassuring hand on her arm. 'He is in a very serious condition. The next few hours are going to be critical.'

'Who could have wanted to hurt him?'

DI Bennett tapped the notebook in his hand. 'We don't know. Is it possible to look in his room, as we asked?'

'If it will help. I've sent Arthur to fetch a key.'

At that moment a stooped white-haired man in a brown overall came towards them. For some reason he reminded Kate of an ancient zookeeper. Thinking of some of the students under her tutelage she wasn't altogether surprised at the thought. He handed the Dean the key with a jerky deferential nod.

'Thanks, Arthur,' she said.

Arthur grunted almost inaudibly and turned, walking away slowly.

'He's long past retirement age but we couldn't bear to see him go,' the Dean explained although no one had made a comment. She held the key aloft and pointed to the buildings on her right. 'Jamil's on the first floor.'

The turfed area in the centre of the building was circular rather than the traditional quadrangle of older colleges and in the centre of it there was a tall sycamore tree, some leaves still just about clinging to its branches.

A youth of eighteen or nineteen, dressed in a workman's overall with a black baseball cap on his head and a scarf wrapped around his neck, was raking the fallen multicoloured leaves into a large pile. Or was trying to. The wind was gusting, sending swirls of the leaves dancing around the grass like animated creatures of myth. She didn't envy him his job, a Sisyphean task if ever there was one – not that he would probably get the reference, she thought.

A young woman's laugh echoed across the grounds and Kate looked over to the main hall where the laughing woman was emerging, duffel-coated and wearing a bright red scarf, flanked on each side by two young men who were hanging onto her every word. All of them clutching textbooks like badges of honour, their eyes bright with the possibilities of their future. She looked back at the man raking the leaves, wondering if he wished he had studied harder at school, or whether he relished the fact that he never had to study again and could work outdoors in the open, fresh and healing air.

Kate snapped out of her thoughts as she realised that the Dean had said something. She smiled apologetically back at her as the woman briskly led the way, skirting around the grass and continuing along to one of the blocks of student accommodation through a pair of wire-meshed glass doors that opened onto a concrete stairwell. She walked briskly up the stairs to the first floor. The stairs opened out into a corridor with a small kitchen area with a red plastic-covered sofa, a small table and some chairs around it. Leading left and right from the kitchen was a small corridor with rooms either side. Each corridor led to double doors at the end.

'The rooms are arranged in groups of twenty,' the Dean explained. 'Each group has its own kitchen area. With a toaster and a fridge, et cetera.' She pointed to the kitchen as they passed and turned to the right-hand set of rooms, fitting the key into the lock of the second room. 'This is Jamil's one.'

She opened the door and led them in. It was a small room. A window directly opposite the door with a bed lengthwise underneath. The walls were brick and painted white. Against the wall to their right was a medium-sized pine wardrobe with the doors closed. There was a small rug on the floor and to the left of the door was a desk and chair with bookshelves above. On the desk was a laptop computer and some stacking files that looked to Kate as though they were filled with paper and correspondence. The books on the shelves were arranged neatly. She looked at the titles. All textbooks, law-related. No fiction, she thought. She looked again and corrected herself: one novel, J.D. Salinger's *The Catcher in the Rye*. The walls were bare, everything was neatly arranged, not a spot of dust in sight.

'You sure a student lives here?' Kate asked dryly.

'I know what you mean.' Sheila Anderson said, looking around the room. 'Like I say, Jamil is a model student. I've never once had a complaint about him or any hint of trouble. Some students, their first time away from home and they see it as a chance to really let their hair down.'

'But not Jamil?'

'Never.'

'He's a second-year student. Isn't it unusual to still be in a hall of residence?' Kate asked.

'What do you mean?'

'Well, when I was at uni, after the first year a group of us on the same course rented a house together. Most second-years seemed to.'

'I'm not sure Jamil has a lot of friends. There's Malik, of course.'

Bennett took a book from the shelves. 'The lad who reported him missing?'

The Dean nodded. 'His cousin. Malik Hussein. From Iraq, studying chemistry.'

'Can we speak to him?'

'I already checked. He has lectures until four o'clock.'

DI Bennett put back on the shelf the textbook that he had been flicking through and turned to her.

'You can think of no reason why anyone would want to hurt him?'

'No, he was a beautiful man.'

Kate reacted. 'Odd choice of expression.'

'I meant he had a very spiritual quality. There was something about him.' The Dean smiled apologetically.

'He *is* very handsome,' Kate conceded.

'Like I say, it's not just that. "Jamil" means charming, you know.'

Kate shook her head. 'No, I didn't know that.'

Bennett's phone rang, the strident ring tone echoing loudly in the small bare-walled room. He pulled it out of his pocket and quickly flipped it open. 'DI Bennett.' He listened for a few moments. 'Okay, I'm on it.'

He closed the phone and nodded to Kate and the Dean. 'Good news. Jamil has just regained consciousness.'

Sheila Anderson sighed audibly. 'Is he going to be all right?'

Bennett shrugged sympathetically. 'They don't know, I'm afraid. He's still in a very critical condition. They're keeping a close eye on him. I am sure he is in the best of hands.'

Kate nodded to the Dean. 'Thanks for your time.'

'Not at all, if I can be of any more help at all, just let me know.'

'Sure.'

*

Bennett fished his car keys out of his jacket pocket and beeped the locks open. 'What did you make of her – the Dean?' he asked Kate as they climbed into the front seats.

'Pleasant enough. Seemed genuinely concerned about Jamil.'

Bennett looked across at her. 'Your university?' he asked. 'Some posh Oxbridge college, no doubt?'

'No doubt at all.'

'Hall of residence during your first year, you said?'

'I did.'

'Same here. Did you socialise with the Dean of your halls of residence much?'

Kate shook her head. 'I don't think I even talked to him.'

'Nor me. Saw him make a speech on arrivals day as we sipped cheap sherry. And saw him about the place here and there, but never had any occasion to speak to him.'

'So your point would be?'

Bennett shrugged as he turned the key in the ignition. 'I don't know. Something seemed a little hinky about her, is all.'

'Hinky?'

'Yeah, something not right. A little off. She called him a beautiful man.'

Kate smiled. 'It's not a crime for a woman to notice an attractive man. Not since the 1970s, at least.'

'*Beautiful*, she said – not attractive.'

'So maybe she has a crush on him. Wouldn't be the first time in a university, would it? Male lecturers have been banging their female students for centuries.'

Bennett looked at her with raised eyebrows and pretended to be shocked. '*Banging* their students. Do you kiss Jack Delaney with that mouth, doctor?'

Kate looked across at him coolly. 'There's a talent night coming up at the local pub on Wednesday. Maybe you should enter.'

'Nah. I may be called Tony Bennett but I can't sing for toffee.'

'I meant as a comedian.'

He started to reply but Kate held up a hand to stop him. 'Just shut up and drive!'

Bennett put up his hands in mock surrender, then put the car in gear and steered it towards the car-park entrance. Kate shook her head and looked out of the window to hide a small private smile. The guy Bennett was replacing, Detective Sergeant Eddie Bonner, he'd thought himself a bit of a comedian too. But then he'd gone up against Jack Delaney and got himself killed in the process. She hoped the new guy would fare somewhat better.

*

Delaney balanced the porcelain saucer a little uneasily on his knee and took a sip of his tea. He looked across the room at the young girl he had taken from the boot of Garnier's car all those years ago. She was sitting next to his cousin on the sofa. Fully grown now, educated, beautiful. The thought of what might have happened to her if Garnier hadn't

112

been arrested when he was still sent a chill to his heart. He looked across at her and smiled, chasing away the thoughts. She was one of the lucky ones. She had been saved.

'I tried calling you on your mobile this morning, Gloria,' he said.

The young woman grinned apologetically. 'It's kaput. Haven't got around to getting a new one. Not top priority with a loan to pay off and I'm between temp jobs right now.'

Delaney pulled out his wallet. 'How much do you need?'

Gloria smiled. 'Nothing, Jack. Really. I've got a new gig starting next week. It's only a small student loan. I was one of the lucky ones who had parents who supported me.'

'How are Henry and Joan?'

'They're fine. And I don't want you mentioning this. They've been really concerned since that man started appearing on the news. They want me to go back to Warwick.'

'But you don't want to?'

'I've got work here, Jack. And a home.' She smiled at Mary. 'And friends.' But it was a small, nervous smile and Delaney picked up on it.

'You say you have been getting some flashes of memory, Gloria?' he asked sympathetically.

The young woman nodded.

'It's since that monster's face started appearing all the time on the news again,' said Mary.

'I've been having nightmares. I see faces, I hear voices. I wake up and I try to remember . . .'

'And can you?'

She shook her head. 'No. But I recognised . . . I recognised his face when he came on television.'

'You hadn't seen any photos of him before?' asked Sally.

'No.'

Mary shook her head. 'We thought it best. Gloria was traumatised by the events. Completely traumatised. She had no memory of who she was. Where she had been. How long she had been in the car, where she came from.'

'It must have been terrible for you,' said Sally.

Gloria smiled and shrugged almost apologetically. 'I don't remember, to be honest. It was all so very long ago . . .' She trailed off. 'But it's happening all over again, isn't it?'

'We don't know, Gloria,' said Delaney. 'Something's happening and we think he is tied in to it.'

Gloria sighed, frustrated. 'I know who I am, I just don't know who I was.'

Delaney's cousin put her hand on the young woman's knee. 'It was the trauma, like I said. You had to hide deep inside yourself.' Mary turned to Sally. 'It was as if her identity had been stripped from her and we had to build it up again.'

Sally, a puzzled look on her face, gestured towards the doctor. 'I'm sorry. I hope you don't mind me asking but . . .'

'Why me?' said Mary.

'Well, yes – why were you involved?'

'Mary's a child psychiatrist, Sally,' said Delaney.

'When Gloria was taken from the car she clung onto Jack,' Mary explained. 'She screamed whenever he put her down, wouldn't let anyone near her. He cleared it to bring her to me. I had done a lot of work with the police in the past. Working with child victims. Helping those without a voice to have one.'

'It took me about six months to find mine again, apparently,' said Gloria.

'And you still have no memory of who you are?'

Gloria shook her head. 'Were,' she said pointedly. 'No. And in some ways that's how I want it. This man coming back into my life . . .' She stopped, blinking back tears, unable to continue the thought.

'It's okay, Gloria,' said Delaney.

'But it's *not* okay, is it?' she said, clearly distressed. 'What if I do remember? What if I remember who I was, what happened to me? What if I can't deal with it? What then?'

'Then we'll be here to help,' said Mary softly, the warm Irish lit to her voice becoming more pronounced.

'I know.' Gloria sniffed and sat up straighter. 'In some ways I want to know. In some ways I hope I never will.'

'Is there anything you can remember from your dreams?' Jack asked.

Gloria closed her eyes, concentrating. 'There are sounds. Music. A song I can almost hear it but every time I think I have it . . . it slips away. It's like trying to catch mist in your hand.'

'Don't try so hard,' said Mary. 'When you are ready it will come back to you.'

Gloria opened her eyes. 'And I hear voices. At least two of them. Sometimes it seems like more.'

'Both male?' asked Delaney.

'Sometimes, yes, I think so. One of them has a

higher pitch.' She shook her head, frustrated. 'I just don't know.'

Delaney pulled a Dictaphone from his pocket and looked to his cousin for approval. She gave him a small nod. Delaney held the Dictaphone forward and pushed the play button. Garnier's voice filled the room, tainting it.

'See, both you and I know that the world is made of chaos, not order, and there is an imperative in the human psyche either to embrace that chaos or to try and tame it. The first is irrelevant and the second is a fool's errand. God knows that. The God of the Old Testament. Our existences are scattered fragments of meaning. You try to fit the shapes together, resolve the randomness of things, like a jigsaw puzzle building bit by bit to make a perfect picture. You have to get each piece in order to make sense of the world, don't you? Like that perfect portrait of Christ and his disciples on the jigsaw your mother bought for you when you were seven years old.'

'Turn it off!' Gloria almost screamed, tears prickling into her eyes as she drew in deep gulps of air.

Mary moved to sit beside her on the sofa, cradling her head into her body and patting her back softly. 'It's all right, Gloria. You don't have to listen to any more. Just take some deep breaths.'

Delaney stood up and walked out of the room. After a few moments he came back with a glass of water. 'Here you go, Gloria. Drink this.'

Gloria took the glass from him. 'Thanks.' She took a few sips. 'I'm okay now. I'll be fine, I'll be fine,' she repeated as if just by saying it she could make it true.

Delaney sat down again, put his hands flat on his

knees and leaned forward, his expression apologising for asking the question.

'Was it him?'

Gloria took another sip of her water and looked back at him. 'I don't know, Jack. I'm sorry.'

'You have nothing to be sorry for.'

'That's just it, though, isn't it?' said Gloria. 'I might have *everything* to be sorry for.'

Delaney nodded.

'And what about that poor kid who's been taken? What has that got to do with him? What's it got to do with me?' Her voice trembled.

'It's got nothing to do with you, sweetheart. You're safe. No one knows who you are. No one knows where you live.'

Gloria looked up at Delaney again, her small hands clasping one another. 'What's going to happen to him? To the little boy?'

Delaney stood up and looked at her steadily. "We're going to find him, Gloria. That's what!'

'You promise?'

'I promise.'

Mary shot him a reproving glance but Delaney ignored it, gesturing for Sally to join him as he stood up.

'We're going to find him and return him home safe to his mother. You have my word on that!'

*

DI Tony Bennett watched as a nurse held a clear plastic cup of water to Jamil Azeez's lips and he took a swallow, his Adam's apple bobbing in his slender neck.

'Not too much, now,' said the nurse, letting him

117

have another sip before she took the cup away. Bennett smiled gratefully at the nurse. She was petite, with midnight-black hair and delicate Asiatic features.

'And not too long!' she said to him reprovingly. 'He is still very far from well and the last thing he needs right now is any added stress.'

'I understand,' Bennett said.

'Good,' she replied. 'I'll be back in five minutes.'

Bennett watched her walk from the room, pulling the door closed behind her and nodding to Danny Vine who was standing guard outside. Then he looked at his watch, pulled the bedside chair closer to the bed and sat down on it. 'Pulled yourself a cracker there,' he said to the patient.

Jamil Azeez blinked his eyes in what could have been a sign of accord and croaked something that could have been an agreement.

'Do you know who did this to you? Do you know who hurt you?' asked the DI.

Jamil shook his head. 'No,' he said in another painful croak.

'Can you tell me anything of what happened?'

The patient shook his head and winced. Bennett put his hand on his arm. 'Okay, try not to move. Try not to upset yourself. I don't want to have that pretty nurse telling me off.'

Jamil swallowed again and nodded almost imperceptibly.

'What do you remember?'

'Nothing. I can't remember a thing.'

Bennett was taken aback a little – Jamil's accent was pure British.

'You speak very good English, Jamil. How long

have you been here? You're in your second year at university, is that right?'

Jamil blinked his eyes. He had long dark lashes. 'Yes, but I grew up here. My family moved back to Iran five years ago. English is my first language.'

'What can you remember?'

'I don't know.'

He closed his eyes, squeezing them shut as if he could somehow press some memories from them. 'I don't know. I can't remember.' He opened them again, clearly distraught. 'I just don't know.'

'It's okay, Jamil,' said Bennett sympathetically. 'It's not uncommon. After a tragic accident it is quite normal sometimes for the brain to shut out memories. Hide them away until you can deal with them. Usually they do come back. That was what the lovely nurse said, and I guess she knows her stuff.'

'But this wasn't an accident, was it?'

Bennett looked at him sympathetically. 'No. It wasn't.'

Jamil blinked back tears, and Bennett was fairly sure it had nothing to do with whatever physical pain the young man was feeling. 'Why would anyone want to do this? Who would want to stab me?'

'We don't know. That's what we need to find out.'

'Were they trying to kill me?'

Bennett leaned in. 'They nearly did, Jamil. I'm sorry but whoever did this to you was in all likelihood trying to murder you. There is no one you can think of who would want to harm you?'

'No one. No. Was it a racist attack, do you think?'

Bennett shrugged. 'It's possible.'

'Where did it happen?'

119

'You don't know?'

Jamil shrugged. 'I can't remember a thing about it. I remember waking up here.'

'What do you remember? Go back to yesterday. Lunchtime – can you remember that'

'Yes.'

'Okay, then. After lunch what did you do?'

'I remember going to the library.'

'The university library?'

'No. At my hall of residence. Whitefriars. It's a small one but it makes a change from sitting in my room. I remember going there. I remember doing the crossword.'

'Which one?'

Jamil looked embarrassed for a moment. 'The *Daily Mail*. I don't read it . . . but I like the crossword.'

Bennett held up his hand. 'It's okay – no one is here to judge you.'

'And then . . .' Jamil concentrated for a moment or two, looking down at the floor to the side of his head. He hesitated for a moment and then shook his head. 'No. Nothing after that.'

Bennett leaned forward. 'You looked as if you might have remembered something then, Jamil.'

'No. Some other students came into the library, I think. But no, that was early evening. You say I was found at midnight?'

'Just about. You were lucky!'

'Lucky?'

'Relatively speaking. The woman who found you is a police surgeon. She was able to keep you alive until the paramedics found you.'

'What is her name, please? I must thank her.'

'Kate Walker. Doctor Walker.' He gestured with his thumb to the general ward outside. 'She's trying to find your consultant, right now.'

'And where was I when she found me?'

'Just off Camden High Street.'

Jamil reacted, surprised. 'Camden. What was I doing there? I've never been to Camden in my life. Why would I want to go there?'

'We don't know, Jamil. Maybe it was a random attack. Maybe it was racially motivated, like you said, or maybe it was just a robbery gone wrong.'

Jamil looked at the side table. 'My wallet?'

'No. Sorry, there was nothing on you.'

'It was a mugging, then?'

Bennett shrugged. 'Most likely. But maybe why you were there in the first place has something to do with the attack on you.'

'Can't see how. Like I said, I've never been to Camden.'

'You've been there once.'

Jamil held a hand to his bandaged chest, his breathing becoming more ragged as he laboured to draw in breath. 'Yeah, and it seems like once was too often.'

Bennett would have replied but the nurse opened the door quietly and came in.

'Okay. Time's up,' she said in a manner that would brook no argument.

Bennett looked at her appraisingly. 'I'm sorry – I didn't get your name?'

'Jessica Tam,' she said.

Bennett held out his hand and after hesitating for a moment the nurse shook it. 'I'm Tony Bennett.'

Jessica Tam raised an eyebrow but before she

could say anything Bennett handed her a card. 'If Jamil remembers anything more be sure to give me a call straight away.'

Jessica put the card in her pocket. 'Okay.'

'Or, you know . . .' he said, with a smile. 'If you just want to give me a call.'

'I'll bear it in mind,' she said coolly, and taking his arm by the elbow she steered him out of the room. She closed the door on him and turned back to her patient. 'Are you okay, Jamil?'

'I've been better,' he said weakly. 'I just wish I knew who would want to do something like this to me.'

'I know how you feel,' she said thoughtfully, remembering a time when she had been attacked by a deranged former patient. 'Sometimes it's just because you're in the wrong place at the wrong time.'

'Why was I there, though? That's what I don't understand.'

Jessica Tam nodded. 'Give it time. Sometimes that's all we can do.'

'I suppose so.'

'And try to get some rest. We need to get you well first. Maybe things will be better for you tomorrow.'

Jamil sank his head back deeper into his pillow and closed his eyes.

Maybe he would find some peace in his sleep, Jessica thought.

But she was wrong.

Very wrong.

*

Delaney pushed the fingers of his right hand through his damp hair. It had stopped raining a short while ago but there was still a stiff breeze in the moist air, and it was cold, too damn cold. He shouldered through the crowd of people who had gathered behind the yellow ribbons sealing off the top end of Carlton Row. Sally Cartwright was sailing behind him in his slipstream and smiling apologetically at the disgruntled members of the public shunted aside by him.

Melanie Jones was shouting something at Delaney as he ducked under the ribbon and he could feel the lights of a video camera trained on the back of his head – a new cameraman stepping into the breach for her, he guessed. But he had had enough of that particular reporter for one day and had tuned her out entirely. However, he couldn't tune out the red-faced man who was even then barrelling towards him, clearly agitated.

'Delaney, where the bloody hell have you been?'

Detective Inspector Robert Duncton of the serious crimes unit based at Paddington Green was a stocky man in his early forties. Delaney had run into him a few weeks back on another case and Duncton had made it quite clear that he regarded Delaney as a dangerous, ill-disciplined throwback with no place in the modern police force. The fact that Delaney had solved that particular case, rescuing at least three people in the process, didn't seem to concern him much and his attitude towards Delaney didn't seem to have mellowed any. Duncton's wide shoulders were straining the fabric of his overcoat as he glared at Delaney, waiting for an answer.

'Traffic was a nightmare on Western Avenue, wasn't it, Sally?'

'Horrendous, sir,' Sally agreed.

'Don't bullshit me, Delaney. What the hell took you so long?'

'You want to dial that attitude down a notch or two, *hombre*?' Delaney asked.

Duncton stepped closer. He didn't raise his voice, mindful of the gathered crowd, but he clearly wasn't happy. 'No, I bloody don't. You might act like the Lone bleeding Ranger out of your hick nick out in White City. But if you are on my watch you do things my way. *Comprende*, *hombre*?' he added sarcastically.

Delaney smiled at Sally Cartwright, not believing what he was hearing, and jerked his thumb towards Duncton. 'Can you believe this guy?' he asked her.

'Let's just get one thing clear . . .' said Duncton, poking Delaney in the chest with a thick finger.

But that was as far as he got because Delaney, turning his shoulder to block his movements out of view, grabbed hold of Duncton's finger and leaned in close to whisper, keeping his face smiling in case any cameras were still trained on him.

'No!' he said. 'Let's get this clear. You ever fucking lay a finger on me again and I will break it off at the fucking joint. I don't work for you. You don't outrank me, so keep the showboating for someone who gives a shit and let's just focus on the matter in hand. Okay?'

He released Duncton's hand and slapped him on the shoulder. 'So what have we got, detective inspector?'

Duncton, now even more red-faced and furious with it, would have slapped his hand forcefully away but was as aware as Delaney of the scrutiny that Melanie Jones was giving them from beyond the perimeter screening and of the camera that was trained on them, the zoom no doubt closing in on their faces. It wouldn't be too hard to get a lip-reader to work out what they were saying, even if they were too far away for the microphone to pick up their conversation. He returned Delaney's smile and spoke through gritted teeth.

'Let's go inside.'

Delaney, followed by Sally Cartwright, accompanied the stocky detective into the house. Duncton pulled them up in the small hallway and shut the door behind him. From the lounge ahead of them they could hear a woman sobbing and another woman making comforting sounds.

Duncton held his hands up in a conciliatory gesture. 'There's a woman in there whose son has been abducted. God knows what has happened to him. Let's focus on that.'

'What I said,' said Delaney.

Duncton nodded and sighed. 'Okay. So bring me up to speed. Garnier. This boy who's missing. What's the connection?'

Delaney shrugged. 'You know as much as I do.'

The other detective shook his head. 'We know the square root of bugger-all. What's this got to do with the sick bastard you've just been to visit?'

'Trust me, it wasn't a social visit. Two children went missing here fifteen years ago. Garnier was involved. We know he is a child murderer and rapist. What has this to do with the child that's gone missing today? Garnier was in police custody.'

'He was with you about the time the child went missing?'

'Yes.'

'Why?'

'He's yanking on our lariat, is all. He had nothing to say.'

But Delaney remembered Garnier asking the time. Remembered looking at his watch at ten o'clock, about the time the boy had gone missing. Had he missed something? There was no way he could have predicted what time the boy would be abducted. Could he? Even if he did have an accomplice.

'Why you?' Duncton asked Delaney, snapping him out of his thoughts.

'Why me, what?'

'Why did he want to see you.'

'He saw me in the woods this morning. Recognised me as the man who . . .' Delaney realised he was about to say Gloria's name but caught himself in time. Although he knew Duncton could track it down his close-mouthedness was a habit he wanted to stick to. The young woman had been through enough without her real identity being outed to the tender mercies of the press. 'He recognised me from the photos in the papers of the time, holding the girl that he'd stashed in the boot of his car.'

'So what did he want?'

'I think he wanted to know what became of her.'

'But you didn't tell him.'

Delaney shrugged again. 'I don't know, inspector. It was all a long time ago. I am sure that she more than anyone doesn't want it raked up again.'

'And he didn't make any mention, however oblique, of what has happened here?'

'If he did I didn't pick up on it. I can't see how he can be involved.'

'You think it's a copycat, then? Someone inspired by all this press coverage to emulate him?'

'It wouldn't be the first time. That's a sad fact.'

'How likely is it that he has got an accomplice from all those years ago starting up again?

'He's only had one visitor, a woman, since he has been in custody, sir, six months ago,' said Sally. 'Just one visit.'

'Who is this woman?'

'Her name is Maureen Gallagher. We're trying to track her down. Uniform have been to the address we had for her but she had moved out quite a few years ago and we don't know where to.'

Duncton shook his head, frustrated. 'Maybe it's just a coincidence. It's only been a couple of hours. If it wasn't for Garnier's little performance this morning we wouldn't be going into overdrive like this. Maybe the boy's at a friend's house.'

'It is possible, sure enough,' said Delaney. 'What exactly happened this morning?'

'The mother left Archie, her child, here under the care of his grandfather at eight o'clock this morning. She had an appointment.'

'What kind of appointment?'

'She's a hairdresser.'

'That's a bit early, isn't it? said Sally.

'She had to get to Abbots Langley.'

Sally shrugged. 'Even so, that's, what, twenty minutes, thirty minutes tops from here. Who has their hair done at that time of day?'

'Brides do, detective constable,' Duncton replied. 'She had a regular client getting married today.'

'So she left the kid with the grandfather. What happened next?'

'The old man wanted a cigarette and his daughter had taken his fags away with her when she left. The doctor's told him he's not allowed to smoke. So. He went out to get some.'

'What, from the shops? He left the kid on his own at home?' asked Delaney.

Duncton shook his head. 'He's got an allotment. He's got a shed there where he stashes some cigarettes. He uses it as a bolt-hole, apparently – doesn't do a lot of gardening any more. He was inside having a smoke and the kid was outside playing, and when he came out to check on him the boy was gone. He swears it was like only sixty seconds, two minutes tops.'

'What about the father?'

'Barry Woods. He's a lorry driver. In France. Due back today.'

'Anybody spoken to him?'

Duncton shook his head. 'No response on his mobile.'

'Possible he came back early?'

'It's possible. We're looking into it.'

At that moment Graham Harper came out of the lounge and looked at Delaney and Sally Cartwright. His face was white, drained of blood, his watery eyes squinting as he focused on them.

'Have you found him? Have you found Archie?' he asked in a tremulous voice.

'No, sir, we haven't. Not yet. I'm sorry,' said Delaney and turned to Duncton. 'Have you got people down at the allotment?'

'Of course we have.'

Delaney turned to Graham Harper. 'Maybe you could show me the way, sir, walk me through what happened.'

The elderly man nodded and went to pick up his overcoat hanging on the newel post at the bottom of the stairs.

Duncton grabbed Delaney's arm. 'Like I said, this is my watch, Delaney.'

'Of course it is,' he agreed affably. 'But Garnier has dealt me into this game and we need to find out why, don't we?'

Duncton sighed and nodded finally. 'We go together. And you don't do anything on this without clearing it with me first. We clear on that?'

'Clear as a glass of water from a mountain lake in the Ring of Kerry,' said Delaney, slipping into a soft brogue.

*

The allotment was a scant six hundred yards or so from Graham Harper's house. It took them just a few minutes to walk there. At the bottom of Carlton Row they turned left into Rowland Avenue at the bottom of which a public footpath led up to a cast-iron bridge built in the early part of the last century. Painted battleship grey, it had rivets like half-marbles studded across it. Wire meshing stretched either side of the bridge, making it into a cage to prevent disaffected youths from dropping rocks onto the passing Underground and overland trains below as they thundered east towards the city.

Delaney paused for a moment, flashing back to a

time in his youth when he'd stood on a bridge at Balleydehob. The river below him snaking out to sea, the dazzling light bouncing off it like a million shattered crystals. He remembered picking up a pebble and lobbing it to send a crow flapping away. He remembered his cousin Mary, whom he had left just a short while back, telling him that it was a raven he had disturbed and that it would bring bad luck down upon him. He looked at where he was today, looking down through meshed wire onto a railway line that carved through an unbroken run of development that stretched from Harrow to Stratford and beyond. He looked at the garbage that littered the sides of the railway, he looked at the grey sky overhead and wondered if his cousin had been right all along. He didn't know what it was that had brought him here, but if it was luck it certainly wasn't of the good kind.

He carried on over the bridge, taking the arm of Graham Harper and helping him down the iron steps on the other side. There was more wire fencing at the base of the steps enclosing what looked like some kind of Second World War memorial. Whatever it was was rusted and overgrown with weeds and tangled growth. The allotments were to the left. A small muddy path ran alongside them, with another wire fence between them and the railway line beyond. In all there were probably about thirty allotments that ran alongside each other for a couple of hundred yards or so before ending in a wooded scrubland. A road bridge above the railway loomed high over the undergrowth. In the wooded area Delaney could see a couple of uniformed officers finger-searching the ground.

Graham Harper led the way along to an allotment near the end of the run. It had two areas for cultivation bisected by a simple narrow shingle path that led up to a wooden shed. A door, with one window to the right, a small porch or step in front, plain wood, the varnish on it peeling, all of it bleached by the sun that was now no more than a distant fond memory. It looked to be about twenty or thirty years old, Delaney reckoned, and like its owner not in its prime, to say the least. Judging by the hacking cough he was listening to it was a toss-up which would stay standing the longest. He walked into the shed with Duncton while Sally stayed outside with the elderly man.

Delaney wasn't sure what he expected to find inside but what he did find didn't surprise him. The weak sunlight barely filtered through the grime- and dust-encrusted window. Delaney placed his feet carefully, mindful that the floor had rotted in places. It was a bare floor with boxes scattered here and there. Vegetable-seed packets, twine, gardening gloves. Against one wall stood a hoe, spade, and assorted plastic plant pots. In the corner was an old-fashioned wing-backed upholstered armchair. A table beside it with an ashtray brimful of fag ends. The air reeked with the smell of creosote and stale cigarette smoke and for once Delaney didn't feel like reaching into his pocket for his own packet.

To the right of the chair, as Delaney looked at it, was a shelf filled with all sorts of knick-knacks and oddments, mostly gardening-related. But there was an old fishing reel as well, along with a clasp knife, some empty jars, a can of rat poison, a few tobacco tins. Beneath the shelf was a box of magazines. Old issues of *Gardener's World*, *Coarse Fishing Monthly*.

Delaney nudged the box with his foot. 'Anyone been through it?'

Duncton nodded. 'Just what it looks like.'

Delaney looked around the shed. 'You got any theories?'

'I read him as genuine. He came in here for a smoke, like he said.' Duncton shrugged. 'Someone took the boy, maybe.'

'Maybe?'

'His mother said he was really keen to be with his mate Johnny. Maybe he ran off. Maybe he'll turn up there.'

'I take it you've got uniform out there looking?'

'As much as we can. Could be he got lost.'

'You don't think so, though?'

'Do you?'

Delaney shook his head. 'No. Peter Garnier is in this somehow. He has to be.'

'How though?'

'I don't know, detective. I wish I did.'

'Why did he really want to see you? He was talking to you about the same time this kid was abducted. Is he telling us something?'

'If he is, I'm sure as hell not hearing it.'

'He lied about taking us to the burial site of his victims.'

'He claims he couldn't remember exactly, that the shot at him put an end to the trip. He might well have led us to them.'

'You think he was telling the truth.'

132

'I don't think he knows what the truth is any more. The man has maggots in his brain.'

'So he had an accomplice back then. Why now? Why start again now?'

'His illness – maybe it all ties in with that.'

'And where do you tie in?'

'I don't. I'm simply a man with a badge, just like you, detective.'

Duncton looked at Delaney and shook his head. 'You're not like me at all, Delaney. You're in this somehow.'

Delaney shrugged. 'You know what I know, which is that a young boy has been abducted. Garnier is in the mix and we are running out of time fast. So what say we put aside your fucking petty politics and concentrate on getting him back alive?'

Duncton would have responded but Sally stuck her head through the open door. 'You better get out here, sir,' she said.

Delaney and Duncton hurried outside. Graham Harper was sitting on the steps of his shed, his body humped and racked with sobs.

A uniformed police constable was holding an evidence bag in her hand, showing it to the elderly man.

'Please look, sir.'

Graham Harper dashed the back of his hand against his eyes and looked up. 'My God, what have I done?' he said, trying to sniffle back the tears and failing.

In the evidence bag was a single black and white trainer. Small – a child's size.

'Is this your grandson's trainer, sir?' asked the constable.

Harper nodded his head, his voice a croaked whisper. 'Yes. God help me.'

Sally looked over at Delaney. His expression was unreadable. 'Show us where you found it.'

The constable led them to the end of the allotments where a gap in the trees revealed a path through the tangled undergrowth to the base of a small slope that led up to the road bridge and pavement above. At the top of the slope the wire fence had been pulled loose from a concrete post, creating a gap. A large enough gap for an adult to have hunched down, squeezed through and pulled a young boy with him.

The female constable pointed to the side of the slope that ran down to the flat ground running alongside the railway track. The ground had been dug over by the looks of it: pieces of broken glass and pottery shards lay scattered around.

'It was down here, sir.'

Delaney looked up at the fence and scrambled up the slope, his feet slipping in the wet mud, but he managed to make it and hold onto a post beside the wall.

'Careful, sir!' Sally called out. Delaney pulled out an evidence bag and used it to pick up a small thread that had snagged on the pulled-back wire. He folded the bag over itself and put it in his pocket. He looked at the wire fence where it had been pulled loose from the retaining post: it was rusted but by his reckoning it would still have taken a bit of strength to rip it free. He put back the fencing and slid back down the slope.

'I think we can safely say he didn't go to Johnny's,' he said, taking the evidence bag out of his pocket and handing it over to Duncton.

'The ground here, sir . . .' said Sally Cartwright, pointing to the slope down to the railway tracks.

'What about it?'

'Looks like it's been freshly dug over.'

'We'll have the place sealed.' Duncton reached into his jacket to pull out his mobile phone. 'Everybody step back. Let's keep the scene preserved for SOCO.'

He looked across critically at Delaney, who was toeing the grass to clean his shoe.

Delaney ignored him and looked back instead at Graham Harper, his head held in his hands between his knees as he sat on the small porch of his shed, his back rounded, his posture almost foetal as he rocked back and forward, his ragged breath still audible across the distance as he dry-sobbed and choked back tears.

Guilt.

Jack Delaney knew all about that.

*

Archie Woods kept his back tight against the wall of the cold room. As tight as he could, given that his hands were tied behind his back. Not cruelly constricting, not so that the rope cut into his flesh, but taut enough so that he could not free himself. The other end of the rope had been tied to an old-fashioned metal radiator beside him. There was no heat coming from the radiator but he had his warm coat on and his jumper with the picture of a giraffe on it underneath and although he was cold he wasn't shivering because of that.

He was shivering with fear.

The man sitting in the chair across the room and watching him had flat black lifeless eyes. A small amount of saliva trickled from the corner of his mouth and he slowly raised a hand to wipe it away, the thick veins standing proud from the liver-spotted skin like worms.

The boy would have screamed had he been able to, but a silk scarf had been tied around his head and mouth, forcing his lips and teeth apart and rendering him mute.

He looked down at his feet, one of them still clad in a black and white trainer, the other in a sock that had once been bright red but was now damp with rainwater and spattered with mud. He made a small whimpering sound and closed his eyes as if to dream what was happening away.

The man watched him for a moment longer and then the corners of his mouth moved upwards slightly. It might have been a smile.

The small boy kept his eyes shut, humming in his head to drown out the sound of approaching footsteps.

'The wheels on the bus go round and round, round and round, round and round. The wheels on the bus go round and round. All day long.'

*

Delaney stood by the doorway, watching as DI Duncton held up the plastic evidence bag with the single trainer in it. Rosemary Woods already had very pale skin but what colour she had leached from her face as she looked at the bag, her green eyes widening with the horror of what it signified.

'Is it his, Mrs Woods?' asked Detective Inspector Duncton.

The woman swallowed and nodded, barely able to speak.

'Yes,' she said. 'Oh my God.'

She teetered on her heels and Sally Cartwright quickly crossed to take the tall woman's arm.

'Oh my God,' she said again, stumbling backwards to sit back on the sofa.

Her father came in and stood beside Delaney, turning the flat cap in his hands like a guilty school-boy, his eyes downcast.

His daughter looked up at him, spots of colour returning to her cheeks now. 'What the hell have you done, Dad?'

Graham Harper looked at her for a moment or two, his eyes wet with grief. He mumbled something inaudible and left the room.

Rosemary Woods looked over at Delaney. 'He's dead, isn't he?'

Delaney shook his head. 'It's still very early yet. We're only talking a matter of hours.'

'He was on the television this morning.'

'I'm sorry?' Delaney asked, puzzled.

'Peter Garnier.' She pointed to the television set in the corner. 'He was on there this morning. I made him change channels. Archie wanted the cartoons and I couldn't bear to look at that man's face.'

Delaney nodded sympathetically.

'He's taken my son, hasn't he? That man has got my son.'

'Peter Garnier is locked up safe and secure in prison,' said Detective Inspector Duncton.

The woman ignored him. Her stare was fixed on

Delaney. 'Why is he doing this? Why now? Why my boy?'

Delaney shook his head. 'We don't know what has happened yet, Mrs Woods. I know you are concerned and you have every right to be feeling the way you do right now. But we have every available person out there looking for your boy. And we will find him. I can promise you that.'

Duncton glared reprovingly at him as Delaney walked out the room, but it had as much effect as throwing a ping-pong ball would have had stopping a determined rhinoceros.

Delaney walked down the hallway to the kitchen that lay at the end of it. It was a kitchen that had been designed sometime in the 1950s and hadn't been updated since. It was clean if not exactly clutter-free. A butler-style sink with a curtain under it stood beneath a double window looking out onto a long back garden.

Graham Harper was filling a metal kettle from the tap. His hands were shaking as though the weight were too much for him to hold. Maybe that was the case, thought Delaney, as Harper put it rattling onto a small gas stove and lit the ring beneath it: the old man looked as though he was made of skin and bone and air.

'I need to ask you a few questions,' Delaney said.

Graham Harper spun round, startled. Delaney worried for a moment that he was going to drop dead of a heart attack because of the way he stared at him. He stood there for a moment or two as if he was really scrutinising him, and then his eyes became mobile, darting left and right as though he'd been suddenly frightened. 'What are you doing here?'

'I'm a policeman, remember?' said Delaney, puzzled at the shift in the old man's attitude, wondering suddenly if maybe he had dementia issues. 'We were just down at your allotment.'

The old man looked at him for a moment or two longer and then blinked as if coming out of dream.

'Yes, of course.' He opened the cupboard and brought out some tea bags.

'I'm sorry to have startled you,' said Delaney.

The man looked back, the skin on his forehead like paper wrinkled into a thousand creases. 'It's been a bit of a day.'

And if that wasn't the understatement of the year, Delaney didn't know what was. Maybe the guy *was* senile. He wondered if anyone had checked with his doctor. Maybe he had left the kid with some relative or friend and had clean forgotten about it. He made a mental note to track down Harper's physician.

'Yeah,' he said and pulled up a chair. It had been a bit of a day, all right.

The scream shrieked in the air as though someone was being tortured.

Graham Harper picked the kettle off the gas ring and the whistling mercifully stopped. 'Would you like a cup of tea, detective?' he asked.

Delaney shook his head. The English. Here was a man who not a few hours before had had his grand-child abducted under his very own nose and was now worried about the social niceties of making tea for his guest.

'No, thanks. I just want to go over what happened with you again.'

139

'I've told everybody a hundred times. I don't know. I was in my shed. Two minutes later I came out and he had gone. I assumed he was playing up in the woods – I let him dig for bottles there.'

Harper moved to the dresser beside the door into the kitchen and handed Delaney a small blue bottle, about five inches high and with hexagonal sides. 'It's Victorian, a poison bottle. They used blue for poison.'

Delaney looked at the object. 'Is it worth anything?'

The elderly man shrugged and took it back from him. 'Not really. But Archie liked to dig, see if he could find any more. I was going to get him a metal detector for Christmas . . .' He broke off, took the bottle back and turned away, busying himself pouring out his tea.

Delaney waited until he'd finished and then asked, 'You say he liked to dig?'

'If the weather was good, yes.'

'What with?'

Graham Harper seemed puzzled as he sat opposite Delaney, supping his tea noisily through discoloured teeth. 'I'm sorry, what do you mean?'

'What did he dig with? There was a spade in your shed but it hadn't been used recently.'

'Well, I told him he couldn't dig today. The ground was too muddy.'

Delaney glanced down at his own shoes. That much was true.

'So talk me through it. You walked down to the allotment and when you got to your patch or plot or whatever you call it, he came into the shed with you?'

140

'Yes, just for a minute, and when I found my cigarettes . . . he wanted to wait outside.'

Delaney caught the slight hesitation.

'He wanted to wait outside?'

The old man hesitated again. 'I told him to wait outside.'

'While you had a smoke.'

'The smoke gets on his clothes. She can smell it. His mum, she's always telling me off.'

'And what did you hear?'

'What do you mean?'

'Did you hear anything?'

'Like what?'

'Like him playing? Singing. Rattling a stick on the fence. Throwing rocks at birds in the trees.'

'No, I didn't hear a thing. But my hearing, it's not so good.'

'I see you have a hearing aid.'

'Yes.'

'Was it turned on?'

'Yes, I had it switched on.'

'How do you know?'

'Because I had the radio on.'

Delaney took out his notebook. 'You didn't mention that earlier.'

The elderly man looked away shiftily. 'I must have forgot. It's not important, is it? I mean, what does it matter?' His voice rose, tremulous and upset.

Delaney leaned forward and spoke softly. 'I don't know yet what's important and what isn't. That's how these things work. But what I do know is that you have to be entirely honest with me.'

'I have been.'

141

Delaney could hear the catch in Harper's voice, could see his gaze slide away whenever he made eye contact, and he didn't know if the old man was holding something back or was just feeling guilty.

'So you didn't hear any voices, anyone talking to Archie?'

'No.'

'You didn't hear a car stopping, or pulling away?'

'A car? There's no road there, just a footpath.' This time Harper did look at Delaney, genuinely puzzled.

'The road above is only fifty yards or so away.'

'I shouldn't have put the radio on – is that what you are saying? I might have heard who took him, he might have called out for help and I didn't hear.'

Delaney didn't answer him for a moment. 'What were you listening to?'

'Radio 3. If I wanted to listen to idiots talking I'd go down the British Legion.'

Delaney consulted his notes. 'And this was about half-ten, you say?'

'Yes.'

'What was on?'

'Strauss.' He coughed suddenly, convulsively. 'I don't waltz much any more,' he added ironically when he had got his breath back.

Delaney made another note. The old man hadn't hesitated when he'd been asked what he'd been listening to, which made him sound genuine. Unless he had an alibi prepared. But that made no sense – Delaney could see how genuinely upset he was.

Whatever had set Graham Harper's hands trembling seemed to be affecting his whole body now. 'So you think Archie called out then?' he asked, tears in his eyes. 'You think he called out and I didn't hear him because of the radio?'

Delaney folded back his notebook, replaced it in his pocket and looked over at the trembling man. 'Maybe. But maybe there was nothing for you to hear. Maybe he didn't call out because he knew whoever it was who took him. Knew him and trusted him.'

*

Sally Cartwright flicked the windscreen wipers on as they pulled out of Carlton Row and turned left into Carrington Avenue. The rain had started up again and the sky overhead was the kind of ominous slate-grey that presaged a deal more of it yet to come. Delaney stared ahead through the smeared wind-screen and spotted, about a hundred yards ahead of them on the corner of Vicarage Road and Carrington Avenue itself, a small pub called The Crawfish. It had been built sometime in the late nineteenth century, when the pub was still very much the heart of the community, before they banned smoking and put the tax on alcohol through the roof. Now people got their booze from the supermarkets and drank at home, turning most of the community locals into little more than pub-themed restaurants. Delaney tutted to himself at the criminal injustice of it all.

'Sir?'

Delaney realised he had actually tutted aloud. He looked at his watch and pointed his finger. 'Pull up outside that boozer, Sally.'

'Sir?'

'I'm starving and that pub used to do the best seafood platter south of my Aunty Noreen's.'

'Oh yeah, and where does Aunty Noreen live?'

'Clacton.'

Sally pulled the car to a stop outside the pub. It didn't look as though people were fighting for parking places.

'I didn't have you down as a fisherman's platter kind of guy, sir,' she said as she locked the car door and walked with Delaney to the pub's entrance.

'I was born by the sea, Sally. I was breathing ozone before I was breathing oxygen. It's in my blood – we Delaneys come from a long line of fishermen.'

'You didn't fancy that yourself, then?'

'Not really, constable. I get seasick in a paddling pond.'

He pushed the door open and stepped inside, steering around a couple of packing crates placed beside the wall. He hadn't been there in fifteen years and the place didn't seem to have changed much in that time. It was dirtier, emptier, more down at heel than he remembered, was all. The photos on the wall by the bar were dustier than he remembered, and the mullet-haired men in them might well all have been dead for all he knew. Maybe it was just him. Maybe moving to Belsize Park had changed him. He looked down at the carpet that didn't look like it had been cleaned in over five years and thought again.

There weren't many punters in. An Indian couple, somewhere in their fifties, Delaney reckoned, sat by the window. The man had a turban on his head and a thick white beard, the woman was dressed in a sari and looked extremely bored. She looked across at

Sally and Delaney and then turned her dead-eyed gaze back to her lap. The bearded man didn't even look up and continued to read a copy of *The Times*. Two other men, one black, one Caucasian, were sitting at separate tables, and another solitary white man was perched on a stool at a corner of the bar. They were all nursing pints and all of them were past retirement age, even allowing for the plans to keep working men shackled for longer in life.

There was only one bar in the room. It was opposite the door and ran the length of the room. The serving hatch was open and as they approached the bar Delaney could see a tall man emerging from the steps to the cellar with a large cardboard box in his arms. He was in his thirties, had red hair and freckled arms, and was about three stone overweight.

'Be with you in a minute,' he grunted and carried the box over to the door where the others were already stacked.

'You got a menu?' Sally asked.

The red-haired man turned round and pointed to a basket with four filled rolls in it. 'Yeah. Full à la carte. Knock yourself out.'

Delaney looked at the basket. 'You've got your choice of cheese or cheese and onion, Sally. Or cheese,' he said dryly.

Sally looked distinctly unimpressed. 'We should have gone to your Aunty Noreen's,' she said.

'What can I get you to drink?' the barman asked, closing the serving hatch behind him and coming back round the bar.

Delaney scanned the beer engines and asked, without any real hope, 'You got any Guinness?'

'No. Just what you see on the taps. And not even that when it runs out.'

'What's happening then?'

'We're closing down. Middle of next week.'

Delaney nodded. 'Your interpersonal customer skills a bit too full of metropolitan charm for the area, are they?'

The barman put his arms on the counter. He was carrying weight but there was muscle behind it and he looked like a man used to violence. 'Are you looking for trouble?' he said.

Delaney pointed at one of the beer pumps. 'No, I'm looking for a pint and a half of that piss that passes for beer, and I'll take two cheese rolls with them.'

'I don't think so, sunshine . . .'

Delaney pulled out his warrant card and smiled. 'Think again, then.'

The barman scowled. 'I had you down as journalists.'

'A lot of people make that mistake, don't they, Sally? It's the air of sophistication we exude.'

The barman grunted again – Delaney guessed he didn't have much call for conversation – and poured their drinks.

'I suppose all the scum have moved off to their next story anyway,' he said. 'Shame, could have done with the business.'

'Nice to see care in the community at work,' said Delaney, taking his pint.

'That's just it,' said the red-haired barman as he handed Sally her glass. 'I don't care.'

Later – but not much – Delaney picked up Sally's roll. She had eaten one bite and declared it unfit for human consumption: the bread was pulp and the cheese was plastic. Delaney didn't care, he was hungry. He demolished it in a couple of bites and washed it down with a swig of beer.

He smiled across at the barman, who was watching them from the bar. The man turned around and went back down to the cellar again.

'Little ray of sunshine,' said Sally.

Delaney nodded. 'He surely is that.'

'So the person who took the little boy—'

'Or persons.'

'Yeah, or persons. How would they know where he was going to be?'

Delaney shrugged. 'Could just have been opportunistic. You know how predators operate. A boy alone. A matter of moments to bundle him in the car and drive away.'

Sally shook her head. 'It's too much of a coincidence – that a boy goes missing from Carlton Row the very morning Peter Garnier is supposed to be leading us to the graves of his missing victims.'

'Archie Woods isn't from Carlton Row, though, is he? He was just staying with his grandfather this morning.'

'Exactly.'

'So what's your point, Sally?' Delaney asked as he watched the red-haired barman coming back up the stairs again, carrying an empty cardboard box.

Sally considered for a moment and then shrugged. 'I don't know, sir. But there is a connection here, there has to be.'

'I guess so.'

The barman started taking down the photos that

were on the wall and putting them in the empty box. Another proper pub gone, Delaney thought bitterly. They should have binned the banks instead. The government was quite happy to save all the fat cats and their fat-cat institutions while letting the honest working man suffer. Banning smoking was bad enough, now they were taking the pubs away altogether. The legacy of Gordon Brown and his puritanical Calvinist attitude, no doubt, *X Factor* fan or not.

He realised that Sally was talking to him and snapped out of his reverie again. 'I'm sorry, what?'

'I was saying, do you remember that missing child, a year or so back? Turned out the mother and her uncle had her all along.'

'Yes. Of course I remember.'

'Maybe something similar is going on. Maybe the mother was involved. She'd taken the old fella's fags. She knew he would have some stashed in the shed . . .'

'Waited for him to leave and then followed him?'

'Maybe. It makes sense. Only her and her father could have known where he'd be with the boy.'

Delaney frowned. 'I'm pretty sure the old man wasn't lying about not realising the boy had been taken. He was pretty eaten up with guilt.'

'I know, and the mother was absolutely distraught.' Sally shook her head. 'You're right, she couldn't be that good an actress.'

Delaney sighed. 'You clock up as many miles on the old shoe leather as me, detective constable, and you'll realise that people are capable of doing the most inhumane things, the cruellest things imaginable, and lying about them straight to your face whilst crying bucketloads of crocodile tears.'

'I guess.'

'That woman you mentioned. How many weeks was she on television looking absolutely distraught and pleading for her daughter's return?'

'True.'

'It's a sick, sad world, Sally. No known cure.'

'What's the point, then?'

'To ease the suffering. Where we can. When we can. It's all we can do, the likes of us.'

Sally shook her head again. 'I don't believe that, sir. And neither do you.'

'That a fact?'

Sally nodded. 'You could take it to the CPS.'

Delaney smiled and took another pull on his pint. 'You sure I shouldn't have a word with my cousin about you?'

'What do you mean?'

'I reckon you'd make a better psychologist than a policewoman, Sally.'

'Rubbish,' said Sally, quite animated. 'It's you who know people, sir. That's why you are so much better than the likes of the chief superintendent in his fancy office. You know what makes people tick and that's why you're such a good copper, such a great detective.'

Delaney looked at her, amused. 'Sometimes, constable, I'm not sure I could detect my own nose if I had swine fever and half a pound of pepper up it.'

'Maybe a while back, sir, when, and you'll forgive me for saying it, you had that nose permanently jammed in a bottle of Irish whiskey. But not any more.'

Delaney laughed out loud. 'See? You know people too, and you're not afraid to show it.'

'Yeah, well, some people are easier to read than others.'

'So what's your take on Rosemary Woods, then?'

Sally frowned thoughtfully. 'What would be in it for her, if she *is* involved? That's what I don't get. She doesn't strike me as a foolish person.'

'Motive, Sally. It's at the heart of everything.'

'True.'

'If we know *why* then we can maybe get a handle on things.' Delaney finished his pint. 'I'm pretty sure the boy's grandad wasn't lying to me. That's about all I know. I'm getting a beer – do you want another one?'

Sally shook her head and Delaney took his glass to the bar. 'Another delicious pint, please, barman,' he said without a hint of irony in his voice. The barman grunted and tossed the last photo in the box: a group of quiff-haired men dressed in Teddy-boy suits and brothel creepers by the look of it. The 1950s, Delaney thought – that wasn't just another country, it was another fecking universe.

*

Jennifer Hickling struggled to breathe but the hand clamped around her mouth was tightening. The woman pushed her back against the wall and leaned in, her voice throbbing with menace.

'You're not welcome here, bitch.'

Jennifer struggled but to no avail. 'Let me go.'

The woman released her and Jenny ran up the road, darting left into Camden High Street.

She took a moment or two to catch her breath but had no intention of going anywhere else. She had a few regulars who were due a little later. Good money for very little work. Just a few hand jobs and one who liked her on her knees down the alleyway she used. But at least he didn't insist on using a condom – she hated the taste of latex – and was clean and she made damn sure he never finished in her mouth. She knew what she was. She didn't like it and she intended to change it. Jenny knew what she was, what she'd been made into . . . but she had her standards.

She looked at her watch and decided to let the foreign bitch have the street for a while while she had a coffee. Wait till the old whore picked up another punter. Any luck it would be a mad bastard who strangled her.

But Jennifer Hickling didn't believe in luck any more. At least, not the good kind.

*

Delaney leaned on the doorbell again and looked at his watch. He guessed Gloria could be anywhere, and in a city the size of London he had as much chance of finding her without a mobile phone as he had of finding a winning lottery ticket. He hastily scrawled a phone number on a piece of paper with the words *There's a hundred pounds' credit on it* below it. He pushed the mobile phone he had just bought her through her letter box and the note after it. He ran back down the stairs to Sally, who was waiting in the car, turning up his collar against the rain and totally oblivious to the pair of eyes that were watching him from across the street. Angry eyes.

*

Several hours later and Jack Delaney put his hand on the cold glass of the window and looked out of the CID office at the car park beyond. It was dark outside now. The neon lighting overhead in the office was flickering and doing little to alleviate the headache that had been building since early that morning. He opened his desk drawer and brought out a jumbo-sized bottle of Advil that he had brought back from a trip to America. He put a couple of the tablets in his mouth and swallowed them dry. Rattling the few remaining pills in the tub and putting it back in the drawer. The car park was about half full. Some people coming in on shift. Some others leaving. All spare hands had been called to the pump but so far the hunt for the missing boy had proved fruitless. The boy's father had finally phoned home – his mobile phone battery had run out – and was even now driving back to England. He'd make it by morning and Delaney prayed to God that someone would have some good news for him by then. Not that He ever listened to him. Or if He did He showed no signs of it.

Delaney looked across at the muted television hanging on the wall across the office. Sky News had been rolling the story all day long, alternating between pictures of Melanie Jones, her injured cameraman, Peter Garnier, and the missing boy and his desperately grieving mother. Making a link between them all but with no explanation to offer.

Delaney didn't entirely blame them. He too was sure there was a link between them all, he just couldn't for the life of him see what it was. The degenerate slug Garnier had got that right at least, Delaney thought: his job was indeed to see how things fitted together. Find the pattern and you can work out what happens next. Find the links and he might work out who had taken the boy, and, more importantly, work out where he had been taken. Work it out in time.

Delaney picked up a half-finished cup of coffee and took a swallow of the cold liquid. What he really needed was a drink. He looked at the flashing cursor on his computer screen and switched the machine to standby. He wasn't going to find any clues looking at his computer, he was pretty damn sure of that. He picked his jacket off the back of his chair, shrugged into it, and walked across the office to another desk, where Tony Bennett was sitting at a computer looking at CCTV footage from various cameras in Camden Town.

'How's it going?' he asked.

Bennett looked up at him, rubbing sore eyes. 'You know how it is. We coppers used to wear out shoe leather, now it's repetitive-strain injuries and gallons of eyewash.'

Delaney grunted. 'I know how that works.'

Bennett gestured at the computer monitor. 'Britain is the most surveilled country in the world. More CCTV cameras per capita than any other country on the planet – for all the bleeding good it does.'

'I don't know,' said Delaney, watching the screen as a drunken twenty-something-year-old woman staggered along the pavement, wobbling on high platform heels and finishing a can of cider which she tossed into the gutter. 'There's been a real crackdown on litterbugs.'

'Yeah, right.'

'You want to call it a day? Come down to the annexe, get acquainted with the most important people you need to know.'

Bennett looked up again, puzzled. 'Annexe? Which people?'

'Bar staff, Tony. Our local, The Pig and Whistle – it's just around the corner.'

'The Pig and Whistle. You *are* kidding me?'

Delaney put a cigarette in his mouth without lighting it. 'I don't kid. Not when it comes to serious matters like your local boozer. I take it you do drink?'

Bennett stood up to swing his own jacket off the back of his chair. 'You take it right.'

As he slipped into his jacket, behind him on the monitor Jamil Azeez walked into shot, stopping beside a lamp-post and pulling out a packet of cigarettes. A young woman with dark hair and quasi-goth clothing approached to talk to him. He gave her a cigarette and lit it for her, she walked off and Jamil put a cigarette in his own mouth and lit it.

Bennett turned back and paused the footage.

'Hang on, Jack, this is my man.'

Delaney looked at his watch. 'As I understand it, he's not going anywhere.'

'True, but I'll just see how this pans out. Catch you down there.'

'Sure.' Delaney headed to the door, slapping a hand on the shoulder of Jimmy Skinner, who was dealing with a pile of paperwork and sketching a

154

farewell wave over his shoulder as Bennett called after him.

'Make mine a pint.'

Bennett turned back to the computer monitor and clicked the cursor to play the streaming footage again. Jamil was clearly in shot: the light overhead and spilling from the shops behind made it a very clear picture.

Jamil Azeez lit his cigarette, nervously flicking the lighter a few times and shaking it to get it to work. His hands seemed to tremble as he took a few quick puffs. Bennett couldn't tell if it was because of the cold or if he was nervous about something. He certainly wasn't dressed for the weather: jeans and a shirt.

Bennett pushed play again and after a moment or two on the screen a young white man, early twenties by the looks of him, walked over to Jamil and raised his hands, shouting something in his face. Jamil stepped back, clearly distressed, and Bennett didn't blame him. The white man was solidly built and was wearing tight jeans, a green bomber jacket and a skinhead haircut. A tattoo at the nape of his neck, just visible through the hair on the back of his head, read B-.

Jamil threw down his cigarette and hurried away. The man turned in profile, watching him, his handsome face now ugly with anger. Then he walked out of shot in the same direction.

Bennett rewound the footage and froze the image again with the man's face in profile. Then he clicked the cursor on file and print. As the wireless printer across the office powered up, Bennett fast-forwarded the footage at thirty times real-time speed. He gave it an hour, up to the time that Jamil had been found by

Kate Walker, but neither Jamil nor the skinhead came back into shot. Bennett closed down the computer and went across to pick up the copies of the screen grab that he had printed off. He looked across at Delaney's desk.

'Help you with something?' asked Jimmy Skinner.

'Yeah,' said Bennett and held out one of the pics he had just printed off. 'Recognise this guy?'

Skinner looked at the photo. 'Can't say I do. No, sorry.'

'No worries,' said Bennett. 'Maybe catch you later down the pub.'

Skinner gestured at his mound of paperwork. 'Maybe.'

Bennett nodded and headed out. Skinner looked after him thoughtfully for a moment and then sighed and picked the next form up from the pile.

*

The Pig and Whistle was crowded. It always was at that time of night, and eighty per cent of the people in it were either on the job or civilian support staff from the station. Delaney was standing at the shorter bit of the L-shape of the bar that ran across one side of the room. Sally Cartwright was perched on a stool beside him, nursing a gin and tonic.

'Are you going to drink that, Sally, or sip it to death?' he asked, finishing his pint of Guinness.

'I'm driving, sir.'

'Very civic-minded of you!' Delaney held his glass up to the Titian-haired barwoman. 'Stick another large one in there for us.'

'Sure thing, cowboy.'

'Where's your Saab, sir?'

Delaney winked at her. 'Back at the ranch. One of the perks of having a doctor girlfriend up the stick is that she doesn't drink. So I have to do it for both of us.'

Sally smiled. 'Up the stick. Nice expression. You'd say that to herself, would you?'

'Of course.'

'Yeah, right.'

Delaney fixed her with a serious look. 'Sure, would the devil not strike me down here in my very shiny shoes if I were to tell a lie?'

'It will be me striking you down, Jack Delaney, you don't watch it.'

Delaney turned round and grinned. 'What did I tell you, Sally? Katy's Kabs. Bang on time.'

Kate smiled despite herself. 'Just get me a large orange juice. I'm going to powder my nose.'

Delaney watched her walking away, the smile lingering on his lips.

'I don't how she puts up with you, sir,' said Sally.

'To be perfectly honest with you, Sally, neither do I!' He gestured at the barmaid again. 'Angela, you beautiful thing, will you be after getting me a large orange juice?' The barmaid grinned back resignedly as Bennett came into the pub and threaded his way towards them. 'And a pint of . . . ?' He looked at Bennett questioningly.

'Lager's fine.'

The barmaid nodded and Delaney pointed at Bennett's foot as he limped over to join them. 'Industrial injury?'

Bennett laughed. 'No, temporary infirmity.'

'What from?

Bennett hesitated slightly. 'I did it playing rugby last weekend.'

'What position?'

'Wing.'

'Same here.'

'You play?'

Sally laughed out loud and covered it with a cough. Delaney shook his head. 'Used to. Long time ago . . .'

'In a universe far, far away?'

'Oh yeah! We're definitely talking light years,' said Sally.

'You can get sent back to uniform very quickly, you know, detective constable.'

'Sir.' Sally pretended to look chastened.

Delaney took the drinks from the barmaid, handed her a tenner and gave Bennett his pint.

'How did you get on with the footage?'

'He finished his smoke and walked out of shot again. But someone did come up and have words with him. Looked like an argument or some drunk having a go at him.'

'Could you make out who it was?'

Bennett reached into his pocket, pulled out one of the prints and handed it over to Delaney. 'Anyone you recognise?'

Delaney looked at it, shook his head and then handed it over to Sally.

'He looks cute for a skinhead, but no. Not ringing any bells.'

She handed the picture back to Delaney, who held it out to Bennett.

'No, keep it. Show it around. Someone might know him.'

'You think he's the man who stabbed your vic?'

Bennett nodded. 'He got right into his face, shouting at him. I couldn't make out what he was saying because he was facing away from the camera. But I could take a guess.'

'Paki go home?' said Sally.

'Along those lines. Except that Jamil Azeez is an Iranian and was born here.'

'Nick Griffin will let him stay, then, so that's all right,' said Delaney, folding the photo up and putting it in his pocket.

'Who was it who said I despise everything you say but I will defend your right to say it to the death?' asked Sally.

'It wasn't George Formby, was it?' asked Bennett.

Sally laughed as Kate came up to join them. 'The new inspector is quite the comedian, Kate,' she said.

'I know,' Kate agreed dryly and pointed at a poster pinned to the wall beside the detective constable. 'I told him he should go in for the talent competition.'

'Fat chance,' said Bennett. 'I've got Van Gogh's ear for music and couldn't go on stage to tell a joke if my life depended on it.'

'That right?'

'It would terrify me. Had to give a best man's speech once. Never do it again.'

'You don't strike me as the bashful type,' said Delaney.

'Trust me, I was more nervous than a pig in a pork-pie factory.' Bennett jerked his thumb backwards at the flyer. 'So what about you, Jack? You going to do us a song-and-dance routine?'

Delaney gave him a flat look. 'Not in this lifetime.'

Bennett slapped his leg. 'And my gammy leg counts me out in that department.'

'So what brought you down to London, Tony?' asked Kate.

'Ambition, I guess.'

'I'm not sure White City is the place for ambition,' said Delaney.

'It's a start and I don't plan to be here too long.'

'Very wise. The sooner you and my brilliant constable get promoted out of here, the safer the public are going to be. Me, I'm just going to count out the days to my pension and settle into obscurity.'

Kate patted her belly pointedly. 'Right. Well, I wouldn't be getting too many ideas about early retirement, cowboy! You've got a few more years on the range yet.'

'Yes, boss,' said Delaney, pretending to be disappointed.

'You're not fooling anybody, sir,' said Sally, amused.

'Anyway, enough shop,' said Bennett, finishing his pint. 'It's my round. Who's for a refill?'

'Not for me,' said Sally.

'Or me,' said Kate.

'I'm in,' said Jack, draining the remaining two-thirds of his pint and holding his glass out to Bennett.

Bennett nodded approvingly. 'You want a large shot of Jameson's with that?'

Delaney threw him a quizzical look.

'Your fame precedes you!' said Bennett.

Delaney looked at Kate and shrugged. 'Just the Guinness, thanks.'

Bennett handed the glasses over to the barmaid.

'So where are you staying?' Delaney asked him.

'Got myself a little flat down in Shepherd's Bush.'

'Handy.'

'Yeah, close enough, and there are enough fast-food takeaway outlets to keep a bachelor boy happy.'

'Couple of nice boozers, too,' said Delaney.

'And that. Did some research.'

'Very wise.'

'And what about you, Jack? Where are you based?'

Kate slipped her arm through Delaney's. 'He's just bought himself a nice little house in Belsize Park.'

Bennett whistled. 'Belsize Park? Nice.'

Delaney shrugged. 'If you like that sort of thing.'

'Must have cost a pretty penny?'

Delaney shifted his feet a little uncomfortably. 'I had some luck with investments.'

Bennett grinned. 'I'll take half your luck.'

'Yeah, well, my wife died. So I sold the house we owned and rented a flat and I put the money together with the life insurance into some investments that did okay, and I pulled the cash back before the big downturn. So I really wouldn't want to wish that kind of luck on you.'

'Sorry, I didn't realise.'

'No reason you should,' said Delaney.

Twenty minutes later and Bennett was clearly feeling at home. On first-name terms with the barmaid and flirting with Sally Cartwright. Delaney finished his third pint and turned to Kate. 'You ready to go home?'

'More than ready.' She held her hand up to Sally and Bennett. 'See you later.'

'Bye,' said Sally.

'Thanks for the drink.' Delaney nodded at Bennett. '*De nada*.'

Kate and Delaney threaded their way through the noisy bar and headed for the door.

'Did I say the wrong thing earlier, about his house and everything?' Bennett asked Sally.

'He's just a little sensitive about his wife, is all. She was shot during an armed robbery.'

'Really?'

'I'm surprised you haven't heard about it.'

'I'm the new boy, remember.'

'It happened some years back. There was an armed robbery at a petrol station. Jack and his wife just happened to be at the wrong place at the wrong time.'

'It happens. Especially in our job.'

'I guess. This was off-duty, though. Jack tried to intervene, his wife got caught in the crossfire.'

'Ouch. No wonder he's a little sensitive.'

'Exactly.'

'They ever catch who did it?'

Sally shook her head. 'No. They never did.'

'Jack Delaney doesn't strike me as the kind of man who lets sleeping dogs lie.'

'He's moved on.'

Bennett nodded thoughtfully. 'I can well imagine that Kate Walker doesn't take any shit, either.'

Sally laughed. 'I'm not sure she'd put it like that herself, but you're probably right.'

'Anyway, enough about them. Let me get you a drink, young Constable Cartwright, and you can tell me all about yourself.'

Sally held up her glass. 'I've had my quota. I'm driving, remember.'

Bennett flashed a grin. 'Then you can have a fruit juice.'

Bennett turned round to the barmaid and held his empty glass aloft. 'Any chance of some refreshment for an honest working man, darling?'

To Sally's dismay the barmaid smiled back at him – she even detected a hint of a wink. Dear God, she thought to herself, just what we need, another bloody Jack Delaney.

*

Jack turned down the corner of a page of the book he was reading, Kate Mosse's *Labyrinth*, and heard a sharp intake of breath. He turned his head to see Kate staring at him in disbelief from her side of the bed.

'What do you think you're doing?'

'Just marking the page.'

'Well, don't do it like that! Use a bookmark or a slip of paper.'

'It's only a paperback book, Kate. It's not an illustrated gospel from Lindisfarne.'

'It's my book. So don't do it again.'

Delaney straightened out the corner of the page he had folded, picked up a petrol receipt from the bedside cabinet and slid it between the pages, making a great display of closing the book gently.

'Is that better?' he asked.

'Much better. You treat your own trashy paper-backs how you like, but my books command respect.'

'You saying I dissed the Mosse?'

'That's exactly what I'm saying.' Kate had a pair of black-rimmed reading glasses perched on the end of her nose, and she peered reprovingly over the top of them at Delaney.

'You look just like the librarian at my old school, you know.'

'Charming.'

'It's a compliment. All the boys fancied her.'

'Really?'

'Oh, yeah. Miss Williams. Very sexy. Very strict.'

'I'll give you strict if you don't watch out.'

Delaney snaked a hand towards her chest. 'Is that a promise?'

Kate slapped his hand away. 'Jack, behave yourself!'

Jack grinned and put his hand under the covers. He looked at the clock. It was nearly midnight. 'I need my goodnight kiss.'

Kate sat up a little straighter as Jack's exploring hand found its target. She smiled and folded the corner of a page of the paperback she was reading and put it down on the matching bedside cabinet.

Delaney threw her his own look of disbelief. 'Oi!'

Kate flapped a dismissive hand. 'That's a trashy crime novel. It doesn't count.'

She snuggled up to him, pulling a mock-stern expression. 'Now then, young man, you were late bringing back that copy of *Lady Chatterley's Lover*. What are we going to do about that?'

Jack moved his hand again and Kate smiled, breathing huskily in his ear.

'Now that . . . is a good start.'

*

Black clouds hung low over the Thames, completely blanketing the moon and turning the water below into dark, impenetrable ink.

The minute hand clicked and shuddered twelve on the clock tower of the Palace of Westminster, and the sound of its historical bell, Big Ben, sounded. As it did so white flashes of light speared through the clouds, thunder cracked and low rumblings spread out like ripples of sound. But miraculously there was no rain.

*

Some twelve miles or so west of Westminster, in Harrow on the Hill, most people were in their beds and already sleeping. In the town centre a few pubs were still open and the youth of the area were singing, dancing, falling in love or settling disagreements with fists or broken bottles. But in one residential side street, a scant mile or so away from the hustle and bustle, away from the street lamps, the lights were all off, save for one solitary building where the multicoloured lights shone forth like a Christmas card.

Maureen Gallagher closed the large oak door behind her and walked into the church, her soft shoes making a gentle whispering, shuffling sound as she paused and knelt painfully, wincing a little as she felt the tendons in her joints crackle. She made a quick sign of the cross and rose again slowly, her knees creaking audibly this time, and Maureen winced again with the pain of it. Feeling much older than her forty-seven years she put a hand on the back pew of the church to steady herself. She straightened the scarf that completely covered her head and looked up at the altar and then around at the large stained-glass windows that marched along both flanks of the building. Ten of them in total. The night sky was coal black outside, but the lights she had put on filled the church with cold if brilliant illumination and picked out the blues and the reds in the windows so that they did indeed seem to shine bright with God's glory. Maureen looked at them for a moment or two and then lowered her eyes, squeezing them shut as though in pain, her breathing ragged.

It was a small church built sometime in the mid-1950s. Utilitarianism winning out over ornamentation. The stained-glass windows with their overtly Catholic themes were the only stylistic nod to denomination. The small local Catholic community that it had been built to service was a far cry from the days when Saint Mary's, the large church that sat on the crest of the nearby hill like a fortress, had been built. Commissioned by Archbishop Lanfranc and consecrated by Saint Anselm in 1094. Its towering wooden steeple was covered in twelve tonnes of lead and was visible for miles around. William the Conqueror built cathedrals and churches and monasteries as hymns to God in stone and mortar and toil. Henry the Eighth destroyed them and his daughter and descendants set about destroying the Roman Catholic Church in England itself, so that long, long before 1956 Roman Catholics had become only a small minority in the country. That had changed in recent years, of course, with the influx of eastern European immigrants, so that there were probably more actively practising Roman Catholics in England now than there were Protestants. But Saint Mary's on the hill was now Church of England, and Saint Botolph's below it in the residential sprawl surrounding the town had been built as a thoroughly modest affair. They were as different, one from the other, as a palace is from a garden shed. It had a plain rectangular shape, and a row of ten pews flanked either side of the central aisle that led to a simple altar, raised on a painted concrete base with a brass rail at the front where the communicants would kneel to receive the wafer.

Maureen Gallagher had been a volunteer at the church for five years but had never taken communion. She found the gazes of the saints and the cruciform Christ that hovered over the altar with arms outstretched almost intolerable. She had taken a pilgrimage to Walsingham once, five years ago, in a desperate effort to make amends. But the weight of the silence and the darkness and the sweet smoky smell of burning candles in the many, many medieval churches she visited had filled her soul with despair and crushed her spirit under the guilt she bore like the carapace of a beetle broken under a workman's heel. Some sins couldn't be forgiven, she knew that. But she came to Saint Botolph's church every morning with her tray of cleaning materials and on her hands and knees scrubbed, polished and buffed the floors and the wooden pews, driving the candle smoke from her memory with the sweet smell of beeswax and the artificial aromas of spray polish. And if she could only bear a glance now and then at the watching figure on the wall, it was nothing like the leaden despair she had felt in the shrines of Walsingham.

Maureen came late each night, summer or winter, long after anyone else, priest or parishioner, had left. She liked the solitude and silence when she worked. She came to Mass alone and sat in the back pew, neither making eye contact with her fellow worshippers nor engaging in conversation after the service. She had barely spoken fifty words to the priest, Father Carson Brown, since she had first volunteered her services five years before. She was so used to being wrapped up in her own quiet world of silent prayer and penance that she didn't really register the sound that night of the door opening behind her as she knelt rubbing an old yellow duster over the brass of the communicants' rail. She didn't hear the soft steps as the visitor approached behind. What brought the presence to her attention was the dark figure and pale face distorted and reflected in the mellow curve of the rail. She turned around and looked up. The lights overhead seemed brighter now, shining on the stained-glass windows and somehow putting a nimbus around the visitor's face like a vision of a latter-day saint. Only the glow in the eyes that looked down on her, with no mercy or seeming humanity, didn't seem to come from the church lights alone. Maureen Gallagher put up a hand to shield her eyes from their glare and brought the face into focus. It took a moment or two and then the breath leaked from her body as the realisation dawned on her. The weight she had been carrying for so very long seemed to rise from her for the briefest of moments.

'It's you,' she said.

Then a thunderbolt hit her in the heart. And the weight was gone for ever.

SUNDAY

Not for the first time in his life Father Carson Brown was feeling guilty. It was a very Catholic emotion, surely enough, he realised, and he was a Catholic priest after all, but it wasn't a strong enough emotion to stop him from returning to the scene of the crime. Or to the woman to be more precise.

Sarah Jane Keeley. She had dark honey-coloured hair that tumbled around white shoulders that were sprinkled with the lightest of freckles, and wide blue eyes that were regarding the priest with the sort of lustful playfulness that Rome would certainly never have approved of.

Father Brown tucked his shirt into his trousers and buttoned them up. 'You are a bad woman, Sarah Jane,' he said.

The woman in question was lying on the bed and smiling languidly up at him, a sheet held to her chest, the tip of her tongue licking the ruby moistness of her top lip in a slow, sensual curve.

'Do you have to go?' she asked, with a coy smile playing now on her perfectly formed cupid's-bow lips.

'I do,' he replied. 'And there's no point pouting like Marilyn Monroe! There's a Union of Catholic

Mothers' meeting this morning and I have to make sure everything is set up for them.'

Sarah Jane grinned. 'John won't be back until tonight, you know?'

'I know.' Father Carson Brown smiled back at her. John Keeley was the reason he was feeling guilty. They had grown up together, best friends through primary school and then secondary school, the Salvatorian College Catholic school, not a hundred miles from the street in Harrow where John Keeley now lived and where he himself would visit whenever his old friend was away on business.

At eighteen John Keeley had gone to university to study law and Carson Brown had gone first to seminary college and then on to the priesthood. The truth of the matter was that the two boys had both been in love with Sarah Jane Keeley since they had met her in infant school. Not that they knew it at the time, of course. Sarah Jane had been a complete tomboy, but the three of them had been inseparable and as they grew into teenagers it was clear that the friendship between them had also grown into something else. But it was John that she clearly fancied, so Carson had kept his distance, never revealing his true feelings for her. In fact, he fell so hopelessly in love with her at age sixteen that he decided if he couldn't have her then he wouldn't have any other woman. He threw himself into his studies and volunteer work at his church, Our Lady and Saint Thomas of Canterbury, and delighted his surprised parents when he announced that he wished to train for the priesthood. It took him many years until he finally made his way back to a position in

Harrow and six months after that before he made his way into a position with Sarah Jane. And it wasn't the missionary one.

'What are you smiling at?' the object of his affectionate recollections asked.

'Life,' he said. 'And all of its rich tapestry.'

'Seems to me you look like the cat that got the cream.'

'If I was a cat I would be purring.'

'*I* certainly am. You sure you don't want to come back to bed and stroke me again?'

The priest laughed. 'Like I say, you're a wicked, wicked woman, Sarah Jane.'

'You're quite right, and I should be spanked for it.'

He laughed again. 'I'd give it a try but I imagine I'd end up with a couple of missing teeth.'

'Yes. You probably would.'

Sarah Jane let the sheet drop, revealing her large breasts, the nipples clearly aroused and as pink as her lips against the creamy white magnificence of her skin. She put her hands behind her neck, arching her back slightly. 'Are you really sure you wouldn't like to linger?' she asked again, breathlessly.

Carson swallowed and shook his head, a look of something like regret passing through his eyes. 'I really can't – sorry.'

Her smile faded. 'You'll have to go and tell a few Hail Marys, I suppose?'

The priest sighed. 'Don't, Sarah Jane.'

'It's not our fault I chose the wrong man.'

'I know.'

'It's your precious God who made him gay. Made him that way but didn't give him the balls to admit it until he had been married to me for fifteen years.'

'Let's not discuss this again.'

'Seems to me your religion can be pretty flexible when it comes to your own moral code but not to others.'

'It's not my religion that dictates celibacy.'

Sarah Jane blinked. 'Come again?'

Father Carson Brown sat beside her and took her hand. 'It's just Church law, not based on any scriptural doctrine.'

'Really?'

The priest nodded his head sadly. 'It was in 1139 when the Second Lateran Council forbade the marriage of priests and declared null and void those legitimate marriages that had taken place before.'

'Nice of them.'

'But it didn't ban sex for them.'

Sarah Jane was sitting up now, the sheet wrapped demurely around her and her forehead creased with a frown. 'What do you mean?'

'The edict made the wives into concubines, is all.'

'Why?'

'So their progeny wouldn't have the right to inherit property. Priests used to travel around before but now churches were being built by communities and parishes were created and the priest was staying.'

'So?'

'So it was all about money. The property was owned by the Catholic Church.'

'So why haven't they done anything about it nowadays, if it's such an old and ridiculous law?'

'They've tried. Ever since the 1960s there has been an enormous groundswell of opinion that the Church law should be changed. There's an organisation called CORPUS that campaigns and represents tens of thousands of resigned priests throughout the world. Trust me, I don't feel guilty about what we are doing because my heart and my soul are telling me it's right.'

'Really?'

'Yes, really. And that's what constitutes faith. It's what religion is all about.'

'So why haven't you told me this before?'

Father Carson took a deep breath. 'Because I am thinking of resigning from the priesthood.'

Sarah Jane looked up at him, shocked and feeling not a little guilty. 'Because of me?'

'No,' he said, shaking his head sadly again. 'Because of me.'

*

The conversation with Sarah Jane Keeley was still running through Father Carson Brown's mind that Sunday morning as he walked past the houses on Westbury Terrace and up to his church. Most of the curtains were closed but he still felt as if he could feel the eyes of his parishioners on him . . . judging him. He held his jacket closed with one hand, shivering against the cold as he opened the small gate to Saint Botolph's. There was a low wall in front of the church that the gate was set in, and beyond that about twenty yards by six of yard. The gravel, still rimed with frost, crunched under his feet, as he closed the gate behind him, but he paid no attention to the sound or to his surroundings as he walked up to and into the small side porch that led into the church. He didn't find it odd that the outer church door was open and he hardly registered the coldness of the holy water as he dipped the first two fingers of his right hand in it and made a sign of the cross on his forehead. The inner doors to the church were also open and the priest had his head bowed, deep in thought, as he entered, knelt and made another larger sign of the cross, touching his forehead, both shoulders and his chest. He rose slowly and walked towards the altar. It took a moment or two for him to notice that something was amiss.

On the altar, which should have been bare, was a white cloth draped over a large object. Puzzled, Carson Brown walked forward up onto the low dais and raised the cloth. He looked down uncomprehending for a heartbeat and then gagged and held his hand to his mouth. He turned away in horror, fell to his knees and threw up into Maureen Gallagher's mopping-up bucket.

Outside on the church's roof a crow took off into the air. Buffeted by the wind, he swirled and banked, his caw shrieking like a prophecy fulfilled.

*

The sound echoed in Delaney's ear as he looked out of the window at the river below him. And time stilled. The water swirling violently now. The rush of it as loud as the wind in his ears. And the little stars of sunlight, which had danced on the water like mayflies, were now flakes of snow, little shards of ice that tinkled in the air like frozen whispers.

It seemed as though time had also frozen. Jack had entered a crossing place between the past and the future. A hiatus. A moment of change that was irreversible and inevitable. Then he blinked his eyes and turned back the way he had come, ran to the edge of the ruined first floor of the mill house, and lowered himself over the edge of the broken floor to dangle for a moment before letting go. Then it seemed like he was falling for ever, the scream ringing in his earls like a knife thrust in his heart, before the cold floor appeared to jump up at him, slamming his knees into his chest as he rolled onto his side, jarring his shoulder as he slammed down. He gasped with pain, rubbing his knee, and staggered to his feet. He could still hear Siobhan screaming in terror and ran across the mill-house floor to the door. His feet slid on the ice-covered concrete and he skidded into the door, clutching it to regain his balance before wrenching it open and charging outside. Siobhan's screams were desperate now and Jack ran towards the river.

A light snow was falling, the fat frozen flakes dancing in the air and floating into Jack's eyes, blinding him. He wiped his hand across them and struggled as fast as he could down the bank, the worn soles of his boots sticking in the slippery mud as he clambered down to the river's edge. Out in the water Siobhan gripped hard to the edge of a long-abandoned half-sunk barge that stuck out from the raging waters at an angle.

'Hold on, Siobhan,' screamed Jack as he got onto the barge and picked his way along the narrow edge that skirted the rotting hulk of the cabin. 'I'm coming.'

'Please, Jack. Please. It's so cold.'

'I know, Siobhan. Just hold on. I'm coming.'

Jack made it to the front of the barge, where the engine would have been housed when the boat had been in use many years before. He clambered up into the small forward deck space and, bracing his feet, leaned over the crumbling woodwork to reach down. He could see the naked terror in Siobhan's young eyes as her frozen hands clung to the rotten woodwork of the hull, clutching at the edges of a gaping hole. The river swirled beneath and around her, like a thing feeding. She whimpered with fear as Jack smiled down at her.

'It's okay, Shiv. I've got you now.'

Jack held his arm out and stretched it as far as he could go, his fingers reaching.

Siobhan shook her head.

'Give me your hand.'

And again she shook her head. Her teeth chattering with fear as she screamed up at him. 'No.'

Jack leaned further down, stretching his arm as far as he could towards her, wedging his feet against the side of the engine housing and straining every muscle in his body. He should never have brought her with him to the old mill house. He was supposed to be looking after her but he'd wanted to search it and knew it might not be safe so he had made her wait outside while he checked it out. He thought she'd be safe but he knew he should never have left her on her own.

He reached out further with his arm. Below him in the water Siobhan was turning blue now with the cold. Her tiny hands were frozen as they clung to the rotting wood of the barge. The water was swirling around her powerfully, tugging at her, hungry to pluck her loose and consume her. Her fingers gripped painfully as a swell raised her and swung her sideways. She looked up at her brother, the tears in her eyes freezing with the cold.

'Help me, Jack.'

And his hands reached her fingers. 'Take my hand, Siobhan.'

And she let go of the wood and grasped at his hand, but the swirl of the water was too much – their fingertips brushed and she was swept out into the river.

'No!' cried Jack as he watched his sister's head bob below the surface of the water. 'No!'

He jumped down from the barge and ran along the river's edge, calling out desperately to his sister. He caught a flash of her faded blue dress as it sank beneath the rough eddies of the water and then she was gone. He could hear the sound of a siren in the distance, a shrill note sounding again and again.

Delaney's eyes flew wide open and as he sat up in bed he looked at the mobile phone on the bedside cabinet. It vibrated again, rattling against the polished wood and making a buzzing sound. Delaney ran his hand over his forehead. It was drenched with sweat.

Beside him Kate stirred and looked up at him sleepily. 'What's up, Jack?'

'Just a dream,' he said hoarsely. He picked up the phone and looked at the caller's ID, then answered it. 'Hi, Diane. This is supposed to be a day of rest, you know.' He listened, his forehead creasing as he did so, squinting at the clock to see the time. It was six forty-five. 'Okay, boss,' he said. 'I'll get there as soon as I can.'

He closed the phone and looked across at Kate.

'What's going on?'

Delaney ran his hand through his hair. 'God knows, Kate. God only knows.'

'Has something happened? Have they found the boy?'

'No. Not that.'

'What, then?'

'The Catholic church two streets away from Carlton Row. Someone's been killed.'

Kate sat up in the bed. 'Do you want me to come with you?'

Delaney grimaced apologetically. 'Would you mind? They've phoned the coroner but he's a few hours away. Might be good to have your opinion.'

'I can't process the body, you know that? We'll have to wait for him to get there.'

'Yeah, I know. I understand if you don't want to do it. This isn't a pleasant one, Kate.'

'It's okay. Give me five minutes.'

*

It was actually just ten minutes later when Kate walked into her kitchen to find Jack dressed and pouring some hot water from the kettle into a Thermos flask.

'Only instant, I'm afraid – short on time.'

'That's okay. It's good thinking.'

At that time of day on a Sunday morning it wasn't busy on the roads and Delaney told Kate to ignore the speed limits. They made the trip in just over twenty minutes. As they turned the corner of Carlton Row it was still dark, although thankfully not raining, and the street was lit up with the blue lights still flashing on top of a number of police cars that had pulled up outside Saint Botolph's. There was also an ambulance, which to Delaney's way of thinking, given the circumstances, was as ridiculous a case of closing the stable door after the horse had bolted as he had ever seen.

He and Kate ducked under the yellow exclusion tape that had already been stretched across the street thirty yards either side of the church. He was pleased to note that the vultures had not yet gathered, but judging by the people looking out of their windows, some with phones held up to the glass, he figured it wouldn't be long. Mobile footage was probably being sent even now over the internet and the real press cameras wouldn't be much longer getting there, he had no doubt of that.

Diane Campbell was standing outside the church with a couple of uniforms beside her, talking to a man with a blanket wrapped around his shoulders and drinking tea from a plastic beaker. Delaney assumed that he was the priest who had made the discovery, and reckoned the tea would be very sweet indeed.

'Diane.' He nodded at her briefly as they approached.

'Jack. Hello, Kate. Thanks for coming.'

'Not a problem.'

'Do we know who she is yet?' asked Delaney.

'We have a shrewd idea but the vicar hasn't been able to go back in and make a formal identification.'

'Priest.'

'What?'

'He's a priest, not a vicar.'

Father Carson Brown looked over at Delaney and Doctor Walker as if noticing them for the first time. He smiled, his face colourless, his lips thin. 'Another true believer.'

'I'm a true something,' said Delaney, a little bit more of the soft brogue sliding into his voice. 'I'm not sure what kind of believer I am any more.'

The priest looked back at him with haunted eyes. 'Nor me.'

Delaney nodded, understanding, and turned to Diane. 'Shall we go in?'

Diane held her arm out towards the door and Kate and Delaney followed her into the church. Delaney held back the urge to dip his hand in the holy water. He wasn't totally sure, but he thought the water might not be classed as holy any more. Would the church need to be sanctified again? As they walked up the aisle to the altar Delaney thought it was entirely possible that that could be the case.

A woman's head had been placed on the altar. Severed at the neck. Her eyes were open in a face that had no colour in it, apart from the eyes. Her eyes were a startling blue. Deep Arctic blue. Her head was as bald as an egg.

Kate stepped forward, putting on a pair of forensic gloves, and placed her hand on the woman's cheek. It was cold. Extremely cold.

She turned back to Jack and Diane. 'She's been frozen.'

'Where the hell is the rest of her?' asked Diane and pointed at the woman's forehead. 'And what the fuck is that supposed to mean?'

Delaney looked closer. The letters *H O R* had been carved on the woman's forehead. 'I don't know, Diane. When I was an altar boy we just had the chalice on the altar and maybe that little bell I had to ring at a certain time in the Mass. Decapitation was a bit too avant-garde for us back in Ballydehob.'

Diane was too used to gallows humour to comment. 'Christ, I need a cigarette,' she said instead.

'Diane!' Despite himself Delaney was a little taken aback.

'What?' she said.

Delaney gestured at the surroundings. 'You know – we're in a church.'

Diane flapped a dismissive hand and pointed at the severed head. 'Exactly. Maybe this is connected to some kind of devil worship.'

Kate knelt down by the altar, examining the cut marks at the base of the decapitated woman's head. 'Maybe the murderer was spelling out the name Horus.'

'Who?'

Kate turned round to look up at the chief inspector. 'Horus was an Egyptian deity. Had something to do with the dead, I think. He was depicted as having a human body but a falcon's head.'

Jack looked back at the altar. 'The fact that her head is shaved . . .'

'Yes?' said Kate, gesturing for him to continue.

'You think she might be a nun?'

Kate considered it. 'It's possible. The priest didn't seem to know a great deal about the woman except he thinks she must be the volunteer cleaner. Apparently she only worked at night, when no one else was around.'

'Maybe she's an ex-nun,' said Delaney. 'Maybe if this is some kind of ritual killing, a Satanist sacrifice or the like, it gives more power or energy to the spell if the sacrificed person is religious.'

'Might make a sick kind of sense, I suppose,' agreed Kate. 'Wouldn't they have painted a pentagram or something, though?'

'Satanists in Harrow on the Hill, decapitating bald nuns and desecrating churches!' Diane sighed heavily. 'Sweet Jesus, as if we haven't got enough on our plates already!'

'So the thing about this Horus fellow having a human body but a bird's head – is it significant, do you think?' Delaney asked Kate.

'It could be. If that's what the letters mean. But we have no way of knowing that yet.'

Diane yanked a packet of cigarettes out of her jacket pocket and snapped one into her mouth. 'Great,' she said. 'So the rest of her body is somewhere having a hawk's head grafted onto it by some devil-worshipping Egyptologist.'

'Don't even think of lighting that, Diane,' said Delaney.

'Jeez, Jack. Of course I'm not going to light it: this is a crime scene. Anyway, I thought your Catholicism was in the lapsed category?'

Delaney looked over at the row of saints marching along both walls, preserved in fractured and coloured glass, their eyes glowing now that dawn had finally broken from outside and shards of light were piercing through the dark clouds that still hung low over the church.

'I'm a betting man, boss, you know that. Let's just say I like to cover the odds.'

Robert Duncton and a woman whom Delaney had never seen before came into the church. The woman was in her mid-thirties, about six foot one or two tall, with short cropped blonde hair. She didn't seem to be wearing make-up and it didn't stop her being strikingly attractive – she had cheekbones you could have sliced cheese on.

'Step away from the evidence, please, Doctor Walker,' said Duncton.

Kate stood up and fixed him with a cool look. 'She's still a person, detective inspector.'

The tall woman held out her hand to Delaney. 'You'll be Jack Delaney?'

'That I will,' he said, almost smiling as he felt Diane's frowning gaze upon them. Her displeasure might not be merely a matter of breach of professional etiquette, he guessed. Diane Campbell admired a pretty woman just as much as the next man.

'Sergeant Halliday,' the tall woman said, introducing herself. She smiled, revealing a row of teeth as neatly arranged as a march by the Grenadier Guards and as white as a Lyons sugar cube. 'Emma. I've heard a lot about you.'

'Ahem,' said Diane Campbell with a stage cough.

'I'm sorry, chief inspector,' said the sergeant. She smiled again, holding her hand out once more. 'I've heard a lot about you as well, this time all good.'

Diane nodded wryly and shook Emma Halliday's hand.

'Well, isn't this lovely?' snorted Duncton sarcastically. 'Shame we can't all have a cup of tea and an iced bun!' He glared across at Kate, who had produced a camera and was firing off shots, her flash lighting up the church like bolts of lightning. 'But now that we've all met, can we stop contaminating my crime scene and keep the area clear for SOCO and the forensic pathologist?'

'He won't be here for another hour at least.'

'The evidence isn't going anywhere.'

'I beg to differ,' said Kate.

'I beg your pardon, Doctor Walker?' said Duncton, incredulous.

'The head – it's already melting.'

'Melting? What on earth are you talking about?'

'The head was frozen. In fact, I would say that the whole body was frozen or at least chilled significantly before the head was removed.'

'Why do you say that, doctor?' asked Sergeant Halliday.

Duncton glared at his assistant but let the question stand.

'The cut marks. The flesh is already softening. Kate took another few shots. 'In an hour's time you won't be able to get this detail.' She stood up again and pointed at the altar cloth under the severe head. 'Very little blood seepage.'

'Because the head was frozen?' asked Delaney.

'Partly. Probably also partly due to the severance taking place post-mortem and the subsequent exsanguinations taking place in a different location.'

'Are you saying her head being chopped off wasn't the cause of death?' asked the female sergeant.

Kate shrugged. 'Impossible to tell at this stage.'

'But it wasn't done here?'

'No.'

'Which is why we need to wait for the pathologist,' said Duncton.

'No . . .' said Kate again.

'It's why we need to find the missing body,' said Emma Halliday.

'Quite so,' agreed Kate and smiled at her as a teacher might smile at a bright student.

'Let's just remember that we are the lead on this investigation here,' Duncton barked at his sergeant, trying to recover some ground.

Delaney's mouth quirked in the faintest of smiles. He was pretty sure Duncton didn't like the fact that his sergeant was taller than him and he had to look up at her when trying to assert his authority. 'Nobody gives a shit whose collar it is, Robert,' Delaney said. 'All we care about is finding the sick fucker who has done this and finding the missing boy.'

'If the two *are* related,' replied Duncton.

Diane snorted. 'Yeah, they're not related – and if my granny grew a cock she'd be my grandad.'

Delaney nodded. 'Garnier is at the heart of all this, depend on it.'

'What I depend on are the facts, inspector. It's called good police work.'

'Do we know who she is?' asked Emma Halliday

Diane Campbell shook her head and pointed at the bucket and the basket of polishes and dusters that was to the side of the altar. 'We think it was the cleaning woman, but the good Father didn't look too closely. We're waiting for him to come in and make a formal identification.'

Duncton walked over and looked into the bucket, grimaced and moved away. 'Let's get him back in, then.'

*

If any colour had returned to Father Carson Brown's face in the time since he had last let his gaze fall upon the severed head that still sat in the centre of his altar like a blasphemous obscenity, it had drained away again now. He still had a blanket draped around his shoulders. The comforting hand of Sergeant Emma Halliday rested on his left one as she guided him reluctantly back up the aisle to the altar.

'Just take your time, Father.'

'Okay.' The priest knelt down and made another sign of the cross on his chest. He stood up, his gaze raised and fixed on the benevolent eyes of the crucified god above the altar. A few steps further and he stopped in front of the small raised dais, took a deep breath and looked down.

He held his unblinking gaze for a moment or two as he stared at the unfortunate woman's head, taking in the absolute horror of it. Her skin had more colour now – some red veins were standing out against the mottled blue skin. Tears formed in his eyes and he did nothing to blink them away. 'Yes, it's her,' he said simply.

'What's her name?' asked Duncton.

'It's Maureen Gallagher,' said Father Carson Brown.

'Sweet Jesus,' said Diane Campbell.

'And who is she, then, apart from being the church cleaner?' asked Duncton, puzzled.

Delaney gave him a flat look. 'She was the only person ever to visit Peter Garnier in prison,' he said. 'She went to see him once, six months ago.'

Duncton blinked his eyes rapidly as he took it in. 'So why in God's name has she ended up decapitated and placed on a church altar a hundred yards from Carlton Row?'

'None of this is in God's name,' said the priest, turning away from the altar.

'Somebody is sending a message?' Emma Halliday speculated.

'To who?' asked Duncton.

Delaney shrugged and looked at the priest who, puce-coloured and breathing deeply, was holding onto one of the pews facing the entrance to the church.

'I guess that's what we need to find out. And quickly.'

*

DI Tony Bennett sat on the edge of his bed and pulled on his right shoe, tying the laces neatly. He put his foot down and winced slightly, leaning forward to rub his ankle. It was still slightly swollen but the pain was easing. He popped a 400mg capsule of ibuprofen out of the foil strip, put it in his mouth and swallowed it with a drink of water from a pint glass that he had by his bed. He put the glass down and picked up the book that was beside it. It was the Good News version of the New Testament. He opened it at random and read a few verses to himself. He put the book back on his bedside cabinet and looked around the bedroom. It was a plain room in a one-bedroom apartment: one window looking out over a back garden that he didn't have access to, a wardrobe, a chair with curved wooden armrests and a red cushion on it by the window. No decorations at all apart from a small wooden crucifix above his bed.

Bennett stood up, wincing a little again, and walked across to his wardrobe. He took out a smart black jacket to match his black trousers and put it on. He looked at himself in the mirror set into the back of the wardrobe door and adjusted his tie, which was blue with red diagonal stripes. He looked at himself for a moment or two longer, his brown eyes serious and thoughtful, and then slid his reflection away as he closed the door.

He stepped through to the living room. Like his bedroom there was little personality in the room: no posters or pictures on the walls, no photographs on display. It was rectangular, a modern design with a sofa acting as a partition from the kitchen area behind it. The sofa faced a television and DVD set up on a chrome stand. At right angles to the pale yellow sofa a matching armchair had been placed, and opposite that was a sideboard with a bookcase above. No books had yet been placed on the shelves but a number of magazines were arranged neatly in a pile at the base of it. Bennett crossed over to the sideboard and picked up the remote control for the television that rested on top of the uppermost magazine, *Fieldsports Quarterly*. He turned on the television.

He muted the sound as a barrage of noise burst from the television and animated creatures danced around the screen. Still holding the remote, he walked over to his kitchen area, which had a beech table that could seat four people, modern matching beech units with a built-in oven, a four-ring gas hob and a shiny metal sink set in a faux-marble work surface. He picked up a mug of coffee that he had made some minutes earlier, took a swig and using the remote he flicked through his pre-set favourite channels to Sky News.

Melanie Jones, wrapped in a bright red thick woollen duffel coat, with a white scarf arranged perfectly around her pretty neck, was addressing the camera. Behind her a few people had gathered at the yellow tape that was cordoning off the street, and further still behind her Bennett could see the numerous flashing blue lights of the police cars parked by the church of Saint Botolph's. Saint Botolph, he thought to himself: another Irishman come to England to preach. Nobody knew much about him, either.

He pressed the mute button again and the presenter's warm honey-toned voice filled the room.

'I am sad to be bringing you yet another bizarre twist to the Peter Garnier story. Not a hundred yards from Carlton Row, which local people are now calling Death Row, where an eight-year-old boy called Archie Woods was abducted yesterday. A woman's body has been discovered this morning in Saint Botolph's church, which you can see behind me. Although the police have yet to release a full statement, they have informed Sky News that they are treating the death as highly suspicious. The discovery was made by Father Carson Brown, priest of the church, and we hope to be speaking to him later.'

Bennett muted the sound again. Turning to the sink, he poured the rest of his coffee away, his knuckles whitening as he gripped the handle of the mug as if to snap it off. His dark eyes were unfocused. Then he blinked, put the mug in the sink, snatched up his overcoat from the back of one of his kitchen chairs and headed to his front door.

*

An hour or so later Kate and Delaney came out of the entrance of the church as a suited team of SOCO went in. Kate nodded to the forensic pathologist, Dr Derek 'Bowlalong' Bowman, a cheerful portly man in his early fifties with a mass of badly managed curly hair atop a large smiling face. He was hurrying up to them at the usual busy pace that had given rise to his nickname.

'Doctor Walker. What a delight,' he said, his smile widening.

'Bowlalong.'

'Thanks for filling in – sorry I got held up. Some teenager turned over his car on the North Circular. Three mates on board. All seventeen.' His smile disappeared momentarily. 'So, Inspector Delaney, I see you couldn't keep the lovely doctor away from the business end of the job.'

'Didn't want to wait. Not with the boy still missing.'

'Quite so.' Bowman turned to Kate. 'Well, what have you found?'

'I haven't processed the scene at all. Just took some

shots – I'll email them over to your office later this morning,' she said.

'I'm led to believe the victim's head was frozen?'

'Or extremely chilled.'

'Could you tell how it had managed to become separated from her body?'

Kate shrugged. 'Cut rather than sawn. I'm guessing a large heavy-bladed implement.'

'Like an axe?' prompted Delaney.

Kate nodded. 'Or a machete – a sabre, possibly.'

'A military sabre?'

'Maybe. We'll know more when Dr Bowman finishes a proper post. I'm just speculating here.'

'But to cut off a human head . . . that's going to take a lot of strength, isn't it?'

'I would say so,' said Doctor Bowman, with an emphatic nod.

'Especially if the flesh was frozen,' added Kate.

'I don't know,' said Delaney. 'If it was partly chilled it would be easier in some ways. Cleaner cuts, less blood spillage. Butchers chill their meat before butchering it, don't they?'

'They do, Jack. They do. Food for thought, I'd say.' The forensic pathologist held his bag up and grinned bleakly again. 'I'd best get to it. I'll be back to you as soon as I can, Jack.'

'DI Robert Duncton is in charge of this one, I'm afraid, Derek.'

'Copy me in, though,' said Kate.

'You got it.'

Bowman bustled purposefully inside and Delaney and Kate walked across the small front yard, through the gate and up to the parked police cars.

Delaney leaned against the bonnet of one of the squad cars and pulled out a packet of cigarettes. As he did so a folded piece of paper fell to the floor and Kate had to bend down quickly and pick it up before it got soaked in the puddle it had landed by.

She handed it back to Delaney who opened it out.

'What's that?' asked Kate.

'Somebody the new boy Bennett is looking for. He thinks he might have something to do with the stabbed Iranian who you found off Camden High Street.'

'Who is he?'

'Don't know.'

Delaney handed her the photo and she looked at it, frowning. 'He looks a little familiar to me.'

'Doesn't look the sort to play tennis at your club,' said Delaney dryly.

'Funny.' Kate looked at the photo again and pulled out her mobile. 'I think I know who he is.'

As she punched in some numbers Sally Cartwright approached, carrying a large brown paper sack. Delaney smiled. The aroma of a bacon sandwich, apparently, was the one smell most responsible for turning ex-meat eaters away from being vegetarians and back to being carnivores. Delaney could see why. Anyway, as far as he was concerned he was as likely to turn vegetarian as he was to turn teetotal.

'They're going to be a bit cold, sir. Got here as fast as I could.'

'Good girl.'

Delaney unwrapped a sandwich and took a hefty bite. Bemused, Kate watched him, wondering how he got away with it. Anyone else who called Sally

194

Cartwright *good girl* would, she imagined, get told pretty quickly what to do with their bacon sandwich – buttered or otherwise.

*

DI Tony Bennett's eyes were fixed straight ahead. The voice filling the air was musical, a deep bass. The words rolling like treacle and echoing from the stone walls.

'Your brother will rise again, he said. And Martha answered, "I know he will rise in the resurrection at the last day." And Jesus said to her, I am the resurrection and the life. He who believes in me will live, even though he dies; and whoever lives and believes in me will never die. Do you believe this? He asked.'

Bennett stared ahead, his eyes shining. He felt a trembling against his thigh, and he blinked, confused for a moment. Then he took out his mobile phone. It vibrated quietly in his hand and he looked at the number, swallowed dryly and used his thumb to click the phone off.

*

Delaney took a last swig of the tea that Sally had also brought.

'Did you see the news this morning, sir?' she asked him.

'No.'

'Your friend Melanie Jones has started calling this area Death Row.'

'Great.'

'After Carlton Row.'

'Yeah, thank you – I got the connection, Sally!'

'She said it's what the locals are calling it.'

'Well, they got that right, I suppose.'

'She also said that the police were fairly sure it wasn't an accidental death.'

Delaney grunted as Kate came over to join them. 'If she knew what had really happened in there she would be shouting it out every fifteen minutes.'

'The press will have to know soon enough, I guess,' said Kate.

'And the chief is stamping up and down, sir,' added Sally. 'Wants to be kept posted on any developments. He thinks there's mileage in your profile on this.'

'Great!'

'He may be right.'

'I've had my picture on the front page of the papers once, Sally. I'm not so keen to have it there again, thanks all the same.'

He looked across at the growing crowd of journalists behind the yellow tape, not at all surprised to see Melanie Jones had now joined their number.

'Death Row,' he muttered and shook his head disgustedly.

Kate was still holding her phone when it rang. Chopin's piano sonata number two, sounding, given the circumstances, like the theme tune to a horror movie. She answered it quickly. 'Kate Walker.' She listened for a moment, tapping her foot. 'Tony, I think I might know who the person in that photo is, the one you gave to Jack. No, I don't know the name but I think I know someone who does.' She listened again. 'You're cracking up, detective. I'll meet you at the station in twenty minutes.' She listened again but there was clearly no response. She closed her phone and turned to Delaney. 'You going to be all right?'

'I'll be fine. I'm supposed to be working, remember? You're supposed to be having the day off.'

'That kid in hospital could still die, Jack. I think this is more important than sorting out the Sunday roast.'

'Course it is – you get on. And don't worry about dinner. I'm cooking tonight.'

Kate headed off towards her car, ignoring the barrage of questions shouted at her.

'I didn't know you could cook, sir,' Sally said, and then held up her hand to interrupt him. 'Yeah, yeah. I know. There's a lot I don't know about you.'

'You'll learn soon enough, Sally. Soon enough.'

She didn't doubt it.

*

Kate flicked the lock shut on her car and walked towards the entrance to Whitefriars Hall. DI Tony Bennett was waiting for her in the archway that led to the square. He was very smartly dressed, she thought as she approached: dark suit, nice expensive-looking tie, shoes polished to a gleam, and hair neatly combed and set with some kind of gel.

'You look like you've just been up in court, detective. I hope I've not interrupted an important date?'

Bennett held up his bare-fingered left hand. 'You know me, doctor. I'm married to the job.'

'What was the meeting, then?'

'I'm sorry?'

'Earlier you said you couldn't take my call. You were in a meeting?'

'I was. A church meeting.'

'Yeah, right.' Kate threw him a doubtful look but he wasn't smiling. He nodded at the photo she was holding in her hand.

'And you are pretty sure it was him?'

'Hard to tell for sure, I only glimpsed him when we were here before, but I think so. Yes.'

They came out of the tunnelled archway and turned left to the Dean's office just as the door to her office was thrown open and a young man dressed in black came out, shouting back into the office.

He said something in a language that Kate didn't understand – presumably Arabic, she thought – and hurried off.

The Dean, Sheila Anderson, appeared in the open doorway and called after him in the same language.

But the youth was gone, flapping a dismissive hand angrily over his shoulder as he disappeared into one of the buildings at the bottom left-hand side of the quad.

'Is there a problem?' asked Bennett.

'He wanted to go into his cousin's room.'

'Jamil Azeez, you mean?'

'Yes.'

'What was he after?'

The Dean shrugged. 'He said something about a book he'd lent him. I said I would have to wait for Jamil to give permission, but Malik became angry. Claiming it was his property and he had a right to it.'

'You speak Arabic?' Kate asked.

'No, Iranian. Not fluently. But I spent some years in Iran as a child.'

'Really?'

'My father was in the diplomatic corps. We were stationed there for a while.'

'When it was still Persia?' said Kate.

'Indeed,' replied the Dean, pleased. 'A lot of people forget that. Persia had become Iran long before Jamil and Malik were even born.'

'What was the book he was after?'

The Dean shrugged apologetically. 'I'm sorry, I don't know. What of Jamil – is there any improvement in his condition?'

'I'm sorry, no,' said Kate.

'But you have a suspect. You think you may know who attacked him?'

Bennett held out the photograph of the man arguing with Jamil on Camden High Street. 'Not yet. Not as such, but we wondered if you might be able to identify this man.'

The Dean took the photo, her forehead creasing as she recognised the man in it. 'Matt Henson. You think he attacked Jamil?'

'He's your gardener?' prompted Kate.

'No, dear,' said the Dean.

'I saw him here yesterday, raking the leaves.'

'He comes for a few hours each weekend to do odd jobs about the place. He's on community service. My husband is a magistrate. I like to help out where I can.'

'What is your husband's name?' asked Bennett, taking out his notebook.

The Dean became agitated. 'Surely you don't need to speak to him?'

'We just need to know where Matt Henson lives, what his offence was.'

'I can give you those details. Come in.'

Kate and DI Bennett followed the woman as she led them into her office. It was a spacious room: a large desk cluttered with books and papers to one side, a large multicoloured rug on the floor – genuine and expensive, Kate thought as she looked around the space. Book-filled shelves lined the walls; it could have been a teaching professor's room rather than an administrator's. Kate looked at some of the books as the Dean rummaged in her desk drawers. There were a lot of directories, academic reference journals and a whole section of American literature.

The Dean looked up to see what she was looking at. 'I did my Master's in contemporary American fiction,' she said and turned to Bennett. 'A large part of it on the detective fiction genre, in fact, inspector.'

Bennett picked up a copy of *The Big Sleep* from the Dean's desk and held it up. 'Wasn't Raymond Chandler educated in England?' he asked her.

'He was indeed.' Sheila Anderson pulled out a sheet of paper from her desk and held it out to the detective. 'Here are Matt's address details. But, like I said, I am absolutely sure he had nothing to do with the attack on Jamil. He's a lovely boy.'

Another lovely boy, Kate thought to herself and reappraised the woman. She was in her fifties but carried herself with a sensual grace. Her make-up was elegant but noticeable, American style, and her hair was immaculately groomed, the cut running to a lot more than the twenty pounds that Kate herself paid for a trim every couple of months or so.

'What was he given community service for?' she asked.

The Dean coloured slightly. 'It really isn't relevant.'

Bennett pulled out his mobile phone. 'It will take me two minutes to find out, Mrs Anderson.'

'Sheila, please. Okay. Okay,' she sighed and ran her fingers through her immaculate hair. 'He was arrested for affray, together with his older brother and his brother's friends.'

'Affray? What happened, exactly?' said Bennett, suspicions already forming in his mind.

'They got into a fight with another group of youths outside a pub.'

Kate could tell there was something else that she wasn't telling them. 'This other group of youths . . .'

'Yes?'

'What nationality were they?' Bennett finished Kate's question for her.

The Dean sighed again. 'They were Indian.'

Bennett nodded, somehow managing to make the movement look sceptical.

Sheila Anderson gestured angrily. 'See? I knew you'd jump to conclusions. He wasn't involved in the fight and from what I gather it was half a dozen of one and six of the other. That's why he only got community service. His brother was given a custodial sentence.'

'How old is Matt?'

'He's eighteen. But I can assure you he would not have stabbed Jamil Azeez. He's not that kind of boy.'

'He's eighteen – that makes him an adult, not a boy, and you seem to know him quite well for someone who only comes a few hours a week to push a broom around your yard.'

'I have been in education all my life, detective inspector. I know young men.'

Kate didn't doubt it, but she didn't make any comment.

DI Bennett pulled out his mobile phone and punched in some numbers. 'Slimline,' he said as his call was answered. 'It's DI Bennett here. I want you to send some uniforms round to . . .' He held the piece of paper up and read out the address that the Dean had given him. 'We'll meet them there in half an hour. We're picking up a skinhead recidivist called Matt Henson and we have good reason to think he may be carrying a knife. Thanks, Dave.' He closed his phone and faced Sheila Anderson again. 'We'd like to have another look around Jamil's room. If that's okay?'

'Of course it is. I'll show you up.'

'No, that won't be necessary. Just give us the keys I'll return them when we're done.'

'I'm not sure—'

'Jamil did give us his permission, Dean Anderson,' said Bennett.

The Dean shrugged, resigned. 'Well, if it's in his best interest . . . but you need to find the real person who attacked him,' she added pointedly.

'Of course it's in his best interests.'

'I'll have Arthur show you up.'

*

The ancient caretaker muttered something incomprehensible, but Kate took it to mean, from some of the words that she could recognise, that he would be waiting for them in the kitchen to lock up after they had finished. He grunted a farewell and closed the door behind him as he left.

Kate looked around the small room. It was in exactly the same state as when they had left it yesterday. 'Did you really get his permission to search the room?'

Bennett shrugged, smiling guiltily. 'I'm sure he gave us tacit approval.'

Kate snorted. 'Extremely tacit. Must have been in sign language when he was asleep.'

'So what was his cousin after, and why was he so agitated?'

Kate looked around her. 'Is there something on his laptop?'

'Maybe.'

'Well, we can't take it with us. That would be going too far.'

Bennett smiled again, swung the bag he had been carrying off his shoulder and put it on the student's desk.

'No need.' He opened the bag and took out a thick matt-black object, about the size of a hardback novel.

'What's that?'

'A portable hard drive. I'll just copy his data across.'

'Is that legal?'

'Not technically. I'll ask his permission later.'

Kate frowned. 'If you are able to.'

Bennett attached a USB cable to Jamil's laptop and turned it on. While he was waiting for it to boot up he opened the small wardrobe standing against the right-hand wall. There were shirts and trousers hanging on rails and jumpers and T-shirts, arranged neatly. At the bottom of the wardrobe were a pair of running shoes and two other pairs of shoes, one casual moccasin type of shoe and the other a pair of black oxfords polished to a shine. He slipped his hand in between the jumpers and shirts and worked his way down the compartments.

'Nothing,' he said to Kate.

'You know what I'm thinking?' she replied.

'Go on.'

'Where's his coat?'

Bennett shuffled the coat hangers and pulled out a smart linen sports jacket.

'Not that one.'

'What do you mean?'

'That's too lightweight for this time of year. Where's the coat he was wearing on the night he was attacked?'

'He wasn't wearing one.'

'It was cold that night. He would have been wearing a warm coat. Where is it?'

DI Bennett shrugged. 'It's not here, that's for sure.' He walked back over to the laptop and dragged the cursor to start copying files across. 'Why don't I see you back at the factory?' he said to Kate. 'I'll let you know how we get on with Matt Henson.'

'I'm not a civilian, Tony.'

'I know. But you're pregnant, and he may turn violent, and I don't want Jack Delaney on my case, thank you very much.'

Kate shook her head. People continually treating her like a piece of porcelain because they were worried what Jack might think was becoming very old. But Bennett had a point, she conceded to herself, she was indeed pregnant and while it was true that she was not exactly a civilian she wasn't part of the armed response unit, either.

'Whatever,' she said simply. She looked again at the books above the young student's desk and pulled out the copy of *The Catcher in the Rye* that she had noticed earlier. She thumbed through a few pages and then went to the front page of the book. Her eyebrows raised slightly as she read what had been written there and held it out for Bennett to see. The handwriting was feminine and graceful and it said '*To my beautiful boy*'.

'Now that might be what you detectives call a clue,' she said.

*

Doctor Derek Bowman took the lid off the refrigerated box and put it to one side. Beside him stood Lorraine Simons, Kate's erstwhile assistant, who was now being seconded to different forensic pathologists until a permanent replacement could be found. 'How was Doctor Walker?' she asked.

The doctor smiled. 'Effulgent as ever. Glowing, almost. They do say that about pregnant women, don't they?'

'They do indeed,' Lorraine conceded.

The pathologist shook his head as if disappointed at the world. 'Quite glowing. Why pretty women such as yourself and she ever wanted to get into the grim world of forensic pathology is quite beyond me. You should be out on the catwalks of Milan or gracing the covers of *Vogue*,' he said, with a raise of one eyebrow.

Lorraine blushed despite herself. She was a strawberry blonde with soft pale skin and a heart-shaped face that betrayed her emotions all too easily. She knew that Bowman was only pulling her leg but she frowned at him, mock serious. 'I should report you to the politically correct police, sir.'

'Please, Lorraine, there are no sirs here. It's Derek, or "Bowlalong" if you prefer – that's what everyone else calls me.'

'Why "Bowlalong"?'

The doctor picked up a pair of latex gloves and snapped his hands into them. 'I had that epithet bestowed on me at school. Always in a rush to get there, that's my trouble, never taking the time to just stop and admire the view.'

'You're a busy man.'

'That I am. That indeed I am. And talking of busy . . . let's see if this poor mistreated creature has any secrets to yield to us from beyond the veil.'

He placed his hands in the box, lifted out the severed head of Maureen Gallagher and placed it on his examining table. The atmosphere in the room changed suddenly, a chill pervading the air as though someone had opened an industrial freezer's door. There was no humour evident anywhere on either the doctor's or his assistant's faces now.

Maureen Gallagher's skin had become even more mottled, the flesh softer, even though the head had been kept in the cooling box.

'The press are saying she might be a nun, sir.'

'The jackals of Fleet Street have got wind of what we're dealing with, then?'

'Just heard it on the radio.'

206

'It's certainly a newsworthy item. I can't blame them for that.'

'Do the police know who she is, then? *Was* she a nun?'

'Just a humble cleaning lady, apparently. A volunteer.'

'And this is what she got for her sins.' Lorraine looked at the woman's head. Her eyes had been closed now and she looked like one of the wax heads that anthropological experts build up over discovered skulls to recreate what the person might have looked like. 'How old do you think she is?'

'Forties, fifties. Hard to tell just yet.'

'Who would want to do something like this?'

'Somebody very strong, somebody very disturbed.'

'The news people are talking about witchcraft.'

'Devil worship, maybe? Satanism, some kind of black magic sect, perhaps . . . but not witchcraft. Wicca is a religion that celebrates the good, the forces of nature. Whoever did this is coming from an entirely different place.'

Dr Bowman picked up his camera and started to take some shots. An hour later he had photographed the head from all angles, weighed it, measured it and taken samples for DNA testing should it be required.

Lorraine had gone to get them both some coffee and Bowman sat at his desk, looking at the printed-out photos he had taken. He compared them with the ones that Kate had sent across to him and concurred with her diagnosis. The body had been chilled and the head separated from it at the neck with the use of a heavy-bladed instrument of some kind. He looked at one of the photos, a close-up of the side of Maureen Gallagher's head, picked up a magnifying glass and studied the shot closer.

Bowman opened his desk drawer and took out a small pair of tweezers. Then he crossed back to the head, pulling his chair across. Delicately, he put the tweezers into one of the ears and pulled something from the opening. He held the tweezers up to the light. They now held a rust-coloured fleck of some substance. He placed it in an evidence bag and leaned forward to look into the ear again. As he did so he heard a faint ticking sound. He leaned in closer, thinking he must be imagining things. But, sure enough, it was still there, a faint ticking sound which seemed to be coming from the head itself. He placed the head on one side and then with both hands attempted to open the jaw. Rigor mortis had set in, so it wasn't easy. He grunted, pulled again and the jaw cracked open an inch or two. The ticking sound immediately grew louder.

*

Diane was standing in her customary position by the open window, smoking. She gestured to Jack to come in as he appeared in her doorway.

'You want one?' she asked, blowing out a smooth curl of smoke.

Delaney shook his head. 'I'm cutting down.'

'Of course you are.' She gestured at her desk. 'Forensics are back on that bullet you found.'

'Cartridge, Diane.'

'Whatever.'

Delaney picked up the file. 'What's it tell us?'

'Not a lot. No fingerprints, no DNA. Standard military issue. Pretty much as you said. A tiny bit of plastic in one of the grooves.'

Delaney took the photos of the cartridge and flicked through them, looking at a magnified close-up of one of the grooves on the cartridge. A small transparent piece of plastic snagged on a minute nick in the brass casing. He flicked to the next photo: an even more magnified close-up of the piece of plastic. It was slightly transparent with a small circular crescent on the right-hand side of it. He flicked to the next photo: an even tighter shot of the crescent shape – it was uniform, regular, obviously not made by the tear. He flicked through the paperwork: a lot of words but adding nothing to what Diane had already summarised.

'Not telling us a great deal, then?'

'Not yet.'

'This piece of plastic? Is it significant?'

'For fuck's sake, I don't know, Jack,' said Diane, tossing the stub of her cigarette out of the window. 'We're pissing in the wind here. And your girlfriend on Sky News isn't making life any easier. We're getting a thousand calls an hour, calling in with so-called information on everything from Satanic cults in Pinner being responsible to terrorist cells operating out of a pizza-delivery service in Stanmore.'

'Don't call her my girlfriend – it's not funny, boss.'

'Is any of this funny? We've got an attempted murder of a serial child killer and rapist, a boy abducted from the same street he took those children from all those years ago, and now we have the head of a bodiless nun placed on a church altar a scant hundred yards from where the boy was taken. What the hell's it all about, Jack?'

'She's not a nun, she's a church cleaner.'

'She was as bald as a billiard ball, so she's either a nun or the nutter cut off her hair before cutting off her head. Any way you slice this cake, Jack, it's not looking too tasty.'

'Some killers do take trophies, you know that, Diane.'

'Yes, of course I know that.'

'Especially if there is a sexual element.'

'A sexually abused nun. Who in hell are we dealing with here?'

'Lots of women shave their heads for all sorts of reasons.'

'Yeah, maybe. But their heads don't turn up on the altars of Catholic churches, do they?'

'No, they don't.'

Delaney looked across as Sally Cartwright came into the room, her expression serious. 'Sally, what's going on?' he asked.

'You are not going to believe this, sir,' she said, her face as white as a snowdrift.

*

The Waterhill estate was a mile away from the Whitefriars Hall of West London University, but it might as well have been on a different planet. An ugly conglomeration of high-rise buildings centred amidst a sprawl of roads and tarmac car parks. A place where the elderly didn't go out after dark and the sight of a burnt-out car was as commonplace as the sight of a Chelsea tractor in Fulham. It was an equal-

210

opportunity estate, though: you were just as likely to be sold drugs, raped, mugged or murdered by a black gang as by a white. There were clear areas of demarcation and, on the drive in, Bennett had flagged several young kids strategically placed to send the signal that the filth had come to visit. Eight years old and they could already tell Old Bill just by the look of them. It was a ghetto, no other word for it, thought Bennett. Like many, many others in a city polluted by its own decay. Being born in a place like the Waterhill was like having your fate marked out for you by a vengeful god, punished for the sins of your forebears. Only it wasn't God who brought misery and degradation to them and Bennett knew only too well who was responsible.

He looked at the face before him and knew all he had to know about hate, fear, frustrated rage, and the wickedness that lives in some people like breath . . . like bacteria.

Adam Henson was in his fifties, five foot six tall and as round as he was high, his body mass effectively blocking the doorway to his flat on the ground floor of Carnegie House, one of the six high-rise buildings that formed the nucleus of the estate. He was wearing shiny black slacks, a white shirt, a severe crew-cut and an expression on his face that would curdle milk. Bennett judged by the smell of him that he probably hadn't washed for several days.

The man crossed his arms and deepened the frown that was creasing his forehead in fat folds of skin. 'I've told you, he's not in.'

'You won't mind us coming in and checking, then,' said DI Bennett, keeping his voice smooth and affable.

'Yeah, I do mind,' said the overweight man, the florid flush rising from his thick neck to his white face like a heart-attack warning, like the spread of red jam on rice pudding. 'You ain't got a warrant, you ain't coming in. Especially him.' He flicked his head dismissively towards PC Danny Vine.

'Why? Because I'm black?' asked the constable, an edge in his voice.

'An Englishman's home is his castle – ain't that a fact, detective?'

Bennett stuck a hard finger against the shorter man's chest and pushed him back into his flat, following him in. 'Not on the Waterhill estate it isn't,' he said.

'You got no right.'

'I got every right. Your son is at liberty on parole, he breaks the conditions of that parole and that makes him a wanted felon. So shut it and get out of our way.'

'He hasn't broken any conditions. He does his community service and shows up every week to his parole officer.'

'He's done something a little more serious than skipping a litter-picking trip,' said Danny Vine.

'Like what?'

'Like sticking four inches of steel into a young student's chest. That's something we rather frown on,' snapped Bennett.

Henson shook his head. 'Oh, I get it. Another fix-up, is it? Not enough you put one of my sons down, you're going to pin something on the other. Never mind he's innocent.'

'Where was he Friday night about midnight?'

'He was here with me.'

'You sure about that?'

'Absolutely positive. I just said it, didn't I?'

Bennett pulled out the photo and shoved it under the man's nose. 'So how come he happens to be on CCTV footage from Camden High Street at the exact same time?'

Adam Henson flapped the paper away.

'That's not my son.'

'What, a doppelgänger, is it?'

'You what?'

'Someone else walking around who looks just like him and also happens to have B-minus tattooed on the back of his neck?' Bennett held the photo up again.

'Let me guess, this geezer who was stabbed, he wasn't white, was he?' Henson threw Danny a withering look.

'He was an Iranian citizen,' said Danny evenly.

'Right.'

'With dual nationality. He was born here.'

'And now he's died here.'

'Not yet,' said Bennett pushing the man aside.

It was a three-bedroom flat with a kitchen and bathroom. The first room on the left was a lounge: a three-piece suite that had seen better days, a coffee table strewn with copies of the *Sun*, a marked-up copy of the *Racing Post*, assorted lager cans, against the opposite wall a three-bar electric fire, all bars blazing, and beside it on a chrome stand a forty-two-inch state-of-the-art plasma-screen television. The sound off and the new *Countdown* assistant pertly placing vowels and consonants on the board.

Henson nodded at the picture. 'You got to keep your brain ticking, don't you?'

'Right. And you on benefits as well, Mister Henson,' said PC Vine pointedly.

'It was a gift.'

'Sure it was.' Bennett opened the door and passed on to the next room, slightly larger and with two single beds in it. It was neatly arranged, no clothes strewn on the floor. No Matt Henson, either. The bathroom and smaller bedroom also proved to be empty, the smell in the second bedroom pretty much making it clear to Bennett that it was used by Henson senior. He backed out of the room and gestured to Danny Vine. 'Check under the beds.'

The kitchen ahead was empty and windowless and Bennett turned the handle on the door of the last remaining room on the left. It was locked.

'You can't go in there. You've got no right.'

'It's okay,' said Bennett, smiling affably. 'I brought a skeleton key.'

He raised his foot and kicked the door at the level of the lock. There was a loud crack and the door flew open. 'Fits all locks,' he said and headed into the darkened room.

'You're going to pay for that.'

'Don't bet on it.'

Adam Henson looked back at Danny Vine as he came out of Henson's bedroom. 'Just keep your hands off his stuff,' he said to the young constable, clearly conflicted about which way to go. Finally he followed Bennett into the darkened room. 'It's not illegal,' he muttered as the detective inspector flicked on the light switch.

Black drapes hung over the front window. The walls were painted black and there was a red carpet underfoot. On the wall opposite DI Bennett was a flag: a red rectangle with a white circle in the middle of it and in the centre of the circle a black swastika. On the adjoining wall were pictures of Hitler and other high-ranking members of the Nazi party. Bennett shook his head at the clichéd stupidity of it all and then stopped and laughed out loud, despite himself. Among the black-and-white photos of Hitler and his generals was also a signed and framed picture of a well-known and glamorous personality.

Bennett looked at the photo more closely, slightly puzzled.

'That's Mariella Frostrup,' said Henson proudly. 'I reckon we're related.'

Bennett looked at the squat, bloated man, thinking that they were probably related in the same way that a toad is related to a human being. Actually, the more he thought about it, Henson had more in common with a toad than he did with a human being.

'And how do you reckon that?' he asked.

'Henson is a Scandinavian name, isn't it?' Henson said.

Bennett shook his head, bemused. 'Yeah – must be true, then.'

There were a number of display cases in the room and the detective inspector crossed the red carpet to look at them. Some with paperwork, others with more photos, one had a hat with a card reading *Early 1932 Schutzstaffel/SS Cap with Death's Head and Eagle*. In the long display case under the flag was a long dress sword, sitting slightly out of its groove, a pair of brass knuckledusters and a knife-shaped depression in the red velvet lining of the case. Danny Vine came into the room. Bennett threw him a questioning look but he shook his head. 'Jesus Christ!' he said, as he looked around the room. 'Not only does the fat frig look like Goebbels, he thinks he bloody *is* him.'

'Your day will come, Sambo,' said Henson, not even attempting to hide the curl to his lip as he said it.

'Sambo?' replied the constable, flashing a wide grin. 'How delightfully retro.'

'You can put a monkey in a suit and train it to dance for a banana. Doesn't make him a human. Just a monkey in a suit—'

'Shut your fucking mouth, Henson!' said Bennett, cutting him short. 'Where's the knife that's missing from this cabinet?'

Henson shrugged, his jowls wobbling but with a definite sheen of sweat on them now.

'I bought the case as a piece. There never was a knife in it.'

'And where's your son? Where's Matt?'

The portly man shrugged again. 'He's free to come and go as he pleases.'

'Not any more.'

'Right, well, do you two want to fuck off now?' Henson looked at his watch. 'I've got an appointment with a pint of lager, if that's all the same to you.'

Bennett shook his head. 'Well, it's not all the same to me. You're coming down the nick. We can discuss things a bit more down there.'

'On what charge?'

Bennett tapped the back of a knuckle on the glass of the display case.

'You have some illegal weapons here.'

'That's genuine memorabilia.'

'The sword, maybe,' Bennett said. 'But, and I quote, Section 141 of the Criminal Justice Act 1988 dealing with offensive weapons lists among other items, "a band of metal or other hard material worn on one or more fingers, and designed to cause injury".' He tapped the display case again. 'To wit, a knuckleduster.' He smiled humourlessly. 'You, my fat friend, are nicked!'

Henson looked at Bennett and across at PC Vine. Then he pushed Bennett, knocking him back against the display cabinet, and charged towards the open doorway. The young constable, however, had the presence of mind to leave a foot strategically placed and the sixteen stone of Adam Henson crashed like a felled log in the corridor beyond, his head slapping against the dividing wall with a sound like a walrus landing on ice.

*

Kate Walker held her index finger up and moved it from left to right. 'Just follow the finger.'

The large man held up a finger of his own and Kate, ignoring it, jotted down some notes. She turned to the uniformed officer standing in the doorway of the police surgeon's office. 'Fit to be interviewed.'

Henson shook his head, an ugly bruise clear on the right-hand side of his swollen head. 'I want a second opinion.'

'Okay, my second opinion is that you need to start

eating more healthily, do some exercise, lose four or five stone.'

'You think you're funny?'

'No, I think I'm bored looking at you. Take him away, constable.'

The uniform stepped into the room, followed by DI Bennett. Henson stood up and glared down at her. 'Nobody is getting away with this.' He looked back at the detective inspector. 'I have been assaulted.'

'The incident will be thoroughly investigated.'

Henson snorted dismissively. 'I have been the victim of a racially based assault and I will get justice.'

Kate smiled despite herself.

Henson stood up. 'You think that's funny? You think Enoch Powell's rivers-of-blood speech was science fiction? It was a prediction that has come true, and you know it. People turn on the television and see every day another knifing, another shooting, another gang-related murder. Black gangs. You tell me it's right for a white man to feel scared to walk the streets of his own town because of them. Scared for his life.'

'Your boys just redressing the balance, are they?'

'I told you. Matt had nothing to do with that stabbing.'

'You'll forgive us if we don't just take your word for that. Come on, Henson. There's some people want to talk to you.'

Bennett nodded to the uniformed officer who led Henson to the door. He stopped and called back to Kate. 'If I'm wrong . . . you tell me why there are over seven times more black people in prison, pro-portionately speaking, than there are white.'

'I can guess.'

'Don't guess, just look at the facts. That Irish scum Jack Delaney puts my eldest boy in prison for defending himself against a vicious attack from a gang of Paki terrorists.'

Kate kept her face impassive.

'My other boy goes in the frame for something he didn't do and everyone involved is going to suffer for it. Mark my words.'

Bennett laughed. 'What are you going to do, Henson? Sit on us?'

The uniform led Henson out of the office.

'Nice family,' said Kate.

'The apple doesn't seem to have fallen far from the tree, that's for sure.'

'You didn't tell me that Jack had arrested the Henson boys.'

'I didn't know. And it's not exactly relevant, is it?'

Kate shrugged. 'Any sign of Henson junior?'

'Not yet. We've got what our American cousins call an APB out on him.'

'He should be fairly easy to spot.'

'True – not many people go round with their GCSE woodwork grade tattooed on the back of their head.'

Kate noded. 'What I wanted to talk to you about.'

'Oh, yeah?'

'While you were off arresting Big Daddy I did a little bit of research on the internet.'

'Go on.'

'B-minus isn't just a grade, is it?'

'Isn't it?'

'No.'

'What else, then?'

'A blood type.'

Bennett nodded thoughtfully. 'True.'

'As a doctor, I should have thought of it before.'

'What's the point of that? Bit like having a tag saying you are a diabetic, that kind of thing?'

'Well, kind of.'

'You telling me that doctors take tattoos on the back of the head as a legitimate indicator of blood type, so that in emergencies they can just go ahead without testing and whack in a pint of B-minus as required?'

'Well, not any more.'

'Not any more? You're telling me they used to?' Bennett was genuinely taken aback.

Kate picked up some pages from her desk and handed them to him. 'I printed off some material from the internet.'

Bennett took the papers. 'Why don't you summarise?'

'You ever heard the word *Lebensborn*?'

'Nope.'

'It translates as "fount of life" in Old German. Set up by Heinrich Himmler originally in Germany, as part of their programme to create a master race. '

'Aryans?'

'Exactly. Tall, muscular, blue-eyed, fair-haired men and women.'

'Which is odd when you consider that Hitler was a short, dark-haired, brown-eyed man.'

'Anyway, it started off as a sort of orphanage set-up but when the war was in its full stride it took on a more sinister note.'

'Like?'

'They set up a *Lebensborn* operation in Norway because they wanted to mingle German blood with the pure Aryan bloodstock that they believed came from Scandinavia.'

'I heard something about that.'

'Some claim there were brothels – Norwegian women forced to breed with SS officers. There is a lot of controversy on the issue to this day. Anyway, remember that the Henson surname is an anglicised version of the Scandinavian name Hansen.'

'Yeah, Henson senior seemed to be quite proud of his heritage.'

'A lot of the children born in that era suffered dreadfully.'

'At Nazi hands, you mean?'

'No. After the war. From their own people. The women who consorted with the SS officers were vilified, their heads shaved, drummed out of town. There have been claims of the children born being used in child prostitution. The worthy and the good lining up in the street to abuse and rape them.'

'But no proof?'

Kate sighed. 'Many of the children were sent to lunatic asylums, where they were tortured or raped. They were officially called rats. Even today, as elderly adults, some still get spat at on the streets. Witnesses say that the Norwegian military experimented on them, making them take LSD and mescaline among other drugs.'

'Are you saying the Hensons are tied up in this somehow?'

'They're too young. Maybe Henson senior's father might have been one of the children sent overseas.

The Norwegian government tried to send eight thousand to Australia.'

'Really?'

'Oh yeah – last year a group of *Lebensborn* brought an action in the European Court of Human Rights, seeking compensation from the Norwegian government of up to two hundred thousand pounds apiece.'

'And did they get it?'

Kate snorted derisively. 'No. They were offered a two-thousand-pound token settlement. And do you know another thing . . . ?'

'Go on.'

'Priests in the country recommended that the Norwegian *Lebensborn* should be sterilised so that they couldn't father any future Nazi children.'

Bennett shook his head. 'Sounds like they were as bad as the Nazis themselves.'

'Exactly.'

'I still don't see what this has to do with Matt Henson, though. The family are neo-Nazi skinheads themselves.'

'Exactly! That's what the B-negative tattoo is all about. The Nazis thought that that was the purest blood group. SS officers had their blood group tattooed onto them. The B-negative tattoo was highly prized. Encouraged in the breeding programme with blonde-haired blue-eyed German and Norwegian women particularly.'

'I didn't know about the blood-group thing. I know they wanted to create a master race.'

'The thing is, they got it wrong again, apparently. Most Nordic people are type A. I remember coming across a book in the Bodleian that was banned by the Nazis. It was a study into Aryanism written by a German and it concluded that the British and Nordic peoples were more Aryan than the Germans, who had too many Slavic genes.'

'So the upshot is that Matt Henson is a neo-Nazi, maybe a descendant of the offspring of a German SS officer and a Norwegian woman.'

'Possibly.'

'And Jamil Azeez is an Iranian British national studying law.'

'With a father who is an international human-rights lawyer.'

'Correct. Who will be here any day demanding answers.'

'Exactly.'

Bennett collected the papers. 'Thanks for these. Not sure if any of it is relevant . . .'

'We never can be, can we, until we fit all the pieces together.'

Bennett looked at Kate thoughtfully. 'Jack Delaney must have you well trained.'

'I hope that's not some kind of prurient joke, Detective Inspector Bennett.'

'Not at all. In fact . . .' He grinned a little sheepishly and sat on the corner of her desk. 'Jack Delaney is the reason I joined the police force.'

'Really?' said Kate, a sceptical smile playing on her lips.

'Really!' Bennett held her gaze, his dark eyes suddenly very serious. 'I remember seeing that photo of him holding the child rescued from the boot of a car, the whole nation cheering him on as a modern-day hero, and thinking . . . yeah, that's what I want to do with my life.'

'You surprise me.'

'See, my heroes when I was growing up were Sir Lancelot and Galahad, rescuing damsels in distress, King Arthur, Robin Hood. Not much call for them nowadays.'

'I'm not at all sure of that.'

'Which is why I went for a squad car rather than a white charger. And your boyfriend was my inspiration. Seems that way to me, anyway.'

Kate looked into Bennett's eyes and couldn't read them – there certainly didn't seem to be any humour in them now. 'You're not joking, are you?' she asked.

'No,' he said. And then he blinked and shook his head. 'So are you up for a bit more detecting?'

'What you got in mind?'

'Another of your observations . . .'

'Go on.'

'Jamil's coat. Why don't we go and find it?'

*

Doctor Derek Bowman slowly turned the wheel on the device he had inserted between the dead woman's teeth. Rigor mortis had set in and hadn't subsided yet. As he turned the wheel the uppermost plate rose, forcing the jaw open. A few more turns and he had a one-inch gap between the teeth. He picked up his tweezers, inserted them carefully into the aperture, and a few moments later removed them. There was an object clamped between them. He put it on the desk and studied it, confused.

'Coffee to go, I am afraid, doctor,' said Lorraine as

she came into the office, her hat and coat still on.

'What?'

'There's been some developments.'

'Hang on a moment,' said the pathologist, picking up his digital camera and firing off some shots.

'What is it?'

Bowman put down his camera and looked over at her. 'It's a watch, Lorraine. A Mickey Mouse watch.'

*

Kate Walker walked out of The Australian, a pub on Camden High Street, fastening her scarf around her neck and buttoning up her coat. There was a definite chill in the air and it was getting colder by the minute. Across the road and further up ahead she saw DI Bennett going into The Star and Garter. She walked, heading in the same direction, towards The Pitcher and Piano, a few yards further on. Camden was turning into the new Islington, she thought, the number of bars and pubs in it. Maybe it always had been, she realised – she didn't really know the area, it had never been her stomping ground. Maybe Islington was the new Camden.

She opened the door of the pub and threaded her way through the crowds of people fortifying themselves with a warming glass or two before heading home for Sunday lunch. The accents in the air were as polished as the new pine floor and the bar glittered with chrome and glass. The young staff in black trousers and crisp white shirts served the customers with smiles that dazzled. Jack Delaney would bloody hate it, she thought.

Five minutes later a twenty-eight-year-old would-be Lothario called Jeremy, his black hair in a pony-tail, informed her that he'd been the duty manager on Friday night and could confirm that no one had left a jacket. He was also fairly sure that the man in the photo had not come into the pub that night. He did offer her his phone number but Kate declined. She didn't smile.

*

Outside, Kate was standing for a moment to do up her belt when a young, slightly built woman charged past her, nearly knocking her over. She instinctively put a hand to her stomach and was catching her breath when an older woman with dark hair, Middle Eastern features and a furious look in her brown eyes raced past her as well and caught up with the first woman, slamming her against a wall. She was shouting something at the girl in a language that Kate didn't recognise and had her hand around her throat.

Kate ran up to them, grabbed the older woman's arms and pulled her away. The woman hissed through her teeth at Kate and threw a roundhouse punch at her. Kate let the punch come, lifting her head back as the fist passed. Swinging the woman around, Kate planted her shoe in her backside and kicked, sending her sprawling and shrieking to the pavement.

'Hey!' Bennett shouted from across the street and tried to cross. But the traffic at that moment was too busy. The dark-haired woman picked herself up and ran up the street away from them. Kate turned to the younger woman but she had flipped her hoodie over her head and was running fast in the opposite direction.

'Oi!' Kate called after her but she was already disappearing, weaving amongst the tourists and locals who turned Camden busy whatever the weather was like.

Bennett jogged up to Kate, ignoring a loud horn being hooted for his benefit. 'What was that all about?' he asked.

'You got me.' She frowned and looked back to where the girl had gone, out of sight now.

'Something?' Bennett asked her.

Kate frowned slightly and then shook her head. Whatever it was she'd remember it sooner or later. She looked down at the pavement, where a purse had been dropped. She picked it up and opened it. Inside, together with some condoms, were a couple of credit cards and a small plastic bag with some white powder in it. She held up the purse to Bennett and he lifted out the smaller bag inside, holding it at one corner between gloved fingers.

'Something to do with this, maybe?'

'Could be.'

'I'll process it back at the factory. And well done, by the way.'

'What for?'

'For the way you tackled that woman. Jonah Lumu has got nothing on you.'

'Just don't mention it to Jack.'

Bennett flicked her a mock salute.

Across the road, and unobserved by either of them, a grey-haired man in a leather bomber jacket, sitting in the back of a Lexus with dark-tinted windows held up an iPhone and pointed it at Kate and Bennett.

He wasn't making a call.

Overhead, a low rumbling roll of thunder sounded in the distance, and the rain that had been threatening to pour out of the swollen sky at any minute began to fall in earnest.

*

Delaney got out of the passenger side of Sally's car, zipped up his leather jacket and put a police baseball cap on his head before throwing another one across to his sergeant.

'Where did you get these, sir?'

'I nicked them. Don't tell Napier, he'd probably fire me for it.'

Sally chuckled as they walked away from the parked car towards the footpath some fifty or so yards ahead. A couple of police cars were blocking the entrance to the allotment, their blue lights flashing. A pair of soaked-looking uniforms were guarding the entrance.

'I don't think so, sir,' said Sally. 'Not with all this going on. I think he can smell promotion and you'll be at the heart of it.'

Delaney shook his head angrily. 'I'm not at the heart of anything, Sally. Trust me, whatever is going on here is nothing to do with me. I didn't even find that girl all those years ago – a bleeding traffic warden did!'

'Yeah, but it was your picture in the papers, sir.'

'Don't remind me, constable.'

'And you are going to find the missing boy. I know you are.'

'Right.'

'You promised Gloria you would.'

Delaney nodded at the two uniforms as they started along the footpath leading down to the bridge but he didn't reply to Sally Cartwright. Across the track a wall of trees shielded the view of the allotment but bright lights were shining through and Delaney could make out the white-suited shapes of scene-of-crime officers as they went about processing the site.

At the other end of the bridge they clattered down the iron stairs and turned left where the allotments started. The ground underfoot was wet and slippery now, the heavy rain turning the once hard-packed earth boglike. They walked a few yards further on to where SOCO were erecting, as quickly as they could, a protective marquee around a large green-coloured tent that had already been set up in the middle of Graham Harper's allotment.

DI Duncton ducked out of the tent as Delaney and Sally approached, his tall sergeant appearing behind him. Duncton's face had the pale cast of a man who had seen things he'd rather not have looked at, and his breathing was a little ragged.

'You still reckon it's not devil worshippers?' he asked Delaney as the Irishman crouched down and looked in the tent himself.

The naked body of a woman had been spread out in cruciform fashion. Large nails had been hammered through her hands and feet to fix her to the ground. She was on her back. Her breasts were flaccid, her pubic hair grey – and she was missing her head.

'Maureen Gallagher,' said Delaney as he stood up again outside the tent.

'We certainly hope so,' replied Sergeant Emma

Halliday, smiling grimly. 'Otherwise we have a head with a missing body somewhere and a body with a missing head somewhere else.'

'Who put the tent up?' asked Sally.

Duncton moved aside as the SOCO photographer and videographer turned on some bright lights and moved in to record the scene. 'It was already here. We assume it was the killer. That's why the body wasn't discovered until now. The old man found her.' Duncton nodded across to Graham Harper, who was standing on the stoop of his shed with a blanket around his shoulders, watching horrified as his one-time haven of solitude was overrun with men in uniforms and white plastic jumpsuits yet again.

*

Kate smiled and looked up at the clock. It was three o'clock in the afternoon now and already it was very dark outside. The black rain clouds overhead didn't show any sign of letting up, neither did the rain which was hammering loudly against the large plate-glass windows of the pub as though they were in a tropical monsoon somewhere far more exotic than Camden Town. 'You're absolutely sure it's him?' she said to the handsome bar manager who was looking at the photo of Jamil that Kate had just given him.

'Absolutely positive,' he replied. 'Hang on, I'll get his jacket for you.' His accent was central-casting Australian and Kate couldn't help wondering how many of them were working in London pubs. He was cute, though, Kate admitted to herself, in his thirties with a surfer-boy physique, blond hair and a perfect tan. He reminded her of the young Robert Redford. If he had offered her his number she might well have had to think about it.

She smiled to herself again and held a hand to her stomach. No, she wouldn't. She'd take the rough Irishman and his gruff ways over a pretty-boy charmer any day.

She pulled out her mobile and a scrap of paper with some numbers on it and tapped them into her phone. 'Tony, it's Kate. We've got a hit. I'm in The Outback pub. Okay, see you in a bit.'

By the time DI Bennett made it across the road, the bar manager had given Kate Jamil's coat. A dark woollen pea-jacket, good-quality wool at that. She rummaged through the pockets and took out a wallet as the detective headed up to the bar. She opened it.

'What have we got?

Kate handed it to him. Bennett opened it and took out a couple of credit cards with Jamil's name on them. He opened the back section and removed a condom, five twenty-pound notes and a handwritten note. The letters were block capitals.

'What does it say?' asked Kate.

'It says "Ten-thirty at The Outback".'

'That's all?'

'That's all. Ten-thirty at The Outback.'

'Which is here.'

'Which is indeed here.'

Kate turned to the bar manager. 'What's your name again?'

'It's Michael.'

'Did you see Jamil Azeez with anybody that evening?'

'Sorry, no. It was rammed here on Friday night. Always is.'

'But you recognise him?' asked Bennett.

'Oh yeah, like I told your colleague here. I served him but he was on his own at the bar.'

'Can you remember what you served him?'

'A Coke and a pint of lager.'

'You seemed to remember that pretty quickly.'

'He came up three or four times, always the same order.'

'Anyone else order that?'

'Not that I recall.' Michael shrugged. 'But like I say, mate, it's pretty rammed on a Friday.'

Bennett pointed to the CCTV camera mounted above the bar. 'You got footage from the night?'

'Yeah, but it only covers the till. We get a few jokers trying the short-change scam. Keeping the till on tape soon sorts them out.'

'Can we get the footage anyway?'

'No worries, I'll do you a copy.' Michael turned and called to a woman sitting at one of the tables by the window, drinking a cup coffee. 'Karin, do you reckon you could give Sean a hand behind the bar while I nip upstairs for five?'

The woman nodded.

Kate pointed at the note. 'It's not the same person's handwriting, is it?

'As in the book?' said Bennett.

'Yes.'

'Could be. These are block capitals. Hard to tell.'

'Maybe that's the idea.'

'Meaning?'

'Meaning that whoever arranged to meet him here

that Friday night didn't want anybody else knowing about it.'

'For personal or professional reasons.'

'Exactly.'

'So how does Matt Henson factor in?'

'He'd seen him in the college. A neo-Nazi made to sweep up leaves and pick up litter. While some foreigner gets to be a student in an English university. There's an awful lot of resentment there. We know Matt's violent. Friday night with a skinful of lager in him and he sees the same student and it all boils up for him. He lashes out. He has a knife in his hand. He stabs him.'

Bennett nodded thoughtfully. 'I can see that happening. So you don't think it was premeditated?'

Kate shook her head. 'You saw him on the CCTV footage. He was worked up.'

'Makes sense.'

A short while later the manager returned with a DVD which he handed to Kate. 'There you go. I burned you a copy of the night shift – nine o'clock through to one o'clock.'

Kate passed the disc over to Bennett and smiled at the barman. 'Thanks.'

'No worries. Come back and see us any time. First one's on the house.' He flashed his surfer's smile again.

'Cheers,' said Bennett as they walked to the door.

Outside he held open the passenger door of his car and smiled at Kate. 'I think you made a new conquest there.'

'Yeah, right,' said Kate. 'Maybe it was you he was interested in.'

'I'm spoken for,' said Bennett without a hint of a smile.

'Really?' said Kate, surprised. 'You said you weren't married.'

'Like I told you . . . to the job.'

Kate got into the car and pulled her seat belt across as Bennett climbed in. 'A telescopic truncheon might be very reassuring to carry down a dark alley but it's not very nice to snuggle up with at night,' she said.

Bennett smiled and opened his mouth to say something but Kate silenced him with a raised finger. 'Don't even think about it.'

'I was going to say I'm blue-beret-trained. I have access to far more interesting weapons.'

'Blue beret?'

'What you might think of as SO19. Specialist firearms command. More likely to wear combat helmets nowadays, mind.'

'I didn't know you'd been with SO19.'

Bennett turned and looked at her. His eyes were unreadable. 'There's a lot you don't know about me, Doctor Walker,' he said.

*

Delaney stood beside the window looking out at the rain and the cars crawling slowly along Western Avenue, heading into London. Their headlights and braking lights splashing some colour into the drab awfulness of the surrounding architecture and urban infrastructure. Paddington Green police station was the grown-up version of Delaney's nick, where the shiny-suited supercops and the serious crime units were based. The sort of station that if you had ambition you would want to be working at. Ambition for yourself, that was. Jack Delaney's only ambition was to solve crimes. To find the rapists and the arsonists and the murderers and the drug dealers and the paedophiles and the rest of the scum that were increasingly allowed to wreak their misery on the world – to find them and stop them. To turn the tide. He was no King Canute, mind, he didn't fool himself that what he did made a whole hell of a lot of difference. But just trying to do so mattered to him. And if what he did made the world even the slightest bit less toxic for his daughter then he was going to continue doing what he did. And that wouldn't happen pushing pens in some supervisory role – he'd leave that to the likes of his Chief Super, who was standing at the front of the packed briefing room, looking on enviously as the serious crimes unit updated the various task forces.

Delaney hadn't been paying attention to what they were saying. He knew most of it anyway but he started listening when Doctor Bowman was summoned forward to stand in front of a display of photographs.

Photographs of Maureen Gallagher's severed head, her cruciform corpse. Her lacerated back, her punctured hands and feet. The letters *H O R* carved into her forehead.

'Firstly, as we all suspected, I can confirm that the head and the body both belong to the same person. A woman we believe to be Maureen Gallagher, as identified by the parish priest at the church where her head was discovered. It's hard to place time of death as her body was partially frozen, that is to say it was chilled before her head was separated. There were puncture and burn marks to the chest consistent with a taser-style stun gun. The head was removed post-mortem and I would speculate that the cause of death was due to a massive heart attack caused by the tasering. I am waiting for lab results to confirm.'

Bowman walked to the next board and pointed at the scarring on the woman's back. 'Her back has been whipped. Some of the scarring is recent, some goes back a while. In her ear I found a small particle that appears to be from the carapace of a crustacean. Probably from a crab shell. And in her mouth the killer had placed a watch. A Mickey Mouse watch that would appear to match the description given of the watch that Samuel Ramirez was wearing on the day he went missing.'

Delaney looked at the montage of photos mounted on the various boards. Photos of the murdered woman, of Peter Garnier, of the murdered children. Someone had obviously helped Garnier. Had kept the watch as a trophy. As a grisly souvenir. But why start killing again now? Why kill the church cleaner and why place the watch in the mouth of her severed head? The killer was sending a message, that much was clear. But why now? And what was the message?

Delaney looked again at the various photos, trying to make sense of them. It was like spot the ball, he thought: maybe all the pieces were there if he could just link them somehow, follow the lines of their stares, see what they could see but what was obscure to him.

He looked at the photo of Maureen Gallagher's headless body on the cold ground of Graham Harper's allotment, and a thought came to him.

'Jesus Christ!' he said.

Delaney became aware that people were looking at him. His boss, her face impassive, and beside her the Chief Super goggling at him in disbelief.

'Something to add, detective inspector?' he barked angrily.

'We need to get back to the allotment and dig, sir.' Delaney pointed at the photograph of the headless Maureen Gallagher, her arms and legs outspread in cruciform pose.

'I think X marks the spot.'

*

Gloria looked down at her hands, which were entwined together and clasped in her lap. She shivered with the cold and put her hand behind her on the sofa to test the radiator. It was on but she didn't feel any warmer. She pulled her bath gown tight around herself and looked back at the television, humming a melody to herself in a low voice. The Sky News crew were back at the allotments in Harrow and the pretty blonde reporter was looking earnestly into the lens of the camera, pointing at her. She could see the woman's lips moving but she couldn't hear what she was saying as she had the sound turned off. A song was playing in her own head, but the melody kept dancing away like a butterfly, like a sea mist slipping through spread fingers, like a dream that didn't want to be caught however hard she tipped her head and tried to catch it.

The shot on the television turned to a series of pictures: Peter Garnier, the murdered children, the church where the head of a woman had been discovered, her own photo as a little girl held in the

237

arms of Jack Delaney. Gloria picked up the Sky+ remote control and froze the picture, staring at herself and the Irishman when he was much younger than he was today, in so many ways, handsome in his uniform, his smile fit to break a thousand hearts.

But Gloria wasn't smiling and her eyes were unblinking at she stared at the television screen. The music in her head was swelling ever louder, like surf at high tide in the depths of winter.

*

Sally Cartwright and Jack Delaney were at the back of the large police marquee that had been erected to cover the whole of the allotment where Maureen Gallagher's mutilated body had been discovered. Several floodlights had been mounted on poles, filling the space inside with a cold bright light. A small trench had been dug in the centre of the allotment and two suitably suited scene-of-crime officers were excavating the ground. They gestured for the photographer and videographer to come forward as they scraped the last few lumps of mud off a green tarpaulin that had been exposed in the base of the shallow trench. With the photographers in position one of the SOCO, took the corner of the tarpaulin and pulled it back.

The first thing Delaney noticed was the feet. One was wearing a sock only and the other had on a small black and white trainer, a match to the one discovered earlier in the scrubland at the end of the allotments, which was now sitting in an evidence bag at the police station at Paddington Green. Delaney barely noticed the high-pitched scream of a woman as the tarpaulin was pulled fully open, or the slump as she fainted into the strong arms of her husband, who was standing beside her, his eyes filling with tears. Delaney was too focused, registering the jeans and the jumper with a picture of a large cartoon giraffe on the front of it. He didn't need to look to know that beneath it there would be a new Chelsea-strip shirt with the word SAMSUNG emblazoned across the front. He looked at the curly hair on the top of the boy's head, so brown that it was almost black, he looked at the closed eyes that would never sparkle with impish pleasure again. He looked at the smooth skin of the boy's face, obscenely pale, and he heard his own words in his head, the promises he had made to another abducted child. One he had been in time to save. He felt the muscles in his heart harden and the hands that were thrust deep into his jacket pockets become fists, the pain of his nails, digging into his own flesh, against the tears that threatened to start in his eyes.

Graham Harper ran past him, tears rolling down his face, as Delaney pulled his cigarette packet out and walked out of the marquee into a late afternoon that was already as dark as the black hole he felt forming in his soul.

*

Standing on the iron bridge above the railway track, Delaney put a cigarette in his mouth. Scratching a match alight he lit his cigarette and held the flame close. But he felt no heat from it. He looked out at the black expanse of the railway track as it headed west into the distance and shivered, remembering.

The snow was falling fast now, the fat frozen

flakes dancing in the air and floating into Jack's eyes, blinding him. He wiped his hand across them and struggled as fast as he could along the bank, the worn soles of his boots still sticking in the slippery mud as he ran along the side of the river. 'Hold on, Siobhan,' he screamed. 'I'm coming.' He could hear her words echoing in his ears as he scanned the swirling waters.

'Please, Jack. Please. It's so cold.'

He had said, 'It's okay, Shiv. I've got you now.'

But he had lied. He hadn't got her at all. And she had fallen into the icy embrace of the water and had been swept out into the river out of his reach.

'No,' cried Jack as he watched his sister's head bob below the surface of the water.

'No.'

He ran harder, calling out desperately to his sister. He caught a flash of her faded blue dress as it sank beneath the rough eddies of the water and then she was gone.

And Jack, throwing off his jacket, ran and dived into the river, not even registering the icy cold of it, his arms swept ahead of him and wrapped around his sister, and freeing one arm he splashed and paddled as powerfully as he could to the side. He pushed his sister up above him and clambered up after her onto the riverbank. He ran back to get his jacket and bundled Siobhan up in it and picking her up he cradled her to his chest and set off for home as fast as he could. Siobhan's teeth were chattering but she laughed as she looked up to him with bright twinkling eyes and said, 'I knew you'd save me, Jack. You always do.'

*

Delaney snapped out of his reverie. The cigarette had burned to the stub and he realised that Sally Cartwright was standing next to him.

'It's not him, sir,' she said.

'What?'

'The boy. It's not Archie Woods.'

Delaney frowned, trying to take it in, and picked on Sally's expression. 'What is it, constable? Who is he?'

'You're not going to believe it, sir . . .'

'Just tell me, Sally!'

'It's Samuel Ramirez.'

She was right. Delaney couldn't believe it.

Seventeen years after the two children had been abducted, one of the murdered children's bodies had finally been discovered.

'Doctor Bowman says the body has been deep-frozen, the skin slightly scalded post-mortem. Rectal damage, and bruising round the throat consistent with strangling.'

'Peter Garnier.'

'His MO, sir. Yes.'

'Someone has kept the body frozen all these years?'

'It looks that way, sir.'

'Who, for God's sake?'

'The same person who has taken Archie Woods. We need to find him, sir. We need to find him quickly.'

Delaney flared another match and lit a fresh cigarette. He thought of the sister that he had saved, living happily in America now, and who his own daughter had been named after; and he thought of the promise he had made to another girl, now a grown woman, whom he had rescued from Peter Garnier all those years ago. A promise he could still keep.

'Yeah,' he said, the reflection of the lit match dancing in his eyes. 'And we will.'

*

DI Tony Bennett yawned. He had been speed-skipping through the CCTV footage that the manager from The Outback pub on Camden High Street had given them earlier in the day. Jamil had come into shot a couple of times but he had always been alone and had seemingly ordered the same drinks both times. As the bar manager had pointed out, the coverage was sketchy at best. It was focused on the till and he had only recognised Jamil by the shirt he was wearing. Certainly no one came into shot looking like the racist skinhead he suspected of attacking the Iranian outside, up the street from the pub. He looked at his watch and yawned again as one of the detectives, he couldn't remember her name, left the office. Five o'clock in the evening and, save for him, the CID office was now deserted. He stood up, took his overcoat off the peg and slipped into it. Time to call it a night. He stood by the window for a moment, watching as a few uniforms coming off shift walked out of the car park and headed towards the pub. He considered joining them for a nanosecond before standing up, picking up a shoulder bag from the floor and heading across to Delaney's desk. Delaney's laptop was open but in sleep mode. Bennett tapped on the *Esc* key and the machine hummed into life. He looked around him and quickly pulled his outside hard drive from his shoulder bag and connected it to the laptop. A couple of quick key strokes and he moved round to stand in front of it. Footsteps approached and he pulled out his mobile phone, starting to speak into it as DC Sally Cartwright came in. He held up a finger to her.

'Hang on, Jack.' He lowered the phone slightly and covered the mouthpiece with his hand. 'Could you be a love, Sally, and get us a glass of water? I'm not being a sexist pig, honest. I'll owe you one. This call is important.'

Sally rolled her eyes a little and nodded at him. 'Too right you'll owe me one!'

She walked back out of the office. Bennett looked down at the computer screen. 'Come on,' he muttered under his breath, looking at the file transfer indicator as it crept forward slowly. In a few seconds more it was done. He had the hard drive back in his bag and had closed down Delaney's laptop just as Sally walked in with the water.

He snatched up a pen and wrote a telephone number on a piece of paper. 'Okay. Thanks for that, catch you later.' He clicked off his phone and smiled at Sally as he took the cup of water from her. 'Dying of thirst here.'

'Talking of which, a few of us are going across to The Pig and Whistle, It's been a hell of a day here.'

'I heard.'

'So if you fancy joining us?'

'I would, but I have a bit of a lead on a case I need to follow up.'

'Was that Detective Delaney on the phone?'

'What?'

'Your call just then. I heard you say Jack.'

Bennett covered, taking a sip of water. 'No. Someone from back home.'

Sally nodded. 'Well, if you change your mind. We'll be down there for a little while.'

'Appreciate it.'

Sally shrugged into her coat. 'Can't see there being a lot of time off just now.'

'The media certainly aren't going to let it lie.'

'No.'

'And there's no leads to where the boy is?'

'Whoever has taken him has been leaving us some clues, obviously. Taunting us. We just have no idea what they mean.'

'And Inspector Delaney?'

'Yeah?'

'He on top of things?'

Sally finished buttoning up her coat and threw Bennett a suspicious look. 'Why wouldn't he be?'

Bennett shrugged and flashed her a guileless smile. 'It's just that it can't be easy with him tied up in it all somehow. What with finding that small girl that Garnier had abducted all those years ago. What was her name again . . . ?'

'I don't know, inspector. Way before my time.' Sally sketched a wave as she headed to the door. 'I'll see you tomorrow.'

'See you.'

Bennett's smile vanished as she left the room. He picked up the cup of water, drained it and lobbed the empty beaker into Delaney's bin.

'Oh, we'll see all right,' he said and smiled again. 'We'll definitely see.'

*

244

Dave 'Slimline' Matthews looked up from the cross-word he was doing as DI Bennett walked towards the exit. 'Hold up, inspector. I didn't know you were in the building,' he called out.

Bennett turned back, puzzled. 'What is it, sergeant?'

'I just tried calling you.'

Bennett held up his mobile phone. 'Sorry, the battery's dead.'

'It's your collar today . . .'

'What about him?'

'We had to bounce him. No charges.'

'Go on.'

'Turns out the weapons are all genuine Nazi memorabilia, including the knuckledusters. Antiques. So he's allowed to have them, sell them, whatever.' Matthews shook his head, bemused. 'At least, in this country he is. Germany, France – we'd have him bang to rights.'

'What about the son, Matt Henson?'

'He's just been brought in.'

'Really?'

'Caused a bit of trouble at The Outback pub earlier, tried to make a run for it and the manager made what we might like to call a citizen's arrest.'

'Meaning?

'Meaning he jumped him and held him down until some uniforms could get there.'

'Very civic-minded. Where is he now?'

'We've got him in holding.'

'Fit to be interviewed?'

'Yeah, bruised ego. Nothing much else.'

'Good.'

'How's the victim?'

Bennett nodded. 'Spoke to the hospital a short while back. He's stable, conscious. Still doesn't remember a thing about who attacked him, apparently.'

The sergeant looked thoughtful. 'Genuine amnesia, you think?'

'What else?'

The sergeant shrugged. 'I'm just plod, you're the man in a natty suit. But maybe he's scared.'

'Scared of what?'

'That if he says anything, Henson will come back and finish the job. Him or another one of his neo-Nazi thug associates.'

'It's a possibility.'

'Wouldn't be the first racially motivated murder in this fair city of ours, would it?'

'Not by a long chalk. Why don't you rustle up a uniform for the interview and settle him down in interview room one, if it's available?'

'It certainly is.'

'Thanks, Dave.'

*

Delaney flicked through the CDs lined up in an old three-tiered pine shelf that stood above a mahogany bookcase in his lounge. The bookcase was half empty. It held some cookbooks – the ubiquitous *Delia Smith's Summer Cookbook*, Nigella Lawson's *Feast* – and the rest was mainly fiction, some crime, some classics. He picked up the best of Dolly Parton and put it back again, finally selecting Górecki's Symphony Number Three Opus 36 also known as the *Symphony of Sorrowful Songs*. He walked over to his CD player and slipped the disc in, using the button to skip to the second movement. Some songs were too sorrowful. They seemed somehow relevant, though, all dealing with motherhood and the separation from a child through war. As the hauntingly beautiful second movement started Delaney poured a couple of fingers of whiskey into a tumbler and added a couple of ice cubes from a crystal bucket with a silver-plated lid and matching tongs that Kate had bought him. He took a sip and let the warmth of the spirit work its way through his body. He felt some of the tension of the day lift as the soprano hit impossibly pure notes. Motherhood and loss. The separation from a child – he couldn't help thinking of Archie Hall and his devastated mother. He couldn't help thinking of the promise he had made to Gloria. That he would find the boy and save him. But he couldn't see any sense in what was happening. There was a pattern forming. There always was. But Delaney couldn't see it. Everything seemed so random. So disparate. Peter Garnier, the only man who might know what was going on, certainly wasn't saying anything. Apart from the killer, of course: *he* knew what he was doing.

*

Bennett was sitting opposite Matt Henson with a uniformed female officer beside him and the recording device already running. Bennett had noted who was present and announced that he was commencing an interview with Matt Henson.

The man in question had his arms crossed and a neutral expression on his face. This wasn't the first police station interview room he had ever been in. Not by a long chalk.

'I'll ask you again. Where were you last Friday night just before midnight?'

The young man grinned arrogantly. 'And I'll answer you again: no comment.'

Bennett slid a photograph of Jamil Azeez across the table. 'Do you know this man?'

Henson hardly flicked his eyes downward and kept his arms crossed.

'Never seen him before in my life.'

'Really?

'What I said.'

Bennett slid the still photo from the CCTV footage of Henson arguing with Jamil Azeez on Camden High Street across to him.

'How come you're seen here getting in his face on Friday night, then?'

Henson didn't even look at the photo. 'It's not me.'

Bennett nodded. 'You have been doing some community work, I'm led to believe?'

Henson glared back at him. 'So?'

'So you've been doing it at the university where the young man here is a student. Just a coincidence, is it?'

'Must be.'

'And someone else who looks just like you also has a tattoo with the B-negative blood-group sign tattooed on the back of his head as well, I suppose?'

Henson shrugged.

Bennett opened the file next to him and made a show of flicking through some papers. 'Only I see from your records that B-negative isn't your blood group, is it?'

Henson shrugged again.

'When did you get the tattoo done?'

248

'It was a birthday present from my dad.'

'Nice.'

Henson didn't reply.

'You sure you don't want a lawyer here?'

'You charging me with anything?'

'Not yet.'

'Don't need a lawyer, then, do I?'

Bennett smiled patiently. 'Do you know what the significance of the tattoo on the back of your head is?'

Henson shrugged again.

'The SS used to have them. B-negative was thought to be the best blood group for the Aryan super-race. Only they got it wrong. The Saxons, the Nordics, type A – that's the Holy Grail when it comes to blood types. Himmler got that wrong, apparently. Type A – just like you, Matt.'

'What the fuck are you talking about?'

'Your dad reckons you have Scandinavian heritage.'

Henson shook his head, puzzled. 'Are you going to make a point here or what?'

'The little armoury in the shrine to Hitler you've got back in your house.'

'What about it?'

'That sword looks like it could do a bit of damage. Oh, I know it's a dress sword, but it works, doesn't it?'

'I have no idea.'

'And there's a little depression where a knife used to sit. Isn't there? Where's the knife, Matt?'

'I have no idea. Dad bought that case off another collector. That's how it was when he bought it and it has nothing to do with me.'

'He was just a filthy immigrant, wasn't he, Matt – no loss to anyone?'

Henson shrugged again. Folding his arms tighter and leaning back in his chair.

'I mean, he comes over here, ponces around the university. Maybe shagging the Dean while he's at it. While you get to clear up leaves and pick up litter after him. Is that what it was, Matt? Did you see him with the Dean? Did you get jealous? I mean, she's got a soft spot for you, hasn't she?'

Matt uncrossed his arms and put his hands flat on the table. He was angry now.

'You don't know what the fuck you're talking about!'

'That's it, isn't it? The filthy Paki immigrant comes over here and cops onto a woman you've got your eye on, the filthy bastard. Is that what you called him?'

Henson smiled contemptuously. 'I thought you said he was an Iranian.'

'I didn't say that at all, did I, constable?' Bennett turned with a small smile himself to the uniform, who shook her head.

'Yeah, well, Jamil is an Arab name, smartarse, I know that much.'

Bennett leaned in. 'I didn't tell you his name, either.'

Henson's surly smile disappeared. He sat back and folded his arms again. 'I want a lawyer, he said.

*

Stella Trent sat at the small table in the corner of her lounge. She ran slender fingers through her gloriously copper-coloured hair and smiled. It wasn't so long ago that her hair had been lank, her skin pale, not the porcelain-cream it was today but sallow, waxy. Her green eyes had been lifeless, those same eyes that now sparkled with mischief and delight. It had been three months since she had taken the cocaine that had wasted her life. Three months since she had been released. Since she had been rescued.

She picked up a gloss lipstick and touched up her lips. They were the colour of coral. If she had been a member of the Pre-Raphaelite brotherhood she would have painted herself, she thought, and then made love.

A lot of people had made the mistake of thinking that Stella Trent was uneducated. That she had fallen into prostitution through circumstances beyond her control. But that was only partly true. She was convent-school-educated and had come to London thinking she could be a model: she was tall enough, had the long, shapely legs that a catwalk demanded, had a beautiful face that screamed innocence and Ireland. Trouble was, there were a thousand girls every day coming to the city with the same dreams. And Stella's looks just weren't fashionable. She wasn't gooky or weird enough. But there were modelling jobs available if you didn't mind going topless. And there were drugs available if you wanted to party all night on the club scene, looking to be spotted. And pretty soon it was more than a sniff here and there, and pretty soon after that it wasn't just the bra that was being slipped off for the photographers. And pretty soon after *that* there wasn't even a camera.

Stella looked at herself and smiled again. She was

pretty much out of that life now and wouldn't be going back, and the good thing about it all was that she didn't feel guilty. She was Irish Catholic and didn't feel guilty – which in the circumstances, she thought, was a bit of a miracle. But she knew it was just sex, that was all. Consensual sex. And she had done it for money, that was all. No one had been hurt except herself – if she had chosen to let it hurt her. She had chosen not to. Maybe she was the exception to the Catholic rule. The man who was due to visit her at any minute certainly felt guilt. He was a walking poster-boy for it, an ex-altar boy who had sinned indeed. A choirboy who didn't make confession any more. At least, not to a priest.

'It's open,' she said, smiling wider and turning to watch the door open and Jack Delaney walk in. God help us, he's a good-looking man, she thought to herself. He had a bottle of wine in one hand and a small case in the other. She nodded at it and said, 'You're getting very serious about this, then, cowboy?'

'I am,' he replied.

She smiled again. 'And you brought wine?'

'Not for us.'

'Oh?'

'I needed an excuse to get out of the house. I'm cooking dinner.'

Stella's smile disappeared. 'Lucky Kate.'

'Don't start, Stella.'

And suddenly the smile was back and with it the mischief in her sparkling eyes. 'Well, at least I get you for half an hour or so. There'd be plenty of women in this grand metropolis who would envy me that delight.'

Delaney put the bottle of wine on the table and the case on the floor and looked at his watch.

'Let's get on with it, then,' he said.

And Stella laughed. 'Jack Delaney, last of the great romantics.'

*

Jennifer Hickling was standing behind the eighteen-year-old youth in the alleyway just off Camden High Street where a man had been stabbed just days before. She could feel the knife that had stabbed him, a reassuring weight in her left-hand jacket pocket. Her right hand was wrapped around a weapon of a different nature, pumping it hard up and down. The youth was making groaning sounds, asking her to be a bit more gentle, but that just made Jennifer grip and pump harder as she leaned in to whisper insults into the youth's hot ear. She knew from experience what made men excited. The boy had wanted full sex with her and she had refused. Telling him it was a hand job or a blow job and that was it. She was a virgin, she had said, and he had laughed.

But it was true. She *was* a virgin. Anal sex didn't count. She knew that. Especially when it wasn't her choice.

The thought made her yank even harder and she realised that the boy was crying out in pain now. He had spilled his seed moments before, staining the cobbled ground that was still marked with the young Iranian's blood.

Not many more to go now, Jennifer thought as the red-faced youth zipped himself up and hurried away, unable to look her in the face. Which suited her just fine. The next one who looked her in the face . . . she was going to use the knife!

*

Delaney felt the guilt. He should be out there looking for the missing boy, not spending time with Stella Trent and trying now to create a cosy picture of Sunday-evening domesticity. A chicken in the oven, wine chilling in the fridge, candles on the table.

The trouble was that he had nothing to go on. With most crimes there was a clear motive. You followed the money, or you followed the sexual jealousy. You looked in the family. But Archie Wood's family was in the clear. His mother was at a wedding, the father's story had been checked out with border control and the French police and it all held true: he hadn't even been in the country when the boy had been abducted. He picked up the bottle of whiskey and poured himself another slug. He took the glass with him to the window and looked out at the dark night. He felt the impotent rage building inside him as he pictured the boy alone out there somewhere, scared, cold, maybe hurt, maybe already dead. He took a swallow of his whiskey and tried to push the thought to the back of his mind. It was just the frustration of it all that he was finding hard to handle. He had made a promise that he should never have made, a rod for his own back that he couldn't stop flogging himself with. He just wanted to get out there and do something. Anything.

He just didn't know what.

He took a slower sip of whiskey as the last of the second movement of the Górecki symphony finished.

He would have turned the music off but Kate walked into the room just then, fresh from the shower and dressed in a fluffy white bathrobe, and her smile chased away his guilt momentarily.

'Are you going to pour me one of those?' she said.

'You drinking whiskey now, Kate?'

'A tiny sip is all. I'm pregnant, remember.'

Delaney poured a measure into a glass and as he reached for some ice Kate took the bottle from him and read the label, raising a questioning eyebrow. 'Armorik, Whisky Breton?'

Delaney shrugged. 'It's a single malt.'

'It's French!'

Delaney laughed and handed her the glass, clinking his own against hers as she took it from him. 'I'm Irish – we don't have to hate the French.'

Kate took a sip. The drink had surprisingly smoky notes but was mellow. She nodded approvingly. 'It's nice.' She gave him back the glass.

Delaney bent forward and kissed her on the lips. 'So are you.'

'Nice, you say?' She ran her hand lightly up his inner thigh. 'There's still time to get on the naughty list before Christmas.'

A timer sounded in the kitchen, its shrill bleeping somewhat ruining the moment.

'Not before dinner, though,' said Delaney, smiling and kissing her again.

'Maybe pudding, then.'

Delaney pulled Kate into a hug and kissed the top of her head. Her hair was still slightly damp and perfumed. 'When we have that baby we're never going to let it out of our sight.'

Kate looked up at him. '*We*'ll be having the baby, will *we*?'

'Well . . . I'll be having the large cigar and pacing up and down outside – that's the hard part, you know.'

Kate laughed. 'That a fact?'

'I mean it, though, Kate. That kid is going to be the best-loved child in the world.'

Kate looked up at him quizzically. 'What's brought all this on?'

'Nothing. I just think when he or she is born we should sell up and move to Ireland. To Cork.'

'You *are* joking?'

Jack shook his head. 'This city destroys people, Kate. It kills them.'

'You can't keep people safe for ever, Jack. Not even you.'

'We have to do what we can, though. And we can do that.'

Kate put out her hand and held it against his cheek. 'You and me. We're good enough for any of them.'

'You are, maybe.'

She patted his cheek. 'I'm going to get dressed.'

Jack took another pull on his drink as Kate headed up to his bedroom. He turned the music up louder.

*

Bennett turned the recording device off and watched as the uniformed officers led Matt Henson out of the interview room. The youth had clammed up, refusing to say another word until he had a lawyer present. Bennett had wished him a good night's sleep in the cell. They'd interview him again in the morning.

When the door closed Bennett took his mobile

phone out of his pocket and looked at the display. A message-alert signal was bleeping on the screen.

He clicked on the button and read the message as it appeared. He nodded, pleased with what he read, a ghost of a smile hovering on his lips.

'Showtime!' he said in a whisper.

*

Delaney crouched down spreading his mittened hands, and opened the oven door to bring out a tray with a free-range chicken sizzling in the middle of it. He took a large metal spoon and poured some of the fat back over the chicken to baste it, then added a slug of wine in the bottom of the tray and tossed in some previously part-roasted potatoes. He was just about to put the tray back in the oven when there was a gentle knocking on his kitchen door.

'Hello,' he called, a little puzzled. The door opened and Siobhan bustled through, running up to hug his legs. She was followed by Wendy, who was dressed in a long dark overcoat and wearing large sunglasses.

'Wendy, what's up?'

Wendy looked over at the table. It was covered with a linen tablecloth and set for two with lit candles, a single rose in a vase, crystal wine glasses and a bottle of Chablis chilling in a bucket.

'Sorry, Jack, this is obviously a bad time.'

Delaney could hear the catch in her voice. 'It's fine. Just doing Sunday dinner. Why don't you have a glass of wine with us?'

'No, it's not a good time. Come on, Siobhan, we have to go.'

She turned back to the door but Delaney quickly

stepped over to her and pushed the door shut. He turned Wendy around to face him and took off her glasses. There was a red slap mark on her cheek and one of her eyes was swollen. Both eyes were puffy and red with recent tears. Wendy looked away, embarrassed.

'This was Roger?' asked Delaney, his voice flat.

'We've been having some problems.'

Delaney nodded and turned back to the oven, putting the tray back in. 'Siobhan, tell Kate this will be ready in twenty minutes and to set one more place.'

'Okay, Daddy,' she said quietly, aware that something was up but not really understanding what.

Siobhan smiled, confused, and Delaney ruffled her hair.

'Jack—'

Wendy started to speak but Delaney interrupted her. 'No, it's all right, Wendy. I'm only going to talk to him.'

Kate walked into the kitchen. 'I thought I heard voices. Hello, Wendy, this is a nice surprise. Hey, Siobhan.'

'We'd better go,' said Wendy.

Delaney shook his head. 'Dinner will be ready in twenty minutes, Kate. Siobhan and Wendy are staying the night. I'll be back when I can.'

'What's going on?'

Delaney kissed her on the lips. 'Something I need to take care of. It won't take long.'

And he was gone.

Kate looked across at Wendy, who sighed and took off her sunglasses. Kate took in the situation for a moment and then she nodded.

'You'll be wanting a glass of wine.'

'Champagne for me,' said Siobhan and the two women smiled. But they were sad smiles. Kate crossed to Wendy and put her arms around her.

Wendy nodded gratefully and sniffed back tears. 'Maybe something stronger if you have it?'

*

Arnold Fraser huddled up tighter against the wall of the doorway where he was sheltering from the rain. In a previous life he had been huddled in dugouts under the fierce heat of a Kuwaiti sun, with shells exploding around him and Iraqi soldiers mere hundreds of feet away who would have liked nothing better than to see his head blown apart by a bullet from one of their snipers' rifles, and as he turned his head against a gust of rain he wasn't sure now which was the better place to be. He pulled his overcoat tight around himself and shivered, taking a sip from the last of his tins of strong lager. It would be a long, cold night if he couldn't get any more.

He heard the sound of footsteps approaching and without looking up saw a pair of Doc Marten boots come into view. Maybe this was the time, Arnold thought, maybe this was *his* time. He didn't die overseas serving queen and country, he'd made it through that, but maybe this was to be his end, this was what was written down for him. Kicked to death in a Camden back street and left to die in the rain by a skinhead thug who wouldn't know duty or service or loyalty if it was tattooed on his Neanderthal forehead. It wouldn't be the first time he'd got a kicking and at least it would be better than being set on fire like so many others had been. Arnold dashed the water from his eyes and looked up. It wasn't a skinhead at all but a young woman with black hair and black make-up and a lacy black skirt under a black leather jacket. Ballerina by the Brothers Grimm and Vivienne Westwood, he thought. Then he held his hand out.

'Spare some tin for a cup of tea?' Arnold Fraser said.

The young woman rustled in her pocket and pulled out some notes.

'I haven't got any change,' she said apologetically.

'That's all right, love,' the ex-soldier said. Then he coughed, his whole body shaking because he couldn't control the convulsion. He felt a note being pressed into his hand.

'Get yourself a six-pack.'

Arnold's coughing subsided and he looked up to say thank you. But Jennifer Hickling didn't hear him – she had already hurried away, her fingers curling comfortably again around the handle of the knife that she had stashed in her jacket pocket. She didn't notice that the man's hacking coughing had started up again and was fading away in the distance as she strode up the road. Jennifer Hickling had business to attend to.

*

Roger Yates sat on the bottom of the staircase in his hall. His head propped in his hands. Lost in dark thoughts.

He jumped as a pounding came on the door, his heart leaping in his chest like a speared salmon on a gaff. He looked up, his eyes wide. The pounding came again and, resigned, he stood up and crossed the hallway to open the door. His expression relaxed a little. 'Oh, it's you,' he said.

Delaney put one hand on Yates's chest and pushed him backwards into the hall, so hard that he almost fell over.

Delaney watched him stumble, picturing him sprawling to smash his head on the cold tiled marble floor. But Yates regained his balance, if not his composure. He was an attractive man, a successful businessman. Delaney knew that Yates was used to getting his way in a corporate world that was not famous for subtle niceties. But he also knew that Yates had no misunderstandings about the kind of violence that Delaney was capable of and that was why he was a little puzzled not to see more fear in the man's eyes. Delaney knew one thing for certain: all bullies were cowards. And the men who beat up women were the worst kind of cowards of all. Yates stood up, an arrogant cockiness to him once more as he walked back towards Delaney.

'I'm sure if we can just talk about this—'

But Delaney interrupted him again. This time by grabbing him round the throat with his left hand and propelling him backwards to smash him up against the wall at the foot of his stairs. A portrait of himself hung beside him, smiling and holding up a gold trophy. His smile was in stark contrast to the genuinely scared face he now presented to the world.

'I don't know what she has told you but—'

'Just shut it, Yates!' Delaney cut him short. He could feel the blood roaring in his veins now, felt the heat of it suffusing his whole body. It was like a drug, pure adrenalin pumping round his system so that the world around him dissolved to a single point of focus.

'I know you fucked her, Jack.'

'What?' Delaney was taken aback.

'Wendy. You fucked her and I knew about it.'

Delaney loosened his hand and Yates leaned back against the wall, his breathing ragged, his eyes wild. 'And that gives you the right to hit her, does it?'

'I slapped her once. It was an accident.'

'Accident, right!'

'You back on your white horse, Jack? Is that it? Riding to the rescue of the innocent maiden, carrying her back to your castle? Well, the thing of it is, cowboy' – he almost spat the word – 'you're not the only one who's been riding another man's mount.'

'What are you saying to me?'

'Your wife Sinead, Jack. She of the blessed, sainted memory.'

Delaney could feel his blood heating again, he could feel it behind his eyes, in his neck, it felt like a blaze consuming his own body and the roaring in his ears made it hard to hear what the man in front of him was saying. But he had heard enough. Roger Yates's mouth continued to move but Delaney had stopped listening – his fist had formed once more. Yates's eyes stared back at him, challenging, like a man who didn't care. And Delaney lashed out, oblivious to the pain in his hand, oblivious to the screaming from Yates. Oblivious to everything except the red mist that filled his head.

*

'And yet another bizarre twist has been revealed in the ongoing Death Row story in Harrow, West London, as the horrors continue to unfold. Police so far have been unable to trace the whereabouts of missing child Archie Woods, who was abducted yesterday morning from this very allotment below, which is two streets from Carlton Row.'

Melanie Jones was standing on the road bridge above the allotments. She stood aside so that her cameraman could cover the police activity below. Then the picture swung back to Melanie Jones.

'As we have reported earlier today the severed head of a bald woman was discovered on the altar of St Botolph's Church, again a stone's throw from this location, and this afternoon the grandfather of the missing boy made another gruesome discovery. The headless body of a woman – naked, cruciform and nailed to the ground. The police have still to make an official statement but unofficial sources confirm that they have little doubt the grizzly find is related to the gruesome discovery at the church round the corner. How this ties in with Peter Garnier, if indeed it does, they are at a loss to understand. A copycat abduction is the most likely scenario but the murder and mutilation of the woman's body doesn't fit into any pattern of Garnier's activities. That the two incidents are not related is a very real possibility and, again, inside sources have confirmed that the killing of the woman as part of a ritualistic murder involving Satanism or some kind of devil worship is being very seriously considered. It wouldn't be the first time that children have been used in gruesome rituals in this country.'

The picture on the television changed to old footage of police processing a crime scene on the banks of the Thames, but the reporter's voice went mute as Gloria Williams thumbed the button on the TV's remote control. She watched the TV for a moment or two longer, the reflected light dancing in her immobile eyes. The she blinked, stood up and turned to face away from the screen.

Her lounge was carpeted in a rich red and green pattern. It was cluttered with small tables and bookcases, green plants on every available surface that wasn't covered with magazines, books, sketch pads. Behind her was a long wall running from the left-hand side of the room where a window overlooked the West Hampstead Pizza Express. It was entirely covered with photos, newspaper cuttings – some yellow with age, some extremely recent – with a map blown up and marked with pins and string, and at the centre of it all a photo of a man in police uniform who was holding a small dark-haired girl in his arms. A girl with scared brown eyes.

Gloria put the fingertips of her right hand to the young girl's mouth and lights danced in her eyes once more.

Angry lights.

*

Tim Radnor had never been a strong man. Neither mentally, physically nor emotionally.

He was thirty-nine years old now, five foot eight tall, weighed just over ten stone and had thin mousey-coloured hair. He was single, with no partner, and had been in the same job for over fifteen years: kitchen assistant in a large public school. A simple enough job that required simple routines. He had never been ambitious and enjoyed the repetitiveness and security of his job. He was neither well liked nor disliked at his place of work – he minded his own business and people pretty much left to him to it. Once a month he would visit an ageing German prostitute called Olga in Shepherd Market. She had cracked skin like an old handbag and the face of an antique doll painted over her features. The crudely drawn lipstick and thick mascaraed lashes were almost a caricature in their clumsy representation of a sexuality long since faded. Miss Haversam as Miss Whiplash. But Tim liked her that way and had been visiting her for over twenty years. He would pay her one hundred pounds in cash for a specialised service that would leave him feeling demeaned but released from the inner demons that consumed him. Released at least for a while. At other times he used the internet to satisfy those desires that tormented him in his dreams and during every waking day. Desires that he kept under control but could not stop. He didn't act on them as others did. He never had. Except once. And even then he hadn't taken part.

He was not to blame.

He had never been to blame.

Tim was a victim. He knew that himself best of all. He knew that what was happening to him now was just as unfair as what had happened to him all those years ago. Just as unfair . . . and he was just as powerless to stop it happening now as he had been then.

As a child he had been one of the first children in the class to get measles, or mumps, or flu. Or whatever sickness was going. At nine years old on his first trip away from home at Scout camp he had not excelled at, nor taken great joy in, the kind of physical exertions that the other kids had revelled in. On the long rope slide, for example, he had fallen off two-thirds of the way down. It hadn't been a long fall but he had landed in muddy ground and twisted his ankle slightly. In truth, he'd exaggerated the nature of the injury, as he was wont to do, and limped his way tearfully to the others, their taunts and laughter in no way unusual for one of Tim's mishaps. He exaggerated his limp as an excuse not to have to go down the rope slide again and to provide a good reason not to go on the hill walk that was planned for later on that afternoon. If he had had his choice in the matter he would never have gone on the weekend in the first place. But his mother had insisted and pleas to his father, as ever, had fallen on deaf ears. In all things his mother had the final word and so Tim had gone to Scout camp like every nine-year-old boy should have been delighted to do. 'And stop your moaning,' his mother had said.

So he had stayed at the campsite while the other members of his troop had gone trekking in the woods and up the nearby hill.

A responsible adult had had to stay behind, of course, and keep an eye on him.

Except that the adult that stayed behind hadn't been responsible. Hadn't been responsible at all.

All these years later Tim still blamed him. And it wasn't just the humiliation and degradation he had felt. It had *hurt*. Hurt more than anything he had ever experienced before. And now it was almost as if he had been training for this moment all his adult life.

And had failed.

Tears pricked in his eyes as he felt the cold metal entering him; he felt his flesh tearing and gasped with the relentless thrust of the weapon. His face was suffused with blood now, his eyes wide with the pain of it, with the fear of what was to come. With the injustice of it all. His hands were tied to the bedstead in front of his kneeling form. His mouth sealed with duct tape so the scream that was boiling in his lungs was contained. The tears running down his cheeks now every bit as useless as they'd been all those years ago.

Tears at the injustice of it all. He had never taken part after all. He had just watched and taken photos.

There was a raspy metallic sound, a loud click, and Tim's heart hung in stasis. And then there was just a rainbow of colour for him. He didn't see, or feel, or hear, or make excuses any more.

His neck and lower jaw made a pattern on the wall above his bedstead like a Rorschach ink blot painted by Hieronymus Bosch.

And then there was silence.

*

Light slanting on the mirror, golds, greens, fractured white light dancing on the glasses, on the glass shelves, on the leaded-light window that looked through to the doorway leading into the bar. And sound surrounding him like a warm fog. Like a coat. Heat from the log fire burning under a copper hood. Irish voices raised in song, and it's no nay never, hands slapping on tables. Money spent on whiskey and beer. Delaney knew how that was. He'd been the wild rover, sure enough. It was all supposed to have changed. Maybe deep down you never can change, not at the heart of you. You had to want it, wasn't that what they said? He looked at the bruised knuckles on his right hand and rubbed some of the dried blood off with his left. He picked up his glass of whiskey, swirled it for a second or two, watching the liquid within tilting and spiralling, then held it to his lips and shot it down, holding the glass forward. The barman picked up the bottle of Bushmills behind the bar, about a third remaining, and splashed a large portion into the outstretched glass. No need to measure it – Delaney had already paid for the bottle. He took another sip, looked up into the mirror that ran the length of the bar behind the optics and sighed. It was like déjà vu. He turned to the two men who were approaching him.

'Let me guess,' he said. 'Another brass been rubbed and you need Jack of the Yard to come and make sense of it all for you?'

'Not quite,' said Sergeant Dave 'Slimline' Matthews. He turned to Jimmy Skinner expectantly.

Jimmy shook his head. 'I'm not going to do it.'

The sergeant nodded, understanding. He turned back to Delaney. 'Detective Inspector Jack Delaney, I am arresting you on suspicion of attempted murder. You do not have to say anything, but it may harm your defence if you do not mention, when questioned, something which you later rely on in court. Anything you do say may be given in evidence.'

Delaney nodded and turned back to the barman. 'Get us another couple of shot glasses here, Sean.' He winked at Jimmy Skinner. 'Might as well finish the bottle, eh, Jimmy? It's paid for.'

'You have to come in, Jack,' said the sergeant, with an apologetic shrug.

'You think I can't take you, Dave?' said Delaney, his voice slurring badly. 'Is that what you think?'

Slimline held his hands up. 'I'm sure you could, cowboy. But we don't want any trouble here.'

'Well, that's where you're wrong,' said Delaney as he stood unsteadily to his feet. 'That's where you're wrong, Slimmio me lad!' he said. Then he threw a punch at the sergeant.

Slimline didn't even move aside. He just watched as Delaney's punch missed by a mile and the Irishman tottered on his feet unbalanced by it before crashing to the floor, where he lay without moving.

Jimmy Skinner picked the bottle up from the bar and put it into his overcoat pocket. 'I think he might need a shot of this in his coffee in the morning,' he said as they bent down to lift up the unconscious Delaney, one to each arm.

'I think we all might,' said Dave Matthews as they drag-walked him through the noisy crowd, who paid them no attention at all, up to the door and out into the cold, wet night.

A few moments later Stella Trent came out of the Ladies and up to the bar. She looked around, puzzled.

'He's left,' said the barman economically.

'Damn you, Delaney!' she muttered under her breath. 'A girl can't turn her back for five minutes.' She picked up her half-finished glass of wine and downed it, then held her glass forward as the barman turned away. 'Oi, barkeep!' she said, her Irish accent getting stronger. 'There's a lady here in need of refreshment.'

'Why don't you let me get you that?'

Stella turned round to the dark-haired stranger who had sat himself on the bar stool beside her. 'And why should I be letting you do that?'

'Because I can't bear to see a damsel in distress,' he said and smiled widely as he held his hand out. 'My name's Tony.'

*

Kate Walker's lips narrowed as she listened to the voice on the other end of the telephone.

'Thanks for letting me know, Jimmy.'

She hung up the phone and looked across at the bruised face of Jack's sister-in-law.

'Your husband has just been admitted to the Royal Hampstead, Wendy,' she said.

Wendy's hand flew involuntarily to her mouth. 'Dear God, no.'

Kate nodded sympathetically. 'I'm sorry.'

'And Jack?'

'He's been arrested. They've just taken him down to Paddington Green.'

The colour had drained from Wendy's face. 'What has he done, Kate?'

'I don't know, I'm sorry. But Roger has been very badly beaten up.'

Wendy ran her fingers through her hair. 'I'd better go to him.'

'I'll stay here with Siobhan.'

'What about Jack?'

Suddenly there was an arctic frost in Kate's voice. 'He can wait,' she said.

MONDAY

DI Tony Bennett was looking down at Roger Yates as he lay wheezing painfully on his hospital bed. A thick bandage ran across his nose, above which two bloodshot eyes blinked painfully from a panda-like face. His lips were cut and scabbed. To Bennett's mind he looked like he'd walked into a threshing machine. Maybe he had.

The man mumbled something again, a wet bubbling sound that could have been words. Bennett nodded and put his hand inside his jacket. Then he froze and looked across the small ward as DI Jimmy Skinner and Sergeant Bob Wilkinson came in and walked towards them. Bennett turned away from the battered man on the bed and walked towards the door.

'What are you doing here, Tony?' asked Skinner, affably enough.

'Checking up on my own squeal across the way – thought I'd look in on Delaney's brother-in-law while I was here. Seems like our Jack's not a man to cross.'

Skinner gave him a considered look. 'No,' he said. 'He definitely isn't that. But fellow-me-lad on the bed over there is none of Jack Delaney's doing.'

'Is that right?'

273

'Trust me, Tony. If the Irishman wanted to kill a man . . . he'd have got the job done.'

Bennett's smile was devoid of humour. 'To protect and serve, isn't that what they say?'

'They do in America.'

'Yeah, well, whatever starts off in America . . . it gets to England eventually, doesn't it?'

Bob Wilkinson pointed over to Roger Yates. 'Like Detective Skinner said, Delaney's not in the frame for this.'

Bennett smiled almost imperceptibly. 'Is that right?'

'That's exactly right. We have a witness seeing Delaney leave and then another man entering the house, with Roger Yates very much alive if not kicking.'

'Well, this is your case, not mine. I'm sure you're on top of things.' Bennett nodded and walked out of the room.

Bob Wilkinson turned to Skinner. 'What's that all about, you reckon? Things starting in America.'

'I don't know, but I reckon he wasn't talking about McDonald's.'

'Something is not quite right about him, you ask me.'

'In what way?'

Wilkinson shrugged. 'I don't know. He says he's from Doncaster, for a start.'

'And?'

'I've got a friend from Doncaster makes glass – for the military, stuff like that . . .'

Skinner raised an eyebrow as they looked down at Roger Yates, whose eyes were now closed but who was still making a faint bubbling sound with his battered lips. 'And your point would be?'

'Bennett doesn't sound like him. That doesn't sound like a Doncaster accent.'

'People move about, Bob. Look at our own Jack Delaney – he ain't exactly North London born and bred, is he?'

'And that's another thing.'

Skinner simply looked at Wilkinson this time and waited.

'The other day he said he was off for some lunch.'

'Yeah, not exactly the crime of the century, you know, Bob.'

'Yeah, but in Doncaster – that's South Yorkshire, that is – they don't go for lunch, see?'

Jimmy Skinner nodded. 'That's right, it's part of their religion,' he said sarcastically. 'That's why they are the slimmest people in the country. The whippet people of England.'

'You're missing my point. They go for lunch all right, but they call it dinner. Do you see what I'm saying?'

'Not really, Bob. Let's see if we can get some more sense out of Roger Yates here, shall we?'

Jimmy Skinner listened to the burbling sound coming from the assaulted accountants lip's and very much doubted that they would.

*

Delaney winced and squeezed his eyes shut.

'Open your eyes, Jack,' said Kate Walker, not quietly.

'Do you want to dial that down a little?' Delaney said, his voice a hoarse croak. 'I'm just here you know, not halfway across the street.'

'You get no sympathy from me. Just open your eyes.'

Delaney opened his eyes a crack and winced again as Kate shone a small but bright torch at them.

'Is this strictly necessary?'

Kate shrugged. 'Not at all. I just like watching you squirm.'

Delaney closed his eyes again.

'I mean, what the hell were you thinking of?'

'I *wasn't* thinking, was I?'

'No, Jack. You weren't.' Kate slammed the torch down on her desk.

Delaney winced and held both hands to his ears. 'Okay. I'm sorry, all right?'

'I've been awake all night long worrying about you. Why didn't you just tell the custody sergeant last night that it wasn't you?'

'I don't think I actually got to talk to anybody. I kind of remember the guys arriving.' Delaney shrugged a little sheepishly. 'I seem to remember taking a swing – it might have been in slow motion. The next thing I remember is you shaking me awake with all the tenderness of a Waterford washerwoman shaking out her laundry.'

Kate wasn't amused. 'I'll give you tender. And why didn't you come home after you went round there? Why go to King's Cross, of all places?'

Jack held his head again, covering it. 'I just needed a drink.'

'We've got drink, Jack. Plenty of it.'

'I know.'

'So why, then?'

Delaney sighed. 'It very nearly could have been me, you know.'

'Could have been you that what?'

'That smashed that man's smug face in. Good Lord, I've wanted to do it often enough before now but last night he gave me the perfect temptation.'

'I know. He hit Wendy. You're an unreconstructed male, we all know that about you, Jack. But the point is that you didn't do it.'

'It's not just that. Not just because he slapped her.'

'What, then?'

'It could have been, though.' Delaney found his hand forming involuntarily into a fist again. 'I swear to God, darling, last night I was this close to smashing my fist into his face and keeping on doing it.'

'I know.'

Delaney looked up at her. 'No, you don't,' he said.

'What do you mean?'

'He slept with her.'

'Who?'

'With my wife, Kate. He told me he'd slept with Sinead.'

'Oh my God.' Kate sat back, thoughts suddenly swirling though her mind as she remembered guiltily.

She shouldn't do it, but, as she sat at her friend's computer terminal she couldn't help herself. She typed in the access code that Jane Harrington had, under duress, given her, and typed in DELANEY to pull up his hospital records. She knew enough not to trust anything the staff at the hospital had told her. She wasn't a relative. In truth, she didn't even know what she was. Girlfriend didn't sound at all right. Partner was a bit formal for what they had. Mother of his child, she decided, that was what she was, and that gave her rights.

The first hit came up with Siobhan Delaney.

Not the right to look at confidential medical records, maybe, but the man she loved was recovering from an operation and she wanted to know how bad the damage was. She justified it to herself: she had every right.

Not the right to read his ex-wife's records, mind, she said to herself again, arguing against what she knew she was going to do. Kate found herself unable to click the screen away and carried on reading it instead. That night had defined Delaney, after all, for the last four years. It had certainly defined their relationship, if such it was. And so, moral qualms delayed if not avoided, Kate read the report.

Everything was much as she knew it to be. His pregnant wife, suffering heavy blood loss, was rushed into theatre. They had performed an emergency C-section. The baby, and subsequently the mother, had both died. The procedures seemed in order, everything apart from the outcome was in order.

Apart from one thing.

Kate read the document again and wished she never had.

Days later, as she held Jack Delaney's hand and looked down at the gravestones of his wife and son, she realised that she would never tell Jack the terrible truth that she had learned about the boy. That when the baby had been born it had needed blood; the surgical team had checked automatically but Jack Delaney was not a match.

He wasn't a match because he hadn't been the father.

*

278

Kate blinked her eyes, realising that Jack was still talking to her. 'He told me that the baby she was carrying when she died wasn't mine, Kate. He told me it was his.'

Kate could feel a flush rising from her neck, burning her cheeks, felt Jack's stare upon her as the realisation struck him.

'You knew this, didn't you?' he asked, taken aback.

'Not all of it. I knew about the baby . . .'

'How?'

'When you were shot, Jack. I looked at your records.'

'Why didn't you tell me?'

She almost couldn't bear to look at the disappointment in his eyes. 'I shouldn't have known, Jack. I'm sorry. Would it have helped you if I had told you?'

'I don't know.' He shook his head as though it were an impossible question to answer. 'It might have.'

'I thought you'd been through enough.'

Delaney looked at her. 'We shouldn't have secrets between us, Kate.'

'It wasn't my secret, was it, though? It was your wife's.'

'Maybe.'

'I'm sorry, truly I am. I didn't know what was for the best. But what about you? I sometimes get the feeling there's things you are not telling me.'

Delaney looked away and sighed. Then he shook his head and immediately regretted it. 'No. You've got nothing to be sorry for.' He rubbed his bruised

279

hand. 'I went to punch his face, just once . . . but I didn't. I smashed his picture instead of his face, you know. Not so long ago and I would have hurt him, Kate, really hurt him. But I didn't . . . and that's down to you.'

'No, it's not.'

'Yeah, it is,' he said emphatically. 'And you and I both know it.'

Kate took his hand and cleaned the crusted blood gently with a wet tissue, then kissed his bruised knuckles tenderly. 'So who did beat Roger up?'

'I don't know, Kate.' He shrugged. 'With all that's going on right now, there's not a lot I do know.' Delaney looked up at her, a determined look in his eye. 'But I reckon it's way past time we started finding out.'

*

'Please, if anybody knows anything about where our boy is. Please, I am begging for you to come forward.'

Archie Woods's mother's eyes filled with tears. Alongside her, behind the narrow news conference table, her husband shifted uncomfortably. His hand was gripping his wife's hand tightly, but his eyes were cast down, his face unreadable.

'Do you want to turn that down, please?' Bennett asked the serving guy behind the counter, who responded with a casual nod before muting the sound on the small television mounted on the wall behind the curved Formica counter.

Bennett was sitting on a tall red-vinyl-topped stool, drinking a large espresso in a small Italian café right in the heart of Soho. The coffee was strong enough to kick-start a dead elephant but Bennett didn't even grimace as he took another sip. The café itself was pretty much as it had been in the 1950s when it first opened. Soho was in a constant state of flux. As fashions and social mores changed so did the architecture of the place, both literally and figuratively. But some places weren't affected: they didn't seem to age and custom didn't stale their infinite capacity for inertia year after year. The coffee bar that Bennett was sitting in, The French House not far around the corner on Dean Street, The Coach and Horses. Bennett approved of that. He didn't like change.

He finished his coffee and looked up and smiled as the person he was waiting to meet walked into the small café.

My God, she was beautiful, he thought. Young, deadly and beautiful. Just like a black-widow spider.

*

The governor of Bayfield prison stood up as Delaney and Detective Inspector Duncton walked into his office.

'Can I get you some tea, coffee?'

'Nothing.'

'Have there been any specific developments apart from what we have seen on the news?'

'You know as much as we do, governor.'

'The good news is that Garnier has agreed to see you.'

'Big of him!' said Duncton.

The governor shook his head apologetically. 'I'm sorry, detective – he's only agreed to talk to Inspector Delaney.'

'That's outrageous.'

The governor held his hands out. 'There's nothing we can do.'

'You are aware that yesterday we found the body of a child he murdered fifteen years ago and kept on ice as a souvenir?'

'I do know, yes. But the point is, inspector, that he has already confessed to those murders, been tried and sentenced. Finding the body now makes no difference. We can't charge him again, can we?'

'He had an accomplice,' said Duncton. 'Somebody who knew where the body was. We know that now and *he* hasn't been charged, has he?'

'Not yet,' said Delaney pointedly.

'He's playing us for fools.'

'Why don't you sit down, Robert? Have a cup of tea. You're going to give yourself a heart attack.'

Duncton was certainly turning an unhealthy shade of red. He sat down and loosened his collar. 'I'll be waiting here,' he snapped at Delaney.

Delaney nodded and turned to the governor. 'You've been through the records and are absolutely sure that the only visitor he has ever had was Maureen Gallagher?'

'Absolutely positive.'

'What about mail?'

'He has never received any mail. He has no living relatives, as far as we know.'

'Did he have any particular friends inside? Anyone who has been released recently?'

The governor shook his head. 'Nobody has been released from the segregated section for over nine months and nobody is due to be released.'

'We'll need the records of all those who have been released from that unit since he has been a prisoner here,' said Duncton.

The governor nodded. 'I'll get on to it. You think he might have . . . what? Trained an apprentice from here?'

'It's possible.'

Delaney shook his head. 'I think he's had an accomplice all along and is somehow getting messages to him. What about the guards?'

'What about them?'

'Is he ever alone with one of them? Is one of them given particular responsibility for him?'

The governor shook his head again. 'There's always a minimum of two guards with him at any time when he is being moved or being treated. It's prison policy.'

'Why?' asked Duncton.

'Should any accident befall a prisoner . . .'

'Which happens,' said Delaney darkly.

'Which happens,' agreed the governor. 'So protocols are in place.'

'And in the interview room?'

'We'll have eyes on you again, inspector, if not ears. The guards will be just outside at all times.'

'If they need to come in, tell them not to hurry.'

*

Peter Garnier had his eyes closed. He was humming a tune to himself. Delaney thought it sounded vaguely familiar but he couldn't quite place it. The door closed behind him. He pulled a chair across, sat down and stared at Garnier without speaking.

After sixty seconds Garnier opened his eyes. Blinking behind the thick lenses of his glasses. 'The first person to speak loses. Is that it?'

Delaney didn't reply.

Garnier smiled. His lips thin, bloodless.

Delaney could picture the disease working its way through him. Destroying the neurons in his brain. Some time in the future and he wouldn't be able to control his balance, movement, speech or even the ability to swallow. The soulless obscenity of the disease. Delaney used to think that nobody deserved it. But Garnier did. He just hoped the drugs they were giving him kept him alive as long as possible. The longer he suffered the better.

'I'll make a deal with you, Inspector Delaney,' said Garnier.

'I don't make deals with pond scum.'

'Then why are you here?'

'To look you in the face and tell you it's over.'

'You're here to make a bargain. You need my help and you know it.'

'You'll die eventually, Garnier. And like I promised, when you do I'll come and piss on your grave.'

'What is it the media are calling my old stomping ground? Death Row, isn't it?'

Again, Delaney didn't reply.

'But we're all living on Death Row, Delaney. We're all going to die. It's when and how that's important.'

'You are going to die alone and in pain.'

'Do you know what the Apache Indians believed?' Garnier didn't wait for Delaney to reply. 'They believed that everybody had a spirit. Or essence. Not what the Christians think of as a soul. More like

284

what Philip Pullman refers to as dust, or stuff. Wasn't it dust that Jahweh blew into Adam's mouth to give him life, after all? Have you read Philip Pullman, inspector?'

Delaney stared flatly at him.

'The Apache warrior believed that the slower and more painful a person's death, the more of his essence the killer took from his victim. Likewise, the mightier the opponent the warrior slayed . . . the better the essence he took from him, or her. Or someone of spiritual significance.' He looked at Delaney pointedly. 'You know, like a priest . . . or a nun.'

'You're a warrior now, are you, Garnier?'

'I'm a collector, inspector. A special kind. I've been collecting life force. It makes me stronger than you can possibly imagine.'

'You're not looking too strong to me just now.'

'I am strong in dust. In essence.'

Delaney shook his head. Whatever he had hoped to get from the man, it was clearly a fool's errand. The sickness had entered his brain. Literally and metaphorically. He stood up.

'Take me back to the woods, Delaney. I'll show you where the final body is buried. The last of the children – and I'll tell you everything you need to know.'

Garnier smiled again, his thin slips sliding over the yellow bone of his teeth.

Delaney shook his head. 'You have nothing to deal with, Garnier. We're done here.'

'Then the killing will continue.'

Delaney looked at him for a long moment. His hands surprisingly still. He stood up, walked to the door and opened it.

'Come back here!' Garnier screamed.

Delaney closed the door behind him.

*

An hour or so later and Delaney stood in front of the display boards in the CID briefing room. The morning meeting was over. Nothing new had been added. Delaney admitted he had learned nothing new from his visit back at Bayfield. Paddington Green had the ball after all, the superintendent had pointed out. White City was just backup, dogsbody work.

The trouble was, Jack Delaney had never been anybody's dog and he wasn't going to start now.

He was alone in the room save for Bob Wilkinson, who was collecting the briefing notes that hadn't already been removed.

Delaney pointed at one of the boards: a blown-up map of Carlton Row and the surrounding areas. A number of coloured markers indicated where the boy had been abducted, the body found in the allotment, the severed head placed on the altar of Saint Botolph's. The addresses of the murdered children from Carlton Row who'd been taken by Peter Garnier fifteen years before. 'What are we missing, Bob?' he asked. 'What's at the heart of it?' He tapped on the board.

Bob Wilkinson joined him at the board, looking at the map that Delaney had indicated, staring at it as if it were some ancient symbol that, if they could only translate it, would solve the mystery for them. In some ways it was.

He pointed to the yellow pin. 'Used to be that the church was at the heart of the community.'

'Not any more,' said Delaney.

'Why the allotment? The boy was taken from there, Maureen Gallagher's body was placed there as a marker for the body of Samuel Ramirez.'

'Maybe it's not the allotment, sir.'

'What do you mean?'

'Maybe it's whose allotment it is. Maybe Archie Woods wasn't a random victim at all. Maybe he was targeted.'

'Because of his grandfather?'

Wilkinson shrugged. 'Maybe. Paddington Green have been all over him, though, and he's sticking to his story.'

'He seemed genuinely upset enough to me.'

Sally Cartwright came into the room at that moment, carrying two cups of coffee.

Delaney looked across at her. 'Do you want to take a rain check on those?'

'What's up?'

'I'm going to have another word with Graham Harper.'

'I thought Paddington Green was running all this now?'

'They are. I'll catch you later, Bob.'

He steered Sally towards the door as Wilkinson nodded at them and picked up the cups of coffee with the look of a man who has lost a penny and found a sixpence.

'Have you seen Detective Inspector Bennett this morning, sir?' Sally asked Delaney as they hurried down the stairs towards the exit.

Delaney shook his head. 'No, and he wasn't here for this morning's briefing either. What's going on?'

'Nobody can get hold of him. And he was supposed to be interviewing Matt Henson this morning about the Jamil Azeez stabbing.'

'Matt Henson?' said Delaney, half surprised.

'Yeah – didn't you know?'

'No, I didn't. I suppose it was only a matter of time before he graduated to his brother's league.'

'His lawyer is demanding that he be bounced.'

'Someone else can cover for Bennett.'

'I guess.'

'What's Henson got to say for himself?' Delaney asked, nodding sheepishly at Dave Mathews as they passed the front desk. Matthews gave him an amused salute and Delaney hurried through the double doors and out into the car park before he got a chance to add any further comment.

'Henson's lawyered up and is saying nothing.'

'Doesn't take after his father in that respect, then.'

As soon as the words were out of his mouth Delaney became aware of the very man heading towards him. His face puce and his fist waving in the air.

'I want a word with you, Delaney,' he shouted.

Delaney turned to Sally. 'Get in the car. I won't be two ticks.'

Sally headed off to her car and Delaney turned to confront Adam Henson, who promptly poked a finger against his chest. Delaney grabbed the finger, turning his back to the station and the CCTV camera mounted on the wall above the entrance, and pushed it back until Henson squealed with pain and dropped to his knees.

'I don't like being poked,' said Delaney and walked off calmly to join Sally at her car.

'Did you break his finger, sir?' she asked evenly.

'Don't think so,' he replied. 'Let's go back to Harrow.'

*

Delaney pressed his finger against the bell again, leaning on it for five seconds this time.

'Maybe he's got his hearing aid in.'

'Maybe.'

They waited a little while longer. 'Come on,' said Delaney. 'Let's go round the back.'

He led the way round the small side alley along the left-hand side of the house, into a small overgrown garden. He tried the handle on the outside door that led into the kitchen but it wouldn't budge. He moved across to peer through the murky glass to see inside and clearly didn't like what he saw. He went back to the door and kicked it. It stayed closed. He raised his foot again and kicked harder. It still stayed closed.

'Do you want me to have a go, sir?' asked Sally.

'No, I don't, constable,' said Delaney, casting his gaze to the ground and looking for something suitable. He spotted a half-brick in an abandoned flower bed, picked it up and used it to smash the window.

A few moments after picking the shards of broken glass clear he clambered through into the kitchen, looked at the motionless figure of Graham Harper seated in his armchair with his eyes closed and then opened the door to let his assistant in.

Delaney put his hand against the old man's neck and felt for a pulse. After a moment or two he shook his head at Sally.

Sally pointed to a scrap of paper by a bottle of pills on the kitchen counter. 'He left a note.'

'What does it say?'

'*It's all my fault. Sorry.*' Delaney pulled his mobile phone out of his pocket and hit speed dial.

*

Half an hour later Kate Walker closed up her medical bag and watched as Graham Harper was stretchered out to the waiting ambulance.

'When did he do it, do you think?'

'Last evening sometime, I'd say. There was nothing anybody could do. He took a massive dose of medication.'

'Definitely self-administered?'

Kate shrugged. 'There was no sign of a struggle, you say?'

Delaney shook his head.

'No sign of a forced entry?'

'No. Apart from mine and that was only because the doors were locked.'

'When did his family last speak to him?'

'Not since the day before yesterday. The mother blames him for her son's disappearance.'

'Looks like suicide, then. That's more your area, Jack, than mine.'

'Actually it's *my* bloody area!' said DI Robert Duncton as he barrelled into the room, followed by his Amazonian sergeant, who had to duck a little as she came through the kitchen door. 'I thought I told you to clear anything through me.'

'We'll leave you to it then, Robert,' said Delaney, smiling and ignoring the way the other man bristled when he used his first name. 'Come on, Sally. The detective inspector has a scene to process and he doesn't need us under his feet.'

'Just you tread carefully, Delaney!' Duncton called after him as they walked out of the kitchen.

*

A few moments later and Delaney was adjusting the heat setting in Sally's car. 'It's colder than a witch's tit in a brass brassiere in here,' he said as the constable fired up the engine and threw him a reproving look. 'What?' he said defensively.

'Nothing, sir,' she said, with a resigned sigh.

'Good. Take us down to Roy Boy's. I need to think and nothing helps me do that better than a fat bacon sandwich.'

'What you said back there to the inspector . . .'

'Spit it out, Sally.'

Sally turned the engine back off. 'About the old man killing himself because he thought his grandson had been killed and it was all his fault.'

'Go on.'

'Well, what if it *was* his fault?'

'The boy we found was killed fifteen years ago.'

'Exactly.'

Delaney looked at her. 'Do you ever do the crossword, constable?'

'Sometimes.'

'Well, let's not turn this into twenty bloody cryptic questions. What's your point?'

'Well, you said it yourself, sir. Why Graham Harper? Why was his grandson abducted, why his allotment? Maybe he was involved fifteen years ago

291

in the murder of those two children. You always said Garnier had an accomplice. What if it was Graham Harper? Maybe that was what he meant by the note: *I'm sorry, it's all my fault.*'

'Maybe.'

'But he didn't take his own grandchild, did he?'

Delaney shook his head. 'I don't think so.'

Sally shrugged. 'Maybe he did just kill himself for the guilt he felt about his grandson being taken when he was supposed to be looking after him, like you said.' She turned the key again and Delaney put his hand on her arm.

'Hold on a minute. Let me think.' He put a cigarette in his mouth, pulled it out again and looked at it thoughtfully for a moment, then put it on the dashboard. He took out his mobile, hit the speed dial and spoke urgently as it was answered.

'Diane, it's Jack. Can you pull up the scene-of-crime report from Graham Hall's allotment and shed?' He nodded. 'The inventory from the shed, Look down it. Is there any mention of cigarettes?' He listened for a while longer. 'Okay, thanks, Diane. I'll get back to you.'

Delaney closed the phone and looked at Sally, an excited gleam in his eye.

'What is it, sir?'

'Graham Harper said he went for a cigarette in his shed while the boy waited outside, didn't he?'

'Yes.'

'Well, there were no cigarettes in the shed. And he didn't have any on him – he said as much when he asked if he could have one of mine.'

'So?'

292

'So where are the cigarettes?'

Sally shook her head, puzzled. 'I don't understand.'

'He didn't just say he had cigarettes in the shed. He said he had them stashed there.'

'Okay . . .' said Sally, clearly still puzzled.

Delaney pointed out of the window. 'Let's go back there.'

*

Back at the allotment the SOCO unit was dismantling the forensic tent. The ground had been dug up and examined and no further bodies had been discovered. Delaney nodded to the crew as he walked up to the shed and ripped down the tape sealing it, ignoring the protests coming from the SOCO unit, who were shouting that they hadn't processed the shed yet. Delaney waved their complaints aside and stepped through the door followed by the detective constable.

Even though it was bright outside, it was still dark in the shed and he sent Sally back to get a torch. It was pretty much as Delaney remembered it, the usual clutter of a gardening shed. No heavy-bladed instruments. Not that he reckoned Graham Harper would have had the strength to cut off a woman's head, but it wouldn't have been the first time he had been wrong on a case.

A short while later Sally returned with the torch. 'They're not too happy us being here, sir. They've put a call in to Duncton. He's on his way over.'

'Great,' grunted Delaney and scanned the floor. The floorboards were old and covered with the kind of ingrained dirt that takes years to build up. He moved the boxes around, paying little heed to the fact that he was disturbing a crime scene.

Nothing.

Frustrated, Delaney let his gaze travel around the room. He looked at the battered armchair, crossed to it and snatched up the cushion. Nothing. He threw it back in place and then shoved the armchair out of the way. The floor was as it was everywhere else, black with dust and dirt. Except there was a small knothole in one floorboard. Delaney bent down and put his finger in it. He gripped under and pulled upwards. The plank came loose. Delaney put it to one side and put his arm through the aperture. 'Bingo,' he said quietly and pulled his hand back up, bringing with it a pack of cigarettes. He reached down with his arm again and felt around. There was nothing there. 'That's it,' he said, disappointed, nodding to the cigarettes. 'At least we know he wasn't lying about those.'

'Let me have a go, sir,' said Sally. 'My arm is thinner than yours.'

Sally knelt down and put her arm through the hole, reaching in almost up to her shoulder as she groped on the floor under the shed. 'Hang on – I think I've got something,' she said excitedly as she forced her arm further in. She reached again and then pulled her arm slowly out. She held in her hand an A4 brown paper envelope, filthy with dust and covered with spider webs and mouse droppings.

She handed it to Delaney, who took it and opened it, sliding out a series of photographs. He took one look at the top photo before sliding the rest back into the envelope and dropping it on the armchair. Then, holding his hand to his mouth, he dashed out of the shed. Sally picked up the envelope and looked inside it.

Delaney put his hand on the side of the shed, leaning against it, and threw up. The bitter acid taste of the Bushmills he had been drinking the night before filled his mouth and he retched again, a dry, heaving retch. A short while later he became aware of Sally standing beside him.

'I'm sorry, sir,' she said.

'Were they all of her?' asked Delaney.

'Yes, sir.'

'And the men . . . ?'

'There were no faces.' Sally's face was ashen too. 'I'm sorry,' she said again.

*

Delaney stood beside Sally's car. He was aware of people moving around him, could hear voices but had no idea what anyone was saying. It was just sound. Meaningless.

Ahead of him the news vultures had gathered again behind the yellow tape. Melanie Jones's assistant fluffing her hair and touching up her make-up. The glamorous face of the news. News that was hitting home to Delaney fifteen years too late. Hitting home like a sledgehammer in his gut.

He fumbled a cigarette into his mouth, grateful at least that the rain that had been falling for days on end seemed finally to have let up. He scratched a match and lit up, drawing deep and holding the smoke in his lungs till they burned.

It was cold but the sky was clear, pale streaks of

salmon pink threading through it like coral in a cobalt ocean. Delaney looked at the street lamp that stood at the entrance to the alleyway, but it certainly didn't lead to Narnia. He remembered the posters of the children that had been plastered all over the area. He remembered the hundreds of hours he'd wasted walking the area. He looked at his watch. Eleven o'clock. He took another pull on his cigarette as Sally Cartwright approached.

'What do you reckon, Sally?' He said. 'Too early for a pint?'

Sally looked at him sympathetically for a moment and then shook her head. 'No, sir,' she said simply. 'The Crawfish is just around the corner. If it's still open.'

'That used to be the best boozer in the area back in the day.'

'Not any more.'

Delaney nodded sadly. 'No. Not any more.' He stood up straight. 'Shit,' he said.

'What is it, sir?'

'Something Bob Wilkinson said. About never mind the church, it's the pub that is at the heart of the community.'

'So?'

'It's the locus. Things happening round here. All those years ago and now happening all over again.'

'I don't follow.'

'The landlord back then had the pub as a sort of nerve centre for the search for the missing children. Organised teams of locals as well as the police who were combing the area. Ellie Peters used to work there now and again, I remember her.'

'And?'

'She was a part-time hooker, an alcoholic, a drug addict. It was a fairly well-known secret that the landlord was giving her more than just three pounds an hour. And she was giving the customers more than a bitter shandy.'

'I still don't follow, sir.'

'The landlord was due to marry his chef who worked there at the time.'

Sally nodded, remembering. 'The woman who cooked the best seafood platter south of your Aunty Noreen?'

'Exactly.'

'And she's important because . . .'

'Because of her maiden name, detective constable.'

'Which was?'

'Her name was Emily, Sally. Emily Harper!'

*

Delaney sat the bar with a pint of lager in front of him as a horde of SOCOs and uniforms headed down to the cellar. Duncton, red-faced as ever, panted as he came up the stairs and into the bar, followed by the red-haired barman, Terry Blaylock. He was clearly less than pleased as he stood aside to let the SOCO get down into the cellar.

'I'm telling you it's a waste of time. There's nothing down there.'

'Anything, sir?' Sally asked Duncton, who shook his head and looked across disgusted at Delaney, who raised his glass back at him as in a toast.

'Your boss is a disgrace, detective constable. Anybody ever tell him that?'

Sally nodded, with a small smile. 'Everyone does, sir – he takes it as a compliment.'

Sergeant Emma Halliday walked in from outside, her mobile phone held to her ear. She finished the call and crossed to Duncton and the red-haired barman. 'They've searched the house.' She shrugged, disappointed. 'Nothing.'

'What I told you,' said Blaylock aggressively.

'Why didn't you tell us you're related to the boy?' asked Delaney from the bar.

Duncton swung round at Delaney, annoyed. 'We'll do this properly down at the station, thank you very much.'

'I've got nothing to hide. My old man died fifteen years ago and my mum hasn't spoken to her brother for twenty years. And neither have I.'

'Why not?'

The man glared, his voice growing more belligerent by the minute. 'I don't know and quite frankly I couldn't give a fuck. Ask her.'

'We're asking you, sunshine, and we'll do it properly,' said Duncton, every bit as bellicose. He nodded to his tall assistant. 'Take him in, sergeant.'

Delaney finished his pint and stood up, gesturing to Sally to follow him as he walked behind Emma Halliday, who was steering Blaylock to the exit.

'Get back to White City and process some parking tickets or whatever it is you're good at, Delaney,' Duncton called after him.

Delaney smiled coldly to himself but carried on walking. Outside, a uniform was holding the back door of a police car open and Sergeant Halliday was about to guide Blaylock in when Delaney called out to her.

'Hold up, sergeant, I know your boss might object, but can I have a word with him?'

Halliday grunted dismissively. 'What Duncton objects to is no longer my problem. I found out this morning that I passed my inspector's exam.'

Delaney smiled. 'Good for you!' Then the smile died as he turned to the overweight barman. 'Where's your lock-up, Mister Blaylock?'

Blaylock shook his head, shuffling his feet slightly. 'I don't know what you're taking about.'

'Yeah, you do. Where is it?'

'Look, I've told you. I had nothing to do with that boy's disappearance. I've never even spoken to the kid.'

'Where's the lock-up?' said Delaney again, pointedly stepping in close to him, getting in his face.

'All right, all right. It's round the corner.'

Halliday nodded. 'We'll take my car.'

Blaylock shook his head, resigned. 'There's no need. Like I said, it's only round the corner.'

Halliday looked back at the pub for a moment and then gestured to the barman. 'Lead on, McDuff.'

As they walked away from the pub Sally fell into step beside Delaney and asked quietly, 'How did you know he had a lock-up?'

'Remember those boxes he had stashed when we were last here?'

Sally nodded.

'Half of them were filled with booze. I think he's been depleting the stock before handing over the keys.'

A short while later Blaylock veered into a small yard that had twenty lock-up garages. Ten on each side, facing each other across a cracked and pitted drive, overgrown with weeds, that looked like it had been laid in the early 1970s and left to rot ever since.

Blaylock walked up to the last garage on the right and reached into his pockets to pull out a key. He put it in the lock in the handle on the centre of the door, twisted it and lifted the door up and in. He gestured with his hand and stood back, his arms folded. 'Knock yourselves out.'

Delaney walked in with Sally and looked around the garage. It was small, piled high with cardboard boxes and packing crates – a lot of them filled, as Delaney had rightly surmised, with bottles of spirits liberated from the pub. There was no sign of an eight-year-old boy. Delaney moved a few of the boxes aside but a couple of minutes later they had to concede there was no evidence of the boy's presence.

Delaney walked out and looked at Blaylock. 'Stocking up early for Christmas, are we?'

Blaylock's already red face flushed an even deeper hue. 'I can explain about that.'

'Don't bother,' said Delaney brusquely. 'Frankly, we've got more important fish to fry.' He gestured for Blaylock to shut the door and watched as he pulled it down again.

'Hang on a minute,' Delaney said as the door was closing. 'Open it up again.'

Blaylock shrugged, puzzled, and did as Delaney asked. The detective strode forward and went to a box near the front of the garage. It was the one that Blaylock had been loading up when he and Sally had been in the pub a few days earlier. He moved a couple of items aside and pulled out a photo. He looked at it for a moment. 'Delaney, you absolute feckin' idiot!' he said softly.

'What is it, sir?' asked Sally.

Delaney handed her the photo and, puzzled, Sally looked at it for a moment.

'Look at the man on the left, Sally. Picture him without the beard and the moustache and the full head of quiffed hair. Picture that and then look who is standing next to him.'

Sally peered a bit more closely at the photo. 'Oh my God!' she said in a low whisper as recognition dawned on her.

*

Jennifer Hickling came out of the HSBC bank on Camden High Street in a foul mood. She had planned to withdraw her savings that morning, get her sister from school at lunchtime, take the Tube to Liverpool Street and take a mainline train out of London for good. She had an older friend called Kelly who had just turned sixteen and had a one-year-old baby. Kelly lived with her boyfriend, a nineteen-year-old apprentice car mechanic called Lloyd who absolutely doted on her. They had a house on a council estate in a small town just outside Norwich. But it was an estate as different from the Waterhill where Jenny lived that it might as well have been in another country. In a lot of ways it was.

The only trouble was that because of her age Jenny had opened the account with some false ID, including a driving licence which she had left back at the flat. Due to the large amount of money she was withdrawing – five thousand pounds – the manager had asked to see the driving licence again. Jenny had arranged an appointment with the woman for two o'clock. It meant an hour or so's delay but her train tickets were valid up to four o'clock and it was only a two-hour journey to Norwich, where her friend and her friend's partner had agreed to meet them.

She ran up the road to catch her bus, showing her real ID to a sceptical bus driver who reckoned she was at least three years older than she claimed but didn't have the energy to argue the matter.

Jenny walked down the length of the bus to sit on her own on the back seat by the window.

She looked out of the grimy window at the brilliant blue sky, the streaks of pale red trailing through it like ink in water. She pulled her coat tighter around her and snuggled into the corner. She put her hand in her pocket, pulled out the two one-way tickets to Norwich and smiled to herself. Time to make a new life for herself and her sister. Time to start again. Time to heal.

Way past time.

She never did make the train.

*

It was a small lounge and Jack Delaney, Sergeant Halliday and Terry Blaylock pretty much filled it. Sally Cartwright stood by the door.

Delaney looked at the woman sitting on the sofa. She seemed to be overwhelmed by their presence. He remembered her as a larger-than-life woman. Big in every sense of the word. The years since he had last seen her had seemed to diminish her somehow. He guessed she was probably in her sixties, with grey hair that had once been a magnificent auburn. She looked up at him quizzically and then smiled.

'I remember you. You were the Irish copper, weren't you?'

'I still am, ma'am,' said Delaney.

'You used to come into the pub for your lunch back in that dreadful time.'

'I did.'

She clicked her fingers. 'The fisherman's platter. Better than your Aunty Nora's, you used to say.'

'You have a good memory, Mrs Blaylock.'

'Only thing I do have nowadays,' she grunted.

'But it was me Aunty Noreen.'

'We don't do food any more.'

'I know.'

'Stopped doing it when my husband died. Didn't have the heart for it any more.' She looked at the picture that Delaney was holding. 'Is that the photo?'

Delaney nodded and held the photo out to her. She took it and looked at it without saying anything for a moment or two. And then she nodded. 'Yes, that's the sick pervert. To think he had been drinking in my pub all those years.'

'He moved away after the children disappeared?' asked Sergeant Halliday.

'That's right. To Ruislip. Where they got him eventually.'

'And that's your brother with him?'

The woman nodded sadly. 'Yeah, that's Graham.'

Delaney picked up on the bitterness in her voice. 'I understand you had a falling-out, hadn't spoken to him in years.'

'That's right. And, quite frankly, when I heard he'd topped himself I didn't even shed a tear.'

'What was the argument about?'

The woman shook her head. 'I don't want to talk about it.'

'Who are the other people in the picture, Mrs Blaylock?' asked Sally. 'Your son doesn't remember them.'

Mrs Blaylock threw her son a dismissive look. 'Yeah, well, it was before his time, wasn't it? When the pub was a successful ongoing business.'

'I didn't ban smoking, Mum. I didn't bring on the recession.'

'No, you didn't do anything, did you? Just like your uncle!' she snapped back at him.

Delaney gestured towards the picture. 'Mrs Blaylock?' he prompted.

Sergeant Halliday's phone trilled. She glanced quickly at the caller ID and switched the phone off.

'They called themselves The Rockabillies.'

Delaney reacted. 'A musical group?'

Mrs Blaylock snorted and shook her head. 'No. They were a pub-quiz team, that's all. They dressed up like that for the final. They thought it was funny.'

'Why The Rockabillies?' asked Sally.

'Garnier's second name was Bill – well, William, anyway. And the guy standing next to my brother was called Bill too. He was always singing some rock-and-roll tune or other. So that's what they called themselves.'

'Bill who?' said Delaney.

'I'm sorry. I can't remember his surname. He was a fisherman. Down on the coast. He inherited a house somewhere in the area. He supplied us for a little while. My husband dealt with him.'

'And who are the others?'

Mrs Blaylock held up the photo: five men all wearing Elvis-style quiffs, some of them wigs. One of the men, wearing a black suit, had his back to the camera. Mrs Blaylock pointed to the fourth man in the group, a young man somewhere in his twenties, considerably younger than the others. 'I know him because he used to work for me as a commis chef. Just sorting out the vegetables, that kind of thing. He was never going to be a cook.'

'What's his name?' Delaney pulled out his notebook.

'Tim Radnor,' the woman replied. 'He left when my husband died.'

'Where did he go? Do you know?'

'He went to work at Harrow School. Up on the hill, you know?'

Delaney nodded. 'Yeah, we know it. And who is the man with his back to the camera?'

Mrs Blaylock looked down at the picture and shook her head. 'I don't know, I'm sorry. '

'You absolutely sure?'

'Yes. Sorry.' She handed the photo back to Delaney. 'What does it all mean?'

'We don't know, Mrs Blaylock.'

'But you think it might be one of those men who have taken my brother's grandson?'

'Maybe,' said Sergeant Halliday.

'Well, it can't be Peter Garnier or my brother.'

'You sure you can't remember the fisherman's name?'

'Sorry, no. It's so long ago now. I just knew him as Bill, I never really spoke to him. I was never front of house much – that was Gerald's area.'

'Gerald?' asked Delaney.

'My dad,' said Terry Blaylock.

Mrs Blaylock threw him another critical look. 'A proper publican!'

Delaney looked over at the tall sergeant. 'Fancy a trip out to Harrow School, *Inspector*?' he said.

She was about to say, 'Sir,' but caught herself and grinned instead. 'Can I borrow your DC?' she asked.

Delaney nodded. 'I want her back, mind.'

*

An hour later and Delaney was standing with Kate at the burger stand around the corner from the station. Kate pulled the zipper of her jacket up to her neck and threw Delaney what he thought of as an old-fashioned look.

'Couldn't we have gone to a proper restaurant for a change? A pub at least? Somewhere inside. You know, a place with four walls . . . and heat.'

'I needed to think, Kate.' Delaney shrugged apologetically. 'And sometimes only Roy's bacon sarnies can help.'

'Right,' said Kate, resigned.

Roy flipped some rashers of bacon on the griddle. Then he put on a pair of catering gloves and started buttering some bread. Delaney smiled to himself: he was pretty sure he had never seen the man wearing catering gloves before and he was also pretty sure that the reason Roy was wearing them now was all to do with Kate Walker. Roy was one of the most

306

irritating men he knew at times, with absolutely no respect for authority, but he seemed to scamper around Kate like a puppy dog wagging its tail.

Delaney winked at her. 'If you play nicely, I'll get Roy to fry you an egg to go with your sandwich.'

'And you can do one of those for me too while you're at it,' said Sergeant Halliday as she walked up with Sally Cartwright to join them.

Roy lifted his eyebrows as his gaze rose from Emma's flat-soled shoes to the top of her head, all six foot two of her. He pursed his lips as if to whistle but Delaney gave him a shake of his head.

'Don't even think about it,' he said.

'Another bacon sarnie it is, then.'

'Good call,' said the sergeant, smiling.

'Any sign of Bennett yet?' Kate asked Sally.

'No. And he's not answering his calls.'

Delaney turned to Sally Cartwright. 'How did it go at the school?'

Sally shook her head. 'Not good, sir. Apparently.'

'What happened?'

'Somebody got there before us. A long time before us,' Emma Halliday said.

'He's dead?'

Sally grimaced. 'You could say that.'

'Someone tied him kneeling to his bed, stuck a single-barrelled shotgun up his arse and pulled the trigger,' Emma Halliday said bluntly.

Delaney frowned. 'And nobody noticed? Nobody heard anything?'

The tall sergeant shook her head. 'His body acted like a silencer, I guess.'

Roy handed a sandwich to Delaney, who took a

big bite of it. He realised that Kate was staring unbelievingly at him. 'What?' he asked.

'I can't believe you're eating that,' she said.

'I told you. I need to think.'

He looked over at Roy as the burger man flipped the bacon again and cracked an egg on the griddle plate. Delaney turned to Sally again. 'You know those pictures of the staircases going up and down? You look at them one way and they are going up, you look again and it seems they are going down, or outside and inside. And you follow a straight path but at the end they've dropped several levels. Like optical illusions. Can't remember the artist.'

'M.C. Escher, sir. Dutch,' Sally said.

Delaney waved his hand dismissively. 'Whatever. The point is, we've been looking at this all the wrong way, whether the stairs are going up and down.'

'And what should we have been doing?' asked the sergeant.

A motorbike turned the corner at the top of the street and headed towards the van. 'We should have been taking the fricking elevator,' Delaney said and turned back to the counter. 'Roy, give us one of those catering gloves, will you?'

'What for?'

'Just give us the fecking glove.'

Roy handed him one of the plastic gloves. Delaney took it and looked across, puzzled, at the motorbike that had stopped on the other side of the road, leaving its engine running. He realised that the rider, who was wearing a dark outfit and a black helmet with a black visor, was swinging something in his hands and pointing it at Kate, who was standing in front of Delaney. Something long and metallic. Delaney processed the information in a split second, shouting for everyone to get down as he grabbed Kate, swinging her round and pulling her to the ground at the side of the van.

The shotgun blast ripped the air apart, the pellets blasting into the trees and the cars and the fencing opposite the van. Delaney scrambled round the side of the van but the motorcyclist was already gunning his engine and racing away back in the direction he had come. There was no number plate on the back of the bike.

Kate stood up, breathing heavily. 'What the hell was all that about?' she said, her face as pale as Delaney had ever seen it.

'I don't know, darling. Is everyone okay?'

Emma Halliday and Sally Cartwright had both dived for cover as soon as Delaney had shouted and they'd seen what was happening. They stood up, dusting their clothes.

'What the hell was that, sir?' asked Sally. 'A warning? Or was he trying to kill you?'

'God knows. Maybe it wasn't me he was after.'

'We thought someone might have been taking a shot at you in Mad Bess Woods on Saturday morning, didn't we?'

'You did. I didn't.'

'There's not a lot of doubt about this one, Jack,' said Emma Halliday. 'Who's got a grudge against you?'

Behind the counter Roy snorted, continuing to cook as though nothing had happened.

Delaney shrugged ruefully. 'How long have you got?'

But Emma wasn't listening. She was looking at Kate, a concerned look on her face. Delaney turned round to look at Kate, who was still deathly pale and holding a hand to her stomach. 'Are you okay? What's wrong?'

Kate smiled and took her hand away. 'I'm fine, just a little bit winded.' She took a couple of deep breaths, the colour returning to her cheeks.

'There's nothing wrong with the baby?'

Kate smiled again and shook her head. 'I'm fine, really. It was just a bit of a shock. Not every day a girl gets shot at.'

'Are you sure you're all right?'

Kate smiled again and rubbed his arm reassuringly. 'Of course I'm sure. I'm a doctor, Jack. I'd know if something was wrong.'

Delaney looked across at the fence that had been peppered with shot. 'Maybe it was me. Everybody connected with Peter Garnier. They're all being targeted – they're all being killed or someone's trying to kill them. Graham Harper. Tim Radnor. Me.'

Sally nodded. 'You could be right, sir.'

'What about the church cleaner, then – Maureen Gallagher? How does she fit into all this?' asked Emma Halliday, brushing some more dirt from her knees.

'I don't know,' said Delaney. 'But she was the only person ever to visit him in prison, so there is a definite connection with the man.'

He took out a copy of the photo of Peter Garnier and the others from his pocket. The child killer, almost unrecognisable in his moustache, beard and ridiculously quiffed hair. 'The men here, I think they're connected with those other photos. One of these two men, the fisherman or the man in the black suit . . . they're cleaning up the evidence and it's Peter Garnier calling the shots.' Delaney stared at the picture, trying to make sense of it all. 'Damn!' he said suddenly. He pulled out his mobile phone and started punching in some numbers.

'What is it, Jack?' asked Kate.

'There's someone else connected too, isn't there? One of his victims.' Delaney listened as the phone rang. 'Come on, Gloria,' he said. 'Answer the damn phone.'

But Gloria didn't.

*

Sally pulled her car to a screeching stop and turned off the flashing lights and siren. 'Wait here,' said Delaney to her as he got out of the car, slamming the door shut behind him and sprinting across the road, weaving through the slowly moving traffic and racing up the steps that led to the first-floor flats. He ran along the balcony that overlooked the road below until he reached the last door on the right. The lights were off in the flat. He rang the doorbell for a few seconds and then rang it again. There was no answer. He pulled out his phone again and punched in the numbers. Again it went straight to Gloria's answerphone. He clicked the phone shut and pressed his finger against the doorbell again, keeping it there for five seconds this time. He waited a while longer and then headed back to the stairwell.

He was just about to descend the steps when the door opened behind him and he turned around to see

311

Gloria standing in the doorway, dressed in a bathrobe with a towel curled around her head.

'Jack, what on earth do you want?'

Delaney turned round, the breath exploding from his body with relief. 'Gloria, for God's sake – you're all right! You had me worried half to death.'

'What are you on about?'

'You weren't answering the door and the phone I bought you has been going straight to answerphone!'

'I was in the shower, the phone was on charge and I don't get a good signal in the flat anyway.'

'Can I come in?'

'No. Like I said, I was in the shower.'

'It won't take long.' Delaney stepped forward

But Gloria held her hand against the door jamb. 'I mean it. I'm busy.'

'Yeah, with a shower,' said Delaney, annoyed. 'This is important, Gloria!'

Gloria sighed, spelling it out for him. 'I wasn't alone in the shower.'

'Oh.'

'For a detective, Jack, sometimes you're not very bright.'

'I didn't know you were even seeing anyone.'

'Well, I am.'

'Have you known him long?'

'What is this? An interrogation?'

'No. I just wanted to know.'

'Is it important?'

Delaney nodded, serious. 'It could be, yes.'

Gloria shook her head, amused. 'Well then, for your information I've known *her* for over two years. Lizzie was always a good friend at university.

Recently we have become close.'

Delaney shuffled awkwardly. 'Right. Mary never mentioned . . .'

'That I'm gay?'

'Well . . . yes.'

'To be honest with you, Jack, I'm not sure what I am. But I am with Lizzie at the moment,' she smiled again, 'and she makes me happy.'

'Good. I'm pleased for you,' said Delaney. 'Really I am.'

'So, then, if you don't mind . . . ?' Gloria arched her eyebrows and moved to close the door.

'It's Peter Garnier,' said Delaney, slipping the name bluntly into the conversation.

'What about him?' Gloria froze, all amusement in her eyes dying. 'What about him, Jack?'

'People who were close to him or connected to him in some way are being killed. We think he had an accomplice. We think that person is taking out anybody who had a link to him.'

'What's that got to do with me? I was his victim, not an accomplice.'

'I know, Gloria. Somebody shot at me earlier today. We don't know why or how it all ties in to Garnier.'

Gloria slumped against the door frame. 'Okay. What should I do?'

'Have you got somewhere you could go? Somewhere you'd be safe for a few days?'

'He doesn't know where I live, does he? This accomplice?'

'We don't know what he knows or who he is. So do you have anywhere you can go?'

'Yes.'

'Just for a few days, Gloria. We'll get him, I promise you.'

'Just like you promised you'd find that little boy.'

Delaney put his hand on her shoulder. 'I don't break my promises. Not any more.'

'Okay, then.'

'And don't answer the door to any strange men.'

'Yeah! Thanks, Dad.' Gloria was trying to smile but was not quite making it.

*

Sally Cartwright was leaning against the car when Delaney returned.

'She's all right, then?'

'Yeah, her phone was on charge, is all. Not a good signal in the flat.'

'I told you that you had nothing to worry about. Nobody knows where she is. Nobody knows *who* she is, Jack! Least of all Peter Garnier.'

'Come on then, constable. Get in the car and let's go.'

*

Gloria stood by the window, looking through a small gap in the curtains as Sally nosed her car out into the traffic and moved off. She continued to lean against the cool glass, feeling it on her forehead. Then she stood back and took the towel off her head, running her delicate fingers through the smooth dry hair.

She tossed the towel aside and walked over to the opposite wall. Looking at her montage of photos and articles. The yellow light from the street lamp outside spilled through the gap in the curtain to throw a slash of sulphur-yellow light across the wall, catching the picture of Peter Garnier and giving his eyes a feral, alien look. She looked at the photo of Jack Delaney holding her when she'd been rescued as a seven-year-old girl. Then she pulled her robe tight around herself and dropped her right hand, letting it come rest on a motorcycle helmet on the side table beneath the picture.

'Turns out you couldn't save them all,' she said as she stared at the man in uniform holding her in his arms. 'Could you, Jack?'

'Has he gone?'

Gloria turned round and nodded. 'Yes, George. He's gone.'

'Good. Get dressed, then.'

*

Sally Cartwright pulled the car to a stop in the White City police station car park and turned off the engine. Delaney snapped his seat belt off and reached for the door handle. Then he looked back at Sally who seemed a bit lost in thought. 'Something on your mind, detective constable?'

'Just wondering how Garnier is getting messages out, sir. He doesn't have access to the internet, he's never alone with a guard. None of them are. He's had no mail, no visitors apart from Maureen Gallagher. Who's now dead. So we know *she's* not involved.'

'Somebody else in there, someone who does have visitors, you think? Somebody from the outside who's carrying messages to one of the two men in the photo?' asked Delaney.

'He's talking to someone, sir.'

Delaney looked at her for a long moment, the synapses in his brain firing as he turned her words over and over. Then he smiled. 'Of course he's talking to someone. And he told me who it is the very first time I visited him.'

'I don't understand, sir. Who?'

Delaney pulled out the photo of the five men and handed it to her. 'Like we thought, it's one of these two men, and I know which one.'

Sally looked at the photo and would have asked Delaney a further question but he held up a finger to silence her. Then he took out his phone and notebook and flipped through it until he came to a number and punched it in. After a few seconds the phone was answered.

'Father Carson Brown? It's Detective Inspector Jack Delaney. Are you in your office? Good. Could you look up for me the name of the priest in charge of your church in the summer of 1995?' Delaney waited for a while as the priest did as he was asked and then wrote down the name that Carson Brown gave him. 'Thank you, Father,' said Delaney and clicked off the phone. Sally started to speak again but once more Delaney held up a finger as he punched in another phone number. He pointed at the photo as he waited for his call to be answered. 'The man in black, Sally,' he said. 'Who wears black suits?'

Sally got it immediately. 'He's a priest!'

'Garnier said he converted to Catholicism six months ago. I knew he was lying but I couldn't see why.'

'Why, then?'

316

'The confessional, Sally. His old associate started visiting the prison and so he got to have a private conversation with him every Sunday. That's who he's been talking to.'

'Oh my God.'

Someone at the other end of Delaney's phone call finally answered. 'Governor, it's Jack Delaney. I've got two questions for you. The priest who visits to conduct the Catholic Mass on a Sunday . . . is his name Father Michael Fitzpatrick?' He nodded, pleased. 'Second question, then: what's his address?'

As Delaney waited for the governor to look it up he flashed a triumphant grin at Sally. 'We've got the bastard!'

Sally blew out a sigh. 'Let's just hope we're in time, then.'

*

Delaney and Sally Cartwright rushed up the pavement. A team of uniformed and flak-jacketed police with combat helmets were approaching the front door of a detached suburban house in Ealing. Half the team crept around the side of the house while the others approached the door. Sergeant Emma Halliday and Detective Inspector Duncton stood behind them at the front gate of the garden.

'Go, go, go!' Duncton shouted – like someone off a cheap television drama, Delaney couldn't help thinking. The lead uniform swung the heavy tubular device into the door and smashed it open. Two of the armed units behind him moved into the house with their semi-automatic weapons raised.

'Armed police!' they shouted, moving into covering positions as their colleagues cautiously entered the house behind them.

'Just stay back, Delaney! This is my collar!' shouted Duncton as Delaney and Sally reached the house.

'Yeah, don't mention it, Duncton. We were just glad to be of assistance, weren't we, Sally?'

'Don't give me that. If you had kept the lines of communication open as you were supposed to do, then maybe we would all have got here a bit sooner.'

'To be fair to Inspector Delaney—' Emma Halliday started to say but Duncton cut her off.

'And you can shut it, sergeant. Given your involvement in all this you'll be lucky not to be back walking the beat come end of play.'

'With all due respect, sir: why don't you go fuck yourself? You silly little man,' she said with a sweet smile.

Duncton's face was turning his usual shade of red but before he could respond one of the armed officers came out of the front door.

'It's secure, sir.'

'You'll keep!' said Duncton to his sergeant and headed into the house.

The others followed behind him. But there was no hurry: even as Delaney approached the door he could tell that no one was there.

'He cleared out some time ago, by the looks of it,' said the armed officer. 'There's mail and papers on the hall floor from the last few days and his wardrobe and drawers have been emptied.'

'Shit!' said Duncton. 'Shit, shit, shit!'

Delaney would have laughed at the disappointment written on the angry man's face, but in fact he felt the polar opposite of amusement. They might know who they were dealing with now, but they had no idea where he was and were no further forward in finding the missing boy.

Truth to tell, Jack Delaney felt sick as he stood in the hallway looking around at the deserted house. Sick to his stomach.

*

Kate held a hand to her stomach and winced a little, breathing heavily. Bob Wilkinson stuck his head around the door and walked in, carrying a cup of tea.

'Thanks, Bob,' Kate said. 'You're a lifesaver.'

Wilkinson shook his head. 'I heard that was Jack Delaney.'

'Still no sign of DI Bennett, I gather?'

'No. Seems like he's fallen off the side of the planet. If he was ever on it.'

'What do you mean?'

'I phoned Doncaster nick. Nobody there has ever head of him.'

*

'Okay. Calm down, Mary,' said Jack Delaney into his mobile phone as he stood outside Sally's car, parked up the street from Father Fitzpatrick's abandoned house. 'We're in Ealing now. So we're not too far away. I'll check back at her house.'

He closed the phone and got into the car. 'Let's get going.'

'Something wrong, sir?' Sally asked as she started the engine and pulled away from the kerb.

'Gloria had an appointment with Mary today. She never showed up.'

'And . . . ?'

'And I don't know. But I've got a bad feeling about this. So put your foot on the floor.'

Delaney leaned forward to flick the siren switch on as they hammered past a bemused-looking Duncton who was coming out of the missing priest's house.

*

Delaney walked across the room and opened the curtains. Bright daylight spilled into the room. Lighting up the display of photos and maps and newspaper cuttings that covered the facing wall. Sally was stood examining the cuttings. The photo of Delaney in uniform holding the young Gloria in his arms had been circled many times in green ink. She looked at the rest of the material, baffled.

'What does it all mean, sir?' she asked.

'I don't know,' Delaney replied, picking up a photo from the table – the same photo that had hung on the wall of The Crawfish pub. The photo of Peter Garnier with Graham Hall, Father Michael Fitzpatrick, Tim Radnor, the unknown fisherman and in the background behind the bar a blonde woman whose identity he couldn't make out.

He turned over the photo and written on the back were the names he had just been running through, and one other. Bill Thompson.

He handed the photo over to Sally, who whistled silently and reached for her mobile.

Delaney put his hand on her arm. 'What are you doing, Sally?'

'Phoning it in, sir.'

'No, you're not!' he said in a voice that cut short any argument. He pointed to the montage on the wall behind her. 'This changes everything.'

Sally looked at him for a moment and then nodded. 'Sir.'

Delaney hit the speed dial on his own mobile. 'Dave,' he said as the call was answered. 'I need an address in Harrow, I need it quick and it stays between you and me – okay?' He listened and nodded. 'I owe you one. The name is Bill Thompson.'

*

Archie Wood's stomach hurt, and every time he closed his eyes he could see the man's hungry eyes staring back at him. He huddled into the corner. He didn't know where the man was. He hadn't seen him in a long while. But he was scared of him. He remembered getting up one morning six months ago, and finding his pet dog, a Golden Labrador called Honey, lying in front of the cold fire in the front room of his house. Dead. Her eyes had been open, staring coldly. No light in them. They'd been like the man's eyes.

Archie put his arms around himself and pulled his knees up to his chest. He wished Honey was still alive. She would have protected him. She would never have let him be taken away from his home, from his dad and his mum. Thinking of his mum made his eyes sting. He blinked, trying to hold back the tears. He just wanted his mum to come through the door and rescue him. He snuggled deeper into the corner, making himself as small as possible. He didn't even have his own clothes. He'd hated the jumper with a picture of a giraffe on it that his mum had given him for one of his birthday presents. But he wished he had it back now. He felt the tears starting again and squeezed his eyes shut hard. Big boys don't cry. That's what his dad always said to him. Big boys don't cry.

Then he heard a key being fitted into a lock and the creaking sound of an old door opening in the hallway outside. He heard the footsteps again and tried to huddle even closer into the corner. He kept his eyes shut and didn't even try to stop the tears that were flowing from them now.

The mantra in his head sounding again and again, trying to blot out the cold and the fear and the pain.

'The wheels on the bus go round and round. Round and round. Round and round. The wheels on the bus go round and round. And round and round again.'

*

Delaney picked his way through the rubbish-strewn back garden of Bill Thompson's house in Hill Road, fifty yards from Carlton Row. The grass, what was left of it, was overgrown and shot through with weeds. There were blue plastic crates dotted throughout, rubble, broken bottles, empty beer cans and a distinctive smell that Delaney couldn't place. It wasn't pleasant.

'What is that smell?' Delaney asked Sally

Cartwright as she followed behind him, stepping carefully over the rubble and garbage.

'I have no idea, sir,' she said, with a grimace. 'But it smells like something's died.'

Delaney nodded. 'That's what I was worried about.'

A short while later and Delaney kicked in the back door of the house. This time it opened easily – the wood was quite rotten in the frame. They stepped into a large tile-flagged kitchen. It reminded Delaney of Graham Harper's, but bigger. Built sometime in the 1950s, probably, and not been much touched since. The smell was stronger inside the house. A salty, fetid, sickly sweet, rotting smell. There were two shop-size chest freezers running along the wall that faced the sink unit, which was long, made of stainless steel and looked industrial.

And in one corner, leaning casually against a cupboard, was a long-handled axe, the blade stained brown with dried blood. Blood that had pooled into a sticky mass on the floor.

Sally Cartwright slipped on a pair of forensic gloves and opened the first freezer. It took a bit of a wrench. Inside were the frozen, broken remains of crab legs and lobster legs and claws and shells.

Delaney looked at it, puzzled.

'It's shickle, sir,' said the young detective constable.

'Shickle?'

'The remains of crabs and lobsters once the meat's been processed or dressed. All the stuff that's left over.'

'So why's he got a freezer full of it?'

323

'It's what they do, sir. They freeze the live crabs and lobsters first before cooking them and they freeze the shickle, like I say, after they have dressed the meat.'

'Why?'

'Because of the smell.'

Delaney wrinkled his nose. 'I can see that.'

'Then the fishermen chuck the frozen stuff back in the sea the next day, before bringing in that day's catch.'

'You seem to know a lot about it, constable.'

'I have an aunt lives on the North Norfolk coast, sir. Used to have our summer holidays there. Not much I don't know about Cromer crab.'

Delaney nodded to the next freezer and Sally opened it. It came open a lot easier.

Delaney looked inside. He didn't speak for a moment and then he said, 'I guess this one is more my area of expertise.'

'Yes, sir,' said Sally Cartwright.

'And it looks like we got it wrong again.'

*

Jennifer Hickling took the thick envelope that the manager gave her and put it into her pocket.

'Are you sure you wouldn't prefer a banker's draft? That is a large amount of cash to be carrying around.'

'This is fine, thanks,' said Jennifer, her voice almost betraying her true age.

She was so close now. They both were. To getting away. To making the Waterhill just a bad memory, a bad dream. Time to wake up.

She nodded at the bank manager and hurried out of her office, through the bank proper and out onto the high street.

As Jenny came out of the bank she looked up at the sky. It was starting to grow dark. The streaks of red that had smoked through the sky during the day were thicker now, darker, almost purple. She pulled the zipper on her jacket up to her neck and looked at her watch. She still had time. She decided to forget about the bus and get a taxi – she had the money now, after all, and she didn't want her sister waiting any longer for her than she had to. Jenny pictured her standing at the school gates with the innocent smile that she herself used to once have. Before her mother was put in prison and she had been placed in the loving care of her uncle.

She walked along the pavement, staring into the distance, craning her neck to see the familiar lit yellow sign showing that a taxi was for hire. She thrust her hands deep in her pockets, one cradling the packet of money, the other curled around the handle of the knife.

She didn't see the dark-haired older woman walking towards her with hate in her eyes or the man in the black suit behind her with a look in his own eyes every bit as full of passion and purpose.

Jennifer never made it to the school gates.

*

Sally looked out of the car window. It was dark now. She knew it was late in the year. But it shouldn't be so dark this early. So cold. She tapped on the car's heating controls and turned the temperature up a degree or two. Beside her Delaney was staring intently through the windscreen, a hundred per cent focused, which was just as well because he was driving with the accelerator floored. She held onto the strap as he swerved in and out of the traffic, overtaking on the left and right, oblivious to the blaring horns and flashing headlights. Delaney never drove if he could help it, which was what was unnerving Sally more than the speed they were travelling at. At least they were in her car, which was fully serviced and maintained. She hated to think what it would have been like if he had been driving his own old and less than fully maintained Saab 900.

She looked out of the window and remembered her childhood trips to the coast. They had travelled in the pitch dark sometimes. That was because her dad had always wanted to leave at the crack of dawn – sometime before it, in fact. Her mother refused to go on the motorway and so they had had to take the longer route and he always wanted to get going early when there ware no cars on the roads. There was plenty of traffic today, though. Plenty of it. And Delaney was zigzagging through it like a metham-phetamine-fuelled maniac in a demolition derby.

Sally shivered again and reflected on how fast things were moving now. Both literally and metaphorically. She just hoped that they weren't too late. They finally had their man: she just hoped that Delaney would get them there in time – and in one piece – to save the missing boy, who had been away from his home for four days now. The statistics weren't good.

She looked down at the invoice that Mrs Blaylock had given her. Dated from the summer of 1995 when this had all begun. But then she realised it had all begun earlier, like everything does. The perpetual cycle of paedophilia and abuse seeding itself through generation after generation after generation. Like cancer, Delaney had said, and he was right. She crumpled the paper in her hand again as Delaney swerved violently again to avoid an oncoming minibus.

A short while previously Mrs Blaylock had been puzzled to see Detective Inspector Jack Delaney and DC Sally Cartwright standing on her front doorstep once more.

'Can I help you?' she had asked.

'When we here earlier you said something to your son, Mrs Blaylock.'

'Yes . . . ?'

'About your husband being a proper publican.'

'He was. Not like that layabout waste of space who's run the place into rack and ruin. That pub was supposed to be my pension. '

'So he no doubt kept proper records?'

'Of course he did. He never fell foul of the law. Any of them.'

It was a shame the same couldn't be said about her brother, Sally couldn't help thinking as the woman led them into the house. Sally willed her hand off the side passenger strap and stared ahead, not wanting to give her boss the faintest idea of how absolutely terrified she was. Thick blobs of moisture fell onto the windscreen. Not quite hail, not quite snow, not quite rain. Fat splashes of sleet, she supposed, and felt the knot tighten in her stomach once more as Delaney blinked, leaning forward and trying to see before flicking on the windscreen wipers and not slowing the car down at all.

Sally shivered a little again, and not just from the cold. She was dreading what they would find at Bill Thompson's house down on the Thames estuary, and remembering what they had seen in his place near Carlton Row.

The small child's bedroom which looked like it hadn't been touched since the mid-1950s. A wardrobe with a young boy's clothes in it. Pictures from annuals pasted on the wall. A bedraggled teddy bear sitting on a small wooden chair. The whole room covered with dust.

And the other bedroom. Strewn with an older man's clothes. A chest of drawers full of pictures of children. Obscene pictures that had brought tears to Sally's young eyes, eyes that had already seen far too much suffering visited on children in her few years with the police. Pictures that had brought tears to Delaney's eyes, too. Tears that he wasn't ashamed to show.

And in the other freezer, next to the shickle-filled one. Frozen in a single clear block of ice. A Catholic priest, his eyes closed, his hands by his sides. Like some bizarre religious relic. Father Fitzpatrick, the fifth member of Peter Garnier's group. Sally couldn't understand how these people found each other out and made their associations. She only knew that they did. And for every paedophile ring that the Met or the international police forces busted, more would spring up around the world. Like fungal growth.

But most of those in this particular ring were either dead or dying and that left only one. Bill Thompson. The fisherman. The crab and lobster dealer. The fragment of shell found in Maureen Gallagher's ear made perfect sense now. Even if how she'd become involved in it all didn't. Sally understood why the severed head had been put on the altar at Saint Botolph's: it was indicating the identity of the priest at the time of the murdered children's capture. Father Fitzpatrick, who would never harm a child again and whom she fervently hoped was even now burning in hell. Sally understood that but she didn't understand why Maureen Gallagher had been killed. Maybe it had just been bad luck. The wrong place at the wrong time. Like Samuel Ramirez and Alice Peters.

Sally turned to Delaney, who was still gripping the steering wheel as if it might come off the column into his hands. 'Sir—' she said but that was all as Delaney snapped back at her.

'Not now, Sally.'

She nodded and took out her mobile, hitting the speed dial. 'Hello, sergeant,' she said as the phone was answered and then she frowned, covering for Delaney. 'I'm not sure where we are and the inspector's a bit busy right now. He just asked me to see if you could chase up Crimint. Did we get any results back on Maureen Gallagher? Has she been in the system at any time?' Sally nodded again. 'Just text back if the signal's out of range,' she said as Delaney entered a tunnel and the phone, true to her prediction, cut straight out.

Sally closed her eyes as the blinding flash of another pair of headlamps swept over them, a screaming horn held down for long seconds as they passed. And she kept her eyes pretty much closed for the rest of the journey, which thankfully wasn't for long. It was probably the quickest journey in terms of speed that she had ever made in a car, but it absolutely felt like the longest.

She whispered a little prayer silently in her head, over and over again. 'Now I lay me down to sleep, I pray the Lord my soul to keep; should I die before I wake, I pray the Lord my soul to take.'

*

Voices were singing in Bill Thompson's head.

The man on the radio walking in a rainstorm, trying to wash the pain and hurt away. Failing. He was remembering the smell of the shickle, ripe in his throat, the sharp cuts in his knees as he was forced to kneel on the slivers of lobster and crab shell.

His uncle singing along to the music. Grunting. Drowning out the sound of Bill's own screams, the tears running down his face, marking him. He looked across at the small window again, fifty-six years later, stained so green with algae that hardly any light filtered through and the bottom of the ocean that he was in was now as dark and as cold as the deepest sea on earth.

He looked down at his twitching right hand, arching it so that the sinews stood out like cord and made the blood vessels move below the translucent skin like thin blue slugs. His fingers curled inward, making his hand a crab once more.

The year of Our Lord 2010.

He moved his head weakly to one side, looking up

at the figure above him, his right eye wet with tears, his left blind, unfocused. He tried to work the muscles in his lips and managed a 'please'. Or what passed for it. But he couldn't manage the words *don't shoot*.

But Jack Delaney was perfectly capable of speech.

'He's right, Gloria,' said Delaney. 'Put down the gun.'

And the girl in the boot spun round to point the shaking gun that she held in her small, perfectly formed hand at her rescuer from thirteen years earlier.

'I don't think so,' she said.

*

Bennett had parked his car further up the beach. He walked across the sand carefully. The sky overhead was dark with rain and the visibility was poor. He was dressed in a black overcoat with a Black Watch cap on his head. If somebody had been standing twenty yards away they probably wouldn't have seen him coming. Which was just as Bennett liked it. Moving unseen. Coming up on people unexpectedly. It was what he was trained for after all. It was what he was good at.

That, and killing people.

*

Delaney held his hand up, placating, putting himself between Sally and Gloria. Gloria's eyes were dancing. Wild with anger. With pain.

'I remembered, Jack. I remembered what he did to me. Peter Garnier appearing on television was like a

331

key turning. Stuff that I had been holding back for so very long came flooding back to me.'

'I know,' said Delaney. Tears pricking in his own eyes as he saw the pain in the young woman's as her mind took in again the horror of what had happened to her.

'And not just him, but Peter Garnier and the priest and Graham Harper and the young one who had the camera and took the pictures and filmed it as it was happening.'

'I know,' said Delaney once more. 'But this is not the way. Look at him. He's helpless.'

Delaney pointed at the frail old man lying on the floor, his right side twitching, the left half of his face slack and unmoving, drool running from the corner of that lip onto his chin. His one watery eye, pleading and pathetic.

'Why did you have to kill them, Gloria? Why kill the woman?'

'She didn't,' said a voice behind him and Delaney looked round shocked to see a single-barrelled shotgun pointing straight at him. Shocked even more to see who was holding it.

*

'Jack Delaney, saviour of little girls, and here you are, finally, in the flesh.'

'I'm sorry – I don't know who you are,' Delaney said, clearly puzzled.

'Oh yes, you do,' said the blonde woman, who had big wide innocent blue eyes. 'I waited for you, but you never came. All these years and you never came for me like you did for Gloria.'

332

'Who are you?'

'She's Alice Peters, sir,' said Sally Cartwright. The thought that had been niggling at the back of her mind during the car journey suddenly came clear to her. 'She's Maureen Gallagher's daughter.'

The woman smiled, and her face softened. Her voice became that of a child. A seven-year-old girl. 'That's right. I'm Alice Peters,' she said and Delaney felt the hairs on his arms and on the back of his neck rise. 'I'm a good girl.'

'Why don't you put the gun down, Gloria?' said Delaney. 'You don't have to be part of this.'

'I didn't remember. Not all of it,' said Gloria, her voice trembling. 'Even after you came to see me and Mary. I had flashes of it after Garnier started appearing on television. But then you led Alice to me – she'd been following you, Jack. And she showed me the photo and told me their names, and then I remembered.' Tears sprang into her eyes. 'I remembered it all. They hurt me, Jack. They hurt me so badly.'

Delaney felt like telling her to go ahead and pull the trigger but he knew that his cousin would never forgive him if he did. It struck Delaney that this was the real therapy that most victims of abuse needed. Revenge. But he looked again at the seemingly angelic face of Alice Peters and changed his mind. There were all kinds of madness in the world. Not all of it could be cured the same way.

But he didn't have to say anything.

Gloria looked down at the sick man, who was twitching on the floor like a crab that had had its back stepped on, and let the gun slip from her fingers.

Delaney could see now that the gun was only in fact a taser, but he wouldn't have been surprised if the shock of it would have killed the man anyway. He didn't look like he had many days of breath left in him and Delaney felt no sorrow at the fact. Gloria crossed to him and Delaney held her in his arms, mindful of the shotgun still trained on him and Sally.

'You don't look strong enough to cut off your mother's head. Did you have help?' he asked Alice as he kissed the top of Gloria's head and hugged her to him, making reassuring sounds as best he could. He was trying to keep Alice talking.

'Yeah. She had help killing the whore,' said a deep voice.

Delaney looked up, surprised once more.

*

Alice seemed to have grown taller, her shoulders thrown back, her eyes full of knowledge now, full of anger.

'I look after little Alice when that old pervert,' she pointed at Bill Thompson, 'doesn't keep me locked up with drugs and tasers and ropes.'

'And what's your name?' asked Delaney, fighting to keep his voice level, the hairs on his neck standing up again, his mind whirling. He looked across to the taser lying at Thompson's feet and knew that he wouldn't have time to reach it before she pulled the trigger.

'George,' she said. 'My name is George. And I know who you are. You're the disappointment.' Her voice was still unnervingly deep.

'And is Alice there, is she with you?' asked Sally.

'Alice is safe, but she doesn't want to talk to you right now.'

Delaney was sure it was his imagination but it seemed that the ends of the young woman's hair were sticking out now too, as if they'd been brushed with static electricity. 'What happened then, George? How did you get free?' he asked.

The woman shuddered and her eyes closed. When she opened them again, they were different once more. 'George doesn't like you, Inspector Delaney,' she said in the voice of the young woman they had first met.

'Why is that?'

'Because you disappointed little Alice.' She pointed at Gloria. 'You were in the papers for rescuing her. She was supposed to be Alice's replacement. Little Alice was too old for him at eleven. But Gloria never came and so he kept her. And as she grew older he drugged her and beat her and made her work. And used her. And every couple of years he made her speak to other children and get them to play. And after a while he killed them. Like Peter Garnier killed the little boy all those years ago.'

'And he kept him in the deep freezer.'

'Yes.'

'Why?'

'He used hot water so the ice froze clear. So he could show the children, you understand.'

'No,' said Delaney, his head spinning.

'He'd show the children the little boy's body so that they could see what would happen to them if they didn't do what he said. And then he made them do things.'

'And why didn't he kill *you*, Alice?'

Alice closed her eyes and then opened them again, her voice once more that of a little girl's. 'Because I was special. I could play with the children. I could bring them to the party. And I always had ice cream.' She shuddered again, her eyes widening, her nostrils flaring, her adult woman's voice thick with anger. 'Gloria never came and you never rescued me.'

Delaney nodded, keeping his voice calm. He could hear police sirens in the distance and wondered who had called them. He needed to keep her talking. 'It wasn't her fault. And if Garnier had brought Gloria down here he would have killed little Alice too.'

The woman's face crumpled. 'But you could have rescued me too,' she said in the frightened whisper of a little girl. 'But nobody ever came. Never.'

She squeezed her eyes shut as tears poured out and Delaney dived for the taser, rolling up to his feet and pointing it at her.

Only her eyes were wide open now and this time they were furious.

'Nobody hurts Alice any more!' she screamed at him.

And Delaney pulled the trigger, sending fifty thousand volts into the woman's body. She staggered back and her body convulsed but she stayed standing and her mouth pulled wide in a rictus grin as she levelled the shotgun at Delaney.

'You'll have to do better than that,' she said.

'No!' screamed Gloria as she threw herself at Delaney.

And Alice Peters pulled the trigger.

*

The scream seemed to hang in the air as if time were suspended. Delaney rolled over and looked around. Alice was lying on the floor with Tony Bennett holding her down. Kate was standing behind him. She rushed across as Delaney and Gloria stood up.

'Are you all right, Jack?' she asked breathlessly.

'I'm fine. What the hell are you doing here?'

'Tony brought me.'

Kate walked across to the body of Bill Thompson. The shotgun blast had removed most of his face. It seemed a ridiculous thing to do but she knelt down and put her hand on his wrist. She was not at all surprised to find that he had no pulse.

Delaney walked to the back of the large boathouse, to the door from behind which the scream had sounded. The door was locked but a shoulder charge from Delaney battered it loose to hang from one hinge. Inside, huddled in the corner, Archie Woods looked up at him with wide frightened eyes.

'It's all right, Archie,' said Delaney. 'You're safe now.'

He held his arms wide and the little boy, sensing that Delaney was right and that he was indeed safe, ran into their enfolding embrace.

Delaney stepped out of the boat shed, the young boy cradled in his arms hanging onto his neck.

A broadside of flashbulbs blinded him momentarily and then he saw the army of news reporters and photographers behind the cordon line that had already been set up. At the forefront Melanie Jones, as ever . . . only this time she wasn't shouting questions at him, she was clapping her

337

hands and smiling. Delaney looked at her for a moment and then nodded.

*

Bennett handed Delaney a cup of tea as, behind them, a squad of SOCO and CID headed into the boat shed. Bennett shook his head, puzzled. 'She could kill all those people. Could cut the head off her own mother, and yet couldn't bring herself to kill the man who had been holding her captive all these years.'

'The adult Alice couldn't – the controlling personality.'

'Stockholm syndrome?'

Delaney shrugged. 'Something like it . . . which was why she brought Gloria here to do it for her, I guess.'

'And she couldn't kill Thompson either?'

'No. And I'm glad. She's had enough to deal with as it is.'

'You'd have pulled the trigger?'

Delaney looked at him for a moment. 'I take it you're not really from Doncaster?' he said, taking a sip of the hot, sweet tea.

'No. Organised crime tactical unit. Right here in this fair city. CO19 before that.'

'So. How did you find us?'

'You were under investigation, Jack.'

'Me?' said Delaney, trying to keep his face neutral. A number of possibilities running through his mind about what he could have been investigated for. None of them good.

'A guy called Alexander Zaitsev. Came here in the early 1990s. Russian Mafia. A major, major player. Drug dealing, prostitution, people trafficking. He's been the focus of our attention for a long time and today we moved to close him down. Multitask forces from the States, Russia, France, Holland and Great Britain all coordinating.'

Delaney's brow furrowed. 'What the hell's that got to do with me?'

'Zaitsev's London accountant.'

Delaney took another sip of his tea and the penny dropped. 'Roger Yates,' he said.

'Exactly. Your brother-in-law. Up to his neck in laundering money for Zaitsev. We weren't sure about your connection. You just bought a house in Belsize Park and paid a very large deposit in cash. Let's just say our interest was piqued. As was Zaitsev's: he wasn't sure if Yates was feeding you information, apparently, so he tried to take you out.'

'The shooter at the burger van?'

'Yep.'

'And the woods?'

Bennett shook his head.

'How can you be sure?'

'Someone like Zaitsev goes down and, believe me, there are all kinds of high-level lieutenants queuing up to do a deal.'

'So who did it?'

'Don't know. But it wasn't the Russians.'

'But it was this Zaitsev who worked Roger over?'

Bennett nodded. 'His people, anyway. Yates wasn't supposed to survive.'

Delaney shrugged. 'This is all news to me.'

'I know, inspector. Yates agreed to give us what we needed. He's turned Queen's evidence. You're in the clear on this.'

Delaney nodded, relieved: he had too many skeletons in the closet for too much close examination. 'I still don't understand how you came to be here.'

'Just in the nick of time, too.' Bennett smiled.

'Well, yes.' Delaney didn't like to dwell too much on the recent memory of a deranged woman pointing a shotgun at him and pulling the trigger.

'After the operation today I was in White City briefing your boss,' said Bennett. 'Kate spoke to me – she was worried about you when you dropped off the radar.'

'And . . .'

Bennett grinned more widely. 'And you didn't drop off *my* radar . . . I had a tracer on you.'

Delaney finished his tea. 'Please tell me your name's not Tony Bennett, at least?'

Bennett held his grin. 'Nah. It's Tony Hamilton.'

Delaney held his hand out. 'Nice to meet you. Thanks for the assist.'

The younger cop slapped him on the arm. 'Well, you're the poster boy for the Met, aren't you? We couldn't have your face plastered over that boathouse wall.'

Delaney grimaced again at the memory. 'What's going to happen to Roger?'

Tony Hamilton shrugged. 'Don't know. Witness-protection programme, I should imagine. You'll probably never see him again.'

Delaney crumpled the plastic beaker in his hand. 'I always knew he was a little shit.'

Hamilton slapped him on the arm again. 'Well, his shit just got canned, Jack.'

Delaney looked at him and shook his head, a slow

smile forming, and pointed at his leg. 'So you really did that playing rugby?'

'Nah. I fell off a pushbike.'

And Delaney laughed.

TUESDAY

Diane Campbell stood next to Delaney's desk by the open window. Outside dawn was breaking. The sky was clear again with only the faintest of red streaks far away in the distance. She blew out a stream of smoke into the cold air, her breath frosting with it, half-listening as Kate Walker talked and watching as a small dark-haired woman barked some orders she couldn't hear at Bennett or Hamilton or whatever his name was supposed to be, and hurried in towards the HQ entrance. Hamilton followed behind carrying a cardboard tray and a guilty grin on his face like an admonished schoolboy. Diane smiled dryly herself, it looked like Hamilton's boss had just as much trouble with him as she did with Jack Delaney. She realised she had missed what Kate was saying. 'Sorry, what was that?' she asked.

'Multiple-personality disorder or MPD is not as rare as some people think,' said Kate.

'And it's usually women?' asked Delaney.

Kate nodded. 'About eight times more frequent in women than in men. Although the figures may be skewed as men with MPD tend to be violent and may never be diagnosed because they are put into prison rather than hospital.'

'And it's linked into the abuse?'

'Absolutely. Alice Peters is a textbook case. Gloria was able to block out the memory of what had happened to her. But Alice clearly couldn't – it was happening on a daily basis. The level of abuse she suffered, and over such a period of time, shattered her. Literally shattered her personality, creating what are called alters to deal with the different emotions. These alters can take on different genders, ages, even nationalities and can speak in foreign languages.'

'Really?'

'Oh yeah. Not only that: their body characteristics can change, different alters can have different heart rates, skin temperatures, different allergies, even asthma, and most pertinently they can have different pain thresholds.'

'Was that why the taser didn't take her down, then? Like someone on PCP?'

'It's possible.' Kate nodded. 'Sometimes the alters aren't even human. They can be animals or creatures from myth and legend. It's to do with disassociation. The emotions like fear or anger or sadness become personalities in their own right. What you saw as George was Alice's anger formed into a completely different personality. A very real person, nonetheless. A very *dangerous* person. When Garnier appeared on television saying that he was going to lead police to the bodies Thompson had a stroke, judging from what Alice has told us.'

'And that gave George a chance to escape?'

'Yes, and the other personalities. But George is the strong one. The one who took revenge for Alice.'

'And how many of them are in her, then?'

Kate shrugged. 'Could be up to a hundred, could be as few as the three you met. Again, women have on average more personalities with the condition than men. The average for women is fifteen but, like I say, given the nature of the abuse and its duration, the drugging, the torture, the degradation . . .' She shook her head sadly. 'God only knows what she went through. But I can understand why she, or George, did what they did.' Kate took a sip of water. It had been a long night but she didn't feel at all tired. 'Ellie Peters sold her own daughter to Peter Garnier. According to Alice she had told her that she was going to be adopted by somebody who didn't have a baby of their own. Someone who could look after her better.'

'Right.' Delaney shook his head, disgusted.

'But I think Ellie Peters always knew what had really happened to her daughter. That's why when she finally sobered up – she couldn't live with the guilt.'

'The scarring on her back?'

'Self-inflicted.'

'Opus Dei?' asked Diane.

Kate shrugged. 'Something like it. I think she was glad to die in the end.'

'Certainly deserved to,' said Jack.

'The thing of it is,' said Kate, 'we make people like Garnier and Thompson into grotesques, into some kind of rare monster. But the truth is that the kind of thing that happened to Alice is happening to kids every day in this country. The Russian outfit that Bennett was involved in closing down, they traffic in people, not just grown women but young boys and girls. Babies even. Babies, born of prostitutes forced

347

into the sex trade as slaves. Their children taken away and used as commodities. It's happening every day in every city all around the world. And what do we do about it?'

'We do what we can,' said Delaney.

'Well, it's not enough!'

Detective Inspector Tony Hamilton chose that moment to walk into the CID room carrying the cardboard tray which Diane could now see had coffees on it, and a paper bag under his arm.

'I bring caffeine and doughnuts,' he said, grinning.

'I didn't think we'd see you here again,' said Kate, smiling back at him.

'Unfinished business,' he said, looking around. 'Where's that pretty young detective constable?'

'Not in yet,' said Diane Campbell pointedly. 'Anything I can help you with?'

Hamilton held the tray forward for her to take a cup of coffee. 'Not unless you plan on changing your sexual orientation, ma'am,' he said with a wink, and put the tray and doughnuts down on Delaney's desk. Then he pulled out a couple of 4x6 photos from his jacket pocket. 'And it's Kate and Jack I came to see.' He laid the photos down.

'I know her,' said Kate, pointing to a picture of Jennifer that was lying next to a close-up photo of a knife wound. 'She's the girl who was attacked in Camden High Street, remember?'

'I do,' said Bennett. 'Her real name is Jennifer Hickling but she was going under false ID. She managed to fall foul of the wrong people working prostitution in the area. My colleagues brought her to me.'

348

Kate picked up the photo of the knife wound. 'They killed her?'

*

Hamilton shook his head. 'Not at all. That's a photo of Jamil Azeez's wound. It matches a knife we found on her when she was arrested alongside the woman who was warning her off her patch.'

'She stabbed Jamil?'

Hamilton shook his head. 'I don't know. I've just got this information. She's being held downstairs.' He looked at Diane. 'She needs to be interviewed, but I don't work here any more.'

'The woman you came with . . .' said Diane.

Hamilton grinned. 'The black-widow spider. Beautiful but deadly.'

'Your boss?'

'Yeah.' Hamilton looked at his watch. 'And I'm due for a debriefing with her and your governor three minutes ago. I better get out of here or she'll have my head.'

Diane flicked her long-finished cigarette out of the window. 'You up for it, Jack?'

Delaney took a sip of his coffee and winked at her. 'I was born up for it, boss.'

Dear God, thought Diane Campbell, and she wasn't the first person to do so. There's two of them.

*

A uniformed guard brought Jennifer Hickling into Kate's police surgeon's office. Delaney was stood by the window.

'Take a seat, Jennifer,' said Kate sympathetically.

The girl was looking her fifteen years now. Her make-up had been scrubbed off and beneath the hard goth exterior that she had worn on the streets was the face of a young, frightened and unhappy girl.

'It's about the knife, isn't it?' Jenny said.

'You don't have to say anything, Jennifer,' said Delaney. 'This isn't a proper interview. You haven't been charged. The doctor here is just going to check that you will be okay to be interviewed properly when we can get you a solicitor and a responsible adult there for you.'

'It doesn't matter,' said Jennifer. 'It wasn't my knife. He dropped it when he ran away. The other man.' She blinked back some tears. 'I thought he was dead.'

'No, he's not dead, Jennifer,' said Kate softly.

'What other man?' asked Delaney.

'I don't know. I heard the man cry out and the other man ran away, dropping the knife.'

'What did he look like?' asked Delaney, having a shrewd idea of exactly what he looked like.

'He was like the first one. An Arab man,' she said, proving Delaney completely wrong.

'What's going to happen to me now?' asked Jennifer. 'I can't stay here. I have to get home. My sister isn't safe.'

'You had a large amount of money on you when you were arrested, Jennifer,' said Delaney.

Jennifer shrank back in the chair. 'It's mine. I earned it. It's so we could get away.'

'It's okay, Jennifer, you don't have to say anything. Not now,' said Kate.

'But I have to. He might hurt her!' she said

'Who?' asked Delaney.

'My aunt's boyfriend.'

*

Dawn had broken an hour earlier on the Waterhill estate but there were very few signs of life stirring.

Angela Hickling, yawning and with tousled hair, opened the front door, puzzled to see Jack Delaney and Kate Walker standing on the doorstep.

'Who are you?' she asked

'We're the police,' said Delaney.

The colour drained from the young girl's face.

'It's okay, Angela,' said Kate. 'Jennifer is perfectly safe – she is waiting for you in the car, see?'

Jennifer was sitting with Sally Cartwright in the back of Kate's car. She waved across to her sister.

'What do you want, then?'

'We came to get you.'

'And I came to have a word with your aunt's boyfriend. I understand you aunt doesn't live here any more?' said Delaney, with a reassuring smile that belied his true emotions as the girl shook her head. 'He hasn't hurt you, has he?'

'No.'

'Come on, then. Let's go and see Jennifer.' Kate took the young girl's hand and led her away as a man stumbled down the stairs and into the hall.

Delaney stepped into the house, pulling the door half shut behind him.

'Who the fuck are you?' said the man, blinking at him.

'You don't know?' asked Delaney.

'No, I fucking don't.'

'Good,' said Delaney and punched him hard on the bridge of the nose, dropping him like a stun-gunned pig.

Delaney looked down at the motionless man for a satisfied moment. 'We'll be back to pick you up later,' he said.

Delaney closed the door behind him and looked across to see Jennifer Hickling, out of the car now, hugging her little sister. Hugging her as if her life depended on it.

Maybe it did.

He pulled out his phone and punched in some numbers, his breath frosting in the cold air as he waited for it to be answered.

'Mary,' he said, 'it's Jack. I need your help.'

*

An hour later and Delaney and Kate stood in Dean Anderson's office, watching through the windows as uniformed police led a handcuffed Malik Hussein across the quad to waiting police cars. Sally Cartwright peeled off from the group, heading towards the office.

'The Outback is very popular with the gay community,' Delaney was telling the Dean. 'I suppose there was a clue in the name.'

'That copy of The Catcher in the Rye in Jamil's room. The dedication in the front . . . ?' Kate asked.

Sheila Anderson smiled sadly. 'I originally gave it to my son in his first year at university,' she said. 'He died last year in Afghanistan. 33 Engineer Regiment. The Royal Engineers.'

'I'm sorry for your loss,' said Delaney.

'Thank you, inspector. So much wasted youth.' She took a breath and smiled. 'I had lent the book to Matt Henson. It is a book that speaks to the young and Matt had difficulty with reading. I was helping him with that.'

'And so was Jamil?'

'It looks that way, yes.'

'Matt has great potential. The potential to be different.'

'Different from his brother and father, you mean?' asked Kate.

'Yes. And different from what was written down for him. It's what education is all about.'

'At least, it used to be,' said Kate.

'True,' conceded the Dean. 'Money seems to be the driving force for a lot of institutions nowadays. But not all. Not all.'

Sally knocked on the door as a courtesy. 'He didn't even deny it,' she said as she came in. 'Seemed proud of himself, in fact, said he was disappointed that Jamil was going to live but there was a death sentence waiting for him when he gets home anyway.'

'They execute homosexuals in Iran, Sally,' said Delaney.

'I know, sir,' the detective constable replied, with a quirked eyebrow. 'I do read the news!' She looked pointedly at the paper on the Dean's desk. It was a copy of the *Guardian* but it could have been a copy of any of them – they all carried the shot of Delaney coming out of the boat shed on the previous evening, carrying Archie Woods in his arms.

'He won't be going home,' said the Dean. 'He'll be

staying in England. What will happen to Matt Henson?'

'He's already been released.'

'Released to what, though? His father will disown him.'

'Strikes me,' said Kate, 'that his is one family he would be better off without.'

'Says something about a country in which a man would rather go to prison for attempted murder than admit his sexuality to his family,' said the Dean.

'Don't get me started on this country!' said Delaney.

*

Kate yawned as the car moved slowly through the busy traffic, heading back to White City. The sleepless night finally catching up with her. 'There's one thing I still don't get,' she said.

Delaney looked across at her from the front passenger seat. 'What's that, darlin'?'

'Tony Hamilton was pretty certain that it wasn't one of those Russian gangsters trying to take you out in Mad Bess Woods?'

'He was.'

'So who was the shooter? Who were they after?'

'Peter Garnier. Like I always said. The shooter slipped as he took the shot. Didn't get a chance to take another.'

'We know it wasn't Alice Peters so who was it trying to kill him, then?'

'I think it was Garnier himself.'

'What are you on about, sir?' asked Sally from the back seat, looking at Delaney as if he were mad.

354

Delaney reached into his pocket and pulled out the catering glove that he had taken off Roy from the burger van.

'I think he got Fitzpatrick to send word about where he would be – and when – to Tim Radnor. That's why he was in the woods that morning: he knew all along that the bodies weren't there. Because he knew it wasn't him that had killed one of the children and that the other was still alive.'

'Tim Radnor was the young one, the catering assistant?' asked Kate.

'Yeah. But Harrow School also trains army cadets. They have access to current fully working field-issue combat rifles. They have a rifle club and Radnor was a member.' He tapped the glove again. 'We found a minute piece of plastic on the cartridge casing that had the edge of one of these little dimples – see? Can't prove it now but I'd bet my life that was what happened.'

'Why, sir?'

'What's it all ever about with people like Garnier, Sally. You said it yourself. Power. The power over life and death. Particularly your own. Garnier didn't much like what was in store for him in his own future. He'd kill himself if he could.' He smiled coldly. 'But I've had a word with the right people.'

WEDNESDAY

Peter Garnier rolled furiously on his bed. He was in a straitjacket. And the walls and the floor of his room were padded. He looked up and shouted as the window in the door of his special cell was opened, as it was every twenty minutes, and a guard looked in on him. The window closed again and tears ran from Garnier's eyes. Soon they wouldn't even need to put him in a straitjacket . . . and it could take years for him to die.

*

The annexe or The Pig and Whistle pub, a truncheon's twirl or two from the White City police station, was always popular with uniform and plain clothes alike. That Wednesday night was no exception. It was packed wall to wall with upbeat coppers. The talent nights were always a big draw but the recent closing of the so-called Death Row murders and the safe return of Archie Woods gave them even more excuse for celebration.

Danny Vine held his hand up to quell the noise – shouted comments, catcalls, even some laughter. 'So I said to him,' he said, 'how was I supposed to know she had a wooden leg?'

An audible groan swept around the pub like a Mexican wave.

'Get off!' someone in the large and merry crowd shouted.

Danny stood closer to the microphone that was on a small stage set up at one end of the pub

'As the bard put it,' he said into the microphone, 'if my jokes have amused, please raise your glass, and if they haven't . . . then kiss my arse!' He swept a theatrical wave and got the biggest cheer of his set. He jumped down to be handed a pint by one of his colleagues out of uniform and was slapped on the back, none too gently, by a few more.

From the other end of the bar Kate could see Sally Cartwright watching him, amused. 'What about you and him, then?' she asked her.

'What about us?'

Kate waggled her hand horizontally. 'Are you?'

Sally laughed. 'Are we what, exactly?'

Kate laughed herself. 'What is the term you young people use nowadays? Walking out, an item . . .' She paused for effect. 'Are you bonking him?'

Sally shook her head. 'No, I am not!'

'Shame. He's a very attractive young man. Fit too, by the looks of it.'

'No doubt . . . but I have had my share of work-based romance, thank you very much. And I have decided to pass.'

'Michael Hills was a very different person to Danny.'

'What . . . a psychotic delusional pervert and a murderer, you mean?'

Kate nodded, smiling. 'Yeah, that.'

'No, I'm going to keep my life simple for a while, Doctor Walker. Concentrate on the job.'

Kate grimaced. 'There's a lot to be said for it.'

Sally looked around. 'And where is the DI, anyway?'

'I don't know. He was supposed to be here half an hour ago but, as you know, Jack Delaney is a law unto himself.'

Sally nodded. 'Literally.'

'So are you going to have a go, reveal your hidden talents, Sally?'

'No way. I am keeping my light firmly under a bushel.'

'Talk of the devil!' said Kate as Delaney came in and threaded his way through the crowds to them. 'Where have you been, Jack?'

Delaney looked uncomfortable. 'I had to sort out a few things.'

'Like what?'

'Something I haven't told you. But I guess you need to know. You deserve the truth. You deserve that much.'

Kate's smile vanished, her heart suddenly leaden in her chest. 'What are you talking about? What's going on?'

Delaney looked over his shoulder and Kate's mouth dropped open as she saw Stella Trent walk through the crowded pub, the case in her hand banging into people as she made her way through them.

'Stella Trent,' said Sally, surprised.

'In the flesh!' said the Irish woman brightly.

'What the hell is she doing here?' asked Kate, little

spots of colour forming on her cheeks as she glared at the man she thought she knew.

Delaney shrugged sheepishly, not responding.

'Sweet Jesus, Jack! What's going on?'

Delaney looked at her. 'Remember what you said, about there being no secrets between us any more . . .'

'Yes,' said Kate, her stomach griping like a clenched fist.

'It's time you knew.'

Delaney took the case from Stella and headed to the stage.

Stella, nonplussed, smiled brightly at the two other women. 'I've been giving him lessons.'

'Oh my God!' said Sally Cartwright. 'He's going to strip.'

Kate turned to look as Delaney popped the clasps on the case and took out a large acoustic folk guitar which he slung around his neck and then walked up to the microphone.

'I don't believe what I am seeing,' said Kate in a low whisper.

'Believe it,' replied Stella Trent, still grinning. 'It's the Man in Black.'

'Ladies and gentlemen,' said Delaney loudly. 'I present to you the chord of A-major.'

He positioned his hands on the guitar and the room was completely silent as everyone turned to look at him. Disbelief written plain on every stunned face. Delaney stepped closer to the microphone, looked straight at Kate and started singing.

'*I keep a close watch on this heart of mine.*'

Then he started to play the guitar.

'*I keep my eyes wide open all the time,
I keep the ends out for the tie that binds,
Because you're mine, I walk the line.*'

And Kate laughed and realised her hands were clapping and she was not alone: the whole pub was cheering and clapping as well.

Delaney smiled and carried on walking the bass with his thumb and picking out the melody with his fingers. His voice wasn't a million miles from Johnny Cash's.

'Go, cowboy!' said Kate, her voice still a whisper but with a smile as bright as a supernova.

And he did.

Death Row is a work of fiction, but the issues behind it are all too painfully real. Research studies show that between one-third and a half of abused children develop psychiatric disorders or other problems in the short or longer term.

Some three thousand children and teenagers under eighteen years old are, at any time, named on child-protection registers in England. Almost twice this number are registered at some point during the course of a year.

Around 40 per cent of these children are considered at risk of physical injury and some 22 per cent are at risk of sexual abuse. A further unknown, and probably large, number of young people experience abuse that does not come to the attention of the child-protection agencies.

More than 2,300 people were convicted in English courts during 1994 for sexual offences involving children under 16 years of age, and a further 1,700 admitted guilt and were cautioned.

Over 15,000 children and young people telephone ChildLine to talk about sexual and physical abuse.

The percentage of adults who experienced sexual abuse as children and have had long-term side effects is not known. However, in one British study 13 per cent of the sample of such adults reported that they had been permanently damaged. In another study, 20 per cent of women who had been exposed to sexual abuse as children were identified as suffering from mental health problems, predominantly depressive in type, compared with 6.3 per cent of the non-abused population. Similar increases in mental ill-health were found in women who had been physically or sexually assaulted in adult life. Another study found that almost half of the psychiatric in-patients studied, including both men and women, had histories of physical or sexual abuse or both.

(Statistics from Mind.org.uk)
From the *Counselling Directory 2009*

ACKNOWLEDGEMENTS

Somebody once wrote that no Man is an Island, which is true unless of course it is the Isle of Man. And in a similar vein a book doesn't just come out of the mind and efforts of one person alone. Many people have bought me drinks and given me copious advice at the bar whilst it was being written, and for the benefit of you, dear reader, I by and large ignored it. Some people, however, were useful: Mark and Maisie gave me the Annexe; John and Helen gave us the use of their lovely seaside home in a difficult time as the novel neared completion; Paul 'Chabal' Durrant gave excellent advice on Northern dialect; and Ron Cornell was adept at spotting continuity errors. Laura, Ellie and Woodsy, the best barkeep in North Norfolk, let me use their names and Robert and Lucy were both as good an egg as any you could find in a country farmhouse.

2009 started wonderfully and ended terribly, but Lynn, my dad and my family made all the difference.

In the main, the guiding lights for the safe passage of this novel came from the celestial beacons at Random House – namely Caroline Gascoigne and the Lone Star legend Tess Callaway!

The reader will note, as ever, that some places are real in the book and some are not.

Jack Delaney is going to try and walk the line, but London indeed is very real – and has a score or two yet to settle with him!

ALSO AVAILABLE IN ARROW

Hard Evidence

Mark Pearson

Jackie Malone has been murdered. Her body lies in a pool of blood in the north London flat where she worked as a prostitute. Deep knife wounds have been gouged into her corpse and her hands and feet are tied with coat hanger wire.

For Detective Inspector Jack Delaney this is no ordinary case. He was a friend of Jackie's and she left desperate messages on his answer phone just hours before she was killed. Despite no immediate leads and no obvious suspects, the fear in her voice tells him that this was not a random act of violence.

Just as Delaney begins his investigation, a young girl is reported missing, feared abducted, and he is immediately tasked with finding her. Delaney knows he must act quickly if there is any chance of finding her alive, but he is also determined to track down Jackie's killer before the trail goes cold. However, his tough and uncompromising attitude has made him some powerful enemies on the force, and Delaney soon finds that this case may provide the perfect opportunity for them to dispose of him, once and for all . . .

arrow books

Blood Work

Mark Pearson

The first victim is a young woman found on Hampstead Heath. Her throat has been slashed and her body mutilated. This horrifying discovery marks the beginning of Detective Inspector Jack Delaney's toughest ever case.

When the expertly dissected body of a second young woman is discovered in a north London flat with a brightly coloured scarf tied around her neck, it suddenly becomes clear that a psychopath is on the loose. There is no apparent connection between the two victims and there are no clear motives – but the crime scenes tell a terrifying story.

Delaney, together with forensic pathologist Kate Walker, needs to act quickly and piece together the evidence in order to uncover the deadly pattern behind the murders. However, violent events from Delaney's past are threatening to catch up with him, and he must stay one step ahead of his enemies if he is to stop the killer from striking again.

arrow books

Adam and Eve and Pinch Me

Ruth Rendell

'Adam and Eve and Pinch Me went down to the river to bathe, Adam and Eve were drowned. Who was saved?'

This old nursery rhyme is a favourite of Jerry Leach, a handsome ne'er-do-well, who sponges off women.

Five women, unknown to each other, are his willing victims. One he even married and abandoned, while promising to marry another. But, with the cruel irony he would be the first to recognise in that nursery rhyme, Jerry becomes the victim of one of his female prey.

'She is to be treasured.'
Anita Brookner, *Spectator*

'Rendell is not only irresistible because of the brilliance of her descriptions of contemporary life and the sad truth of her characters. She is a great storyteller who knows how to make sure that the reader has to turn the pages out of a desperate need to find out what is going to happen next.'
John Mortimer, *Sunday Times*

'Unequalled ability to build and sustain suspense'
Peter Guttridge, *Observer*

arrow books

Portobello

Ruth Rendell

'Found in Chepstow Villas, a sum of money between eighty and a hundred and sixty pounds. Anyone who has lost such a sum of money should apply to the phone number below.'

The chance discovery by Eugene Wren of an envelope filled with banknotes would link the lives of a number of very different people – each with their own obsessions, problems, dreams and despairs. It would also set in motion a chain of events that lead to arson and murder.

'It is Rendell's superb sense of place that counts. She makes you smell the excitement and the desperation. *Portobello* is as brilliant as anything she has ever written' *Evening Standard*

'Rendell has a Dickensian empathy, informed by a prodigious love of London life. Her account, bursting with colour and vitality, is a treat to read'
Independent

arrow books

Cold in Hand

John Harvey

Two teenage girls are victims of a bloody Valentine's Day shooting; one survives, the other is less fortunate . . .

It's one of a rising number of violent incidents in the city, and DI Charlie Resnick, nearing retirement, is hauled back to the front line to help deal with the fallout.

But when the dead girl's father seeks to lay the blame on DI Lynn Kellogg, Resnick's colleague and lover, the line between personal and professional becomes dangerously blurred.

As Lynn, shaken by this very public accusation, is forced to question her part in the teenager's death, Resnick struggles against those in the force who disapprove of his maverick ways. But when the unimaginable occurs, an emotional Resnick takes matters into his own hands. No one could have foreseen where this case would lead, and this time Resnick will need all his strength to see justice done . . .

'Reveals modern England in all its most depressing messiness while engaging the reader with characters whose warmth and humanity give real pleasure'
Times Literary Supplement

arrow books

ALSO AVAILABLE IN ARROW

Gone to Ground

John Harvey

Will's first thought when he saw the man's face: it was like a glove that had been pulled inside out . . .

Stephen Bryan, a gay academic, is found brutally murdered in his bathroom. Will Grayson and Helen Walker, police detectives investigating the case, at first assume that his death is the result of an ill-judged sexual encounter: rough trade gone wrong.

But doubts are soon raised. Bryan's laptop has gone missing – could the murder be connected to a biography he was writing on the life and mysterious death of fifties screen legend, Stella Leonard?

Convinced there's a link, Bryan's sister Lesley sets out to prove that Bryan had uncovered a dangerous truth, and that – desperate to keep it hidden – Stella Leonard's rich and influential family have silenced him.

But soon both Lesley and Helen Walker find themselves victims of the violence that swirls around them, as gradually the investigation uncovers the secrets of a family corrupted by lust, wealth and power . . .

'Harvey is a master craftsman.'
Guardian

arrow books

THE POWER OF READING